Africaville

Africaville

A NOVEL

Jeffrey Colvin

Amistad

An Imprint of HarperCollins*Publishers*

AFRICAVILLE. Copyright © 2019 by Jeffrey Colvin. All rights reserved. Printed in the United States of America. No part of this book may be used or reproduced in any manner whatsoever without written permission except in the case of brief quotations embodied in critical articles and reviews. For information, address HarperCollins Publishers, 195 Broadway, New York, NY 10007.

HarperCollins books may be purchased for educational, business, or sales promotional use. For information, please email the Special Markets Department at SPsales@harpercollins.com.

FIRST EDITION

Designed by SBI Book Arts, LLC

Library of Congress Cataloging-in-Publication Data

Names: Colvin, Jeffrey, author.
Title: Africaville : a novel / by Jeffrey Colvin.
Description: First edition. | New York, NY : Amistad, [2019]
Identifiers: LCCN 2019017430| ISBN 9780062913722 (print) |
   ISBN 9780062913715 (ebook)
Subjects: LCSH: Slaves—Fiction | African Americans—Migrations—History—
   20th century—Fiction | BISAC: FICTION / African American / Historical. |
   FICTION / Sagas. | FICTION / Family Life.
Classification: LCC PS3603.O4685 A68 2019 | DDC 813/.6—dc23 LC record available
   at https://lccn.loc.gov/2019017430

19 20 21 22 23 LSC 10 9 8 7 6 5 4 3 2 1

*For my mother Ruby and
my sisters Debra and Cynthia*

There is no moral distance between
the facts of life in San Francisco and
the facts of life in Birmingham.

—James Baldwin

Author's note: This quote is taken from the film *Take This Hammer*, a PBS documentary (1963). The program premiered on public television on February 4, 1964 on Northern California's KQED Channel 9 in the San Francisco Bay Area. The station had produced the film for National Educational Television (NET)—the predecessor of WNET and THIRTEEN in New York City, Baldwin's home town.

Ships to Halifax

PART ONE

Woods Bluff

Dogtrot Fever

Nova Scotia, 1918

Newborns are never afflicted with the malady. The swollen tongue, the reddish throat, the raw cough seem to afflict only babies older than six months. By the spring, in the village situated on a small knuckle-shaped peninsula just north of Halifax, all five of the stricken babies have now developed a high fever.

Having no luck with sweet milk and lemon bitter, worried mothers administer castor oil mixed with camphor, then a tea of beer's root steeped with beech ash and clover. When desperate, they even place a few charms under the mattresses of the beds where the stricken babies lie crying.

Nothing works.

In mid-April, with three more babies now suffering from the malady, health department nurses visit the village, their faces frozen even before they have examined a single new case. Why our children? several mothers standing in the yard of one house want to know. Hadn't

Halifax already given enough babies in the fire that leveled ten square blocks of the city months before, when the munitions ship exploded in the harbor? Then again, those had been white babies. No colored babies had died in that explosion. Was it now Woods Bluff's turn to lose infants? And if so, how many—five, ten, all twenty-two?

The following week, after two of the feverish babies die, the mothers turn to the grandmothers, though many are leery of this option. Already several grandmothers have suggested that since the home remedies haven't worked, and since neither nurse nor doctor has useful medicines, the afflicted infants must be bad-luck babies.

It is an expression the mothers haven't heard since they were children, though the fear of having a bad-luck baby has terrorized mothers on the bluff as far back as 1790. That was the year the first groups of cabins sprang up across the bluff, displacing the foxes, hare, and moose that ran through the thick Christmas ferns and sheep laurel. Back when no medicine could reinvigorate a baby whose body had begun to show the outline of bones, smothering was sometimes recommended. Take no action, and bad luck might infect the entire village. Best to end the child's suffering midday, when injurious spirits would likely be bedside, feeding on the moisture of a weak baby's last breaths.

Yet several mothers are unconvinced the deceased infants are bad-luck babies.

And even if the now-suffering babies are saddled with bad luck, who's to say those old tales of smothering are true? Had anyone actually seen a mother place a blanket or pillow over a child's face? And most important for these new cases: by what evidence will we make the diagnosis?

The grandmothers have ready answers. For several descendants of the Virginian who came up to Nova Scotia in 1772 as a messenger in the British army, a feverish baby had to be put to sleep if its father had recently had a limb severed above the knee or elbow. Death was also imminent if the baby's fever came during the same month as the mother's birthday. For the granddaughter of the Congolese woman who, in 1785, dressed as a man, sailed into Halifax Harbour on a ship out of Lisbon, Portugal, a feverish baby had to be smothered if the newborn was smaller than a man's hand.

And for the largest group of grandmothers, those descended from the nearly two hundred Jamaicans who landed in Halifax Harbour in 1788 after being expelled by British soldiers from their island villages for fomenting rebellion, a feverish baby's fate was sealed if the child coughed up blood during the same month a traveling man arrived on your stoop selling quill turpentine, goat leather, or gunpowder. Hadn't such a vendor made the rounds in Woods Bluff the month before? Why continue to nurse such a child? Death already had a square toe on the baby's throat. It was only a matter of days, a week maybe, if the baby were a girl.

The mothers nod as they listen to the explanations, but over the next weeks only one baby is smothered, although Lovee Mills denies doing it. Near the beginning of May, however, another mother on the bluff seriously considers taking the grandmothers' advice about ending her baby's suffering. Her afflicted child is the cousin of the first baby that developed the fever. Adding to the mother's exasperation are the noisy groups of neighbors that have been gathering outside her home each day at sunset, a few of them knocking on the door and asking outright if the bad-luck baby had been relieved of its worldly suffering.

By now the malady has a name. It refers to the style of cabin where the woman and her extended family live. A dogtrot cabin's construction— two rooms connected by a short breezeway in the middle—had confounded the villagers for years. Some suspected the man who built the cabin wanted a reminder of his home in Virginia. But a breezeway in a dwelling in Nova Scotia? Pure stupidity.

And now living in the cabin has caused two babies to get sick. Many blame the parents and the other members of the large extended family that lives there. Tight living made sense in 1782, they say, but this is

1918. If parents, grown children, and grandchildren are going to continue to jungle up in quarters that tight, what was the use of leaving prison? Even in the best families, sleeping foot to head too long breeds animosity. And if lies, jealousy, and ill will erupt easily in close quarters, why not a virulent fever?

"Will she do it?" someone in the crowd that has arrived at the dogtrot cabin this evening asks.

"If you mean smother the child, she had better," another replies. "Or else one of us will."

The cabin's odd construction had also puzzled several of the rebellious Jamaicans who arrived in Halifax Harbour in 1788. Of course, by the time they first saw the odd dwelling, their minds had been addled by two years of confinement in the military prison on the western edge of Halifax. It took that long before Canadian military commanders believed they had sorted out which of the prisoners were combatants or abettors, and which were mere residents of the Jamaican villages torched by British soldiers.

The wait had been a horror in the cramped underground magazine and provisions spaces.

Eighty-two prisoners were moved to cells aboveground. From this group, squads of men were conscripted to repair damaged sections of the Citadel, help guard the city against French soldiers raiding its perimeter, and do road repair. One warm October day, a group of men on a road detail snuck off to walk the foot trails of Woods Bluff.

Most of the men had heard by then that the money being sent from London and Jamaica to house the prisoners had slowed to a trickle. With no firm offer yet from the government of Sierra Leone to accept them and their families, the men walked the trails looking for the cabin where military officials said a few families would soon be offered housing.

The first two families released from prison and driven by mule wagon out to the bluff never learned what happened to the family from Virginia that had lived there. But with the almanac predicting a heavy snowstorm within the week, they set about gathering dried grass and mud and fieldstones to repair the roof, chink the gaps in the logs, and mend the chimney. The men and women had their freedom. But they were facing a winter on their own in a cold, unfamiliar place. To them, this oddly built cabin seemed a present from God.

With the fever threatening another baby, villagers in 1918 have a different view of the dogtrot cabin. After hearing that the infant suffering inside the dwelling was not smothered but died on its own, they want nothing more to do with the cabin. Fearful that it is harboring bad air that might kill another baby, they chase out the families living there and set the cabin ablaze.

But what had their actions accomplished, the villagers wonder one afternoon in June, when word spreads that little Kath Ella Sebolt, who lives at 68 Dempsey Road, has developed the fever.

By now seven babies have died.

Fearing her daughter might be the eighth child to die of the fever, Kath Ella Sebolt's mother, Shirley, goes in search of the handmade dolls she had purchased the previous winter. All ten of the dolls made by the neighborhood leatherworker were imitations of the Lucky Beatrice doll that had been fought over by a platoon of fathers in a pistol-shooting contest at the most recent Pictou County Exposition. What can it hurt, Shirley Sebolt figures, to slide her daughter's doll under the bed where her daughter suffers?

That evening Kath Ella's fever breaks. The next morning Shirley carries the doll to a house down the road. The next afternoon, similar dolls are slipped under other beds all across the village.

"Could be the fever just tired itself out," George Sebolt tells a neighbor visiting with the news that his previously ailing infant has sucked down a full bottle of milk. "And maybe the nurses are bringing better medicine."

"No," Shirley insists. "That lucky doll under the bed did the trick."

Kath Ella Sebolt's doll is made of dark-brown nettle-cloth and has whalebone-button eyes. Its hair is fashioned from the tassels of a freemason's cap. Its burgundy dress matches burgundy shoes made from the leather upholstery of discarded car seats excavated from the municipal dump, which by the eve of Kath Ella's tenth birthday has nearly reached the southwestern edge of Woods Bluff.

It becomes customary for Woods Bluff girls reaching their tenth birthday to present their handmade dolls to a younger girl in the neighborhood. A gesture of thanks, mothers tell their daughters, because you dodged a death with the fever. The evening before Kath Ella's birthday party, she puts new ribbons in her doll's hair and dresses the doll in its freshly washed jumper. But several hours before the party, the doll goes missing.

"Fine if you don't want to give it away," Shirley says after retrieving the doll from under the mattress of Kath Ella's bed. "But I won't let you hide it."

With that, Shirley places the doll on the shelf beside Kath Ella's bed.

Several years later, on this warm spring afternoon of Friday, March 17, 1933, Kath Ella lies across her bed surrounded by her schoolbooks, while Kiendra Penncampbell, who lives down the road, sits on the floor with the doll in her lap.

"Didn't you hear me talking to you just now?" Kiendra says.

"Didn't you see me writing just now?" Kath Ella replies.

"You always get the highest marks. Why are you studying French?"

"I'm not studying French. I'm using the book to hold my paper while I write this."

"That looks like a letter. Are you writing to some boy?" Kiendra frowns. "Is it Omar Platt? It better not be."

"I am not writing to Omar Platt. I am writing a composition Mrs. Eatten says I have to write for the ladies who give the VMO scholarships." Kath Ella holds up the page. "See?"

Kiendra rises to her knees, leans forward, and stares at the page. Several shades of brown darker than Kath Ella, she wears two long braids that reach to her shoulders. Her school outfits, hand-me-downs her mother gets from the women whose houses she cleans, are always well coordinated. No plaids or prints or stripes, she only wears solid colors. She arrived at school several days last week wearing the same blue skirt, but with a different blue blouse. The green dress she wears this afternoon is faded and threadbare, the loud green socks too thick for the warm weather.

"We don't have school for a whole week," Kiendra says, sitting back down. "You have plenty of time to write to the committee. Have some fun today, why don't you?"

"I will. Just give me a few minutes of quiet, pretty please."

Kath Ella writes with her brow furrowed, hoping Kiendra will get the hint. She ignored the tapping at the window earlier, suspecting Kiendra had come over to show off some trashy thing she had picked up on Cornhead Beach or at the municipal dump, where she often scavenges with her brother. Or else Kiendra was there to show off some new rock she found. Why the girl litters her room with rocks in a village where stones are plentiful is anybody's guess. At the window, Kiendra must have seen that Kath Ella was working. Still, she lifted the window higher and climbed inside.

Kiendra is right that Kath Ella has plenty of time to complete her composition. Although Mrs. Eatten is making the whole class of seniors write a composition, everyone knows that only the students who do well in the interviews will be asked to submit their compositions to the scholarship committee of the Victorian Maternal Order.

For the last three years, with money dried up all over Canada, no student graduating from Woods Bluff Elementary and Secondary has gone off to a residential college. Word this year is that three students might get a scholarship. Imagining herself dressed in a wool skirt walking the leafy campus of Saint Agnes Rectory or Halifax College makes Kath Ella beam with joy. But what she wants badly is to attend the Teachers Seminary in Toronto. Her father, George, says it makes him tired as a bull-ox to imagine his daughter as a traveling gal, like the ones she reads about in books. With relatives who uprooted themselves from Jamaica and Trinidad, not to mention those who left Halifax for unknown parts in 1822, why would a Sebolt child want to travel far from home?

The first paragraphs of Kath Ella's composition for the scholarship are her attempt to answer that question. But the task has not been as easy as writing about whether she prefers spearmint or peppermint wax candies, or which prime ministers of Canada she admires the most. This question is personal. She does not like revealing herself to strangers, especially people who do not live on the bluff. The ladies at the VMO already know that she is poor. Why else would she want the scholarship? She suspects they would like to hear how getting far from Woods Bluff would be beneficial to her life. Her father should understand that, too. Talking with other neighborhood men who are also angry about the municipal dump expanding toward Woods Bluff, George says it is not always the air from the municipal dump that people smell. He says though his neighbors may be hardworking, the bluff itself sometimes stinks badly of poverty.

"What I was asking you just now," Kiendra says, undoing the last of the doll's four hair braids, "is whether you are going to the jamboree tomorrow."

"Of course, silly," Kath Ella says. "I'm helping Mr. Ovits judge the tumbling contests."

"The girls will be happy. They are sick of you winning most of the blue ribbons."

"If I didn't volunteer, I probably wouldn't go."

"I'll bet you would go, if only to see what prank the boys do this year. Remember last year when they glued a whole ream of colored construction paper on Mr. Geedish's Ford?"

Kath Ella laughs. "The man yelled so loud, I was afraid he was going to burst a throat vein."

"I don't know why he was so torn up. The car cleaned up nicely." Kiendra scoots closer to the bed. "I have an idea."

"Imagine that."

"How about this year the girls do a prank?"

"Halt the bus right there. I am getting off."

"But wait. Let me finish."

"Halt the bus, I said. You are finished."

Kath Ella begins another paragraph, hoping the soothing task of combing the doll's horsehair tresses will keep Kiendra's grumbling from escalating into a full-on hissy fit, like the one she threw in her yard last Sunday before church. The trouble was that Kiendra had just learned that she had to spend all five days of the school vacation helping her mother, Rosa, clean houses. Given the shrieking Kiendra did, it is clear that shrill noises still do not bother her like they do several other teenagers on the bluff who survived the fever.

The malady raged longest in Kiendra, but she also does not suffer the occasional headaches that plague Kath Ella. Her doctor says, however, that her fever may have harmed her brain in other ways. Kiendra's mother disagrees. Rosa says her daughter has a sound brain, but sometimes doesn't use it properly. "Starting all this mess out here in your father's yard is a waste of time," Rosa had said as she jerked Kiendra's arm and directed her toward the road. "Hard work next week will keep you out of devilment."

Kiendra has parted the doll's hair into two sections, and on one side she has finished a fat braid. "Will you at least let me tell you what happened to Old Mister?" Kiendra asks, tying a ribbon bow at the end of the braid.

"Who is Old Mister?"

"The man who lived in a house my mother cleans. He fell out of bed the other day. Hit the floor flat as a teacake. The son came running out to the backyard, where Momma was beating rugs. She helped haul Old Mister off the floor and back onto the bed. Old Mister only lived to see two more sunups. The son and his wife are moving into the house next week. I haven't seen their baby, but I helped carry in the crib. The baby must be a girl because I saw a little pink peek-a-boo bonnet and the play-pretties. That's how I got my idea for the prank."

"That again?"

"See, while everybody is at the jamboree, we could sneak downtown to the house."

"And do what?"

"Steal the play-pretties."

"How many?"

"All of them. Then after we take the play-pretties out of the crib, we'll leave this doll there. Wouldn't that be a hoot?"

"It wouldn't be a hoot if we got snookered."

"We won't get snookered."

"You might not but I would. Whoever discovers the doll in the crib will soon find out it belongs to me."

"You'll say you loaned the doll to me. I'll say one of the boys stole the doll. One of the boys must have overheard me say where the family hides the door key. This is a boy's prank. They'll never believe a girl would do this."

"Where is the house?"

"In the South End. I could tell you the address, but you probably wouldn't know it. You don't get out and about in Halifax like I do."

The smirk on Kiendra's face as she combs the hair on the other side of the doll's head irritates Kath Ella. She feels envy every time Kiendra mentions another day of riding the bus by herself to meet her mother at some house in a strange part of the city. There would be hell to pay if Kath Ella took the bus unaccompanied by her sister or another neighborhood girl. Kiendra is correct to say she knows the city better than any of the other girls on the bluff. But does she have to brag about it all the time? "I think your idea is ludicrous," Kath Ella says. "Now, will you please leave so I can get back to work?"

"For your information, I was getting ready to leave anyway," Kiendra says. "I'm only staying because I have to finish this last plait."

Kath Ella returns to her composition feeling herself getting more annoyed with each new sentence she writes. Instead of finishing the last braid, Kiendra fiddles with a loose button on the doll's dress. Kiendra was there in the rear of the classroom yesterday with the lower-level students when Mrs. Eatten had given stern instructions that they were to be quiet while the graduating students completed the four booklets of the scholarship examination. Only five students would be going downtown to the scholarship interview. Midway through the hour and a half, giddy about having completed the science and the grammar booklets, Kath Ella had peeked at the nearby desk where Betty Addison sat. Betty Addison and her sister, who are nearly light enough to pass for white, were always going on about how they would not spend their futures scrubbing floors. Kath Ella did not plan to either.

Betty had also finished the first two booklets. And she had finished the questions in the civics booklet and seemed to be working on the geometry problems. Kath Ella had not dared peek again but she could sense Betty there with her head down, biting her lip as she usually did when drawing a triangle or a rhombus.

Betty Addison will probably get a scholarship. So will Buddy Caulden. Kath Ella is certain she needs an excellent composition to ensure she gets the third one. Why on earth had she allowed Kiendra to crawl in through the window? Even more exasperating is the thought of how easily she gave in to Kiendra's begging to play with the doll. She should have left the doll up on the shelf with the eleven volumes of her *Lucy Kirchner in the Mountains* books. There used to be twelve. A few years ago, Kath Ella was certain she saw Kiendra slip the first book of the series into her jacket. Had the doll been smaller, Kiendra probably would have tried to steal it, too. Before her tenth birthday, Kath Ella had considered passing her doll to Kiendra. But by then the boys had started to tease the two of them about spending so much time together. You and Kiendra are joined at the lips, one of the boys joked.

Kath Ella is patient with Kiendra. She knows the bond between the two of them runs deeper than the substance of a silly joke. That fact should be obvious to the boys who at least pretend to respect Kath

Ella and Kiendra's place of honor during the ceremony held every November at the graves of the seven infants who died of dogtrot fever. Kiendra rarely dressed properly for the chilly air that often hung over the cemetery during the ceremony. Though Kath Ella appreciates the accolades she gets for being the first child to survive the malady, she finds it an unearned honor to stand near the graves, stealing heat from the girl who fought the longest against the fever. Last November with her mother sick in bed for nearly two weeks, Kiendra stood for the entire ceremony with her eyes cast down at the frozen soil. Despite the doctor's assurance that her mother would be up and about soon, Kiendra had apparently asked God every night to take her life instead of her mother's.

That news revealed a selfless side of Kiendra that Kath Ella had never seen before. She always assumed that most of the prayers spoken in the Penncampbell home were done for Kiendra's benefit. On Monday morning, having seen Rosa at the bus stop coughing and sucking on a peppermint candy, she decided to accompany Kiendra home from school to try to find out if Kiendra was worrying again about her mother's health. But that was before getting to school and being told by Mrs. Eatten that the scholarship exam this year would be given before the school recess.

Kath Ella finishes another paragraph of her composition, realizing that, with the stress of preparing for the scholarship exam this week, she has barely spent a minute with Kiendra. Her guilt about that is probably the reason she let Kiendra climb in through the window.

Half an hour later, Luela, Kath Ella's older sister, enters the bedroom. At the bureau mirror Luela admires herself, wearing one of the refurbished hats Mrs. Breakstone, from down the hill, has been selling at the baseball games. The recent winter has lightened Luela's skin nearly to the color of her younger sister. The color of toasted almonds, she likes to say.

"Shirley says this chapeau looks good on me," Luela says, fussing with the fabric flower on the side of the hat. "Anybody here agree?"

"No, she didn't say that," Kiendra says. "Your mother told you to stop coming out there bothering her."

"Shirley did not say that."

"Yes, she did," Kiendra says. "I heard her. And she told you to come in here and take off her hat." Kiendra scoots closer to the bed. "Why don't we do it, Kath Ella?"

Luela shakes her head. "What silliness are the two of you up to now?" she asks as she lowers the hat gently into a cardboard box.

"That's for me and Kath Ella to know," Kiendra says. "And for you not to."

Luela marches across the room. "I will never understand why your mother lets you out of the house by yourself," she says, looking down at Kiendra. "I imagine Rosa is already mad at you for all the fidgeting you did in church last Sunday. And now you want to get into some devilment? Give me the doll."

Kiendra tries to scoot away, but Luela has grabbed one of the doll's braids. "Let go this minute, Miss Kay," she tells Kiendra. "Or I will send you home."

Luela places the doll back on the shelf and returns to the bureau. "Don't give me that hurt puppy face," she says, tossing a clamshell bracelet to Kiendra. "You're not fooling anybody."

With a wide grin, Kiendra rattles the bracelet as she waves to Luela, who walks out of the bedroom. Most of the quarter-size shells on the bracelet are chipped. But any old bangle suits a girl whose child fever had her thrashing so badly one evening that she cut her wrist on the rusty rods of an iron headboard. Kiendra adjusts the bracelet on her wrist so that it covers the mess of tiny scars.

After several minutes of trying to get Kath Ella's attention, Kiendra stands. "Are you coming with me to do a prank or not?"

"No chance, Miss Kay."

Kiendra takes off the bracelet and drops it onto the bed. "Yesterday,

I saw you reading Betty Addison's answers during the test," she says. "You're not supposed to cheat."

"I wasn't cheating."

"I saw what I saw."

"So?"

"So what if I tell?"

When Kiendra reaches for the bracelet again, Kath Ella picks it up. "You can play with this some other time," she says and slips the bracelet onto her wrist. "But I really must finish my schoolwork."

Kath Ella opens her French textbook, but only pretends to read as Kiendra climbs out the window. Maybe she ought to accompany Kiendra downtown. But if she does go she will know why. Despite what her sister says, she does not often fool herself when it comes to Kiendra. She would not go downtown because she is afraid Kiendra would snitch on her. Kiendra knows how much getting the scholarship means to her. She would never destroy that. It would be because her being there would help keep Kiendra from getting into too much harm. If she does go downtown, she will not go inside the house. If anyone asks, she can say she had no idea Kiendra had carried in the doll.

Unlike in the North End neighborhood of Halifax, where the blast from the munitions ship explosion in December of 1917 leveled all the mature trees, in the South End, the trees are large and leafy. On this sunny Saturday afternoon, two ancient maples shade the back patio of a two-story brick house on quiet Henry Street.

With the sounds of the Spring Jamboree bands she heard from afar before leaving the bluff still resounding in her head, Kath Ella follows Kiendra across the patio of the house. Inside, they hurry toward a ground-floor bedroom.

"Why are you still out there?" Kiendra asks Kath Ella, who has halted at the doorway. "Come in here with me."

Kath Ella leans her head in. On one plum-colored wall, along with several religious figures, is a framed picture of a young man in a Canadian Forces uniform. Is he the man who died in that four-post bed?

The bright-red object she sees across the room is the shopping bag Kiendra carries with the doll inside. But why is Kiendra standing at the crib? Why hasn't she put the doll inside the crib?

Kath Ella rushes across the room. "We didn't come to tarry," she says, approaching Kiendra. "Take out the play-pretties."

Kath Ella pokes Kiendra in the shoulder, and Kiendra turns around.

"Why did you poke me?" Kiendra asks. "Do it again and I'll sock you."

The outburst from Kiendra is familiar. But not the odd way Kiendra's face is contorted. What is the matter with this girl? Why is she looking like she does not recognize her friend? The early evening sunlight streaking in through the window has weakened. In the dimness Kiendra seems to be studying the shiny items nearby on the bureau. "Come out of that trance and pay attention to your schoolwork," teachers are constantly telling Kiendra. Yet this does not seem to be one of Kiendra's schoolhouse trances. Something long hidden within her seems to be showing itself. When Kiendra gives a mischievous smile, Kath Ella recalls the taunts of their schoolmates—*Kiendra did it, Kiendra said it, Kiendra took it, Kiendra stole it.* Why on earth had she come to this house with Kiendra?

Kath Ella steps around Kiendra and moves to the crib. Something is moving in there. When she looks down, she sees a sleeping baby.

The baby's soft gurgle brings Kiendra out of her stupor and she turns around. Both girls are quiet, watching the baby's chest rise and fall.

"Never been this close to a white baby before," Kiendra says. "Where's the mother?"

"Coming back soon," Kath Ella says. "We'd better go."

"Not yet," Kiendra says. "Let's do the deed first."

"I don't think we should."

"Stop being a Scaredy-Louise. Let's do the deed."

Kiendra reaches into the crib and takes out a string of furry pink cubes. The baby emits a long gurgle. When the infant is quiet again, Kiendra lays the doll into the crib.

"The doll doesn't look funny in there," Kath Ella says.

"Think how mad the mother will be," Kiendra says. She turns the doll onto its side, so that its eyes are directed at the baby. "That's funny."

Kath Ella picks up the shopping bag and rushes out of the bedroom. Halfway across the kitchen, she realizes Kiendra is not behind her.

She returns to the bedroom, where Kiendra is holding the baby.

"Put that child back, dum-dum."

"I wouldn't hurt her," Kiendra says. "She's a good-luck baby."

Kiendra rocks the child in her arms.

Hearing a door opening at the front of the house, Kath Ella turns, her face feeling hot. She opens a nearby door, but it leads to a closet. At the window, she tugs on the sash. But the window will not budge.

"Now you've done it," Kath Ella says, returning to the crib.

"Not me," Kiendra says, lowering the baby onto the small mattress. "I didn't want to do this. You did."

The man turning the ignition key to start the dark green sedan parked at the curb has wavy hair, just like the soldier in the picture on the bedroom wall of the house from which Kath Ella and Kiendra have been rudely ejected.

"Are we going to see the constable, sir?" Kath Ella asks from the back seat. "Are we?"

"Be still back there, girl," the man says. "I'd appreciate no more words from you."

As the car pulls away from the curb Kath Ella turns toward Kiendra, who is quiet as a church cat. She had talked up a blue streak inside the house when she was being interrogated. The man said he didn't believe a syllable of her story that she had come into the house because she heard the baby crying, especially after he saw the doll in the crib. If they are going to the constable station, the officers there probably won't believe Kiendra's story either.

With each passing city block, the back cabin of the sedan feels more confining. What a relief to realize that the car has not turned off Gottingen Street. When the lights of the city give way to dark forest, Kath Ella leans over toward Kiendra. "The man is taking us to our parents," she whispers. "What are we going to tell them?"

Every few minutes Kath Ella taps Kiendra's knee. But Kiendra keeps her eyes closed. Soon Kath Ella gives up and stares out the side window into the darkness. Kiendra must be terrified about what her father will do when he learns about this mischief. She has good reason to be terrified. Mr. Penncampbell can swing a mean hand when he is angry.

The crunch of the car tires as the sedan rolls onto Dempsey Road startles Kath Ella. Calm down, she tells herself, gripping the door handle. You need to think. Never mind what Kiendra will say to her parents. What on earth are you going to say to yours?

Calming down will be difficult now. Already she has spied the bushes that mark the beginning of the village. The tall cluster of wild Labrador grows on the site where the old dogtrot cabin was torched by angry neighbors attempting to stop the spread of the fever. Last month when the blossoms were bursting with fragrance, Kiendra came to school for several days with pink and white flowers pinned to her hair and her blouse. In the back of the sedan now, that memory gives Kath Ella an urge to backhand Kiendra across her mouth. If this foolish girl ever took the time to think the matter through, she would recognize that if her lingering fever had persisted a few days more, one of those ash-loving Labradors might today be feeding on the remnants of her torched house.

It's every girl for herself now, Kath Ella concludes. She alone must decide what she will tell her parents about how she got into trouble.

And she is not even sure how it happened. Her afternoon had begun so well. With the nickel Shirley had given her to entice her to leave her books and head over to the jamboree, she left the house thinking that a bagful of butterscotch jawbreakers would be a nice treat. She had also planned a detour up Beach Road to see if one of the cute Higgins boys was out in the yard helping his father repair a neighbor's car.

Instead, Kath Ella had spent the afternoon at the Penncampbells' house, helping Kiendra and her sister mop the floors, which had been neglected because their mother was under the weather. The only treat she got for helping was a hard biscuit with a smear of canned raspberry preserves. No, thank you, was what she should have said when Kiendra offered her a bite of the paraffin disk from the opened jar, especially when she realized Kiendra was being generous only because she wanted to use Kath Ella's nickel to pay their round-trip bus fare downtown.

Kiendra is still fifteen years old, Kath Ella thinks, when the sedan has moved past the wild Labrador bush. But children like her, who are older than sixteen, go to jail for trespassing. Kath Ella leans back in the seat, trying to calm her thoughts. Too soon a light-green bungalow appears out of the darkness, like a trawler out of dense fog.

K ath Ella lives beyond the church and schoolhouse in a part of the bluff called the Hindquarter, named by the first builders, who complained that the land there was as tough as hindquarter meat. Most of the houses are small bungalows, many with rooms or back porches appended wherever the slope allowed. Many houses have unobstructed views of unfamiliar cars driving onto the bluff from the paved road. At this hour, however, by the time neighbors begin discussing the dark-green sedan parked near the mailbox at 68 Dempsey Road, the man in the panama hat is seated on the sofa in the front room of the Sebolts' house.

"A misunderstanding is what's happening here, Mister," George

Sebolt says, glancing in the direction of the bedroom where Shirley has taken Kiendra and Kath Ella. "Our daughter's never been in a lick of trouble. Are you certain it was our daughter?"

The man moves his panama hat from the coffee table and drops it rudely onto the dark-brown sofa cushion. "My wife wants me to call on the constable in the morning," he says, emptying the contents of Kiendra's red shopping bag onto the coffee table. "Can you blame her?"

George turns up the wick in the kerosene lamp and leans over the mess. The doll's severed head has fallen onto the floor. But its severed limbs are there with the body, everything covered with the doll's innards of rag and straw.

"Both of the girls will be punished," George says. "You have my word on that, Mister."

George offers another long apology. When he presents his tobacco tin and a stack of cigarette rolling papers, the man shakes his head and reaches for his hat. After leading the man across the porch, George lights the front steps with the kerosene lamp held low. Descending, the man keeps his eyes directed toward the noise of boys gathering on the dark road.

"I will inform my wife of your promise," the man says, when he reaches his sedan. "But I cannot say for certain that will calm her down."

George remains in the yard until the rear lights on the sedan have disappeared. On the porch he finds Kiendra alone, her legs crossed at the ankle, her eyes directed down at her blistering patent leather shoes.

"Whatcha loitering around here for, gal?" George asks. "Get your tail on home."

"I can't go to my house by myself, Mr. Sebolt."

"It's just a short walk, child."

"But I don't have a lamp."

The boys are now gathering at the front steps. George calls the oldest to the porch and tells him to accompany Kiendra home. "Kerosene cost a pile of pennies," George says, handing the boy the lamp. "Be back here lickety-split, or else I'll beat your head so bad Jesus won't recognize you."

Holding the lamp above his head, the boy leads Kiendra across the yard toward the side path. The other boys follow, jostling but keeping their voices low.

A few yards down the path, the boys break into a loud song: *What the fella gwine do? What he supposed to do. What the man gwine do? What the law say do. What the fella gwine do? What he supposed to do. What the fella gwine do? What the law say do.*

I n the house down the hill, Kiendra Penncampbell's father, Guivalier, does not add his voice to the call-and-response the boys have taken up again as they leave his front yard. Why would a man from Haiti chime in on an old Jamaican tune?

Tall and lean, Guivalier strides into the living room, where Kiendra stands with her back exposed and the front of her dress held against her chest. Kiendra's mother, Rosa, has not bothered to get out of bed. Her brother and sister have been warned: Come out of the bedroom and I will beat your black head to the white meat.

Guivalier feels the warning to his other children was too harsh. Fearing his anger might get the best of him, he doesn't select the cricket mallet from the trunk in the bedroom. His father used to swing the bat in the yard at the school in Port-au-Prince, before the family was forced back into the countryside and later onto the boat to Canada. The year he came with his family to Halifax as a four-year-old, many times he suffered the handle of the cricket mallet against his back. Never so many licks that he could not go to work the next day. When he was Kiendra's age, by this hour he was dead tired from a day of pulling potatoes on the fields in Annapolis County. This evening he chooses for punishment a strap cut from a belt that once turned gears at the gristmill where he worked in his early twenties.

Near the mantel, Guivalier opens the Bible his father used to recite from before meting out punishment. Flipping the pages, Guivalier feels his daughter's brazen eyes watching. He has never told her how brash he was the evening he refused to offer his back to his father's belt. That time he would not even acknowledge any wrongdoing. The cracked ribs he got in the tussle gave him the fortitude to pack his belongings and leave the cabin. At his father's funeral, his job was to place the Bible in the casket, along with his father's two French pistols. The pistols he hurled into the basin. But the Bible would not leave his hand.

Unable to find a suitable passage, Guivalier closes the Bible. He reaches for the strap again, hearing the mannish boys return to his yard, rousting again, though they know full well that early evening calls for quiet in a Haitian yard. Guivalier raises the strap, recalling the voices of the parents of those boys, the residue of Jamaica, yes, but also Portugal, Trinidad, and the lower states in America. Sometimes, after he has thumped Kiendra's noggin at the bus stop or whacked her neck with the edge of a cardboard hand fan during church service, one of the parents will come up close to say Kiendra deserves more leniency. They remind him of the medical treatments Kiendra endured when she was ill with the fever, as if he hadn't been present during those weeks his daughter suffered, as if he hadn't suffered, too. Blame gravity, his father often said before lowering the strap or the rod. Blame gravity and the creator who is working through me. But as his arm falls, Guivalier blames his own angry agency for the downward jerk of his arm as the strap strikes Kiendra's back.

A Way Out

A shriek of delight erupts in the Sebolt living room the following Tuesday afternoon as Kath Ella reads the note from Mrs. Eatten. It states that Kath Ella is invited to travel downtown this coming Thursday, March 23, for a 10:00 a.m. scholarship interview. Her eyes shut tightly, her shoulders tensed, Kath Ella cannot stop her body from shaking.

"Take a breath, child," Shirley says, picking up the note from where it has fallen onto the floor, "or else you're going to pass out."

The lingering exasperation Shirley still harbors over the trouble Kath Ella got into the previous Saturday is evident in the quick rub she gives to the girl's back before sending her off to tell her father the good news. Out back near the shed, George reads the note with pursed lips. "You're going to bring your narrow behind home right after your interview," he says, handing back the note. "Or I will tear your hide good."

Both of my parents will be proud of me again, Kath Ella tells herself two days later in the study room at the Victorian Maternal Order, where she sits admiring the wood paneling and brass wall lamps. At a shiny oak table in the library, her conversation with the two scholarship matrons is a delight. One of the ladies seems to know every pleasant reason Kath Ella wants to be a teacher.

Outside the building later, Kath Ella walks down the sidewalk toward the other students from Woods Bluff Elementary and Secondary who have come for an interview. All three are there, several blocks away waiting for the bus. When the students have boarded a bus, she pretends to hurry down the sidewalk, but lets the bus depart without her.

Walking by herself, the afternoon sun warming her arms and neck, Kath Ella likes the freedom she feels after having traversed so many city blocks alone. She hopes her pleated dress and white gloves will deter strangers she meets in the South End from accosting her to ask why she is in the neighborhood. Her father will be angry that she has disobeyed his orders to come directly home after her interview. After what Kiendra told her yesterday evening, she feels she has a good reason.

Having snuck out of her house, after her father had grounded her, and sprinted up the hill, Kiendra climbed through the window of Kath Ella's bedroom talking up a streak. "You should have seen the look on the wife's face there at the house in the South End when her husband said that me and my mother could come inside and get back to cleaning," Kiendra said, nearly out of breath. "Then the wife told the husband, 'If you know what is good for you, you better dismiss Rosa and hire a new housekeeper.' Fat chance of that," Kiendra said. "My mother practically raised that man."

But, Kiendra said, the wife has now threatened to visit her bigshot cousin at the Wales and London Hotel, where Kath Ella's mother worked in housekeeping.

"Oh, dear," Kiendra said, climbing out the bedroom window. "I hope the wife's not going to convince her cousin to fire Shirley."

The uneasiness that welled up in Kath Ella yesterday as she watched Kiendra leave returns now as she spies the marker for Henry Street. Shirley had taken a week off from her job at the hotel years ago, when Kath Ella was suffering with dogtrot fever. For that she lost her position serving the hotel's wealthiest customers. To show that she is a daughter worthy of her mother's sacrifice is one reason Kath Ella works hard in school.

Now my mother might lose her job altogether, Kath Ella concludes, knocking on the front door of the house. As she did yesterday, she tries to banish that thought from her head. She has heard that, these days, even jobs cleaning houses are difficult to get.

I didn't come back here to cause any more trouble," Kath Ella says, inside a bedroom on the second floor. "I came to apologize."

The bedroom is sparsely furnished. Besides the large bed, there is a padded armchair and a dressing table. A full-length mirror leans against a beige wall. The mother, seated in the padded armchair in her undergarments, looks younger than she did last Saturday evening. She cannot be more than a few years older than Kath Ella. "Kiendra didn't seem very sincere when she apologized," she says, spreading talcum powder on her ankles. "Why should I believe you?"

Kath Ella tries to think. The woman's husband had escorted Kath Ella to the bedroom, then hurried out. But has he gone back downstairs? The baby's crib sitting in the far corner also distracts. Is the baby asleep there? Kath Ella is also irritated that the first words the woman says to her are about Kiendra. Kiendra had said she would be here. Where is she?

As Kath Ella begins to speak, the woman raises her hand. "That will be plenty," she says, pointing. "Bring me that."

Kath Ella reaches for a green-and-gold gown lying on the bed. Now she is confused. This woman said she could come upstairs to apologize. But the woman has cut her off before she can finish. Perhaps the woman allowed her to come upstairs simply because she wanted to show off this expensive dress.

After opening the back of the dress, Kath Ella inspects the lining for hidden buttons or hooks. With the top of the dress draped over her shoulder, she kneels and holds the dress open. "This is how you hold the dress," she says. "Isn't that right?"

The woman steps into the dress without answering. "I hear you're finishing your schooling," she says, turning to let Kath Ella fasten the back of the dress. "I imagine you'll get married yourself."

"Not soon. I plan to attend college."

"You're sounding grown up this afternoon. So why were you so stupid the other day? Hand me that brush."

At the dressing table, Kath Ella picks up the brush, wondering if it was a mistake to brag about going to college. So few children from the bluff do. "But I might not go to college," she says, presenting the brush. "I might get a job at the Wales and London like my mother. My sister works there when she's not at the trade school. My grandmother used to work there, too."

"Your grandmother worked at the hotel?"

"Before she died."

The woman accepts the brush with a softer face. "I never get to visit my grandmother anymore," she says. "Nor any of my friends down the coast. My mother says I must be grown up and settle in here in Halifax. She complains when I miss mass. But I don't intend to raise my daughter the way she raised me. My husband agrees."

"I'm sorry I came here uninvited the other day," Kath Ella says. "Please don't make trouble for my mother about it."

The woman runs the brush through her wavy brown hair a few times, looking deep in thought. As she lowers the brush to her lap, her face hardens again. "I wanted my husband to let Rosa go," she says. "I'll wager Kiendra didn't tell you that. But did my husband comply? Not hardly. Philip does nothing I tell him. Nothing."

On Monday, March 27, when classes resume at Woods Bluff Elementary and Secondary, Kiendra Penncampbell remains missing the entire school day. She is absent the next day, too.

"I know very well that Kiendra has missed two days of school," Guivalier tells Kath Ella on Wednesday morning on the front porch of the Penncampbells' house. "I am her father."

"Is she sick?" Kath Ella asks, clutching her schoolbooks closer to her chest.

Guivalier sits on the banister peeling a hard-boiled egg, but with his eyes cast down the hill. He claims he can hear the rumble of the gray-and-white Acadian bus he takes to work miles before it has reached the municipal dump. "Kiendra's going away," he says.

"Where's she going?"

"Rosa is sending your partner in trouble to her aunt in Wells Bridge."

"For good?"

"No, for bad." Guivalier chuckles and takes a bite of the egg. "This was not my decision," he says, looking a bit helpless, "but I support it."

"When will Kiendra be back?"

"When her mother tells her she can come back."

Kath Ella steps toward the front door and tries to look inside the house, but Rosa pushes the screen door open and comes outside. "You got what you came for," she says, pulling her housecoat closed. "Now scoot on to school before you stir up more trouble."

Kiendra's mother has never spoken to me like that, Kath Ella tells herself, heading off. She must still be under the weather. By the end of the second period, with the one-piece metal-and-wood desk assaulting her body as she corrects her scholarship essay, Kath Ella's shock at Rosa's words has turned to anger. How dare that woman talk to her that way?

"Your composition is the strongest, my dear," Mrs. Eatten says, handing Kath Ella her essay at the end of the day. "Still, I'm afraid it is not yet good enough to send downtown. I suggest you stay for an hour after school with the others and work on it."

Usually when Mrs. Eatten has instructed her students to rework an assignment, she paces the classroom in her busy print dress, her plump brown arms hanging heavy at her sides whenever she stops to check a student's work. But the hour ends without Mrs. Eatten having gotten up once from her desk to examine the corrections Kath Ella has made to her essay. And later, after she gives Kath Ella the messy job of changing the sticky ribbons on the two school typewriters, Mrs. Eatten talks with several students standing at her desk, asking questions about their essays.

"I do hope you are not planning to serve as ringleader for any more pranks, my dear," Mrs. Eatten says at the door, where she makes hurried corrections to Kath Ella's composition. "And to think I once believed Kiendra was the prankster."

Has someone cranked a handle to turn on a new world where everybody thinks she is a bad girl? Kath Ella wonders. Rosa and Mrs. Eatten believe so. So do her parents. But what sane person believes Kiendra wasn't the girl who planned the prank? Nobody, that's who.

Kath Ella carries no schoolbooks home, just the two marked-up pages. A ways up Dempsey Road she can hear behind her the boys from the high elementary rows, racing toward Nobody's Acre carrying oversized baseball gloves. She envies their freedom. Yet, so far, her only punishment for the mischief she got into has been to come home directly after school. Her father knows that being confined to her bedroom is no penance for a girl who is perfectly content to be alone reading a book or perusing old letters. It has been over a week now since she got into trouble. When will she learn about the real punishment? And what will the real punishment be?

Answers to Kath Ella's questions about her punishment seem to be imminent when she arrives home to find the leather-bottom chair in the living room placed to face the sofa.

"I hope you have enjoyed your leisurely walks home from school these last few days, young lady," George says, ashes falling off the cigarette he waves, motioning Kath Ella to sit. "Because from now whenever school lets out, you will have exactly fifteen minutes to get home."

Kath Ella nods, but the tone of her father's voice makes her uneasy. In these situations Shirley usually sits beside George on the sofa. But Shirley stands rigid in her housecoat, guarding the doorway. "Your mother was let go from her job at the hotel today," George says. "And I believe you know why."

Kath Ella looks up. "Momma was let go?"

George shoves his cigarette lighter into the pocket of his work pants. "No more trips to the gymnasium or the swimming pool after school for a while, young lady," he says. "I am not spending another gray nickel on the bus for your entertainment. Do you follow?"

Shirley uncrosses her arms and moves to the sofa. "First you talk Kiendra into going on a prank. Then you go back to the house and bother the mother again? What possessed you to do that?"

"I didn't talk Kiendra into going on the prank."

"You didn't talk her out of it," Shirley says. "And you didn't talk yourself out of going back to that house. Has someone stolen your senses?"

George puts a hand on Kath Ella's knee. "Now your mother and I have to go back to the hotel and ask her boss to change his mind."

"I doubt he will," Shirley says. "Which means we'll have less money to run this house."

"I'm sorry," Kath Ella says.

"Not as sorry as you're going to be," Shirley says. "I'm putting you to work this summer. You're going to find a job."

"At the hotel?"

Shirley's open palm lands hard against her daughter's cheek, and Kath Ella winces at the sharp pain. With a hand on her cheek, she looks at the doorway. Her sister must be there in the hallway, out of sight, because she has heard a gasp. Now footsteps bring Luela closer.

"Just look at all the correction marks on this whatchamacallit thing you are writing for the scholarship," Shirley says, pointing at the page on Kath Ella's lap. "I want this schoolwork fixed before you get a bite of dinner."

Kath Ella looks at George, who also seems startled at the force of Shirley's blow. "If I was you I'd skedaddle out of your mother's sight," he says. "And I would do it lickety-split."

One of the benefits of rereading her scholarship essay this evening is that Kath Ella can turn her mind to her deceased elders. Not a single grandparent that she can remember was ever as mean as her parents. At least that is how she feels at the moment. Her paternal grandfather, who built the house she lives in, was still alive when she was born, but try as she might she doesn't remember him. She knows her grandfather used the old Sebolt family home, the narrow cabin behind the house, as a woodshop. There he made tables, chairs, and wooden utensils on a workbench he constructed using railroad ties. He earned good money repairing shutters, floors, and other house parts during the year before he died of a heart attack. She and her sister spent plenty of afternoons in the storage shed rummaging through trunks and crates, looking for dress-up clothes or items to use for made-up games. After her grandfather's tools were sold and the bulky workbenches cleared out, there was room to play jacks or skip rope in bad weather.

Mrs. Eatten says the scholarship committee would also appreciate reading about Kath Ella's maternal great-grandfather, Mordechai. He got on at the Wales and London Hotel the same week he arrived in Halifax from Trinidad. For years he rode the coal trucks that rattled day and night up the long hill into the backside of the hotel. By the time Mordechai retired as a hotel steward, he had gotten his daughter Pallis and his granddaughter Shirley jobs in the laundry. Kath Ella wrote about the time she visited the laundry room at the hotel. The noise from the dryers was deafening and every breath she took seemed to burn her lungs. Pallis and Shirley often laughed together in the laundry, until the day the heavy dryer tumblers broke free and knocked Pallis to the floor. After getting out of the hospital, Pallis was transferred to the kitchen. Though her back often gave her trouble, she rarely complained.

But Kath Ella has been having trouble following Mrs. Eatten's suggestion that she write about how she felt during the months before her grandfather died. She does not want to recall seeing him sweating in a chair on the porch, his body swollen from diabetes. Her failure is obvious in the paragraphs on the second page, where there are more blue corrections than on her earlier attempt.

After a few moments Kath Ella realizes that she has torn a corner of the page. Staring at the small jagged triangle makes her fearful of how much better Betty Addison probably did on the mathematics section of the scholarship exam than she. Earlier, she had seen Mrs. Eatten in the school doorway, offering what seemed like pleasant advice to Betty and several boys who took the scholarship exam. Just how generous are Mrs. Eatten's new corrections to her composition?

Kath Ella tears off more pieces and soon the whole composition is a pile of paper shards on the bedspread. Good, she thinks, taking two lined pages out of her notebook. Without the distraction of having to look at Mrs. Eatten's half-hearted notes, it will be easier to start over.

Kath Ella writes the date at the top of the page and then lies back on the bed to gather her thoughts. For this new effort she wants to go back further in the Sebolt family line. But to do a good job she will probably have to interview her father. No way is she stepping into those angry jaws anytime soon. And besides, members of the scholarship committee have probably already read compositions from students whose relatives left the military prison in 1782 to start a life on Woods Bluff.

After working for more than an hour, she has written only three paragraphs. But not one of them does she like. Now she is starting to wonder if it was a good idea to tear up her earlier work. Despite all the blue marks of corrections, Mrs. Eatten had said that her composition was nearly done. Maybe she should have listened.

Kath Ella resumes her writing, hearing the warm greeting her sister is receiving from her parents in the living room as she returns for dinner. Gathering the shards of paper, Kath Ella wonders when she herself will be the good daughter again.

Centervillage, the place on Woods Bluff where Kath Ella's parents have been hinting she will most likely be working after school, is a bustling area. Nearly half the shops are operated by families of colored men and women from the southern United States who moved to the bluff almost a hundred years ago. They arrived when barely half the houses were occupied. Neither cholera, nor typhus, nor yellow fever caused them to vacate those houses. Those who left the bluff for unknown parts did so as the newcomers had arrived—imprisoned aboard a British ship.

One of Kath Ella's relatives was among the neighbors who snuck downtown on November 14, 1822, to get a look at HMS *Perspicacious* and HMS *Angel Pequod*, two ships anchored in the harbor. A Nova Scotia official had visited the bluff the day before, saying the government of Sierra Leone was finally offering to take in the black residents living on Woods Bluff. Were the two ships really going to Sierra Leone? the men asked one another on the way back to the bluff. Or were the tall sails going to fly the families to another British prison in the Caribbean or the Australia Antilles?

Kath Ella has read an account of the departure of the ships written for the church records. But she does not know the details of the evening before they departed Halifax Harbour. A family story recounts what happened the evening her ancestor, four-year-old Kipbo Sebolt, awoke to find his parents packing.

"Where you going?" Kipbo asked from the floor pallet where he slept.

Kipbo's father, Ephram, had been moving about the cabin, laying a hand on the furniture he had made with discarded wood from the carpenter's shop where he was a janitor. He would be leaving behind his favorite items, two rope-seat chairs and a walnut table. Ivy, Kipbo's mother, was at the bed laying out clothes. Her blue dress with stitched patterns on the front would go with her. So would her yellow hat with the shell comb attached and her high-top shoes. The last thing packed would be her grandmother's snuff tin, which had remained in Ivy's possession during the long months in prison.

When Kipbo began asking more questions, his mother gave him a thumb-size portion of dried goose dusted with bee sugar. Kipbo chewed the treat by the hearth, where he played with the wooden animals his father had carved. When he began to nod, his father carried him to the bed, where he fell asleep.

Outside, the bluff was noisy with the sound of soldiers shouting at villagers starting the trek downtown, the grunts of livestock being confiscated, and the hard yelps of dogs being executed with military lances.

Kipbo slept through the commotion. He awoke several hours later and realized he was alone in the cabin. When he began to cry, Vitsay Ovits, a distant aunt and his new guardian, pushed the cabin door open but remained outside looking at the road. "Get up from there, country man," Vitsay said. "No time for sleeping."

Because the governor of Halifax had insisted that the *Perspicacious* and the *Angel Pequod* also haul away the men in the crowded military prison, a quarter of the residents who had been marched downtown to board the ships returned to their homes. Months later, when no word had come from those who had left the bluff, residents asked military officials, What happened to our families and neighbors? "We're investigating," they were told.

"Throw us back in the jailhouse if need be," one resident said, a year later, when another ship docked in Halifax and two platoons of soldiers arrived on the bluff. "Why should we get on the ship?"

Soldiers whipped the man who had made the threat, and over several days government officials threatened to whip more. Still, no other residents left their homes to board the ships.

W hy did you ask Mr. Platt to give me a job?" Kath Ella asks her father this morning, when they are having their sausage and potatoes at the breakfast table. "I don't want a job there."

"Nobody wants to go to their job," George says. "That's why they call it work."

No longer afraid of her father's reactions, Kath Ella rushes past him after breakfast and stands in the living room between him and the front door. "But Mr. Platt's place is a smelly mess," she says. "Don't make me work there."

"As I remember, you used to love smelly messes," George replies, stepping around Kath Ella and reaching for his hat.

"But I was a child then."

"You still are."

C hevy Platt owns the establishment where Kath Ella will begin her after-school job. He and his wife live in the house of a distant relative who had moved there when the bluff was partially cleared in 1822. The long journey up from the southern United States did not bring Chevy Platt directly to Halifax. He left the south in the fall of 1889, heading for a job in the rich coal country of Cape Breton.

After his long journey up from Mississippi, the first train nineteen-year-old Chevy boarded carried him across Nova Scotia a hundred miles northeast of Halifax to the terminus at Mulgrave Station. There he settled his tired body on the floor of the ferryboat *Guysborough* as it departed for the three-mile journey across the Canso Strait to the island of Cape Breton. Hard rain beat the wooden roof of the ferry as it tossed in the surf at the pier at Point Tupper. There, Chevy and a hundred or so other colored men departed the ferry and trudged a quarter mile to catch another train, this one to Glace Bay.

"Last leg," Chevy said in a rear car at dawn, waving a deck of playing cards, trying to round up a game of Gimme-takeme. "Git up for it, y'all."

Around him, while the train rumbled farther east, men roused from where they slept on wooden benches or on the floor, their knees or elbows resting on suitcases or canvas bags with the belongings they had brought from Texas, Mississippi, and Alabama.

"Your brother done died," said one of the men who lowered himself to the floor beside Chevy. "Don't that call for quiet?"

"Quiet ain't for the living," Chevy said as he dealt the cards. "And quiet ain't never brought a man back from glory."

Chevy picked up his cards without glancing rearward, as he had often the evening before. Miles behind the train was the field where a pile of stones marked the grave of his brother, Tommy. His brother had also been taken with the words the white man had said to get them to board the train in Jackson, Mississippi: that the coal vein at Collier 8-W in Glace Bay was richer than in any other mine in Canada, that at the end of one large shaft the canopy was big enough for two dozen men to stand under, that he hadn't seen coal that rich since he was a boy in Scotland, that coal out of 8-W burned cleaner and coughed up less soot than product from any other mine in Cape Breton. Hell, even the residue from Collier 8-W sold for a pretty nickel.

At the mine office at Glace Bay the next morning, Chevy was the first man in line at the supply and requisition hut to sign the IOUs for his work boots, pants, and hard hat. In the weeks that followed, Chevy often approached the mine's entrance laughing and imitating the blast of the mine horn, the whistle of a far-off train, or the horn of a ship in the bay. He loved how the light struck the tin roof on the engine house, how the coal dust bit his nostrils as he approached the timber arches at the mine entrance, how the hitched-up miniature ponies worked their shoulder muscles before moving forward into the black air. At the end of a twelve-hour day, Chevy even liked the feel of the grime scratching his ankles as he walked down Viceroy Road to the boardinghouse. In the letters home to Mississippi, Chevy said how much he appreciated his job. Work, he wrote, was the best way to cure his homesickness and to honor his buried brother.

A decade later, when the haul at Collier 8-W had plummeted to a tenth of what it had been in 1889, Chevy and his wife moved south to Woods Bluff. There the Platts lived in the back rooms of a cabin and used the front room for a new business, selling handmade brooms and galvanized tin buckets, dishpans, and bathtubs. By the time Kath Ella Sebolt was born, the establishment was doing such brisk business that Chevy Platt moved his family out of the back rooms and offered lodging there as incentive on the advertisement he posted for an employee to mind his store, which was now called Platt's Hardware Barn.

K ath Ella can no longer stall. Her composition for the VMO scholarship has been approved by Mrs. Eatten and driven downtown. She has taken the last part of the yearlong battery for the French college certification exam. Her final exams are still a month away. Still, Friday, April 14, the day she has reluctantly agreed to begin her job at the Hardware Barn, comes much quicker than she had imagined.

Thankfully she has to work at the store only three days a week. Still, during her first weeks there, she hates the tedious tasks of creating new price tags to put on the refurbished appliances, comparing stacks of IOUs with entries in the business ledgers, and, especially, giving hard glances at loitering visitors.

But to her surprise she enjoys doing inventory. She likes scouring the merchandise to see if any of her grandfather's old tools are there. She scrutinizes the chairs, carved ducks, and picture frames to see if any bear his etchings. Kath Ella also enjoys gathering similar merchandise in orderly clusters, nesting the tin buckets, arranging small appliances on the shelves, or lining up the used work boots along the sidewall. By the middle of the third week, she no longer curses when her hands are soiled with soot or her skirt brushes against the rusted seed spreader in the back corner.

A continuing irritant, however, are the boys that come to the store with their baseball bats and gloves, looking around, and buying nothing. When she is away at college next fall, she will miss Clemmond Green; the tall Eatten boys; wooly-headed Buddy Taylor, now chasing after Kiendra; Seth and Graham Teakill; Daniel Steptoe; No-Hips Eddie; even that rascal Tristan Griffin. But for now these visitors are only an annoyance, especially the ones claiming Kiendra will be coming home from Wells Bridge any minute. All the news they have passed on about Kiendra has been dead wrong.

With the warmer weather, the next week of school and the afternoons of work seem to drag on. One afternoon, with her upcoming graduation on her mind, Kath Ella is in front of the store lining up the brooms when she spies Kiendra seated between her aunt and uncle in the back seat of M. T. Everson's jitney as it races by on Dempsey Road. She tries to run after the car, but the road is too muddy.

Was that you I saw today in the back of M. T. Everson's jitney? Kath Ella writes in the evening to Kiendra. *Why didn't you come by the store or my house to say hello?* She mails the letter to Kiendra in Wells Bridge.

The next week Kath Ella receives a reply. *I'll be home for a visit before you can spell Newfundland,* Kiendra writes. *I promise, I promise.*

For the rest of May, if Kiendra does visit, Kath Ella does not see her. At the beginning of June, Kath Ella writes Kiendra with the good news that Shirley has been rehired at the Wales and London. *Thank God,* she writes. *Now I can quit this job soon.*

But a few days before graduation, Shirley announces she has asked Chevy Platt to keep Kath Ella at the store all summer. *I can't wait to get off to college,* Kath Ella writes to Kiendra. *I cannot tell you how happy I will be to get away from Shirley. I hate her.*

So where did the two ships that left Nova Scotia in 1822 finally drop anchor? For years Kath Ella's great-grandfather Kipbo Sebolt asked Vitsay Ovits that question. Before she died in 1843, Vitsay had written letters to Ottawa, to London, and to the governor in Freetown, Sierra Leone, trying to get an answer. The *Angel Pequod* had probably drifted off course in a storm, Kipbo learned, and was never heard from. HMS *Perspicacious* had run aground, but was close enough to the shore of Sierra Leone that passengers had waded in. But did the Jamaicans on board then travel north or south along the Pepper Coast? Or did they go into the interior?

On a spring day in 1858, Kipbo Sebolt left his cabin on the bluff carrying a letter he hoped would reach someone who could give him answers. He was nearing forty and typhus had taken his wife; cholera, all three of his teenage children. The letter had been written by his future bride, seventeen-year-old Jubilee. She often read to him the article in the *Colored Freeman* about a Christian mission in northeast Sierra Leone. Near the mission was a village where a number of residents claimed to have had relatives who had emigrated from the Province of Canada. But the Province of Canada is big country, Kipbo thought, riding into town on a mule-drawn wagon to mail the letter. Would any person in Sierra Leone know the whereabouts of his parents?

Kipbo's letter also mentioned several other family names written in the big ledger book stored near the altar at Basinview Baptist. The Ovitses, the Taylors, and the Cauldens. With a child on the way, Kipbo left the post office convinced that knowing the whereabouts of even one former neighbor would lift his heart.

Several months later, Kipbo sat near the hearth of his cabin, unable to believe he was holding a reply from the mission in Sierra Leone. But the letter was thin and weightless. He ran the tip of his boning knife along the top of the envelope, fearing another disappointment.

His wife, Jubilee, asleep on the bed, had agreed to marry him after he promised to lay a wood floor in the cabin. His father had wanted to lay a floor himself. But wood was scarce on the bluff back then. And any wood his father obtained was used to make furniture to sell or to do repairs on the houses of neighbors.

Kipbo unfolded the letter, fearing the thin paper might crumble in his shaking hands. In nearly half a century, he hadn't heard a word from abroad about a Sebolt or a Gordonell, his mother's family. As far as he knew, he was alone in the world. Holding the letter closer to the flame of the whale-oil lamp, Kipbo stared at the first two lines. He had heard his father also lacked the patience to sit while the woman he loved tried to teach him to read the Bible. He himself had learned to recognize only a phrase or two. After scanning the letter, his eyes went back to the top. There, in the first few lines, were two words he understood: *so sorry.*

Kipbo laid the letter over the smoldering coals in the hearth and stretched out on the woven-grass rug. As a small boy he had hated his mother, Ivy, for making him sleep on the dirt floor. But now the hard ridges were a soothing reminder of his boyhood. Drifting off to sleep, he wondered if Jubilee was correct that the child riding low in her belly was a boy. If her prediction were true he would name the child George. True, it was the name of the king who ordered all those villages burned on Jamaica. But it was also the name of the last Sebolt male to have been buried on Jamaican soil. His grandfather. There was good history in the name, too.

Kipbo did not sleep well that evening. And he woke hating the dirt floor again. Still, it took months of Jubilee's begging before he began gathering wood for a new floor. He had gotten a letter from another mission in Sierra Leone. Again there was no mention of Sebolts, but the letter said some of the names in Kipbo's letter were familiar in that part of the country.

There may still be hope, Kipbo thought as he laid the first plank in the floor. Putting in more planks, he imagined his parents returning to Halifax. He recalled the symbols his father had etched into the wooden chairs, bowls, and utensils he had made to sell to neighbors.

At the board ends, Kipbo etched every other plank with little designs. In a corner he nailed a tiny brass square with the date the floor was laid: 1858.

George Sebolt also named his son George. Nobody called the son Junior. He was always called Little George. Each time Little George asked his grandfather if he would ever go to Sierra Leone or to Jamaica, Kipbo shook his head. "Nothing over the seas for us anymore. We must make do here in the tough land of the Hindquarter. Rocky land, after all, is better than none."

Near the middle of June, Mrs. Eatten herself arrives to deliver the news. On the Sebolts' sofa, wearing another busy print dress, her wide patent leather belt disappearing into the folds of her midsection, she leans forward to speak. "I have always felt Kath Ella was the smartest girl in her class," she tells Shirley. "She got the highest score on the French exams. Her scholarship essay was a struggle, but in the end was first-rate. But the decision was not mine, you understand?"

Mrs. Eatten says that although Kath Ella did not get a scholarship, the committee wrote a nice letter about her. The following day, seated next to the principal's desk, Kath Ella unfolds the letter. It is the same hard wooden chair where, two years earlier, Luela read her disappointing news. Having seen how the white ladies on the scholarship committee nodded as she explained what she had learned from the trouble she had gotten into with Kiendra, Kath Ella was certain she would get the scholarship. But unlike Luela, she will not even be a finalist.

Kath Ella leaves the dinner table later in the evening and goes directly to bed. For several days she imagines her life withering up like a dried beach creature. Buck yourself up, George says. But how can she? With no scholarship, what college can she attend?

"I've been thinking about a woman who used to work with me at the shirtwaist factory," Shirley says to George the next evening at the dinner table. "I believe I remember her saying a college out in New Brunswick was always on the lookout for smart colored students. Let's take Kath Ella out there."

Later in June, after the family has visited the campus, a scholarship is offered. But the amount is not enough. When the only option seems to be the local trade school, Shirley writes a letter to one of the women on the selection committee that had denied Kath Ella a scholarship. On June 23, three days before the graduation ceremony for Woods Bluff Secondary's Class of 1933, a letter arrives from a college in Montreal. A representative from the college will be coming to Halifax in late July. An interview is a mere formality. They already believe Kath Ella will be a nice addition to the campus. A full scholarship is a very good possibility.

"Will she want to go to Montreal?" Shirley asks George.

"She is always going on about traveling," George says. "Of course she will."

The Memory Cabinet

When Kath Ella arrives at Sainte-Marie College in Montreal in September, she is told that only three other colored girls have ever attended the school. What she is not told is that none of those girls graduated. Near the end of the school year, Kath Ella learns from a nice lady in the office of the newly installed president that her late acceptance and scholarship came about because the school was in a panic. Two colored girls who were supposed to enroll that fall chose other schools.

"Your job is to be one of the first colored girls to graduate from that college," Shirley says when Kath Ella is home for summer vacation. "Study hard and you will be."

Kath Ella returns for her second year, determined to study even harder than she had during her first. The classes are more challenging and little annoyances still make some days difficult. Instead of being satisfied that most girls at school are nice to her, she constantly fumes about the few who call her names, keep her out of school clubs, and openly refuse to invite her to parties because she is colored.

By the time Kath Ella begins her junior year, three more colored girls have been admitted. And there is even talk of the college appointing a colored trustee.

Three weeks into the fall term, Kath Ella is pouring herself a drink from the water pitcher in the dormitory hallway when she notices a flyer on the bulletin board announcing an upcoming Deerfield Lecture. Oscar Mislick, a businessman who will be giving the lecture, is a colored man and a childhood acquaintance of the previous college president. Apparently he has helped many students find positions in Toronto after graduation. A South African shipping magnate, an American general, and a nine-year-old mathematics prodigy have all delivered Deerfield Lectures. The first ever given by a colored man will be something to write home about.

"I like going to lectures," Kath Ella tells her roommate, Yvette. "But afterward nobody talks to me at the reception."

"Stand by the refreshments table," Yvette says with a wave of her freckled hand. "After listening to another windbag lecture, *tout le monde* will rush toward you *rapidement.*"

Kath Ella became friends with Yvette last year when they studied together for their French exams, which were extremely difficult at this bilingual college. Yvette has already passed the exam and is now a know-it-all, Kath Ella thinks.

But on Saturday evening after the lecture, Yvette's advice seems prudent. Standing near the refreshments table, Kath Ella is in the middle of her third conversation, when she realizes that the lecturer is approaching her and extending his hand.

"I knew a man who lived in Halifax," Oscar Mislick says. "His name was Joseph Craigsmore and he lived over in Dartmouth. Have you ever had the chance to become acquainted with him?"

"Dartmouth's across the basin," Kath Ella says. "I live in Halifax."

"Where?"

"Woods Bluff."

Oscar's large face is a few shades lighter than Kath Ella's. His silver-gray suit reminds Kath Ella of the suit Daniel Steptoe, one of the young men from the bluff, wore at his wedding, the week before she left for Montreal. A bit of friendliness seems to leave his eyes, as if he is disappointed to hear that she is from the bluff.

Oscar shakes the hands of several students who approach but continues to speak to Kath Ella. "Glad to hear you want to be a teacher," he says. "Shaping young minds is God's work."

"Young children are my favorite," Kath Ella says. "Six- or seven-year-olds. At that age children have capacity and desire."

"Why not join me for lunch tomorrow?" Oscar asks, pressing a card into her palm. "We could discuss getting you a teaching job."

Oscar drains his cup of punch and follows one of the deans back into the crowd. Kath Ella wishes she could have better read the grin on his face as he left. But she recognizes the boyish way he glances behind him when he is a few steps away. Every schoolgirl recognizes the clumsy saunter a boy has after talking to a girl he finds interesting. Kath Ella slides the card into the sleeve of her dress, suspecting the college's social director is watching from somewhere in the room. Mrs. Wittenberg, who takes an interest in all the colored girls at the college, will soon be over to find out Kath Ella's version of her conversation with Oscar Mislick. With so many of the social director's spies in the room, Kath Ella has no choice but to tell the truth.

Through the large picture window Kath Ella can see the lights of Montreal spread out like embers tossed onto a dark plain. Dinner is not mandatory for upper-division students this evening, so the corner suites in the dormitory will be quiet later. Many of the girls will be getting into the freshly washed cars parked near the quadrangle and heading to restaurants, parties, or secluded places around the city. A modern woman can go wherever she wants with whomever she pleases, the girls say. She can be alone with a gentleman she has just met. She can be intimate with a man if she wants to.

Turning from the window, Kath Ella searches the crowd, but Oscar seems to have left. She noticed the wedding ring, of course. Within a week of arriving at the college, she knew the names of all the divorced professors who still wore their wedding rings. Apparently, plenty of professors think it makes them more desirable. Descending the front steps of Deerfield Hall, she realizes she could have asked Oscar if he is married. She could also have found a sly way to ask Mrs. Wittenberg. Why hadn't she?

W e'll go down to lunch in a minute," Oscar says the next afternoon, even before Kath Ella has said hello. After she steps into the hotel room, he closes the door. "I want to talk to you here first."

Oscar's large hands grip her elbow as he directs her further into the room. The maroon rug smells of rose-scented pipe tobacco. The matching curtains, pulled tightly, block the fall sunlight that warmed her on the walk to the hotel. Oscar leads her to a seat on the divan, next to an antique desk.

"Have you seen the little artifact they wrote about my lecture?" Oscar asks, picking up an open newspaper from the desk. Without waiting for an answer, he reads aloud a paragraph praising him for being one of a handful of colored men to have fought overseas with a Canadian Army battalion.

"Were you really fifteen when you joined the service?" Kath Ella asks.

"Ashy-kneed and stupid," Oscar says.

Oscar folds the newspaper and walks to the bed. "Come here a moment," he says, sitting down on the striped bedspread.

Four new blouses were in the suitcases Kath Ella brought with her to college last September. For this visit, she has chosen her pink blouse. The material feels heavy as she sits beside Oscar. He has taken off his tie and is unbuttoning his shirt. A voice in her brain is telling her to keep her blouse on.

But Oscar is already working at the buttons. Feeling the material, his hand rubs against her breast. When he slides his hand down to her stomach, Kath Ella sits up straighter. Talking to him after the lecture, she believed he was around forty years old. Today he looks older. With his shirt open, he shows that he carries his weight on his chest. She never thought she would find something appealing in a mature body. But she does.

He gives her a long kiss.

"This is a nice skirt," Oscar says, his hand now on Kath Ella's thigh. "Let's free you of it, so we don't damage the material."

Kath Ella steps out of her skirt, feeling a nice swelling in her chest and neck. A similar feeling rose up in her several summers ago, when Daniel Steptoe put a hand on her thigh. Though she frowned and pushed his hand away, a nice feeling lingered for several minutes afterward. At Daniel's wedding last August, she thought about that feeling, wanting it to return. And now here it is.

But Daniel Steptoe never relieved her of her blouse and skirt. Nor did he ever lean her back onto a soft bedspread. Lying with her head against the spread, she studies the ceiling, which appears to move almost imperceptibly, like the surface of one of the interior lakes on a day when the wind is quiet. She imagined she would first offer her body to a man in a college dormitory room or a library alcove. He would be a professor. The lovemaking would occur in late fall, with orange sunlight streaming in through leaded windowpanes. She never thought her first time would be in a hotel room with the curtains drawn.

Oscar's tongue feels rough on Kath Ella's neck. But his two fingers feel pleasant as they push into her. Oscar licks her breasts and her jaw clenches. But she does not speak, not wanting to interrupt her lightheadedness. A heat seems to be rising through her and up toward the ceiling. Oscar positions himself between her legs. He kisses her neck and rubs his penis against the lips of her sex. Kath Ella opens her legs wider. Oscar turns her over and rubs his penis against her buttocks. When she lies on her back again, he puts his fingers back inside her. He works his penis with the other hand.

Oscar's fingers now push more roughly inside her. How did he know she would like that? She did not know herself. Each time she relaxes her shoulders, as Oscar's fingers move inside her, her shoulders stiffen again. Oscar's body jerks and then relaxes. Kath Ella relaxes, too, letting the calm sweep over her.

Lying beside Oscar, she finds more pleasure in trying to match his labored breaths. She watches him turn on his side and begin taking in her body again, rubbing her chest and stomach. She is disappointed later as Oscar bounds from the bed and walks to the lavatory.

When he returns, Kath Ella is still on her back, letting the sensations linger. She dresses quickly and the lightheadedness is still with her on the walk back to her dormitory. Seated at her desk, she recalls a few of the strange moans she made during their time together. She opens her French history book, imagining new conversations she will have in the dormitory and back home in Woods Bluff. She is happy she went to the hotel.

S ebolt family lore is rife with stories about the letters Kath Ella's ancestors wrote to officials in London, Jamaica, and Sierra Leone, trying to locate the Sebolts who left Halifax on those two ships. And she has heard how many of the letters went unanswered. She agrees with her father: if somebody writes to you, have the decency to write them back.

Several months after her visit to the hotel room with Oscar Mislick, she wakes up one day with the thought of writing to him. By now the happiness she felt about meeting him has vanished, replaced by distracting feelings that seem to rise in her at least once a day. Each time she imagines him standing before her in the silver-gray suit, he seems just out of reach. But could she write to him?

What is the matter with her? she wonders late one morning, leaving a classroom after a geography exam and recalling not a single map she has drawn. She has met Oscar only once. Why does she worry about the possibility of never seeing him again? She must get her mind firmly on her studies or her school marks will suffer. And then where will she be?

The end of the school year comes with no letter from Oscar. Clearly he does not have the same attitude she has about answering letters. Or perhaps he was reluctant to mail a letter to her at the college, Kath Ella thinks, when she has returned home in early June. Yes, he will respond to a letter if she writes from Woods Bluff.

The thought of this correspondence sends Kath Ella to the shed looking for the four-drawer chest her father made for her twelfth birthday. The year she got the cabinet, she asked her relatives to send mementos in their letters: bits of ribbon, newspaper clippings, portions of school or church programs. If nothing came with a letter, Kath Ella sometimes placed items inside the envelopes herself: a drawing she made, a ticket stub from a bus trip, a dried blade of seagrass. She calls it her memory cabinet.

The shed is in such disarray that it looks as if her father has not straightened up here for several springs. She decides to help with that. After clearing the interior, she pours scalding water over the floor, uncovering etchings on the planks that she had not realized were there. With an ice pick and a wire brush, she excavates sawdust and oils from the grooves in the etchings. With charcoal chips and sheets of onion paper, she lifts a copy of each unique pattern. The twelve sheets contain helixes and the heads of animals and sea creatures, designs she recognizes from the underside of furniture and on the wooden toys her grandfather made for her and her sister.

The memento letters, once stored in drawers of her memory cabinet, are now in boxes. Kath Ella places the charcoal transfers in the bottom drawer of her memory cabinet, leaving the other drawers for her letters from Oscar. There may be many over the next year. No need to put the tiny padlock back on yet. She assumes that Oscar will be discreet in the letter he sends here, just as she has been in hers.

But during June and July, not a single letter that Kath Ella stores in the memory cabinet is from Oscar Mislick. Why hasn't he written?

she wonders, when her summer drifts into August. She addressed the two letters she wrote before leaving Montreal and the letter from here in Woods Bluff to his office in Toronto. She had been circumspect. She wrote about her classes. She reminded Oscar about her desire to teach. She hadn't said anything improper. Did all three letters fail to reach him?

An odd September heat wave beats down on Montreal when Kath Ella returns to the campus. On several afternoons after classes start, she returns to her sweltering dormitory room feeling more depressed than on the day she returned. Finally, in the middle of October, a letter from Oscar arrives.

The typed letter is barely half a page. Oscar asks about the weather in Montreal and what classes she is taking. As the school term progresses, Kath Ella peeks at the letter again every few days before going to bed. In early December, she is elated when another letter from Oscar arrives. He will be in Montreal in February.

They spend two days together, visiting places mostly on the outskirts of Montreal. "The college does a spring excursion to Toronto," Kath Ella tells Oscar on the second night, after she has dressed to leave his hotel room. "I'd like to visit you. May I?"

Oscar, stretched out naked on the bed, rubs his mustache, his eyes directed at his bare feet. "That might not be wise."

"Are you saying you don't want me to come?"

"It will always be better if I visit you. I'm a busy man in Toronto, you understand."

Kath Ella gives a reluctant nod as she slips on her boots. She puts on her coat, wanting to understand, but she does not. For the next few days she walks to classes wondering if it was wise to have gone to the hotel room the first time. Yes, she decides, it was.

Several weeks later, Kath Ella leaves the campus on an excursion bus filled with students from the college. In Toronto, after barely thirty minutes of strolling through the Ontario Museum of Art, she steals away from the chaperone and catches a bus going up Yonge Street.

For an hour she stands across the street from an antique, three-story building. Then she spies Oscar coming outside with a tall man in a suit. The man rides off in a taxi, and Oscar is about to head back into the building when he sees Kath Ella.

"I'm in town on a school trip," she explains as he approaches with a stiff face.

Oscar takes Kath Ella's hand and seems to let himself smile. "Give me the name of the hotel. I'll come by tonight. I will park down the street. Can you get away at six thirty?"

"We're leaving today to go back to Montreal."

"Then why did you come to visit me?"

"I wanted to see you, even for a few minutes."

Something about the statement seems to touch Oscar. But after glancing toward the building, he leads Kath Ella down the sidewalk. They halt near a tall delivery truck. "Perhaps you shouldn't write to me anymore," he says.

"Why not?"

"It would hurt my wife to believe there's something inappropriate between us."

Unable to form words, Kath Ella turns away from Oscar, not looking back as she heads away from him. On the long walk back to the museum, she tries to imagine what she could have done to make him welcome her. She has never met Oscar's wife, yet she feels such hurt each time she recalls his face when he mentioned her.

The streets back in Montreal are covered in a dusting of snow. Kath Ella steps off the bus, wanting to appreciate the sight, but she feels a headache coming. Oscar's words confuse her. Trudging across the campus, she can't help wondering what would have happened if she had stayed overnight in Toronto. In the dormitory lobby she wipes the slush from her boots, concluding that she needs to forget about Oscar. If he cared for her, he would not have mentioned his wife.

This third year of classes is exhausting, especially her French courses. Both professors speak quickly and use big words. When the weather improves she goes only to a few of the popular parties in the Outremont district. And she does not accompany Yvette to any of the athletic matches at the nearby military college. Still, a week after March exams end, she carries a disappointing grade report to the academic building. She has come to ask the matron of students if she can make adjustments to her course of study.

"I'm afraid that is not possible," the matron says. "Your scholarship requires that you study French culture. You can manage, my dear. Work harder."

The matron of students sounds like Mrs. Eatten, Kath Ella thinks later, on the way to the dining hall. Ordinarily that would be a good feeling, but not today.

After dinner, Kath Ella wants to lie down, but she feels nervous and energetic and decides to write a few letters. The first letter is to Philippe Mallachoy, a young man she has been meaning to write for weeks. Philippe has been leaving notes for her at the reception desk downstairs, but she has not picked up any of them. She met him last year at a memorial service for his father, who had been the college's chaplain. Last spring she told Philippe she was being courted by a man who lived out of town. Still, Philippe insisted on escorting her to the fall social. At the Ice Breakers carnival he bought her a large Strawberry Cassandra and said she was the only girl he thought of night and day. But one afternoon, as she was strolling along Rue Saint-Hubert and thinking of giving her body to Philippe, she saw him a few blocks away, kissing another girl from the college. Watching them in their fur coats, smiling at a troupe of jugglers that had wandered over from Rue Saint-Denis, she was hot with anger.

Kath Ella finishes her letter to Philippe while the last bits of sunlight strike the enormous oak limbs outside the window. *Seeing the kiss is not the reason I no longer want to keep company with you*, she writes. *I simply must be attentive to my studies now.*

Then she opens the most recent letter from Oscar. It had arrived several days ago. Written with the hard strokes of an expensive fountain pen, the letter explains how disappointed Oscar feels in recognizing he could never care for her the way she wants. Reading the letter again, Kath Ella recoils at how much pain the words cause her.

Eventually she places four sealed envelopes along the edge of her desk. She feels no compunction about mailing the letters to Oscar and Philippe. And she will certainly mail the letter home to Shirley. But what about the letter she has written to Oscar's wife? She was so satisfied with herself when she had the idea of not including a return address. But now she feels bad. Should she send that letter, too?

At a piano recital in Byerly Hall the next afternoon, Kath Ella waves at Philippe across the room. She feels happy to be done with him, or at least resigned to never spending time with him again. Leaving the auditorium, she heads across campus, realizing that no new letters from Oscar Mislick will make their way into her memory cabinet back home. She is happy about that, too.

Her father also says that you should always answer a person's letter even if your response is that they should go jump in the basin. Later in the day, Kath Ella carries the four letters to the postal bureau. Standing before the letter bin, she drops in the letters to Oscar, to Philippe, and to Shirley. Turning to leave, she walks a few steps, returns to the bin, and drops in the letter to Oscar's wife.

Back in her room, Kath Ella recalls her criticism of Oscar and realizes he is not the only one guilty of failing to correspond. There are a number of unanswered letters stacked on her own desk. In the evening she skims a few from Kiendra Penncampbell. Based on what Kiendra writes in the letters, Kath Ella has evidently been revealing plenty about life here in Montreal. She wrote to Kiendra about the joy she felt when she took a boat trip up the Saint Lawrence River with Oscar, and of being a teacher's aide at the Saturday education program at the

East Lawrence Community Center. She even wrote about how Ursula Branbower called her a dirty nigger monkey after she beat her out for junior class stentorian. Kiendra knows about the professor Kath Ella had let fondle her breasts during evening office hours, and, of course, about the troubles with Oscar Mislick and Philippe Mallachoy. My goodness, the things she probably should not have written.

You have never come to see me when I'm home from college, Kath Ella writes in a letter to Kiendra. *If you do not come up to Halifax this time, you will miss seeing T-House Patton. I just happen to have two tickets to his sold-out show in July at the China Tavern. If you do not come up from Wells Bridge, I guess I will have to give the other ticket to my sister, Luela.*

The day she returns home to Halifax, Kath Ella forgets about Kiendra for a few hours. She is elated to learn she won't have to toil in the Hardware Barn. Chevy Platt says that in honor of her becoming a senior, she can have a job at his other business downtown. But she is hesitant to tell her father.

"What does Chevy Platt do at that office these days?" she overheard George ask Shirley the previous summer. "Other than take money from jailbirds?"

"Chevy Platt runs a legal business," Shirley replied.

"Well, legal isn't necessarily legitimate," George said.

To Kath Ella's astonishment, neither George nor Shirley raises objections to her taking the new job. And neither objects when she asks if she can live with Luela for the summer, to be closer to the job.

Am I the favorite daughter again? Kath Ella wonders on Tuesday morning, beaming as she carries her suitcases up the stairs to Luela's third-floor apartment in Simms Corner. Shirley and George must think three years of college have matured their daughter.

Two days later, Kath Ella and her sister are preparing to sit down to a very early dinner when the doorbell rings.

"Kiendra?"

"Hey, girl."

Kath Ella holds her friend in a long embrace. "What happened to your long hair?" she asks when she lets go.

Kiendra plays with her bangs and then pats the side of the full-volume waves. "Why are you crying?" she asks. "My hair will grow back."

"I'm not crying about your hair, silly," Kath Ella says. "I suppose it finally feels like I'm home."

"Simms Corner isn't home," Kiendra says. "The bluff is."

While Kiendra helps Luela set the table, Kath Ella lifts the cover off a pot on the stove. Her sister cooking a nice meal on a Thursday before going to work? She should have suspected a surprise visitor. Spaghetti with clams is Kiendra's favorite dish.

Kiendra had written in a recent letter that she had lost a bucketload of weight. But she doesn't look thin. She moves easily in Rosa's beige dress and red suede shoes. Luela is right, Kath Ella thinks, watching Kiendra slide onto a chair at the table. Kiendra is looking shapely like her sister.

"Wells Bridge was too quiet a place for this gal," Kiendra says, during the meal. "When I skedaddled from there, I stayed at a few places I shouldn't have. But now that I'm seeing Buddy Taylor again, I'm trying to get right with Jesus."

"That is a tale you've been telling all over the Hindquarter," Luela says. "I hope you mean it."

For dessert there is a four-layer lemon cake. Watching Kiendra use a fork to separate the sections of her slice of cake like she used to as a child delights Kath Ella. That is a sight she wishes she could capture for her memory cabinet. But the sight also dredges up a few sad childhood memories. Later, while they clear the table, she is tempted to ask Kiendra if her mother still believes the trouble the girls got into a few years ago in the South End was Kath Ella's fault. Kath Ella wishes she didn't concern herself with that matter any longer, but she does.

In the living room, Luela presents two tickets for the Thursday matinee at the downtown cinema. "I can't use these," she says. "I have to work."

"I've got a present, too," Kath Ella says, reaching into her purse. "This one's just for you, Kiendra."

Kath Ella takes out a silver-plated bracelet with two dangling charms. "You gave me a present for my birthday once," she tells Kiendra. "But in all these years, I never gave you one back. The bracelet holds twelve charms, but I could only afford two."

Kiendra reaches for the bracelet, as if she is afraid it might take flight. With a broad grin, she lays it across her wrist. While Kiendra puts on the bracelet, Luela tells her and Kath Ella the news about the apartment building being erected a few blocks down Gottingen Street. "I heard they want twenty dollars a month for a tiny two-bedroom," Luela says. "Now who in the Hindquarter has that kind of money?"

Kiendra does not seem to be listening, too busy grinning as she inspects a charm on the bracelet. Later, when she and Kath Ella are preparing to leave to catch the bus downtown, she shows the bracelet to Luela, shaking it near her face.

"Yes, gal, I see the trinkets," Luela says. "Now quit jangling them at me. God does not like a show-off."

Outside, instead of crossing the street to catch a downtown bus, Kiendra halts on the crosswalk, looking in the direction of the construction site of the new apartment building. "The fence has come down," she says. "Let's go take a peek."

Kath Ella has to step quickly to keep up with Kiendra, who is rushing down the sidewalk. At the construction site only the length of chain link that fronts the sidewalk has been removed. Three sides of the work site are still fenced. Kath Ella studies the redbrick building, whose front is covered in a fine dust. No grass has yet been planted in the front yard.

"My daddy says the city hall big shots are putting up this rat-hotel to stop more house building on the bluff," Kiendra says. "They are trying to get people off the Hindquarter."

"Plenty of people need to get off the Hindquarter," Kath Ella says.

"Yes, but why can't it be to a place with nice bedrooms *and* a nice yard?"

Kiendra heads along the side of the building, which is littered with empty paint buckets, broken floor tiles, and piles of discarded bricks. "We don't want to be late for the picture show," Kath Ella says, walking behind her.

"Then we better put some fire in our feet," Kiendra says, starting to stride faster.

Three wings jut out of the back of the building. At the rear door of the nearest wing, Kiendra presses her face against a small window and looks inside. When she turns the knob and pulls, the door opens.

Kiendra wheels around and looks at Kath Ella with a wide grin. "Well, what do you know?"

"We don't have time to go inside," Kath Ella says, turning to head back. "We have to hurry to make it to the picture show."

Heading toward the front of the building, Kath Ella hears the back door shut. What a relief to see Kiendra round the back corner. But why is she carrying a half brick?

Before reaching Kath Ella, Kiendra halts and holds up the half brick. "How much you want to bet me I can't bust that high window?" she says.

Kath Ella watches with disbelief as Kiendra stretches out her arm and points at a third-floor window. She could give a laugh, as if she suspects Kiendra is just kidding, but she cannot manage it. That she has let herself again arrive someplace where Kiendra plans to do mischief angers her. She recalls the look on Kiendra's face by the crib the evening they carried the doll into the house in the South End. She remembers the doll as it lay in the crib next to the baby. Later the doll was a mangled mess—head, body, and limbs yanked apart and tossed back into the shopping bag. She left the bluff for college, believing Kiendra was mangled, too. Yet in none of Kiendra's letters from Wells Bridge had there been any hint that the reckless girl still existed. But now here she is, wearing grown-up hair and suede shoes.

"I'm sure that you are beyond childish pranks," Kath Ella stammers, then resumes her way toward the front of the building. "I'm sure you will drop that piece of brick and we can get going."

Kiendra remains near the back corner. She weighs the brick in her hand the way her aunt in Wells Bridge used to weigh cantaloupes at the market. Its coarse surface reminds her of the patch of rough skin on her aunt's arm. Her aunt says an elderly relative she once cared for had spilled a pot of boiling water on her arm, not knowing who she was. Kiendra has never believed that. For most of the first week she lived in the house in Wells Bridge, she went to bed crying about how horribly her aunt treated her uncle. And not once during the two and a half years she lived there did her aunt offer a kind word to her.

A hazy reflection moves across the surface of the high window. Kiendra frowns. She recently heard that Gussie Mills has been telling former neighbors that when Kiendra went missing from the bluff years ago, she had been carried off to a crazy farm. Her aunt certainly thought the girl's head was scrambled, because during the first few months Kiendra lived in Wells Bridge, the woman took her to the doctor several times for observation. The doctors found nothing unusual in her head, so she must be cured of whatever the fever did to her brain. Still, the reflection moving across the high window disquiets Kiendra. Is it real or is it a trick of her mind?

Kath Ella looks back just as the brick leaves Kiendra's hand. It arches high but misses the window. After striking the side of the building it tumbles to the ground, where it lands with a thud. Kiendra is about to toss it again but she hesitates, looking toward the sound of someone yelling near the front of the building.

A constable is coming.

Rushing forward, the constable motions for Kath Ella and Kiendra to approach him. "I'm not going there," Kiendra says. "He saw me throw the brick."

"What are you going to do?" Kath Ella asks.

"Go in the back and out the front. Easy peasy."

The constable yells for Kiendra to halt, but she disappears around the back. At the curb, a younger, pudgier constable has gotten out of their vehicle. After a signal from the older constable, the younger one takes off toward the far side of the building. "Your little friend thinks she is smarter than me," the constable says, approaching Kath Ella. "But my buddy there will catch that little imp when she comes around the other side. Meantime, you get to that vehicle and wait there until I return."

Kath Ella takes a few steps, but then looks behind her at the constable running after Kiendra. Should she go wait at the vehicle as she was told? Or should she go see what is happening at the rear of the building?

Now a racket comes from the front of the building. Kath Ella rushes to the entrance. Through the small window in the door she can see Kiendra, banging on the door to get out. Kath Ella reaches for the doorknob, but there is a metal plate where the knob should be. Three boys arrive and help Kath Ella push the door. But it will not budge.

Kath Ella looks through the window again. The lobby is empty. *Come back here, Kiendra. Come back.*

Kath Ella runs alongside the building trying to shout again to Kiendra, but though she opens her mouth, no words come. At the nearest wing the rear door has been flung open. Somewhere inside, Kiendra is yelling. The constables are inside, too, barking orders. The commotion seems to be happening on the second floor. Have they cornered her there?

When one of the boys tries to enter the building, Kath Ella shoves him back. "All of you had better stay right here," she yells. Her voice has come again, but it is thin and brittle. "If one of you tries to come inside, I will knock your head."

She hears a crash inside the building. Has Kiendra thrown something at the constables? A loud pop, like a firecracker, echoes inside. Then she hears Kiendra scream.

Kath Ella rushes into the building. Her legs feel heavy as they carry her up the stairwell. With each step she feels her face grow hotter. In the air, thick with dust, it is a struggle to breathe.

On the second-floor landing she sees the pudgy constable approaching out of the gray dimness. Breathing heavily, he looks ten years older than he had outside.

"Afraid I can't let you go any farther, ma'am," he says. "Go back down the steps and exit the building."

"Not without Kiendra."

When Kath Ella steps forward, the constable raises his pistol. He sticks it so close to her right eye that when she blinks, her eyelash brushes the barrel.

"I said back on out the door, ma'am. Do it before I blow your damn head off."

The Ladies Club

Over the years, Oneresta Higgins has served on numerous committees working to improve the lives of Woods Bluff residents. The notice she sent last winter, announcing the dates for the 1936 Woods Bluff Spring Jamboree, included a note informing residents that Platt's Hardware Barn was offering a nice discount on house paint. The note came after the long speech Oneresta gave at the last Woods Bluff Citizens' Advisory Meeting about how nice the bluff would look if neighbors painted their houses vibrant colors. Chevy Platt didn't have the paint in stock at the Hardware Barn, the note said. But if enough neighbors placed orders (and paid in advance) they could purchase the paint at wholesale.

It is now the second week of June, and the only structures that have been freshly painted are a few sheds and one outhouse. During the jamboree, residents told Oneresta that they liked her idea but that it would take a while to gather the funds. Even with the discount, the paint is very expensive.

Oneresta can't disagree. She promised Chevy Platt that she would order four gallons of sea-green paint. But she has only found money enough to afford three of the four gallons she will need to paint her house. Visitors coming by the gray two-story bungalow Oneresta shares with her niece Marcelina might well remark that her property could stand a bit of color. In the front yard, two rosebushes, bordered by a circle of white gravel, have stopped blooming. And although jars of white trilliums and purple violets (the few flowers that will tolerate the rocky loam in the backyard) sit on window ledges in the kitchen and the front rooms, those plants wilted days ago.

For the first time in weeks, however, Oneresta has not once worried about where she will get the money to buy the last gallon of house paint. Yesterday she learned that Kiendra Penncampbell, the girl sent to the Halifax hospital on Thursday with a gunshot wound, is fighting a virulent infection. Having already visited the hospital and gone shopping with Kiendra's mother, Oneresta is now arranging a meeting of the Woods Bluff Ladies Club. Only one item is on the agenda: what to do about the incident that put Kiendra in the hospital.

The club used to meet monthly, like the Peacoat Ladies, the Garden Club, and the Sisters of Heavenly Stars. Most of the ladies in those other clubs are from families that have been in Woods Bluff less than fifty years. The women of the ladies club are from long-back families—Higgins, Ovits, Steptoe, Tipps, Sebolt, Teakill—families that lived in Woods Bluff when Sadie Caulden's great-grandmother convened the first meeting in 1820. Now the club meets only when there is serious business.

"Is that a peach jam icing I see over the Jump-Up cake?" Marcelina asks Oneresta on the front porch.

"Best fix I could think of," Oneresta says.

Marcelina sits down in a nearby chair, fussing with the plastic cap over her damp hair. "I guess I'll go on over and see Rosa," she says.

"Why are you pestering Rosa?" Oneresta asks. "She's got plenty to do. Why don't you get Steppie Caulden to curl your hair?"

"Rosa told me to come," Marcelina says. "She's going to do

Donnita's hair, too, before they go back to the hospital. She said pressing hair takes her mind off her daughters."

"We're all worried about Kiendra. But why is Rosa worried about Donnita?"

"Donnita isn't taking things too well. She's been saying her sister was pushed down the stairs after the bullet hit her. Didn't you hear that, too?"

"Here-say-there-say is what that is."

Marcelina dabs at her damp temples with a hand towel. "I heard the constable tried to touch Kiendra the wrong way. That's why she slapped him."

"She slapped him?"

"What I heard. You think it's true?"

"What's thinkable's possible. Of course the girl should have known better than to tussle with a constable." Oneresta turns a pincushion several times, hoping her big-eye needle has not gotten lost again. "Now I'm not saying Kiendra's to blame for what happened to her. But she shouldn't have been at the building in the first place. Guivalier told her to stay away. This is what happens when a child doesn't listen to her father."

"Or her mother."

From the box at her feet, Oneresta takes out a square of cloth. She lets the square glide across her arm. Two or three years earlier she scoffed at the girls selling combs or packets of flower seeds, the young men peddling lye soap, and especially that distasteful Clemmond Green, who she heard was selling numbers. But these days, with everything costing more—and with her need to set the example and complete her order for house paint—she has no choice but to start sewing again. Today's job is a stack of handkerchiefs, silk ones to distinguish her merchandise from those coarse hats Lucille Breakstone still peddles at the baseball games.

"Guess I'll get going," Marcelina says.

Oneresta examines the square for imperfections, knowing Marcelina's eyes are still on her. The child knows she's too young to attend a ladies club meeting. But that hasn't stopped her from asking. The big-eye needle is not in the pincushion, so Oneresta plucks another one. "I suppose you're right," she says, picking up the spool of thread from her lap. "You should get going."

After her niece has gone, Oneresta sits a moment, unable to decide what stitch to use to edge this square. With a raised hand, she shields her eyes from the sun and looks down the hill. In Centervillage, a truck has pulled up to the bus stop where the men gather to be picked up for evening work at the sugar refinery or the cotton factory. The truck idles less than a minute before driving off, leaving two men standing.

As Oneresta threads the needle, her eyes blur. When she closes her eyes, her nose is assaulted by the vinegary scent of the blue pines encroaching on the side yard. People thought her relatives were crazy to build this house and the one across Dempsey Road. It took back-breaking labor to put pilings into the hard rock. Digging the garden was no cakewalk either. The two houses are a testament to the Campbell brothers, who had made something of nothing. That was why it was such a loss when the influenza menace killed both brothers. When her husband died five years ago, Oneresta considered joining Marcelina in the smaller house across the road. The checks from her dead husband's city pension were being eaten by the cost of winter coal. Money got especially tight after Marcelina's trade school hiked its tuition. Even with Marcelina working, Oneresta is considering closing off the top floor of the house next winter and raising the rent on the house across the road.

The aunt who left Marcelina the other house couldn't put three stitches in a straight line. It was her uncle Bishop, a tailor, who taught her to stitch. Oneresta almost laughs thinking about Bishop, but she remembers she's selling these scarves to assist a grieving mother. She visited the hospital yesterday with a red-and-gold scarf for Kiendra. But Windsome Taylor offered cash for it, not credit the way folks these days operate. The news from Windsome wasn't good, so Oneresta let go of the scarf and now she is making something green for Kiendra. Isn't green the color of epiphany or redemption? If the color green doesn't bring Kiendra good luck, might the simple act of sewing?

Oneresta can't be sure. The quilt she sewed years ago for her ten-year-old grandson didn't help him survive the day the munitions ship exploded in the basin. She was drinking then—nobody knew how much—and was napping the afternoon the boy snuck off the bluff with his friends and ended up in the North End. Judging from his injuries, the doctor said the blast must have thrown her grandson half a city block.

Drinking hadn't stopped Oneresta from doing the community work needed to get into the Woods Bluff Ladies Club. And now she is co-chairwoman. In the bedroom, while searching for her eyeglasses, she hears voices in the front yard. The ladies are early, she thinks, kneading the pillows on the living room sofa. That's a good sign. Still, what deep work can they do for Kiendra? The important work is now in the hands of doctors.

For the third time in two days, Kath Ella turns over in her bed and buries her face deep in the pillow. As with the last two times, her memory of what happened at the building in Simms Corner is hazy. She recalls a scream, the shrill shriek of a young boy. At least it sounded like a young boy. If she stays awake, some vision of what is causing the screams may come to her. But does she want to remember? She closes her eyes tighter. If she tries, maybe she can will herself to sleep again.

She woke up thinking she heard someone tapping at her bedroom window. But the tapping must be in her head. Yesterday, when George and Shirley were visiting her bedside, she heard one of them say that Kiendra had lost a bucket of blood. If that is true, no way could Kiendra have risen from the hospital bed, let alone walked here for another visit. What Kath Ella needs now is another hard sleep, like the one she fell into after arriving home, still trembling and barely audible. She remembers refusing the buttered bread and soup Shirley offered. Maybe that was a mistake. Some nourishment would have soothed the dull aches and intermittent tremors that have plagued her every time she opens her eyes. Had anyone heard her a few hours ago when she woke suddenly and screamed?

When the tapping starts again, Kath Ella lifts her face from the pillow. Noticing a figure at the window, she almost screams again. But she realizes it is not Kiendra. It is Kiendra's sister, Donnita.

"I knocked at the front door," Donnita says, raising the window higher. "Nobody answered."

Kath Ella sits up in the bed, listening for noises in the house. There are none. She notices that the bed she has been sleeping on is still made. And she is dressed. "How is Kiendra doing?" she says, rising.

Donnita is only four years older than Kiendra. But today she looks much older than twenty-two. Her freshly pressed hair has rows of large stiff curls, yet to be combed out. She seems to be thinking over her answer. "Rosa and Guivalier say she is resting."

"That's all they said. What happened to her?"

Donnita looks at Kath Ella with eyes that suggest she hasn't been getting adequate sleep.

"You were there," she says, a bit sharp. "Don't you know?"

Kath Ella shakes her head.

"The girls are having a meeting," Donnita says. "Us girls need to talk about a few things."

"I don't feel up to going to a meeting today," Kath Ella says.

"Not today. Monday. We're meeting at the Bowl."

"The Bowl is where the boys congregate."

"Girls can go there, too."

"Not if they want any peace."

Kath Ella moves to the window as a car groans down the hill. Eventually the vehicle will pass the Bowl. Dusty in summer, the Bowl is covered in the fall and winter by mud that can sometimes be treacherous. Last year Clem Sasser's dog was chasing a woodchuck across the Bowl when both dog and woodchuck slid into a deep crack in the rocks. Buddy Taylor had the idea of lowering a gunnysack. To everyone's surprise, the dog climbed right inside.

"The boys say they are going to collect money," Donnita says.

"What for?"

"To buy firecrackers. They want to throw a party for Kiendra when she gets out of the hospital."

Kath Ella frowns.

"Don't bring that face," Donnita says. "Kiendra likes firecrackers."

"Yes, but the constables don't. Nobody is going to give those boys money for firecrackers. The boys ought to have learned a lesson from the time they nearly burned down the schoolhouse. Remember that?"

"The neighbors might give the girls some money." Donnita sets a tall cylindrical tin on the window ledge. On it are the words OTTAWA'S BEST BUTTER COOKIES and below them a picture of a horse covered in a plaid stable blanket. "At the meeting on Monday we'll decide what to buy for Kiendra. It will be something nice. After the meeting, us girls are going to the hospital. Can you come?"

"I have to go to work on Monday."

Donnita reaches out her arm and presents her wrist, pretty brown and not scarred like Kiendra's. "My sister is missing the bracelet you gave her," she says. "Her boyfriend broke into the building in Simms Corner looking for it."

"I doubt he'll find it."

Donnita looks as though she is about to leave the window. Instead she places a hand on the ledge. "Are you afraid one of the girls will say something smart to you?"

"Like what?"

"Like that Kiendra wouldn't have gotten shot if she had not come up from Wells Bridge to see you. I heard one of the girls already said that." Looking mildly angry, Donnita stiffens her body and looks at

Kath Ella, as if knowing her words hurt. Recognizing that Kath Ella is too weak to manage a response, she slackens her shoulders and lowers her eyes to the tin can. "Of course, if I hear that at the meeting on Monday," she says, "I will point out that Kiendra came up here to see Buddy Taylor. And to see about getting a ticket to the T-House concert at the China Tavern."

Donnita's last words give Kath Ella a bit of strength and now she wants to respond. But as she is gathering words, Donnita jumps down from her perch and disappears toward the front of the house.

Later in the afternoon, Oneresta is putting the last stitches on another scarf when the Reverend Clifford Steptoe and Hezekiah Eatten walk through her front gate. Both men mount the porch steps brazenly, like owners come round to collect late rent.

"Warm today," Oneresta says, putting her thimble aside.

The men sit down.

"Sunshine's a blessing, sister," Reverend Steptoe says.

Hezekiah, the darker of the two men, nods and opens the copy of the *Colored Freeman* that was lying in the chair. Not wearing his eyeglasses, he scans the paper as if content to let Reverend Steptoe lead the interrogation. Heavy and round-chested, Reverend Steptoe talks with a deep, half-hoarse voice Oneresta had once found appealing. "Sent word for you yesterday," he says. "Why didn't you come see me?"

"Been busy."

"Busy going downtown, I hear. Talking to white folks."

"We ladies decided to go downtown a few times, yes."

Seeing the men exchange glances, Oneresta puts aside her cloth and goes inside for iced tea. In the kitchen she stabs at the block of ice with a pick, trying to decide how to handle these men. Aside from the fight the two had years ago, when Hezekiah threatened to marry the reverend's ex-girlfriend, they've been thick as syrup since childhood. Neither seems pleased that she is butting in with regard to matters concerning Kiendra. No doubt they will give her another lecture about what their fathers have done for Woods Bluff, how an Eatten and a Steptoe got city officials to supply wood to build a bigger church. But men from other families did the work of building the church. Bettie Ovits's savings paid for the new pulpit and pews. Why isn't her name on the front plaque along with that of Hezekiah's grandfather?

On the porch, after filling two glasses, Oneresta leaves them on the tray for the men to serve themselves. "Mrs. Klacafee agrees that tossing a brick ought not get a young woman shot," Oneresta says, picking up her sewing again. "She says somebody in Halifax will pay for Kiendra's hospital bills, even if it has to be her."

"Not all bank checks promised from downtown get written," Reverend Steptoe says. He takes a long drink of tea. "Don't you think this is something the men ought to handle?"

"Whatcha doing to handle matters?"

"We talked to the head constable," Reverend Steptoe says. "Told the mayor we feel Guivalier ought to get compensated. The mayor listened."

"Yes, but did he hear?"

"Plain as rain. And if the mayor keeps hearing, maybe we can get us electricity at the elementary and secondary school. The houses, too. And we're going to get a water line out here. Leave it to us, Sister Higgins."

"You gonna get the dump moved, too?"

"Anything's possible. Our fathers believed that."

Hezekiah Eatten finally reaches for a glass of iced tea. He got his broad shoulders from his mother, who used to stand over Oneresta and the other students doing summing and subtraction on those rough-hewn benches in the old church. Who knows where he got the long face or sharp chin.

"Want you ladies to butt out of things," Hezekiah says. "Let the men handle matters."

"Right now all I'm doing is helping Rosa," Oneresta says. "Don't have time for butting in."

The men exchange glances again. Then, as if to lay the matter to rest, each drains his glass. Hezekiah rattles the ice in his glass, but Oneresta does not rise to pour more tea. Last year, for the first time, she didn't vote for Hezekiah to become co-chair of the community board. She wanted pigheaded Samuel Ovits, or even Raymond Griffin, someone who still lived in Woods Bluff. Hezekiah was elected by two votes, one probably from Marcelina. That girl never could be depended on to do what she was told. Watching the men reach for their hats, Oneresta realizes she forgot the lemon slices. Ordinarily she would apologize for the oversight, but right now she feels no compunction to do so.

Half an hour after the men have gone, Marcelina returns. "Back so soon?" Oneresta says. "And why isn't your hair pressed?"

"When I got there, Rosa and Donnita were fighting about what to do with the money some of the girls have already collected. Donnita has it, but when Rosa asked for it, Donnita tried to hit her."

"I don't believe a word of that. The girls just started collecting. Steppie Caulden didn't have that much money in the tin she carried when she came by here."

"Yes, but down in Centervillage, she had several of the proprietors in tears. Bound to have gotten more than a nickel or two there."

Oneresta shakes her head. "That girl tried to hit her mother? She's lost her mind now, too. Just like her sister."

In the shed in the backyard, the interior structure is sound, but the front is riddled with bruises from years of enduring too many harsh Nova Scotia winters. Even on the interior of the front door, the nail heads are bleeding little ferric currents down ashen and pitted planks. But the floor planks, with the wonderful etchings on the ends, are still in good shape. They easily support the heavy worktable in the corner, where Shirley, in an old dress and straw hat, is binding bunches of onions with twine.

"Get away from here, girl," Shirley yells when Kath Ella walks to the table. "Do you want the smell to get on your clothes?"

After using her hips to push Kath Ella away from the table, Shirley reaches for the ball of twine. "You're not going back to work today, are you?" she says.

"I wanted to. Why did you let me fall asleep again?"

"Because you should rest another day."

"I've rested all weekend, and yesterday. That's enough."

"Do you remember what happened?"

Kath Ella shakes her head. "Why is my luggage in the living room?"

"George brought it home."

"But I'm spending the summer with Luela."

"Not anymore." Shirley takes off her hat and fans her neck. "George wrote to the college, asking if they'll let you come back early."

"I need to earn money this summer," Kath Ella says.

"Yes, but you have shown that you can't manage to stay out of trouble long enough to make any."

"I'm not going to quit my job."

"Your father's not asking you to quit your job, just end it early."

"I wasn't doing anything wrong in Simms Corner."

"Nothing you can remember. But something wrong put Kiendra in the hospital. And now your father and I have to bring you downtown for a hearing with the peace officer. George wants you on a bus soon as the hearing is over."

"This is madness."

"Quite the contrary. Your father is trying to send you away from madness."

Kath Ella picks up her father's Beretta knife and begins cutting lengths of twine. What little energy she had after her nap has dissipated. But she cannot bring herself to lie around the house, afraid of remembering what happened at the apartment building. "Daddy doesn't have to get me a ride to see Kiendra," she says. "I can ask Omar to give me a lift to the hospital."

As Kath Ella expects, the mention of Chevy Platt's great-nephew, Omar, who also works at the business in Simms Corner, causes Shirley's back to stiffen. She takes the knife from Kath Ella and shoves it into the pocket of her dress. "Did you know Omar Platt is behind in his studies?" she asks. "That's what I learned when he was here yesterday."

"Omar was here yesterday?"

"Barely a few minutes."

"Why didn't you wake me?"

Shirley shrugs and ties another bunch of onions. "That boy may be smart," she says, inspecting her knot. "But he does not apply himself. What kind of young man is that for you? Wasn't there a college boy in Montreal? Philip somebody?"

"Philippe," Kath Ella says. "You wouldn't like him either. He has too many lady friends."

Kath Ella walks out of the shed quickly. She crosses the yard, surprised by the anger she feels at hearing mention of Philippe Mallachoy. There will be no going back to that boy.

Shirley may be right about her being too exhausted to go to work today, she tells herself in the bedroom, but Shirley is not right about Omar Platt. If her mind had been right in the shed earlier, Kath Ella would have mentioned that she had seen a brand-new *Strengths of Materials* textbook on the desk Omar shares with the assistant office manager. Shirley would be pleased to hear that Omar is back in school. But after the headaches Kath Ella has had with those men in Montreal, she is not ready to sing the praises of another man. And Shirley needn't worry about her daughter having strong feelings for Omar Platt. Since arriving in Halifax from Mississippi at six years old to live with his great-uncle, Omar has been visiting the bluff for years. Yet Kath Ella barely knows him. Still, seeing him last night might have helped her feel better.

Trying to think what she might give Kiendra to replace the lost bracelet, Kath Ella reaches for the rosewood jewelry box. The imitation pearl brooch might be the thing. But if it's true that the bullet barely missed Kiendra's heart, is a chest brooch appropriate? Kath Ella reaches into another compartment, afraid of recalling too much how she felt when she learned the extent of Kiendra's injury. She wants to feel better, so she lets herself recall the rush of heat to her face the day Philippe Mallachoy placed the earrings with tiny blue stones into her hand. If she gives them to Kiendra, each time she sees them on Kiendra's ears she'll regret lacking the strength to send back the earrings in the letter she mailed to Philippe before leaving Montreal.

For years Kath Ella and her sister, Luela, have admired their grandmother's jewelry box. Yet her sister had surrendered their grandmother's treasure to her, as a present for graduating from Woods Bluff Elementary and Secondary. Each time Kath Ella returns home for the summer, Kiendra's sister, Donnita, has acted like a generous older sister. Unable to choose a new present for Kiendra, Kath Ella closes the jewelry box. Why can't she be generous, too?

From the bureau, she picks up the cookie tin with the horse on the front, wanting to throw it out the window. What on earth would compel one of the girls to say that Kath Ella is the reason Kiendra got shot? That is patently wrong. But, then, is it?

Later, bright sunlight bears down on Dempsey Road as Kath Ella enters a neighbor's yard carrying the tin. Word has probably gotten around that she doesn't remember what happened at the building. Still, some neighbors will ask anyway. She might well sit for a moment in a neighbor's living room or on their porch and explain that she hopes to remember more after her visit to the hospital. She will say the best thing the neighbor can do for the Penncampbell family is to pray for Kiendra's recovery. Even if you have already given a little money, she will say, a little more would be a great help.

Omar Platt and the American Nurse

K ath Ella gets off the crowded and noisy city bus in front of the building in Simms Corner, missing the two days she had walked to work from her sister's apartment. Each day, refreshed from her leisurely four-block walk, she began work swollen with the mature pride of a young woman soon to be a college graduate. She left work late last Thursday afternoon a bit tired but eager for a summer at her new job. There were to be new experiences living in Simms Corner, plenty of them more fun than spending the summer at her parents' house on the bluff. But what a horrible few days it has been since. And now that she has once again lowered herself in her parents' eyes, they want her out of their sight. Especially her father. When has that man ever corresponded with anyone at the college? Clearly he's got a rock in his claw to ship her off to college early.

Given all the stern warnings her father has been giving her these last few days about how she should comport herself when traversing the city, Kath Ella half expected him to suggest that she needed a chaperone again to ride the bus. But knowing how upset she was about having to move out of her sister's apartment, perhaps he decided not to push his luck.

Platt's Insurance and Surety does business in Simms Corner at 654 Gottingen Street, a two-story, beige brick building that also houses a dentist, a dry cleaner, and a beauty shop.

"Not today, sugar," the office manager tells Kath Ella in the small lobby, where she is about to sit down at the reception desk. "Go on to the back. We'll find something else for you to do today, rather than deal with the customers."

But sorting papers and making files brings Kath Ella no relief. She is in no mood to sit in the back office. Omar's older cousin, Kiryl Platt, who runs the office now that Chevy Platt is retired, always finds a reason to come back there. And invariably when he does, out of the prying eyes of the office manager, he asks her if she has a boyfriend in Montreal. He has already hinted that if she wants more money he can make that happen. It isn't just that Kiryl Platt is older. She has heard that he can be very petty and mean.

As noon approaches, she wonders when Omar will get in. If he does not come into the office today, as he usually does, how will she get to the hospital this evening? Was it just talk when Omar told Shirley he would give her a ride? The day she started to work here at this office he told her that if she needed to go someplace after work, she should say the word and he would borrow his great-uncle's Lincoln. A long bus ride home from the hospital after seeing Kiendra would be very gloomy, so today she would be happy to accept the offer.

Omar finally arrives at half past noon, carrying a large bag of food from the deli up the street. He and Kath Ella take their sandwiches outside and walk up the stairs to the second-floor balcony. Kath Ella sits on the bench with her sandwich while Omar unwraps his standing at the railing. Tall and lanky, he wears an off-white shirt, with the usual hurried-looking knot in his necktie. This summer she has been trying to be nicer to him, after finding out he was the person who asked Chevy to give her a job here at the insurance business. Being nice to him is not easy, given how he confounds her. She dislikes how quiet he is during the first moments they are together. Last summer he badgered her for several days until she said yes to his invitation to accompany her to the San Gennaro festival. She was dressed and ready on Sunday afternoon, but he never showed. She later learned that on the Friday before the festival he had taken the several-hour drive to Preston to visit a distant aunt and uncle. Watching him peel back the wax paper from his pork chop sandwich now, she is dying to ask him what happened during his recent visit. Omar's face looks hard, so something heavy must be on his mind. Why does time spent with those relatives always put him in a foul mood?

"I saw a few letters in your back pocket," Kath Ella says, when Omar sits beside her. "You are sitting on them now, you know? They must be getting wrinkled."

"Don't much care if they do."

"Every letter's important. Don't you think?"

Omar takes a big bite out of the sandwich. He chews, watching a delivery truck speed past on Gottingen Street. There is a cool wind, but his brown hair sticks to his sweaty forehead. "There was a disturbance," he says, after a while.

"In Preston?"

"No, at the prison in Mississippi. My father was killed."

"My goodness."

When Omar turns toward her, Kath Ella drops a fried potato wedge onto the waxed paper. Now the sun seems to hit every hard angle on his narrow face. "When did it happen?" she asks.

"Three months ago."

"Is that what's in the letters?"

"The news came from my aunt. My mother never wrote to me with any news about my father," he says. "All she ever tells me in her letters is 'Be good, find some work, keep your senses about you.' I wonder why she writes at all."

While they continue eating, Kath Ella tries to recall the few grainy pictures she has seen of Omar's father. She knows his name, Matthew. In every picture she has seen of Matthew Platt, he is smiling. No resemblance to Omar there. Omar rarely smiles.

Across Gottingen Street, an elderly woman in a red rain slicker strolls up the sidewalk, followed by a boy pushing a girl on a tricycle. The group is heading for the archway over the entrance to the parking lot of the Battleship Inn. Mounted atop the archway is an anchor as tall as Omar. Folks say that, years ago, you could see the corona from the lit-up anchor at night from way over on Woods Bluff.

"I suppose you missed the funeral. I'm sorry."

Omar nods. "Chevy's going to pay my way down to Mississippi. And when I get there, I will ask my mother why she didn't write to tell me Daddy had died."

Kath Ella wants to ask more questions, but she sees Kiryl Platt coming out of the family house next door. If he sees her with Omar, he will have something smart to say as he tells them to get back to work. "Maybe we can talk in the car," Kath Ella says, standing. "Can you still give me a ride to the hospital?"

Heading down the stairs, Kath Ella feels sorry about the news that Omar's father has died. Still, she has asked him for a ride to the hospital anyway. The request seems to make Omar smile a little. Going to see Kiendra this evening might be a needed diversion for him. His difficulties are not as bad as what Kiendra is facing. And more important, Omar knows it will be a treat for Kiendra to see him.

When Omar first began coming out to Woods Bluff to play softball, Kiendra was the only girl who chased down and tossed back the balls he fouled over the fence behind home plate. When Omar talked about the mischief he got into at the school run by the Evangelical Adventists, Kiendra laughed louder than anyone else. When Omar got older and began ignoring Kiendra and chasing after the girls over in Dartmouth, Kiendra still returned his errant fouls. Omar is my buddy,

Kiendra said. Kiendra was also the person who informed Omar that Bullyboy Griffin was telling lies about why Omar had left Mississippi.

On October 12, 1916, Matthew Platt married seventeen-year-old Zera Bradenburg in a large ceremony in Jackson, Mississippi. Several weeks after their wedding, Matthew became assistant principal at the colored high school in Jackson, a job that required him to attend community events with the county superintendent. One evening at a dinner, Matthew and Zera were seated at a large table in the back of the auditorium with a coterie of retired colored soldiers in well-worn Confederate uniforms.

"May I ask why you served, sir?" Matthew asked the colored man seated next to him.

"The South is colored country, not the North," the veteran said. "The South's where we live, where we raise our children." He was a small, dark man missing several teeth but with all his hair. He took a draw on his cigar, glancing at the two white men rounding the table and shaking hands with the other colored veterans. "Things were bad in the South, but they were getting better. The invasion by the North threatened that."

Doubting the veteran's logic, Zera resumed the conversation she had started with the veteran's daughter. "My father's done his duty for the Old South," the daughter said, pressing a folded notice into Zera's hand. "Will you come see about doing something to help the New South?"

Matthew was offended that the woman assumed he and his wife had not already done something to help the South. As a college student, he had spent summers traveling the state of Mississippi with his father to raise funds to build schools for colored children.

"But where are the new colored schools we've been promised?" the veteran's daughter asked Matthew when the dinner was ending. "Not a single school has been built in Mississippi during the last five years. Several have been built in neighboring states. Two in Alabama, for heaven's sake. Radical action is what is needed here."

On the drive home, Matthew admitted to Zera that he was frustrated with how few new schools had been built in Mississippi. Several weeks later the two sat in the auditorium of the Mechanics' Building, listening to the veteran's daughter tell those assembled that the group of people she represented had a surefire plan to get more schools built. On the wall behind the woman was a large banner proclaiming THE NEW CONFEDERATES—WE GET IT DONE WHEN OTHERS CAN'T OR WON'T.

The daughter turned the podium over to a young white man. He asked for volunteers willing to travel the state with the group, raising funds and recruiting new members. One man stood up. But it was to remind the audience about the reports of the gang of colored teenagers on the loose, robbing and destroying property all over Mississippi. Four boys in one gang had already been lynched.

"Good riddance for those troublemakers," someone responded.

"All right," the man said. "They have God to answer to. But what about the other twenty colored boys who have been lynched this year with no due process? And the ten adults? With all this trouble about, is it wise for a colored man to travel outside a county where he's known by white and colored alike?"

The speaker replied that members of his group were irate over the lack of government commitment to educating the colored representatives of America's future, and over the lack of government attention to a whole host of societal ills.

"The youth of the New Confederates have passion and commitment," the young man said. "We will not fail you."

Matthew Platt's parents had warned him to be wary of the New Confederates. Interrupting political speeches and handing out sleeve patches on college campuses was one thing. But throwing blood on government officials and damaging private property was a serious matter.

Matthew and Zera joined the group anyway. During the first years they were members of the group, Matthew did little more than give talks at churches in Jackson and surrounding counties. When their son Omar started walking, Matthew and Zera were promoted to the education and orientation committee. Using a handbook titled *Tactics for Recovery*, they gave seminars as far south as Gulfport and as far north as Tupelo. Both were still uneasy about joining in the group's more radical activities, but one day they agreed to go along on a protest. That evening, several members of the group were painting a message on the side of the governor's houseboat when a white dockworker attempting to chase them away slipped off the pier and drowned.

The trials for Zera and Matthew were held on the same day, August 18, 1923. And both lasted less than a quarter hour. The judge pronounced the same sentence to Zera and Matthew: death by hanging.

Several weeks later, while an appellate court was considering the appeals, six-year-old Omar visited his mother at the county jail. The waves had fallen out of Zera Platt's tea-colored hair, and her tense face was unpowdered. Though she and Matthew were light enough to pass for white, both were quick to tell strangers they were colored. She offered no reassuring words to her son. All she wanted to discuss were the items Omar should take with him to Canada.

"That herringbone bracelet I'm sending with you was the first present I ever got from your father," Zera told Omar. They faced each other across the foot-high wall on the long table of the visitors' room. "One day you should give it to the woman you plan to marry."

"I ain't going up to Canada," Omar said.

"*Ain't?*" Zera said, looking cross. "You mean you are not. And yes, sir, you are going."

"I want to see Daddy."

Zera opened the heavy Bible on the table. She flipped several flimsy pages to reach the end, where she read from the Concordia: "It was said that you should love your neighbor and hate your enemy. But I say love your enemies, bless those who curse you, do good to those who hate you, pray for those who spite and persecute you."

"I want to see Daddy."

Zera closed the Bible and glanced toward the hallway, where her white lawyer was chatting with the white guard. When she reached across the divider and touched Omar's plaid shirt, the guard came to the doorway. She quickly drew her arm back.

"I doubt your grandparents wanted to buy you that new shirt," Zera told Omar. "They're not willing to raise you. That's why you're going to Nova Scotia."

Omar boarded the bus in Jackson, angry with his mother for sending him north. Why had she been so mean? he asked himself on the long bus ride through Atlanta and Washington and New York. And why had he not been able to see his father? The day the bus pulled into Augusta, Maine, Omar hoped the doctor who came to the terminal to examine him would pronounce him too sick to be let into Canada.

Omar did as his mother told him and kept quiet about being colored. In Halifax he remained at the terminal until his great-uncle, Chevy Platt, came to meet him. His mother had said relatives in Halifax were going to drive him farther north, to live with relatives in Glace Bay. But leaving the bus terminal with his great-uncle, Omar learned that he was staying in Halifax.

A re you going down to Mississippi soon?" Kath Ella asks Omar. "I'd go next month," Omar says, "but I want to stay for Kiendra's party."

They are in the Lincoln on the way to the hospital. For ten or so blocks Kath Ella—whether staring at the floorboard or out the windshield at the thin traffic—has been thinking about Kiendra.

"Do you think she'll be well enough for a party?"

"Hope so. I'm rigging some rockets. That girl loves herself some fireworks."

Talking about rigging fireworks for Kiendra seems to put Omar in a good mood. But the more Kath Ella hears about this party, the less she likes the idea. "I should remind you about the rocket the boys fired two years ago out on Nobody's Acre," she says. "One of those fool rockets made a U-turn and scraped the side of the schoolhouse."

"That was Kiendra's brother Dominion's blunder," Omar says with a chuckle. "What you get when you use store-bought pyro. I'm a working professional. Nothing will skid off course if I'm rigging."

"Fireworks are still illegal in Halifax."

"It's also illegal to shoot an unarmed girl."

"Do you want to go to prison, too?"

"You mean, like my father?"

"I didn't mean that."

Omar looks like he accepts her explanation. Still, Kath Ella regrets her offhand comment. In her lap is a bouquet of gardenias Shirley sent. If Shirley had woken her the other day, Omar would not have wandered down to the Bowl and let the young men bend his ear with party foolishness. Chevy Platt brought Omar into the business several years ago, hoping he would quit his job at the fireworks company and focus on his studies. But Omar skipped classes for a full semester to continue working with the fireworks. Well, at least Omar and the other young men were doing something. Not one of the girls accompanied Kath Ella around the village to collect more money for Kiendra.

During Omar's first years in Canada, the children of Woods Bluff shunned him. It was to be expected, given all the bragging he did about how the appeals court had overturned the death sentences of his parents, and how the judges knew his parents were right in wanting to do good in Mississippi. The year Omar turned twelve, the boys he played softball with on Saturday afternoons seemed to enjoy listening to him brag about how his parents would be out of jail before his fourteenth birthday. Yet those boys rarely brought Omar along with them to participate in mischief after the games.

But attitudes changed after the dispute Omar got into one day with Bullyboy Griffin. At fourteen, Omar was already nearly six feet tall. Still, Bullyboy towered over him. After striking Omar across the head with his baseball glove, Bullyboy pushed him to the ground. Omar sprang up and tackled Bullyboy. On the grass, Omar gripped Bullyboy's head in the crook of his arm. Bullyboy struggled a while before clutching his chest. "He's got your breath cut," one of the boys yelled. "Raise your hand, Bullyboy. Give up."

But Bullyboy did not raise his hands, Kath Ella recalls, as Omar turns off Robie Street and into the parking lot at Halifax Regional Hospital. Omar later said that if he had not held his grip, Bullyboy would have attacked him again. Was that true? During the two weeks Bullyboy was in a coma, Omar came to the hospital every day. And for every boy who walked out of the hospital room when Omar entered, two or three stayed and wanted to be his friend. And how did Omar respond? Instead of enjoying the company of new friends, he began instigating fights—fights that got him several nose fractures. Chevy says it's a miracle Omar enrolled in the technical college with all his brains intact. Those young men who say they are Omar's friends are not impressed by his plan to join the civil engineer service, Kath Ella believes. They only respect Omar's ability to rig up devilment. And they take advantage of the fact that while he has outgrown the fighting, he has not outgrown his desire to fit in.

R oom 200 at Halifax Regional Hospital has an imposing, wide entrance, which affords a view into the noisy ward. From the hallway Kath Ella can see the three long aisles that run to the back wall, where a row of high windows lets in the last rays of early evening sunlight. Light-green curtains hide many of the narrow cots, which the kids in Woods Bluff call loony boats.

"Couldn't we just go down and take a quick peek?" Kath Ella asks the two men in matching pullover sweaters blocking her path.

When the men say no, Kath Ella marches toward the freckle-faced woman seated at the attendant's desk. "Please let us see Kiendra," she tells the woman. "We promise we'll be quiet."

The attendant directs Kath Ella and Omar toward two chairs near the wall. Seated, Kath Ella hears a woman down one aisle calling "Attention, everyone. Attention, everyone." In one corner, a man bursts into song. The shouts and antiseptic smells don't bother Kath Ella as much as the sight of the green curtains. Rosa said there is a gash on Kiendra's forehead. Is her head swollen? Is that why the attendants are not allowing visitors?

Several minutes later, noticing a tall, brown-skinned woman coming up the hallway, Kath Ella sits up rigidly in the chair. Yesterday, walking the Hindquarter collecting money for Kiendra, Kath Ella had gotten an earful from several neighbors about her bad behavior. Seeing the hard look on Windsome Taylor's face as she approaches now, Kath Ella suspects she will probably get another lecture, this time for acting out at the hospital. But that can't be helped. She wants to see Kiendra.

Windsome Taylor is quick to tell anyone who asks that, of course, she knows who started calling her the American Nurse—a name she hates. The name makes no sense, Windsome often points out. For one thing, any sensible person seeing her full figure in her blue-and-red-striped uniform would recognize that Windsome Taylor is a nurse's aide, not a nurse. No hospital in Nova Scotia or anywhere else in Canada would hire a colored nurse. Secondly, Clem Sasser knows full well that the only reason she was born in Ohio was because her parents were attending a funeral there. She is Canadian through and through. And though she now lives in Simms Corner, she grew up in Woods Bluff. Her father's relatives came to Nova Scotia in 1811. Later than the Jamaicans, but still. Her mother is descended from blacks who have lived across the basin in Hammond Plains since 1790. She is a distant cousin of Sadie Caulden, for heaven's sake.

Windsome walks past Kath Ella and Omar to the attendant's desk. When she turns from the desk, Kath Ella rushes to her. Windsome is as dark as Kiendra. She smiles slightly, exposing the small gap between her front teeth. "You must listen, dear," she says, running a hand down Kath Ella's hair. "The doctor sedated Kiendra. Her relatives went home for a meal and a change of clothing."

Kath Ella raises the bouquet of gardenias. "I'm not leaving until I see her."

Windsome takes off her glasses and lets them hang on the string around her neck. "A hospital is a place for civility, young lady. You will do as you are told."

Windsome grips Kath Ella's elbow and leads her into the hallway. "Kiendra has a high fever," she whispers. "She's being moved to the critical care unit. The doctors have called the family back."

Kath Ella opens her mouth to speak, but instead of words she bursts into tears. When Omar steps forward, Windsome motions for him to step back. "Let her cry," Windsome says. "Then take her home. And put those flowers in some water. They'll smell as sweet tomorrow."

The next day, sitting between her parents in the back seat of the jitney as it drives away from the bluff, Kath Ella sees an unfamiliar black Chrysler idling beside the road in Centervillage. On the return home after another visit to the hospital, she sees the car again. This time it is parked on the road in front of her house.

Could it be Oscar Mislick? Kath Ella wonders. As she gets out of the car, she feels her chest swelling. It is.

Inside the house, Kath Ella carries several shopping bags into the bedroom. She remains there a moment, waiting for the energy she needs to return to where the others are talking. It was a disappointing visit to the hospital—again she was refused a visit with Kiendra. And now this. When the energy comes, Kath Ella marches into the living room. She halts by the arm of the sofa, where Oscar sits telling George about his line of work. Even in her agitation she has the presence of mind to study Oscar well. With the weight he has put on, he hasn't so much sat down on the sofa as fallen into it. When she first saw him get out of the car, she couldn't imagine why he had come. Now, as she watches him nervously smooth the front of his necktie, she recalls the letters.

"You came all this way to see me?" Kath Ella says. "Why?"

Oscar takes a handkerchief from the pocket of his suit jacket. He looks as if he is about to address Kath Ella. Instead, he turns to George. "Kath Ella told me she wants to teach," he says. "I offered to help her. I told her that teaching is God's work." Oscar's face stiffens. "But she has repaid my generosity by writing inappropriate letters."

George lights a cigarette, looking confused. "What did our daughter write that was inappropriate?"

"Things my wife would rather not read," Oscar says, wiping his neck with the handkerchief. "I've been nothing but honorable toward your daughter. That is why it comes as such a surprise that she would write to my wife and suggest otherwise."

Shirley enters with a glass of water. She hands it to Oscar and then remains by the sofa, gripping Kath Ella's arm. Before going to the hospital, it was Shirley's idea to shop for another charm bracelet to replace the one Kiendra lost at the apartment building.

"Have you been writing to this man's wife?" she asks Kath Ella.

When Kath Ella does not answer, Shirley shakes her head.

"Kath Ella's a nice young woman," Oscar says. "I believe she wanted more help from me than I could give. So she got angry."

"That's not true," Kath Ella says.

"Did you write to his wife?" Shirley asks.

"Yes."

"Tell us why you wrote the letters."

Feeling Shirley's grip tighten on her arm, watching Oscar unbutton the jacket of his suit, Kath Ella wants to insist she put nothing inappropriate in the letter. She wants to say Oscar has come here to spread lies. But she can only manage to look down at her feet.

The room is quiet for a long while. Kath Ella remains seated on the sofa arm, but when Oscar clears his throat, she bounds up and hurries out of the room.

"Please forgive our daughter," George tells Oscar. "One of her girlfriends is doing badly in the hospital."

"Would you go after her?" Shirley asks George. "I'll finish the talk we're having here."

After George leaves the room, Shirley stands by the sofa, looking at Oscar.

"George seems reasonable," Oscar says. "I figure he can fix matters before they get too bad."

"George may be a while," Shirley says, picking up Oscar's hat. "I'll say your goodbyes."

Outside, as they cross the yard, Oscar steals glances at Shirley, who has not yet handed over his hat. "I see that Kath Ella comes from a decent family," he says at the car. "I'm not here for trouble, not here to blame."

Shirley opens the car door and flings Oscar's hat inside. "I'm glad to hear that you're not here to blame," she says. "Because my daughter is not accepting any."

Shirley is on the porch when she hears a noise behind her on the front steps. She turns to see Lick-the-Bottom run up onto the porch, trip, and fall.

"Get you skinny body up from there, boy," Shirley says. "What is the hurry?"

"I'm suppose to tell you about Kiendra."

"What about Kiendra?"

"She passing."

"Passing what?"

"She died."

Honoring Kiendra

Among the young men in Woods Bluff, friendship is a tempered thing, hardened as much by a shared laugh as a slap to a shoulder blade. It is the remedy for a sputtering alternator. It is a conversation, sometimes taut and unbending, other times loose and yielding. Sometimes the pauses are thin as worms' silk, other times they are frozen and split with a crackle, like ice thawing in the waters way north in the bays of Labrador. And when a friendship wavers or becomes unwieldy, young men know it's sometimes wise to leave it alone, as a woman might leave alone a loose braid on her way to the hairdresser. Every young man in Woods Bluff surrenders to a need for friendship—except perhaps Willard Teakill. But a twenty-year-old man with a girl's voice who keeps to himself doesn't count anyway, does he? What other choice is there for most young men living on the bluff in 1936, cordoned off from Halifax proper?

But the bluff itself also surrenders, especially to the shifting Canadian elements, the icy-warm autumn wind followed by the long winter of covering snow. The snow sometimes hides what the bluff has accumulated, including the billion-year-old outcropping—a long ridge of gray-green rock that reminds the villagers of the limits of how far west they were allowed to build. Geologists tell the schoolchildren that the composition of the outcropping is unusual for eastern Canada, that it took tremendous heat, pressure, and the intrusion of special minerals to compress ancient sand and lava into this great arm of stone as hard as iron and deeper than any well.

Though boulders rise out of the long stretch of rock in places, the center is mostly flat, with a slight depression, as if the heel of a large, powerful hand had pressed gently there. Small children, when teenagers do not chase them off, sometimes kneel on the floor of the Bowl, examining the tiny claw prints of a skittering sandpiper or the iridescent shards of a clamshell dropped by a feeding gull. One teenager, before he was chased off by a group of young men, left the Bowl holding a fallen starling chick, panting in his hands as he searched the tree line for the nest. Today the young men who will gather in the Bowl know they might be chased off by one of the constable cars that have been drifting through the bluff since Kiendra's shooting.

This afternoon, Clemmond Green lounges on a flat boulder, watching Kiendra's boyfriend, Buddy Taylor, cross the Bowl with his arm extended. "What the devil is that?" Clemmond Green asks, staring at the small mangle of gold and blue in Buddy's palm.

"One of those doohickeys from Kiendra's bracelet," Buddy says. "What's left of it. That girl of mine gets crazy about the littlest things. I hear when she woke up she asked about this doohickey before she asked about me. Found it inside the building."

"You broke in?"

"How else?" Buddy climbs onto a nearby boulder. "Guivalier told me a redheaded fella pulled the trigger. I went to the constable station. When the constable came outside, I threw a brick at him." Buddy frowns. "The son of a bitch ducked. Then I hightailed it. If I see him again, I'll throw something else at him."

Buddy's mood seems to sour as he puts the mangled trinket back into his pocket. But he and Clemmond Green are laughing again a few minutes later, when Kiendra's brother Dominion arrives carrying a sack.

Dominion takes a single rocket out of the sack and stands it on three spindly legs. The lettering down the side of the rocket says RED BEAUTY. The apex of the rocket reaches Dominion's waist. "This baby gives plenty of flash," he says.

"But none of the tit-rattling noise like the rockets Omar's getting," Buddy says.

Dominion frowns. "We've heard plenty about Omar's plans," he says to Clemmond Green. "But I ain't heard the country boy give no particulars. Is you?"

While Dominion refolds the legs on the rocket, Clemmond Green and Buddy look up the hill, where Omar has made it halfway down the path. Lick-the-Bottom is calling down from the road, but Omar keeps walking.

"Whatcha getting for us?" Clemmond Green asks before Omar has even stepped into the Bowl.

Omar, wearing a very nice shirt, saunters across the Bowl and takes a seat on the boulder next to Buddy. "I'm no longer employed with the rocket company," he says. "But if Lady Luck is with us, we'll get a flight of Big Stellars. You'll have to cover your ears when they explode. Red and yellow, boys, red and yellow. We'll use them as the finale."

Clemmond Green gives an approving smile and then turns to Dominion. "Where's the money the girls collected?"

"Donnita had it," Dominion says. "But then Rosa took it."

"Well, go get it back."

"Has Omar brought any money?" Dominion asks. "Old man Chevy Platt has plenty."

"He doesn't give it to me," Omar says.

"You could ask Kath Ella to get some from him," Buddy says. "I hear he's keen on her. I'll bet she could get us as much as forty dollars."

Omar frowns, but no one speaks for a moment, as if letting the echo from the talk of that much money reverberate off the rocks.

"I'll get everything this weekend, including the platforms and the rigging," Omar says. "Dominion can drive me out there in his boss's truck."

"Nice of you to volunteer me, country boy," Dominion says. "But there's a big trunk on Chevy's Lincoln. Why don't you take that?"

"The trunk will hold the mortar casings but not the platforms," Omar says.

"Well, we might need the truck to do some work for Kiendra."

The mention of Kiendra seems to jumble Dominion's thoughts, because he has trouble getting the rocket back into the sack. "I'll try to get the truck," he says, closing the canvas bag. "But Omar had better be ready when I come to get him. My boss is tight about his truck on the weekend."

Up the hill, Lick-the-Bottom takes a few steps down the slope. Everyone knows why he has not come closer. He has seen Buddy Taylor, who more than once has dangled him over the large crevice in the Bowl. After taking another step down the hill, Lick-the-Bottom turns and runs off.

The young men head up the path in a single file, their heads down, each deep in thought. Behind them a soft wind blows grass, leaves, and dust across the hard floor of the Bowl.

On June 22, 1936, two days after Kiendra Penncampbell's death, get-well cards arrive from as far away as Ottawa. Many are from relatives and old neighbors promising to visit while Kiendra is home recuperating. Rosa collects the condolences in a big soap-powder box for the remembrance display Oneresta Higgins erects at every funeral.

Now that Kath Ella has stopped crying, she needs to decide what she will contribute to the display. In her memory cabinet, she has half of the construction-paper bunny rabbit she and Kiendra made one Easter. During an argument about which of them should take the bunny home, she took a pair of scissors and cut the rabbit in half.

"Whoever has a child first can have both halves," she said. Kiendra accepted her half of the bunny, pretending she wasn't mad. But Kath Ella could tell she was. It will be nice to reunite the two halves on the remembrance board, Kath Ella thinks this morning, on the way to the Penncampbells' house.

"Would you take a look at these?" Rosa says, showing Kath Ella several pictures she has taken out of the soap-powder box. "Some of these pictures don't even have Kiendra in them. Kinfolk from all over, wanting their pictures pinned on Oneresta's board. As old as I am, people still surprise me."

Kath Ella also carries a small bag with a new charm for Kiendra's bracelet. She expects Rosa to open the gift in the living room, but Rosa keeps walking.

"I don't want to see Kiendra's room," Kath Ella says, remaining near the console radio.

Rosa turns. Her slightly swollen face has a look Kath Ella recognizes from childhood, a mother intent on making her sick child swallow a spoonful of bitter medicine. "Come on, girl," Rosa says. "Stop acting foolish."

Kath Ella does not know which part of her body is pushing her forward. She remembers the odd discoloration that showed in the part when Kiendra's hair was freshly plaited. She thinks about the time Kiendra cut up her brother Dominion's favorite girlie magazine, about the time they laughed as they kissed on the mouth. She remembers the day Kiendra lost a tooth while biting into a hunk of saltwater taffy. She enters a bedroom she has not been in since Kiendra left for Wells Bridge years ago. Two beds and three dressers occupy most of the space. An unfamiliar pink dress hangs limp on a wire hanger. The shelf near the bed is still littered with odd rocks.

Kath Ella's half of the bunny is still a grayish brown. But Kiendra's half, taped to the wall, has faded to a mild ash color. Kath Ella touches the brittle construction paper. There is no use trying to hold back tears. "We made it for Easter," she says. "Kiendra and me."

Rosa holds a stack of spiral notebooks. "The girl wrote letters to herself when she should've been writing what the teacher told her. No wonder she was always half a term behind in school."

As Rosa hands her the faded half of the bunny, Kath Ella cries even harder. Rosa also gives Kath Ella one of the stones from the shelf. "I'm going to send some of Kiendra's stuff to heaven with her in the casket," Rosa says. "But you may as well have one of her favorite stones."

K iendra had told her mother and father that if she died, she wanted her funeral to be outside.

"Impossible," Reverend Steptoe says when Rosa broaches the matter. "Miss Penncampbell is a daughter of Basinview Baptist. I'll say a few words outside at the burial, but inside the church is where our daughter's life should be celebrated."

Rosa shows Reverend Steptoe one of Kiendra's notebooks. He reads a page from the notebook, turns to the next page, and reads another. "Our daughter had a way with words when she was talking to herself," he says, closing the notebook. "A pity."

On the day of the funeral, a group of men carry the church pews onto the grassy spot between the church and the cemetery. At ten o'clock, ushers begin seating visitors. By eleven, the air above the crowd is heavy with the smell of perfume, rose aftershave, moth repellent, and fragrant throat lozenges. Teenage boys give up seats to elderly or female visitors and stand on the grass between the last row of benches and the remembrance display.

Reverend Steptoe refuses to allow the piano to be carried outside into the salty air. So, a little after noon, the air fills with strains of an a cappella hymn sung by the Five Preston Boys. When it is time to visit the polished pine casket, Kath Ella has to be assisted. The rich pink blooms of the tall irises hurt her eyes. So does the sight of the rose-colored shoes Kiendra wears. Neither the keepsake bracelet nor the earrings nor the imitation pearl necklace from the ladies club are on the body. Showy jewelry on a child who died so sadly would be an insult to Jesus, Rosa says. But isn't this pink dress showy? Kath Ella wonders, heading back to her seat. And is it not also an insult to Jesus to let a child die so young? She holds on to George's hand. No longer, she thinks, will he have to convince her the world is a harsh place.

Because Kiendra had not yet passed her twenty-first year, Reverend Steptoe says, a child will read from the book containing the names of the deceased children of Woods Bluff. The girl has barely read the first few names when Donnita Penncampbell springs up from the front row and runs down the aisle. At the back of the gathering she leans on the remembrance display, her chest heaving with every loud breath. When a church usher grabs her, Donnita screams. When the usher attempts to pull her off the display, Donnita struggles, sending her, the usher, and the display crashing onto the grass.

Members of the Woods Bluff Ladies Club have gotten Kiendra's funeral expenses paid for. Reverend Steptoe and Clarence Eatten have gotten one of the white men downtown to give Guivalier a better-paying job. The boys are planning a big party. But what has Kath Ella done for Kiendra?

Kath Ella would not worry so much about that, if it weren't for the fact that it seems every tongue on Woods Bluff has been gossiping that she was the person who lured Kiendra into the trespassing that ended up getting her shot. Not one of the girls has said that to Kath Ella's face. And not a single neighbor has said Kiendra's death was Kath Ella's fault. But she believes that is what everyone is thinking.

It has been two weeks since the funeral and Kath Ella still has trouble concentrating during work at Chevy Platt's business. Today in the office, when she ought to be organizing and filing documents, she is staring at an article in the newspaper. She is startled by the sound of a gray leather bank pouch hitting the desk with a thud.

"If you hurry, you can get to the bank before it closes," Kiryl Platt says.

Kath Ella listens to Kiryl stomp down the hallway and then reaches for the pouch. She dumps the receipts and bills out onto the desk. She counts the money, feeling the minutes pass quickly. She will have to work quickly to make it to the bank before six. She has been wondering when Kiryl would show his annoyance. On her first day back at the office, his comforting words soothed the feelings she had—that the world had thrown her face-first down the old community well. When he started saying she would feel better if she spent time with someone other than family and neighbors, she agreed. Yet each time he asked her to accompany him downtown on an errand for Chevy, she said she had work to do.

Since the funeral Kath Ella hasn't been that nice to Omar either. "You would be grumpy, too," she says when Omar comes by the desk. "I'm going to have to sprint to reach the bank before it closes."

"I'll drive you," Omar says.

Kath Ella motions for Omar to come closer to the desk. "But Kiryl already asked to drive me there," she whispers. "I told him no. He will think I don't like him."

Omar laughs and looks as if he agrees. "He went next door. If we hurry we can go before he gets back."

On the drive, Omar seems to sense that Kath Ella's mood has improved. "Why don't we take a drive out to the beach one of these days," he says.

"When?" Kath Ella asks.

"As soon as I can get the car from my uncle."

"That would be nice."

In the middle of the following week, at the small quiet beach at Vicksham Cove, Omar spreads out his great-aunt's Mexican blanket on the warm sand. After dipping her toes in the surf, Kath Ella lies down and closes her eyes. Feeling the warm sun on her face, she decides a picnic is just what she needed. After they eat their cold fried chicken, Kath Ella is drifting off to sleep when she feels Omar's hand sliding under her skirt. They begin to kiss.

After the long, slow lovemaking, Kath Ella falls asleep. She wakes up disoriented by the sight of the ragged granite in the overhanging roof of the cove. On the drive back, the dull ache that has plagued her head since Kiendra's funeral starts to recede.

The next morning, Kath Ella arrives at the office feeling better than she has in weeks. Gone are the hard memories of those men in Montreal. Seeing more of Omar will be good for her, she thinks. Refusing his past invitations seems silly now.

Several times during the day, Kath Ella finds herself daydreaming about what she might do in Kiendra's honor. Whatever she decides will require money. On the bus ride to the office she had considered asking Kiryl to give her an early paycheck. But Kiryl is as tight as his father, Chevy. And besides, she saw the look he gave her first thing this morning. Perhaps he knows about the trip she made to Vicksham Cove yesterday with Omar. Clearly Kiryl's feelings about her have cooled.

Kath Ella stands in line at the bank, the hot air from the ceiling fans blowing onto her head. The closer she gets to the counter, the heavier the pouch she's carrying feels. To her surprise, the office systems at Chevy's business in Simms Corner are sometimes in more disarray than those at the Hardware Barn. Would anyone at the office notice if a few bills were lost? By the time the teller is counting the deposit from the pouch, Kath Ella has filled out a form to make a withdrawal from the Sebolts' account. My, how well she imitates her father's signature. She withdraws thirty dollars, fifteen of which is her savings.

Here she is acting out again, Kath Ella tells herself outside the bank. Just like the trouble she got into with Kiendra. For the trespassing she now has an upcoming hearing with a peace officer. Her parents will tell the officer that their delinquent child will, in the future, be dependable and trustworthy—but not if George discovers she has stolen family money.

It is hot in the office later, so Kath Ella and Omar carry their lunch to the house next door. It feels good sitting next to Omar on his grand-father's parlor sofa. With the window fan cooling her body, she listens to Omar tell her that he has already gotten the money for the fireworks. "I asked my great-uncle and what do you know, Chevy said yes."

Watching Omar count the bills, Kath Ella feels the sadness drain-ing from her body. What she feels now seems even nicer than what she felt at the beach, lying on the blanket beside Omar. It has been months since such feelings have filled her body.

"I've gotten some money, too," Kath Ella says.

"What will you do with it?"

"I don't know. But I also want to do something for Kiendra."

Omar places a few of the folded bills into Kath Ella's dress pocket. He listens for sounds from the upstairs bedroom to indicate whether Chevy is asleep. Before Omar can turn, Kath Ella has leaned forward and placed her head on his chest. These are good feelings she will miss in the fall, when she is away at school. But going away is the only thing she can do to promote a lasting heal from Kiendra's death. The long kiss feels good. But a kiss won't keep her in Woods Bluff. Not here with all these fresh memories ruining her days. She intends to go back to Montreal.

Nearly an hour's drive northeast of Halifax, Exposition Fireworks operates out of a former gristmill beside a slow-running river. This morning at the beginning of August, Omar steers a white truck close to a side door of the business. He is humming as he loads the wood-and-metal platforms, the double line of mortar sleeves, and the crate containing a dozen rockets.

"Those Big Stellars will arc wide as a moon rocket for the show for Kiendra," he says, climbing into the driver's side of the cabin. "There's more bang in one of those than in a thousand of those cheap fireworks the other boys are buying."

Beside Omar on the front seat, Donnita Penncampbell looks over her shoulder, through the back window at the haul. When the truck arrived in Simms Corner, Omar was surprised to see her at the wheel and not her brother, Dominion. He was not surprised to hear that Dominion had gotten home at daybreak and was still passed out drunk. But he did not believe Donnita could drive the truck as well as her brother.

"Party, party is all my knucklehead of a brother does these days," Donnita says. She looks out the windshield of the truck as they speed along a stretch of highway with wide fields on both sides. "Daddy says he's irresponsible, but I think Dominion doesn't like being at the house anymore. You'd understand if you lived there these days. Rosa and Guivalier have been nasty to each other since Kiendra's funeral. Lord, give me a break."

The cab is quiet for several minutes. "I heard you're quitting your job at the cafeteria to attend beauty school," Omar says.

Donnita nods, looking now at a red barn in the distance. When the barn is no longer in sight, she turns from the window. "And I heard you're going to Mississippi."

"In a few weeks."

"Miss-ee-sip-ee. Miss-ee-sip-ee. Where-it-is, I-cannot-tell-thee."

Omar downshifts and the truck slows behind a tractor. Donnita is biting her lip and seems to be counting to herself, using her fingers like a child. He'd once seen Kiendra do that. This is the first time he and Donnita have been alone together in a long while. Without the other girls around, Donnita seems mislaid. The church ushers earned a spot in heaven, given how much work it took to calm Donnita enough for her to attend the burial. Omar has already noticed that her blue blouse has several buttons loose at the top. She must know he would take note of the bit of chest visible through the parted blouse. Like Kath Ella, Donnita will need time to warm the bones that have gone chilly with Kiendra's death. Kath Ella seems to be ready to allow him to help her cope. But he is not sure what to say to Donnita. A few summers back, before he decided to work hard to get Kath Ella's attention, he entertained the idea of asking Donnita to one of the Elks Lodge dances. Billy Ovits was chasing after her at the time, but what did that matter?

His arm out the window, Omar feels the air hitting his palm. He wishes he wasn't so prone to thinking about Kath Ella. Chances are good she will not return to Halifax when she graduates college. Given all those books he used to see her reading on the bleachers at baseball games, she may well become a teacher. He knows there is more work for a teacher in Montreal or Toronto. Did Kath Ella have to say it? Omar closes his palm, trying not to look at Donnita. Maybe he ought to have tried harder with some other girl these past two summers. Donnita is no traveler. He appreciates that today.

There is only forest beside the road now. Omar drives on, wondering if he ought to stop thinking about these bluff girls and do what Chevy advises: put his mind on his future. Platt's Insurance and Surety already has a manager. And the only other job he imagines himself doing is repairing machines at a factory. Or begging Chevy for a loan to buy one of those portable kitchens to sell snacks at the Negro league baseball games. Neither of those options is appealing.

After they have filled the tank at a gas station, Donnita takes over the driving. "Let's go by the apartment building," she says when they are on the city streets again. "I want to show you what the girls did to the windows."

"I hope they didn't break any."

"Just threw some paint is all. But if I'd been there I would've broken all the windows."

When the truck turns onto Gottingen Street, Omar notices a return of the solemn face Donnita wore at her sister's funeral. With each passing block, she stares at the windshield with a harder face. When the apartment building comes into view, Donnita stomps on the accelerator.

The truck is roaring at forty miles an hour. At first Omar laughs, but when Donnita runs through a stop sign, he places his hands on the dashboard. "Slow it down, girl."

Though the truck starts to rattle, Donnita keeps her foot on the accelerator, her eyes ahead. Gray smoke pours out of the front of the truck and begins rushing into the cab. After the next intersection, when the truck weaves into the adjoining lane, Omar reaches over and turns the ignition key. The engine dies, but the truck races on, heavier smoke now flowing into the cab.

Omar yanks one of Donnita's hands off the steering wheel, but with the other she gives the wheel a hard turn. The truck jumps the curb and hurtles toward the building. After pushing Donnita's knee out of the way, Omar stomps on the brake. Brakes screeching, the truck skids across the grass and crashes into the corner of 920 Gottingen.

This Monday sunrise begins a week that Kath Ella fears her body is in no shape to endure. She lies awake in bed believing that in some ways it might be better to be flayed alive. In the afternoon she can make no sense of the words in Reverend Steptoe's sermon during the services before Donnita Penncampbell is laid to rest. The following day she wakes up feeling numb, but the numbness does not insulate her body from the pain that seems to chew at her insides as she sits through the funeral for Omar Platt.

And the next afternoon, still numb from watching the pallbearers lower Omar's casket into the ground, Kath Ella ascends the granite stairs to the second floor of the courthouse, feeling as though the earth is trying to pull her down into it, too.

She has come downtown for her hearing with the peace officer about the trouble she got into with Kiendra at 920 Gottingen Street. In the hot hearing room, she tries to formulate coherent answers to the peace officer's questions. But it is difficult to concentrate. She should have eaten the egg sandwich Shirley offered before they left the house.

But she was too busy pleading with her parents to attend the hearing without her. That was a foolish request. She knew they would refuse.

"I have half a mind to send a letter to your college," the peace officer tells Kath Ella.

A thin man with narrow shoulders, he sits at the head of the long table. He does not seem at all swayed by the letters George has brought from teachers and neighbors. "But because of all the stress you've endured," he says, "I'm going to put this matter of trespassing to rest without any punitive measures. Don't expect the same leniency if you come before me again."

"She understands, sir," George says. "She has learned."

Kath Ella tells the peace officer what she has learned, but on the bus ride home, she cannot recall what she said. What has she learned? If she has all this new knowledge, why do the streets look unchanged? Next week she will be downtown to shop for school clothes. A week after that, she will return to Montreal. At first, she saw George's decision to have her leave the bluff and go back to college early as impossibly cruel. Now, after all these funerals, she cannot wait to get away.

But she has a few things to do first.

One thing Rosa got right at the funeral, Kath Ella believes, was the matching colors: pink and rose everything. But what about the other colors Kiendra wore? Kath Ella asks all over the bluff in the next few days. By the end of the week, she has twenty or so young men and women waiting in line at the Hardware Barn to pick up the cans of paint she has purchased with the money she took from the Sebolts' account. Over the next few days, practically every shed on the bluff is painted white and green and blue and yellow. "Use red for the outhouses," Kath Ella says. "Kiendra never liked that color."

By the end of August, a visitor to the bluff also sees plenty of color on the houses. When there is too little paint left in one can to finish a job, colors are mixed, producing nice blends. The schoolhouse gets one of these mixtures, a bluish-plum color some neighbors say reminds them of homes on the islands.

September 17, 1936, comes much more quickly than Kath Ella had anticipated. In the afternoon she goes over to 920 Gottingen Street. It is a cool, sunny day and the lawn is coming in deep green. The corner of the building wrecked by the truck has been repaired. At a window on the ground floor, Kath Ella presses her face to the glass. The bedroom looks clean, but dirt must be hiding there someplace.

A strong wind greets Kath Ella at the back door, where the men carried Kiendra out on a stretcher. The exterior wall has been cleaned of the paint the girls threw the day after Kiendra's funeral. Kath Ella tests the doorknob, thinking some feelings ought to rise in her. But none come.

Kath Ella carries the rock that Rosa gave her in the bedroom before Kiendra's funeral. The farther she walks from the back of the building, the heavier the rock feels in her hand. Obviously, Rosa did not realize that Kiendra once swore this beautiful reddish-blue stone would never leave her bedroom.

At the side of the building, Kath Ella halts and examines the rock. On the bus ride here, she had admired the gold specks in its smooth surface. In the sunlight she can see what looks like the oily impression of fingerprints where Kiendra once gripped the rock.

She opens her hand and the rock shifts and comes to rest in her palm. When she grips the rock again, she squeezes tightly. Her fingers begin to hurt, but she keeps a tight grip. She takes a step back from the building and looks up at several high windows. The sunlight blazing off one pane is so strong it hurts her eyes. Could that be the window that Kiendra wanted to break?

Before she realizes it, Kiendra's favorite rock has left her hand, arching upward in an angry flight.

PART TWO

New Jamaica

New Assignments

Montreal, 1952

*H*ello, class. I am so happy to be starting school again.
I am happy in autumn because I get to see all your happy faces.
I see a few new faces, but I see plenty of familiar faces, too. I see
you peeking there, Miss Allison. Sit up straighter, dear. Some of you know
me already. And before I tell the rest of you my name, I am going to tell you
something else about me. Years ago, before any of you were born, I moved
to Montreal from Halifax, where I grew up. Halifax is a city on the map of
Canada. You learned that in the first or second grade, didn't you?

I came to Montreal to go to college. The college I attended is not far from
here. Sainte-Marie College. Mrs. Teggleston was a student there also. Of
course, she is younger than I am, so we didn't know each other there. I have
a sister, Luela, who works at the Wales and London. That is a gigantic
hotel in Halifax. Sometimes my sister spends her entire night at work typing
up bills for hotel customers. My mother, Shirley, worked at the hotel. So did
my grandmother, Pallis. My father, George, used to work at the speedway

in Halifax. A speedway is where the cars race around fast. Now my father is retired. He's old.

This year of our Lord, I will begin my tenth year teaching the fourth grade here at Greeves Adventist Primary. I've also taught second and third grade. Never the first grade though. I wish I had. Of course I like teaching the fourth grade the bestest. That's a made-up word. You can make up a word from time to time in my class. I don't mind, as long as you tell me you know the word is made up. My favorite dish is beef Stroganoff. I like the gravy. My favorite color crayon is—well, I can't decide on a favorite crayon. But I like tangerine and all the glitter tones. I love to go ice-skating in the park on Mount Royale.

My husband, Timothee, works for a firm that makes drawings that show workers how to put together bridges and ice-skating rinks and the buildings at airports. My son's name is Etienne. He attended primary school here at Greeves Adventist. But now he is in the tenth grade at Bratt Argonne International. Etienne is much taller than I am. He is this tall. Isn't that something?

As a child I loved my Lucy Kirchner in the Mountains *books. Look there, you'll see the newest editions. I hope you all will love reading them this year.*

What else? Oh, yes, silly me, I haven't told you my name. When I was younger, they called me Kath Ella. During my last years of college, my classmates started calling me Kath. That is what I go by now—just Kath. But you will call me Mrs. Peletier.

T he passing of the months from fall to spring is more exhausting than Kath expects. By the end of May, she cannot wait to begin her summer trip. The plan is to begin on a large cruise ship out of Halifax. It is a vacation she has wanted to take for years.

This morning in Halifax, in the crowded reception area of Arcadia Travel and Leisure, Kath and her son, Etienne, have been standing for nearly an hour, but finally a family relinquishes one of the long benches.

"Why are you sitting so far away?" Kath asks Etienne after they are seated. "Slide over so other people can sit down."

When Etienne moves closer, Kath grabs a brass button on the leather bomber jacket draped over his shoulder and lifts one side. Underneath, the small red-and-gray snake wrapped around Etienne's thin wrist lifts its head and flicks its tongue.

Kath glances around the waiting area. Bad weather last winter delayed many departures. But in three days, hopefully, she and her husband, Timothee, will be boarding the ocean liner she saw by the docks yesterday, when they arrived here from Montreal. There are no faces she recognizes, even though most of the travelers yet to be assisted are colored.

"I distinctly remember telling you to leave that pet in the car," Kath whispers to Etienne. "Why didn't you?"

"It's too cold in the car."

"It's quite pleasant outside."

"Not for a snake."

Kath lets go of the button and opens her purse. The cover of the small book she takes out reads *Easy Italian Phrases*. She has told her husband and son that she doesn't need to study the book, but she does. The date of their cruise departure—Monday, June 8, 1953—is a week before Timothee's birthday. What a surprise to hear several weeks ago that in addition to visiting Gaeta, Italy, to celebrate with his maternal grandparents, they will also be visiting Morocco. The side excursion is a present to her from Timothee for her speedy recovery from an operation last year. The doctor said he had lifted the spot from her lung as easily as lifting lint from a sweater. Political trouble in Casablanca and Tangier means the ship may dock farther down the Moroccan coast, in the city of Mogador. She does not mind the change. She is eager for a stroll down the stone streets and alleys in the charming historic city.

"Do you see that gray thing there?" Kath asks, showing Etienne a grainy black-and-white photograph of the port at Mogador.

"Everything's gray," Etienne says.

"Over there. That's an American ship."

"Why can't I go to Vancouver?"

Kath puts the photograph back between the pages of the phrase book and then feels around in her purse. "Go wait in the car please," she says, dropping the car keys into Etienne's lap.

"Aunt Luela's bringing me a treat from the candy shop."

"Off you go."

Etienne tries to work the car keys back into Kath's hands, but she keeps a clenched fist. "Bean shit," he says.

Etienne stands, letting the jacket slide off his shoulder onto the bench. As he walks off, a boy points at the snake and says, "Wowie."

Finally, a moment to herself. Perhaps now she can select the pictures she intends to bring to the picnic on the bluff later. In the winter of 1945, when she received an invitation to Marcelina Higgins's very first picture party, called A Splash of June, she wrote back to say her end-of-the-school-year obligations made it impossible for her to attend. That was not exactly true. Though it had been a decade since the horrible summer when she lost Kiendra, Omar, and Donnita, and though she missed her neighbors, she did not yet feel up to celebrating on the bluff.

The children in my monthly Weekend Academic Enrichment Program will be doing a project on Sierra Leone later in the summer, Marcelina had written in the letter that came with the invitation to this year's party. *You're a teacher. Bring me some ideas for the classroom when you come to the picture party.*

Despite being a teacher, Kath hates it when people give her assignments. Still, Marcelina's request had some appeal. If she developed a lesson about Sierra Leone for Marcelina's enrichment program, she could use it for her own students. But a bout with a nasty flu and several colds put her behind, and just managing her own schoolwork was a chore. She hopes the stack of fold-up maps of western Africa she found in a shop on Rue Bel-Air will be of interest to the students. There must be some future wanderers in the program.

What could be keeping her sister? Kath wonders. Looking through the large window into the travel office, she sees no sign of her husband either. Given how irritated Timothee was by the long wait, he may well be complaining to the office director. When they first started going out in public—a colored woman with her tall white husband—the slightest sideways glance by employees in hotels, restaurants, or retail stores would merit a grumble from her. These days Timothee is more easily roused. Earlier, when a clerk told the crowd that some customers with reservations on the cruise ship might have to make the trip to Europe by airplane, Timothee demanded to see the office director.

Kath returns to her phrase book, hoping that while the family is away, the neighbor checking on the apartment in Montreal will properly attend to her plants. When misting her three orchids, she likes calling their names: Cindy, Lindy, and Mindy. The first orchid she ever fussed over was a present from Timothee a week after they met. He now has a nice job as a projects manager, but he says he wants even better for Etienne. She appreciates the fact that Timothee cares so much about Etienne's future, especially since the boy is not his biological son.

How could she be pregnant? she wondered that year on her visit to the college infirmary. She left the infirmary and crossed the campus back to her dormitory in a daze. All three times she and Omar had been intimate, he had been careful to pull out before discharge. Then again, how trustworthy was her memory of the horrible summer she had just had? After Kiendra's funeral, her thoughts were scattered but she knew she wanted to be held. One day while she and Omar were in the car heading to the bank, she had boldly reached over and squeezed his thigh. He drove to a secluded section of Haverill Park. Was that the afternoon it happened?

She wanted a child but thought it would happen after she graduated. She would have gotten a job. And she would already have traveled to Morocco and Aix-en-Provence. Instead, with a baby already growing inside her, she would have to leave college. The thought made her head throb. She ought to have been more attentive. With a child, what type of man could she interest in marriage? Certainly not a well-educated professional, as she had imagined.

She was grateful that she had wandered into East Campus, with its tall hedges and paths down which she could hurry if she spied someone she recognized. The warm September breeze did nothing to improve her mood. And then she began to fear that any minute a former neighbor from the bluff would jump out from behind a hedge and remind her of some mischief she had gotten into as a child. One neighbor might say the pregnancy came because Kath grew up in a neglected neighborhood. Another would put the blame on her wanton behavior. Where is your soul now? So much promise, and now look. And perhaps one would say she had become the one thing she feared becoming. A failure.

She went to bed that evening imagining her future turning as brittle as a sand dollar. The next morning, among the chatting students in the dining hall, she felt an even worse fear. What did she know about raising a child? Luela always babysat the infant cousins. She had never even changed a diaper. She was making her own family, but she hadn't a penny to her name to provide for it. Staring at her toast and curried eggs, she recalled the last time her future was threatened. Back then her parents had found a way for her to attend college. Now, she needed to find a way out of this pickle herself.

In Byerly Hall after breakfast, she ascended the steps with her stomach empty but her brain full of reasoned thoughts. She would say to the matron of students, *I'm going to have to leave the college. I don't want to, but what else can I do? I don't think I will ever return to finish my*

*degree. Without a degree, I can't get the job I need to raise a child properly. I
had hoped to make my parents proud of me. Now I have disappointed them.*

Seated on the brushed-leather chair in the matron's office, at first
all she did was cry.

"Let us not be rash, dear," the matron said, after hearing a few
blurted-out sentences. "With a bit of rationality, these matters can be
managed."

And manage she did. The day after she returned home to the bluff,
she started working again at Chevy Platt's business. She got a few sideways looks when a stranger learned that she did not have a husband.
But many seemed sympathetic when she told them the father of her
baby had died. In the spring of 1937, two weeks after little Omar was
born in her parents' house on the bluff, she was selling insurance plans
at the business so rapidly that Chevy was able to hire a new employee.

Several of Omar's former schoolmates came by the office to ask
about his son. One of them brought a note from the school's principal
inviting her to come for a visit.

"Do you have plans to return to college?" the principal asked in
his office, where he gave her several boxes filled with baby clothes,
diapers, and powdered milk.

The envelope of money was a surprise. So was his question asking if
she were still interested in teaching. "Yes, sir, I still hope to teach," she
said. "Do you think you might have a position for me here?"

Seeing the principal's face redden, she quickly said, "Oh, I'm sorry.
Did I misunderstand?"

"I don't have a position here in Halifax," the principal said. "But
I would be willing to put in a good word at one of the schools in
Montreal."

She left the school building unsure how she felt about the principal's counsel. By then, the idea of finishing college had receded deep
into her mind. Over the next few days, however, she began to realize
how unfulfilling working at Chevy Platt's business had become without Omar there. Chevy no longer smiled when he saw her. And his

son, Kiryl, was even less friendly, especially after she declined his offer to take her to a dance.

Hearing someone suggest she might go back to college and become a teacher had made her feel wonderful. Leaving her infant son in Halifax with her parents just as he was beginning to recognize her would be difficult. But in short order, the decision was made.

Walking the campus in Montreal, a mother now, she wanted everyone she encountered to notice how different she was in the world. But most of the women she knew had graduated. No longer could she cross the campus at a certain time of day, knowing which friend might exit a building to stop for a chat.

During her last month of studies, she raced up the dormitory stairs to tell her roommate that she had been hired at Greeves Adventist Primary. She would start as a part-time teacher's aide and would have to wait a year for a teaching position, but still she was elated. Those first months of work, she lived in a basement apartment, every day growing more determined to bring her son to live with her.

One mild November day she was delighted to read an advertisement by an elderly couple willing to look after her son during the day, in exchange for a bit of housecleaning. At noon Kath left her other part-time job and was rushing to view the apartment when she was startled by a voice behind her on the street.

"Excusez-moi, madame."

Kath turned to see a man whom she probably would have overlooked even if she hadn't been in a rush. Timothee Peletier wore one of those fur hats young professional men were fond of wearing with suits, but which Kath thought looked silly. Appearing disoriented, he asked for directions to Javier Street. Only later would Timothee admit he was a draftsman at a construction firm just a few blocks from where they were standing. But his sly grin told Kath he had invented the street name to delay her on the sidewalk. She liked the gentlemanly way he handed her the slip of paper she had dropped, the patient way he stood there shivering as she tugged on her gloves, pretending to be

thinking over the matter. Two months later, she moved into his apartment. A year later, they were married.

Little Omar was barely walking when Kath brought him to Montreal. Timothee was happy to adopt her son, but before the marriage
he asked her to change the child's name. They settled on four names:
Etienne Omar George Peletier.

G irl, why did you buy only peppermint?" Kath asks, peering into
the paper bag her sister has tilted toward her. "You know full well
butterscotch is my favorite."

In the reception area of Arcadia Travel and Leisure, Luela has
taken a seat on the bench beside Kath, scooping Etienne's bomber
jacket onto her lap. Inside the bag are shiny red-and-white candies that
look like little pillows.

"Butterscotch cost double, girl," Luela says. "And don't look at a
gift horse sideways."

Kath takes two candies from the bag. "I hope that son of mine is
on his best behavior later today," she says, dropping the candies into
her purse.

"Hope will get you far."

"He's a little sore because I won't let him go on the school trip with
his friends."

"Vancouver's awfully far for a teenage boy to travel without a parent along."

"Most of the way is by train, only a few days are by bicycle. But
Timothee and I let Etienne go skiing with his friends, what was it,
three months ago? Those bandits busted two lamps and broke the legs
off a side table at the lodge. I do not want to imagine all the devilment
our son would get into in Vancouver."

Sucking loudly on a peppermint, Luela looks through the stack
of photographs Kath has brought with her. "Eh-tinne doesn't sound
happy about going to the camp."

"He doesn't get to make those decisions."

"Now you're talking sense. Will Eh-tinne be going to that school in the fall?"

"His name is Eh-*ti-enne*. Not Eh-*tinne*. I hope when you talk to him you say his name correctly. And yes, indeed, he will be going to the school in the fall."

"When are you going to tell him?"

"That's his father's job. This is all his idea."

Luela chews the remnants of her peppermint candy as she traces the initials E. O. G. P. stitched above the right front pocket of Etienne's bomber jacket. While it may have been Timothee's idea to send Etienne to a camp run by the private school from which he graduated, it was probably Kath—who brags about the school's rigorous academics—who filled out the papers to enroll their son there. But why further anger the child who has been a terror since he found out he was adopted? George and Shirley wanted to tell Etienne years ago, but Kath forbade that. You'd think the boy, as inquisitive as he is, would have discovered the papers sooner than last year.

"He doesn't like it when we snoop," Kath says, noticing that Luela has retrieved two movie tickets from the front pocket of Etienne's jacket.

"My French is rusty," Luela says, presenting the tickets. "What does it say?"

Kath shakes her head and takes a peach-colored compact out of her purse. As she suspected, the small mirror reflects a face that looks as tired as she feels. Timothee should not have let her sleep this morning until after ten. Now they are going to be late getting to Shirley and George's house. Just spreading the talcum onto her cheeks with the sponge is tiring. Despite her doctor's disapproval, a cigarette would provide a nice jolt. On the walk here from the hotel she did not need a few puffs to wake her up, since hearing the rattle of a streetcar on Barrington Street gave her a burst of energy. She had never seen such large crowds at the pier. As a teenager she used to dream of boarding an ocean liner to begin a journey with a man she loved. And now she will.

"I'd like to ask a favor," Kath says, tossing the compact into her purse.

"Oh, what's the trouble now?"

"No trouble. But when Etienne finishes at the camp, I'd like for him to stay with you."

"Didn't Momma and Daddy ask to take him?"

"They didn't ask. They agreed to. But I'm not sure Etienne will like living with his grandparents."

"You mean living with George." Luela hands back the stack of photographs. "Why didn't his grandparents in Montreal offer to take him this time?"

"What do you mean?"

"They usually look after Etienne when you and Timothee are traveling."

"Do you have reservations about looking after him?" Kath asks.

"It's just that the child hardly knows me."

"He will if you look after him. You only have to watch your nephew, what, a week and a half? Most of the time we're away he'll be at camp." Kath frowns. "Given the way you're acting, you'd never know the boy was family."

Instead of answering, Luela places the movie tickets into a pocket on the sleeve of Etienne's jacket.

"You've put the tickets back in the wrong place," Kath says as Luela zips up the pocket. "He'll know you've been snooping."

"I know he will."

When Kath turns her head toward the ticket office, Luela really notices for the first time the discolorations bleeding through the powder on her sister's cheeks. "Oh no, no," Timothee had said when Luela offered to put the family up with her or at Shirley and George's place. "We don't want to be a bother. We'll get a hotel." But one of the big shots at the Wales and London helped Luela secure the Bay of Fundy

Suite. Luela hoped the hotel's nice beds and room service would help Kath recuperate after the long car ride from Montreal. Kath will need her strength to get through this afternoon. There will be a few people at the picnic she will be none too happy to see.

K iryl Platt called me at the hotel yesterday," Luela says later, when she and Kath are exiting the travel office.

Kath halts on the sidewalk, looking at Timothee, who is walking ahead. "What did that boy want?"

"You don't have to say it like that," Luela says. "He was calling to say Chevy's gotten worse. Could be any day now."

"My goodness. I didn't know."

Luela carries Etienne's jacket. "Kiryl asked if you were coming to the picnic this year," she says. "He said if you were, he'd try to come by for a brief visit."

"I hope you told him to stay at the hospital."

"I told him what I knew. I said you would be at the picnic."

"Can we talk about something else?"

"We can as soon as I am finished with this. It is plain to me that Kiryl wants to see you."

"Did he mention seeing his nephew?"

Getting no answer from Luela, Kath starts walking again.

"You said yourself you want Etienne to get to know where he came from," Luela says at the crosswalk. "Isn't that the reason you're here to attend this year's picture party?"

"I meant the old neighbors," Kath says. "And the relatives who care about him." Kath looks across the street to the next block, where Timothee is disappearing around the corner. "Kiryl had plenty of chances to see his nephew when Etienne was an infant," she says. "Why didn't he? Can you answer that question?"

"I believe you know the answer to that question."

"I never led Kiryl Platt to believe there was anything between us."

"Maybe not between, but probably on his side there was something."

"Even if he were angry with me, why did he take it out on his nephew?"

"If you are still mad about that you need to quit it."

Kath grabs Etienne's jacket out of Luela's arms. She walks on again, angry with her sister. But she knows she shouldn't be. For the year and a half her son lived on the bluff, Luela was there nearly every weekend to bathe him and change his diapers. Luela had also been in Montreal last year, cleaning, cooking, and looking after Etienne during the two weeks Kath recuperated after her operation. But had Luela not heard what Kiryl said years ago? That if she had let him escort her around town, she wouldn't have gotten pregnant out of wedlock, that she would now be a better woman? The nerve.

As Etienne grew up, if anyone in the family wanted to see him, they had to come to Montreal. As a result, Etienne knew little about the place where he was born. Regret about that is one of the reasons Kath is here today. Despite her anger at Kiryl, she would have made an exception and brought Etienne to Woods Bluff to see his uncle. But Kiryl Platt has never asked.

And did Kiryl really want her? Or were his advances merely stupid competition with his cousin Omar? No matter. In Nova Scotia, Etienne's other relatives—the Platts—are few and far between. Chevy Platt is definitely short for this world. Though Kath's memory is somewhat vague, she seems to recall that Omar appreciated his great-uncle.

Now Kath gives herself another assignment for this trip home. For the picture party, she will keep all the nasty things she would like to say to Kiryl Platt out of her mouth. She will keep her tongue so that she can begin to repair the estrangement between nephew and uncle. She will do so to honor Omar's memory.

I told him to wait at the car," Kath says to Timothee, when they arrive at the Regent parked at the curb on Barrington Street.

"Clearly he didn't listen," Timothee says.

"I have three-quarters of a mind to leave without him."

"He's got the car keys."

Kath steps close to Timothee. "You didn't bring the other set?"

"Didn't you?"

"Well, now one of us should go find him."

"The boy's sixteen. I'm not chasing after him."

Timothee leans against the car door, rubbing his necktie with his hand. Kath grumbles as she grabs Luela's arm. "Let's go see if the little imp went down to the water."

Mother and aunt are several blocks away when Etienne saunters up to the Regent. After he takes the car keys, Timothee throws the bomber jacket into Etienne's chest.

"Get in the back seat with that snake you had no business agreeing to look after," Timothee says. "And do not let that creature out of the cage until I or your mother say you can."

Etienne climbs into the car without argument. He is quiet in the back seat when Kath and Luela return to the car. But at the curb in front of the drugstore, as soon as his mother and aunt exit and head up the sidewalk, he rolls down the window. "I want a cream soda, a bag of pommes frites, and three hi-fi records."

The women continue without responding. When they near the front of the drugstore, Etienne jumps out of the car.

Timothee rolls down the window. "Where do you think you're going, captain?"

"Out here."

"Get back in, please."

When Etienne doesn't comply, Timothee gets out of the car. He used to be as skinny as Etienne. But eating the big meals the woman who comes over three evenings a week to cook has caused his waist to spread. "Do you want me to cancel your mother's trip?"

"No."

"I will do it. And if I cancel your mother's trip, you will get to go back to Montreal. But you'll have to forget about that new stereo. And that new bicycle you brought with you will be going away."

"You can't send my bicycle away. You didn't buy it. Grandmother did."

Timothee steps close to Etienne. He pokes Etienne in his chest with the car keys. Etienne knocks the keys out of Timothee's hand, and they bounce against the car tire and land on the sidewalk.

Standing up with the keys, Timothee seems to recognize how tall Etienne has gotten. "I hope you like Saint Richelieu this summer," he says, "because you may be going there in the fall."

"Mother won't make me go."

Timothee laughs and gets back into the car. After Etienne has slid onto the back seat of the Regent, Timothee turns to watch Etienne undoing the latch on the glass cage. "Don't you dare let that creature out again, captain."

"Why not?"

"Because I said so."

"Mother's not afraid of it."

"Yes, but your grandmother Shirley might be. And I don't want any unnecessary trouble when we get over there."

The Newcomers

Who's to say why white residents began moving out of the eleven houses in the West Slope?

Some say the decisions began in March of '38, the month bulldozers began clearing land to double the size of the municipal dump. By December of that year, two houses had been left empty. Three more families moved out in 1940, after logging opened up a passable road that enabled traffic from Centervillage and the Hindquarter to clatter through the West Slope, along the new shortcut to downtown. Some bluff residents say if logging were to blame for the white exodus, the final leaf fell in the autumn of '42, when the residents of the last two occupied West Slope houses realized that the bare forest gave them a clear view of Centervillage. Center of whose village? Certainly not theirs.

For a few dollars more than the cost to rent an apartment, Shirley and George Sebolt rented a whole house in the West Slope. Only three other families from the Hindquarter joined them there. The remaining houses became occupied by families who arrived in Halifax from the Caribbean islands. Most new families attended Basinview Baptist and all painted their houses in bright colors, like the houses on the rest of the bluff. But the new bluff residents were quick to correct anyone who suggested they lived in Centervillage or the Hindquarter.

The newcomers considered the deal good, even though they had to use their own funds to finish installing the indoor plumbing. "Our rental agreements give us the option of purchasing our homes," they pointed out. And buoyed by the promise of new services by the city government, many of the new arrivals wanted to call their neighborhood New Halifax. But across the bluff, and even downtown, that area of the bluff became New Jamaica.

Following a brief rainstorm, the lights in Shirley and George's house have been flickering all morning. Afraid the electricity will go off altogether, Shirley plans to serve iced tea and cake to Kath and her family on the small back patio.

"Get up and move over to this chair," Shirley tells George, who is stretched out on a pinewood lounge chair on the patio, drinking a cocktail of prune and apple juice.

"Why?"

"The back on this one keeps slipping. Do you want our company sitting in a broken chair?"

"If the chair's good enough for me to sit in, it's good enough for company."

Shirley wipes the matching pine table with a damp cloth, inhaling the bitter-orange scent of her blooming sweetspire bush. She likes it when the air is thick with that fragrance and the smell of her flowering plants, all confined to pots. Her knees are up to the task of working a garden, but not her arthritic shoulder.

"Are you going to move or aren't you?"

"I will in a minute."

Shirley watches George take another long draw on his cigarette and then marches off, grumbling. Inside the house, Shirley searches the hallway closet, looking for a present to give her grandson. But there are only nicked ashtrays, imitation Tiffany lamps, and embroidered hotel towels. Nothing suitable. But she does locate the pack of double-D batteries she has been looking for all morning. What in the world could be keeping Luela and the others? she wonders, pressing the last battery into the back of her portable AM radio. It is well past one o'clock. She and George could have taken the bus to Marcelina's party. But Kath had insisted on giving them a lift. Too much longer and she will miss the children's singing program. Hearing those young voices is always a joy. The wait may be worth it though. Their grandson has not been on the bluff since he was a baby. George would never admit it, but he also wants to spend time getting to know his grandson.

"I'd like to give this to our grandson," Shirley tells George on the patio. "Do you mind?"

George picks up the striped maple candle box Shirley has placed on the pine table. It is one of the few items passed down from his grandfather Kipbo. Shirley has applied wax in the small grooves to help the top slide back easier. He always did that.

"The closet's full of a whole heap of whatsits," George says. "Give the boy some of them."

"You mean the hotel junk? I doubt your grandson will want any of that."

"That boy won't appreciate whatever you give him."

"He appreciates that brand-new bicycle."

"You don't have to compete with his other grandmother."

With the box resting on his lap George stretches out again on the lounge chair, hearing Shirley's house slippers flap as she leaves the patio.

When George opens his eyes, he realizes Shirley has carried off his cigarettes. Just as well. An hour from now the next cigarette is bound to taste sweeter. Before the operation to dislodge a gnarled growth in his trachea, he worried his raw cough meant trouble with his lungs.

He once thought having a lung ailment would help him understand his younger daughter better. She knocked him dumb as a doorstop years ago, when she brought Timothee home and announced they had gotten married. "This is the thanks your mother gets for taking care of your child while you finished school?" he said to Kath. "You don't bother to invite her to your wedding? Or even tell her you're getting married. What madness has overtaken you?"

Several weeks after his daughter and new son-in-law visited, George sat by the living room window, peering out at the drifts of snow, reliving the visit. *When Kath and I did this, and when Kath and I did that, and when Kath and I did the other.* Did the man she married ever shut up? Soon George felt he knew what madness had seized his daughter. That French college in Montreal had corrupted her mind, made her believe she could live happy married to a white man. That French college was the reason Kath added insult to injury by announcing a done wedding. What about a mother's wish for her daughter? Many neighbors agreed. When another daughter from the bluff won a scholarship to the college in Montreal, the father said no way was he going to allow his daughter to attend.

"I have to give the boy something," Shirley says, returning to the patio to find the box still on George's lap.

George places the box underneath the lounge chair, lies back, and closes his eyes again. "You're giving him lunch."

I n Centervillage, two rooms have been added onto Woods Bluff Elementary and Secondary. Yet the school looks smaller than Kath remembers. From the side window of the Regent, she can almost see Mrs. Eatten in the front doorway, calling the lower grades in from recess. The post office has been moved across the road to what looks like a rooming house. And Mrs. Tee Tee's Sundries has a new owner. But the Hurricane Lamb Café and the Hardware Barn are still run by the same families. Beyond the tree line up the road, where they get out of the car, comes the noise of a pickup baseball game on Nobody's Acre.

The brief afternoon rain shower has forced Marcelina to move the tables of food and the small stage from the lawn of Basinview Baptist to the church's basement. The better tables down here have been reserved for the elderly neighbors who still live in the Hindquarter or Centervillage.

"The nerve," Shirley says, when she realizes that her family is being led to a back corner with several small card tables holding handmade signs that read RESERVED FOR OUR NEIGHBORS FROM NEW JAMAICA. "How dare Miss M put us this far from the food and the stage. And where are our tickets for the buffet? When I see Marcelina, I'm definitely giving her the what for."

Kath cannot be bothered to complain. She takes the seat at a table that offers the best view of the crowd. It took a while to get down here with all the hugs she gave upstairs. And to think she was worried her former acquaintances would chastise her for being gone so long. All the old neighborhood kids and the former school classmates wanted to talk about was her son, Etienne. Few of the elders—the parents and grandparents down here—have recognized her yet. But they soon will.

Marcelina descends the stairs, followed by several men carrying trays of pies and cakes. Barely an inch over five feet tall, she moves in a green-and-red dress with a large silk bow on the front pocket. With a laugh, Marcelina ignores the grousing from several New Jamaica residents, not happy about their seats. She also ignores Kath, heading straight for Etienne.

"And this must be little Omar," Marcelina says, practically pulling Etienne out of his seat. "The boy looks just like his daddy."

"I don't use the name Omar," Etienne says, looking at Timothee.

Marcelina does not seem to have heard. "Come with me, son," she says. "Let's meet some folks."

Threading through the tables behind Marcelina, who is presenting Etienne as if he were her own son, Kath tries to remember the basement as it was when she was a Sunday school student. The table holding the fish cakes, meat pies, and lime punch is where she, Bonnie Ovits, and Steppie Caulden used to loiter at the water pail. In one back corner there once stood a large globe where she used to point out Jericho and Mesopotamia City and the River Damascus.

They reach a table where neither Marcelina's aunt Oneresta, wearing a small prissy hat, nor Reverend Steptoe, in a rumpled gray suit and a bright-yellow tie, seems to understand when Marcelina presents Etienne to them. "We remember you, boy," Opal Bennington says as her sister Gussie nods. "You came out of your momma fat as a goose."

Eventually they drift to a table not far from the picture display. A tall plywood board sitting on A-frame legs, it is covered in a light-blue crepe paper. Big letters across the top of the board spell out A SPLASH OF JUNE MEMORY CELEBRATION 1953.

"Remember what I told you, sister," Marcelina says, leaving Kath and Etienne. "Only one picture per family on the board today. We don't have room for more."

Kath heads toward the board later carrying several pictures, not at all happy that she can pin up only one. She will pin up the picture of Etienne standing at his school desk wearing shorts and suspenders. But she can't help wondering if there will be pictures of Kiendra on the board. She has seen no Penncampbells today. Since Guivalier died, she has heard, Rosa rarely leaves the house. And nobody has heard from Dominion in more than a year. Could she sneak up the picture of her and Kiendra?

"Is that a light-skinned colored man sitting with George and Shirley?" a woman asks the man standing with her and blocking Kath's path to the board.

"Must be," the man says. "I don't imagine George would bring a white man to this party."

Neither the man nor the woman averts their eyes as Kath steps between them. Nor does either look embarrassed by what they have said.

"I remember your boy's name used to be Omar," the woman says as Kath pins the picture of Etienne on the board. "Now they tell me it's something else."

"Do you imagine Omar would have minded his child being raised by a white man?" the man asks Kath.

"Don't give my husband that sideways glance," the woman says. "He was just speaking his mind."

"I don't remember asking what was on his mind," Kath says.

Kath pins up the second picture—of her and Kiendra in the cutouts at the Pictou County Mining and Cattle Fair, their dark faces on the bodies of the children of a white couple. The woman studies the picture with a scowl. "What kind of nonsense is this?" she says.

"It is an odd picture, I admit," Kath says. "But it has Kiendra Penncampbell in it."

"I know who Kiendra Penncampbell was," the woman says. "But it's a dumb picture. Take it down."

One of the perils of being estranged from the old neighborhood is that Kath is rusty in the ways of pleasantly disagreeing with her elders from the bluff. The dark-brown woman could be an Ovits, a family in which laughter disarms. Then again, she could be a Higgins or a Shuttlesworth, families whose members can be swayed by a biblical argument about love and friendship. The light-skinned man in the coat and tie looks like Clemmond Green's uncle. To argue with that man was always a waste of time.

Kath asks the couple their names. Before they can respond, a woman steps up to the board.

Kath lets out a loud scream, causing heads to turn at nearby tables. She gives her former school classmate Steppie Caulden a long hug. Kath and Steppie get to talking loudly as the couple moves away. "What were those old chickens walking off looking so mad about?" Steppie asks Kath.

"Maybe that they've spent their lives somewhere nobody wants to be."

Steppie gives a hard face. "I know why some of the neighbors have a bee in their bonnet about you," she says. "They say you're ashamed to have lived on the bluff."

"I am not ashamed."

"Then where have you been?"

Steppie shows Kath a picture pinned to a corner of the board. In it, Steppie sits with a group of boys on the gymnasium bleachers at the community center. A warm feeling erupts in Kath when she realizes that Omar is in the picture.

"Wednesday evenings were colored night at the gym," Kath says.

"And most of the fun was had after we finished playing volleyball," Steppie says.

"My, how young you look, Steppie."

After Steppie goes, Kath moves closer to the picture. She has already noticed that Steppie's hand is on Omar's shoulder. But does she see Omar's hand on Steppie's thigh? She knew Steppie and Omar had gone on walks together. Had they done more? Were they ever together?

Why on earth has Steppie put up that picture? Kath wonders, heading back to join her relatives. Was it jealousy? Could be. After all, Steppie has no husband. But no woman deserves criticism for telling the truth about her relationship with a man. Kath began to believe that during the troubled months after her relationship with Oscar Mislick ended.

S omebody outside wants to see you," Marcelina tells Kath a little while later, as Kath is coming out of the small toilet in the basement.

"Who?"

"Go up and see for yourself."

Exiting the side door of the church, Kath looks out toward the basin. The rain has stopped. Out there on the bluff a man sits on a large protruding boulder. The wind is heavy, and she tugs on her sweater as she walks across the wet grass. The man wears a light jacket and has a thick beard with a bit of gray in it. Behind him is the expanse of Dartmouth across the bay. As Kath approaches she gets a good look at the man's face. It is Clemmond Green.

After hugging Clemmond she sits on the boulder. It is damp, but she doesn't care.

"You still married?" Clemmond asks.

Kath presents her hand. While Clemmond studies the ring, she notices the scar on the side of his head. He got that the day he ran into a post at the bus stop. He was seven at the time.

"I'm on at the docks now," Clemmond says. "Big money. Enough for a family."

"I heard you don't have a wife and kids."

"Some women think I'm too old." Clemmond unzips his jacket. "I've been thinking about you. I wonder what it would have been like if you and I had been better friends."

"You're just reminiscing too much. Do you forget how much you taunted the younger kids? Have you seen Jessup, or Bonnie Ovits? Just wait until those two get here."

Clemmond laughs and looks toward the church. "Marcelina's parties are all the same," he says. "Just the punch is different."

"My first attendance has not gone as well as I planned," Kath says. "Not everybody is happy to see me and my family."

"Folks don't know you because you've made yourself scarce."

"Steppie Caulden said as much. But I haven't meant to be a stranger."

"You sure about that?"

Clemmond holds Kath's elbow and they walk back toward the church. Several people standing near the doorway watch them approach. Kath knows she ought to tell Clemmond to let go, but his hand feels good touching her elbow. Before they reach the church doors, Kiryl Platt approaches. It is obvious to Kath that Kiryl wants a word with her. When he was her supervisor at the Platts' business in Simms Corner, the impatient look like the one he wears now used to make her nervous. But not today.

The boldness of her approach with Clemmond seems to have disarmed Kiryl. No doubt Clemmond has heard the Platts' businesses are not doing as well as they did when Chevy Platt was vigorous. Kiryl has purchased two of the vacated houses in the West Slope, living in one with his wife and renting the other. But while he lives in New Jamaica now, compared to Clemmond he is a newcomer to the bluff. Perhaps Marcelina has it right. In many matters here on the bluff, the newcomers will have to wait their turn.

"Just a minute," Kath tells Kiryl as she grabs Clemmond's hand and directs him toward Dempsey Road. "I want to walk Clemmond to his car."

T he three giant punch bowls have probably half a ladle of lime punch altogether. But this end of the long food table is the only place in the crowded basement where Etienne can be alone.

Hey, boy, whatcha know good?

Etienne looks over his shoulder, thinking someone from one of the tables has called out to him. The crowd has quieted, though, some attendees dozing as they await another speech now that the children's musical performance has ended. Etienne rakes the bottom of one bowl with a ladle, wishing he could blow this old-folks shindig. Why can't he go upstairs where his mother seems to have disappeared to? But then he doesn't know any of the teenagers hanging around up there. Also, his mother says there are a few more people here he must meet—including the man walking beside the long table.

He approaches, not looking in Etienne's direction. Fanning his neck with a paper plate, he scans the scraps of fried cod and stewed chicken and the paltry traces of rice and greens clinging to the large bowls and platters.

"You probably don't know who I am," he says, arriving near Etienne with an extended hand.

"Yes, I do. You're my uncle."

"And not a good uncle, I guess."

Etienne tilts another bowl to ladle up more punch. Earlier, at the car, Kath had pointed out this man. Etienne had taken note of the small figure up on Dempsey Road, wearing pleated khaki-colored slacks and a short-sleeve shirt with a wide collar and talking to what looked like a young woman in front of a business establishment. Mentioning the man, his mother's voice had been friendly. She sounded as if Kiryl Platt was a man Etienne just had to meet. What a change from the times he overheard her complain about how Kiryl rarely saw him when he was an infant and how Kiryl was one of those no-good uncles. It was one of the few times Etienne heard her use the word *motherfucker.*

"Shirley told me you're going to summer camp," Kiryl says, dropping the empty paper plate down on the table. "The woods will be a change for a city boy."

"The camp is not in the woods," Etienne says. "It's on a school campus."

Kiryl looks out at the crowd. When he turns to Etienne, a long, awkward silence ensues, as if he does not know what to say. "I thought I had a picture of your father somewhere at my house," Kiryl says. "I tried to find it so you could put it up there at the board, but dang thing just wouldn't come out of hiding. But I will find the picture before you head back to Montreal."

"You will?"

"But to get it, you have to come see me when you get back from the camp. Then you can meet my wife and your cousin." Kiryl looks down at his shoes. "And you will meet my daddy, too, if he is still with us. Will you come see us when you get back?"

"If you want, I guess."

When Kiryl gives a satisfied grin, it is as if the face in one of the photographs Etienne has seen of his father has come to life. Something in what Etienne sees goes straight to his brain. Too often lately, he finds himself looking for similarities between his mother and himself. He stares at Kiryl's hands. The long, nervous fingers and knobby wrists are just like his. But can he trust his eyes? With solid certainty he used to tell his friends in grade school about the similarities between him and Timothee. But that was all in his head.

Etienne takes a drink of punch, feeling the sting of a slap to the middle of his back. His uncle heads for the table where Timothee sits with his aunt Luela and his grandparents, everyone laughing with yet another elderly couple. Today the only thing more annoying than another kiss on his cheek would be another slap on the back from another strange man. So Etienne heads upstairs to look for his mother.

Black as I Want to Be

Northumberland County, New Brunswick, 1953

A s he stands crouched on the starting block inside the natatorium of Saint Richelieu, the clap of the starting gun sends a jolt of energy through Etienne's body and he leaps off the block and into the water.

Twenty meters into the race, he can sense himself pulling away from the other boys. Yesterday he won every round of the fifty-meter races. Of the defeated boys, only one shook his hand. Reaching out for another stroke, he intends to massacre these same boys over seventy-five meters.

The cool water feels refreshing. Shouting voices drift up to the high, cantilevered windows, open to let in more chilly morning air. This newly built natatorium was all his father talked about during the drive across Northumberland County two days ago. That and his time as co-captain of the Saint Richelieu swim team. His mother was quiet for most of the drive, although, when they stopped for gasoline, she returned from the restroom animated. Beside her during the orientation in Divine Hall, he could smell the perfume she had sprayed on her arms. It did not totally mask the scent from the cigarette she must have smoked in the bathroom at the roadside station.

When Etienne recognizes that he might be swimming in this pool for two more years, his desire to avenge yesterday's slight by the boys diminishes with each stroke. Sensing a swimmer starting to catch up, he imagines Timothee, yelling from the bleachers. *Lengthen your strokes. Swim harder. Come on, captain.*

A swimmer is nearly upon him, yet Etienne stops his strokes. He sinks, and when his feet touch the coarse floor tiles he opens his eyes. He lets his body sway with the moving water. A frigid current runs over his feet. Above him on the surface, a laggard is plowing behind the other swimmers.

When his body drifts up, he flails his arms, pushing his body back to the bottom. Now the water stings his eyes. Irritating bubbles drift out of his nose. His chest feels tight, but there is no problem there. He can stay underwater for quite a while. In his family, his mother is the one with the frail lungs. He never used to fret about her health. However, from four in the morning until the call to athletics at six thirty, he lay in the dormitory bed imagining his mother's health getting worse in Italy. He does not want this campus to be a reminder of that. Of course, he cannot tell a single boy here on this campus about his fear. The boy will tell the others that he is *un fils à maman*.

Etienne did not like the strained smile his mother gave him last year as she lay in the hospital bed, reading the get-well cards made by her pupils. He wanted to see the broad smile she gave when reading a postcard from one of her college friends living overseas. Since leaving the hospital, his mother rarely talks to him about her health. During dinner all she talks about are her students.

Drifting to the surface of the pool, Etienne tries to forget the goodbyes last Sunday outside Divine Hall. After a hug, he asked his mother if he'd have to come back here in the fall. Getting no answer, he walked to the curb, where Timothee sat in the Regent with the windows up. As his head clears the water's surface, Etienne recalls that nothing he said enticed his father to roll down the window to listen.

In the dining hall later, Etienne eats his cheese sandwich and stewed figs, watching the large clock on the wall. At exactly six thirty, he heads for the exit.

"I waited for you this afternoon. At the handball court," says the boy who has followed Etienne outside. Orlando Quay, in a denim vest and tan-and-black rock-and-roll shoes, is a thin boy with a red patch of acne across his forehead. "Why didn't you show?"

"Didn't feel like playing," Etienne says.

"That's not a good reason. You want to go play Ping-Pong?"

"Don't know if I feel like it."

"Well, I guess we'll just walk then."

The boys cross the South Lawn down one of the long diagonal brick walkways. At the center of the lawn, Etienne leaps over a row of tulips. A few yards on they approach the Hindu temples. There, Tyrell Levesque is leaning against the lip of the fountain, emptying a pebble out of his loafer. As they get closer, Tyrell puts on his large sunglasses and starts speaking French with his cousin, who arrived late on Monday from Saint Lucia. Despite the cool air, both of the boys' dark faces are shining.

"Well, what do you know," Tyrell says when Etienne gets close. "Here comes Stringer-Beaner."

"That's not my name," Etienne says.

"Philippe Casson called you that at dinner yesterday."

"What do you want, Tyrell?"

"Is your mother coming back to visit?"

"How many times are you going to ask me that?"

"Three hundred."

"She's in Italy."

Tyrell slaps his cousin on the stomach with the back of his hand. "Wait until you see her. She'll break your heart."

"His mother's sick," Orlando says. "She's been in the hospital."

For a moment Tyrell looks like he's wondering what to say. As Etienne and Orlando continue on, Tyrell and his cousin follow.

"Did you tell him you think his mother ought to drop that white man?" the cousin asks Tyrell.

"You've never met his father," Orlando says.

"Still think she ought to drop him," the cousin says.

Tyrell glares at his cousin. "You better not say that when she comes back."

"Why not?"

"Because then his mother won't speak to me."

"But you've already said it yourself," the cousin says.

Tyrell punches his cousin's shoulder. Then he steps to Etienne. "Aren't you embarrassed to have a white father?"

"Aren't you embarrassed to have a bald-headed one?"

The cousin and Orlando laugh.

"You ought to be embarrassed, Stringer-Beaner."

Etienne stares at a little spit bubble in the corner of Tyrell's mouth. Yesterday, when he returned to the dormitory from orchestra lessons to dress for afternoon sports, he discovered that someone had sprinkled cinders from the running track into his underwear drawer. It must have been Tyrell. "I think you need to get a new game, Tyrell. Why don't you tell me something I haven't heard before?"

"Etienne looks white himself," the cousin says.

"But he's not," Tyrell says. "He's black. Aren't you black, Stringer-Beaner? Aren't you black, Etienne?"

Tyrell and his cousin stand straighter, both sets of shale-colored eyes demanding an answer. The gummed-up zipper on his bomber jacket has been bothering Etienne all day. With a quick jerk now, the slider moves all the way up. "I'm black if I want to be."

"You can't choose to be black," Tyrell says.

"You can if you look white like Etienne does," Orlando says. "Look, his arms are as light as mine."

Tyrell makes a face. "I'm glad I'm black."

Etienne laughs. "You don't mean that."

Tyrell lands a fist to Etienne's chest, sending Etienne stumbling back. When Etienne recovers, he swings, knocking the sunglasses off Tyrell's face. Orlando and the cousin back up as the boys wrestle down to the walkway.

The two boys continue tussling on the grass until a young camp assistant rushes over. The assistant hesitates, unsure which boy to reach for. Finally, he seizes Tyrell's arm.

"You know you're black," Tyrell says as the assistant helps him to his feet.

Etienne frowns at the tear in his jacket sleeve. He looks over at Tyrell, still in the assistant's grip. "You can't tell me what I am. I can be whatever I want."

Wresting free, Tyrell picks up his sunglasses. He puts them on his face, which is now as hard as the stone walkway. "Believe that and you're a fool."

The following Thursday, no one at Saint Richelieu can explain exactly why Etienne is being sent home—at least not to Luela's satisfaction. Someone called the hotel on Tuesday evening to tell her about the scuffle Etienne had gotten into earlier with the two boys from Saint Lucia. Had there been another fight? On the ride back to Halifax she doesn't chastise Etienne too much. But several days later, on Monday morning, tired from having worked two overnight shifts to make up the time she missed going out to Northumberland County, she wants answers. Noticing how upset Etienne still is, she decides to wait a few more days.

"Couldn't you at least have stayed out of trouble for a little while longer?" she asks on Saturday, after Etienne has eaten his fried eggs and potatoes. "You only had a few more days to go."

Etienne does not answer, so Luela follows him out of the kitchen.

From the bedroom doorway she watches him fall onto the unmade bed. "Tyrell kept pestering me," he says. "So I told him where to put it."

"Is talk all you did?"

Etienne does not answer.

"I'll bet that boy's mother's going to take a belt to him," Luela says.

"She should whip him," Etienne says. "He's a fool."

"I ought to do the same to you."

When she moved back into her parents' house, Luela replaced the twin beds in the bedroom she had shared with Kath. But the bureau is still here, although it now holds the unnerving sight of the reptile case with glass on three sides. The hump of straw at the far corner of the case means the serpent is still resting. Still, Luela hesitates a moment before entering the bedroom. She shakes her head as she steps over dirty pants, underwear, and socks strewn about the room.

"You always hang this up," she says near the bed, where she has picked up the bomber jacket. "Why was it on the floor?"

"Can't wear it anymore. The sleeve's torn."

"I patched the sleeve, did you look?"

"The boys will make fun of me."

"Not here in Woods Bluff."

"But we are going downtown."

"Boy, you have an answer for everything, don't you?" Luela drops the jacket on the bed beside Etienne. "Put on your shoes," she says, heading out of the bedroom. "We have to go pick up Shirley soon."

Etienne rolls off the bed and onto the floor, where he lies using the jacket as a pillow. On Wednesday, his first night in this bedroom, he fell asleep in his clothes with his body sprawled diagonally across the bed. The next morning, beneath the blanket someone had thrown over him, he opened his eyes expecting to see the dull gray dormitory walls of Saint Richelieu. Instead his eyes were assaulted by colorful birds swarming in a field of light-blue wallpaper. When his eyes adjusted, he recognized the two postcards leaning against the mirror on the bureau. They were from his friends who would be going to Vancouver. One postcard showed a dozen girls in bikinis, all staring up at a billboard of a large ketchup bottle. Etienne is certain one of the camp counselors at Saint Richelieu held on to the postcard several days before handing it over. Etienne had masturbated himself using the postcard one evening in the dormitory bathroom. His best friend, Fabrice, had written something on the back of the postcard in French, using lots of exclamation points. Etienne could only make out two words: *beaucoup d'amusement.*

Upon first meeting Fabrice's parents, people are surprised when they learn that the couple is colored. If you look carefully, you might suspect something in his father's tanned face. But Fabrice's mother has skin as pale as Etienne's. Fabrice often says his parents are hell-bent on keeping him colored. In a ski lodge last March, he complained that his parents had dragged him to another lecture by a colored man at the Publik Common. Lately, however, Fabrice seems to resent his parents. "I don't want to be like them," he said a few weeks ago. "I blow my own whistle."

Etienne rubs at a scuff mark on his shoe. Probably put there by Tyrell Levesque, he thinks. He meant it when he said he didn't believe Tyrell was glad to be black. Nobody's glad to be black. They put up with it. He loves his mother and appreciates his relatives in Halifax, but he has no desire to live in the skin they have. He dislikes how some bus drivers and store clerks in Halifax bark at his aunt Luela. Store clerks in Montreal sometimes speak just as rudely to his mother. Tyrell must have witnessed his parents being treated like that. What dullness in his mind prevents him from seeing the trap of his dark skin?

There must be a way for him to get out of going to the drugstore today, he thinks as he puts on a shoe. His parents will be very upset when they find out that he has been sent home early from the camp. What harm would it have done to tell Tyrell Levesque that he was black? Then he wouldn't have gotten into this new trouble. But would Tyrell have been satisfied with that answer? Etienne thinks as he picks up the dirty clothes from the floor. No, he would not. With his short attention span, Tyrell would soon have moved on to other foolishness. That idiot would have just started telling the other boys: *Etienne isn't really black.*

Downtown, Luela's husband, Chamberlain, has parked the car around the corner from the drugstore where they will go to call Italy. "All right," Luela tells Etienne. "Because you have picked up your room, I will not say anything to Timothee and Kath about you being kicked out of the camp. Not yet."

But as they get out of the car, Luela starts to worry that she will not be able to keep the secret. "Could you go with Etienne to make the telephone call?" she asks Shirley.

Shirley looks up the block to where Etienne has already reached the corner and is looking back. "Why?" she asks. "Are you and your sister fighting?"

"No, we are not. Kath called me at the hotel a few days ago. I figured I'd give you the opportunity to speak with her."

"I'm too old to be walking around downtown by myself."

"Etienne will be with you. You've heard about all the fistfights he gets into."

"Yes, but does he win any?"

"Can't you do me this one little favor?"

Shirley ponders the request for a moment. "No. I think you should come with me and the boy. I don't know how to operate a telephone."

Inside the drugstore, Luela sits in the telephone booth, not sure what she will say when her sister asks how things are going with Etienne. She lifts the receiver with a smile, hoping that will cheer her up.

Thankfully, Timothee comes on the line first. But his voice sounds heavy. "She's not doing well today," he says. "The doctor says she may need a day or two in the hospital."

Luela shifts on the stool with her back to Etienne and Shirley. "Can I speak to her?"

"Of course."

Kath comes on the line. "How's my child doing?"

"Rather talk about you."

"The doctor needs to go in and clear out some fluid is all. Is Etienne with you? Did he like the camp?"

"You should ask him when you talk to him."

"I'm asking you."

Luela hesitates. "Timothee's gone off to talk with the doctor," Kath says. "We can talk. Did my son get into trouble?"

Luela turns slightly. When her eyes meet Etienne's, his face tightens. She turns away from him. "Yes, I'm afraid he did get into trouble."

Kath's voice is now calm and steady, which means Timothee must be back in the room. When Timothee comes back on the line, his voice is calm, too. "I guess I'm ready for him," he says.

Luela holds out the phone to Etienne. "Your father doesn't know yet."

Etienne sits in the phone booth. "Hi."

"We've only got a few minutes," Timothee says. "Did you like the camp?"

Etienne grips the receiver tightly. "When are you coming home?"

"You're not giving your aunt and grandparents any trouble, are you?"

"How's my mother?"

"Here she is, talk to her."

Kath comes on the line. "Hello, baby. We've got to be quick."

"How are you feeling, Mother?"

"I'm feeling fine. Be even better in a few days."

"Better? What's the matter?"

"We've got lots of presents for you. But you'll have to wait."

"Can't wait until you're back. Then we can all go home."

"Goodbye, baby."

Waiting for Timothee to come back on the line, Etienne rubs the stitching on his jacket. He should have stuffed the torn jacket into the garbage bin behind the arts building, where he discarded his torn trousers. "I'm out of money," Etienne tells Timothee. "I want to buy a new jacket."

"Are you getting along with Luela?"

Etienne looks over his shoulder at Luela, who is down the aisle pulling something off a low shelf. "She's fussy."

Timothee laughs. "What else have you been doing?"

"Went to a baseball game on the bluff with Chamberlain."

"Your mother needs a little more time. Another week or two to rest."

"Grandmother's been writing. She wants me to come back to Montreal."

"I've got to hang up now, son. You behave for your mother."

"Why? You said yourself she's doing good now."

The next morning, Luela is finishing another overnight shift when she receives a telephone call at the hotel. "Why didn't you tell me he was sent home from the camp?" Timothee asks.

"Figured Kath would."

"He's got to be punished."

"I made him stay in his room. I locked his bicycle up in the shed. It's pretty dry in the area where the roof doesn't leak."

"Not good enough. Get rid of the bicycle."

"Don't have the money to send it back to Montreal."

"Sell it."

"No kid in Woods Bluff can afford to buy it."

"Some kid in Halifax will want it."

"I suppose I could put up a notice at one of the bulletin boards near the hotel. Maybe at the YMCA or the library."

"Now you're talking sense. Do it quickly."

A few days later, still in his pajamas, Etienne answers the front door at Luela's house to find a man and a teenage boy standing on the front porch. The man looks like Mr. Wong, his social studies teacher, except he doesn't speak with a heavy French accent. He speaks English like he's from Britain. "We've come to see Luela Sebolt," the man says.

Etienne yells over his shoulder. But when Luela's husband, Chamberlain, does not come out of the bedroom, he steps close to the man. "Aunt Luela's not home from work yet. What do you want?"

The boy hands Etienne a note he says was tacked up at the launderers. "The advertisement says the bicycle is for sale," the boy says. "We've come to get it."

"Nobody's selling a bicycle," Etienne says, handing the note back.

When the boy steps forward, Etienne is about to shut the door, but Chamberlain appears. He gently pushes Etienne aside and steps into the doorway. He looks over his shoulder toward the clock sitting on the television. "Come back this afternoon, maybe two or three to be safe," Chamberlain says, keeping a hand on the sleeve of Etienne's pajama shirt. "Luela will straighten this out."

When his mother first led him to the shed behind the Sebolt house—gabbing about a workbench and etchings in floor planks, Etienne barely looked inside. This afternoon, however, he visits every corner. He even bends down and peers into the dark area underneath the long worktable.

As he feared, his bicycle is not there.

"Damn her," he says.

He crosses the backyard feeling as if his swelling forehead is trying to tear itself from his face. Not once since arriving here in Halifax has he gotten the chance to ride his bicycle. He sits on the back steps, trying to calm down. But all he can think about is how to get back at Aunt Luela for selling his bicycle. He'll slice the pom-poms off those patent leather boots she likes so much. He'll hide her name badge one evening when she has to be at the Wales and London Hotel for an

early morning shift. While she's in the shower, he'll slosh baby oil on
that tacky hallway linoleum hoping she'll slip and break both of those
scrawny legs.

Later, in the bedroom, knowing his aunt is afraid of his pet, Etienne
lets the snake wrap itself around his wrist. But he hesitates before
bringing the snake out to the living room where Luela and Chamberlain sit listening to a radio program. What if Luela is not the person
who decided his bicycle had to be sold? What if his mother was the
culprit? He sits down on the bed but is unable to be angry with her.
Not with his brain invaded by the memory of her fighting back tears
as she gave him a goodbye hug on the campus at Saint Richelieu. And
did he overhear Luela tell her husband that his mother is seeing a doctor in Italy?

The next morning, with Etienne still sulking in the bedroom and
Chamberlain doing a roofing job in Saint Johns, Luela takes a
seat in the living room, grateful for the peace. She likes to sit in her
living room among the large sofa, the standing brass lamps, the thick
worsted throw rugs, the gold-framed mirror, and the side tables. All
were retrieved from the large storage room in the basement of the
Wales and London. It helps to keep telling herself that the furniture
shows very little fire and smoke damage.

But when the last dregs in her coffee mug have gone cool, Luela
finds the quiet disorienting. Today she doubts she will be content too
long sitting among these pieces by herself.

A walk through the Hindquarter and Centervillage will be good
for her, Luela thinks, and for Etienne, too. After all, he was born on
the bluff. Thinking about what she would point out to her nephew, it
occurs to Luela just how much things have changed since she was a
teenager. In Centervillage alone there are four new businesses.

Perhaps these two postcards that came in the mail from Italy may
cure the boy of his gloomy attitude, Luela thinks later in the day.

The postcard addressed to her has a picture of her favorite Italian actress. *You wouldn't believe the fun we're having,* Kath has written on the back. *I don't know why in the world we waited so long to do this. I feel wonderful.*

The postcard addressed to Etienne has a picture of a cowboy boot with tiny stars indicating the large Italian cities. In the border around the boot, Kath has drawn an arrow pointing to the location of the village of Gaeta.

In the living room, when Etienne sits down to look at the postcard sent to him, Luela assumes he will read his mother's happy words aloud. But Etienne reads them to himself. There is no postmark on either of the cards, but Luela thinks he suspects as she does that the happy words were written before his mother got sick.

Witnessing Etienne's gloomy slouch as he lowers himself into a chair for dinner makes Luela even more convinced that getting out of the house will help him feel better. His uncle Kiryl has been asking after his nephew ever since Etienne returned from the camp. The day before yesterday, when she ran into Kiryl's wife in Centervillage, she said Kiryl had not yet found the pictures he promised to give Etienne. Perhaps Kiryl will look harder if Etienne visits, his wife suggested.

Luela spoons rice onto Etienne's plate, worried about the news that Chevy Platt's health has taken a turn. There is no greater joy than seeing elderly relatives while they are still alive, George taught his daughters. And it is something that Luela can pass on to Etienne. Tomorrow morning, rain or shine, sour face or happy, she will make sure that Etienne walks over to New Jamaica so that Kiryl Platt can take him to see his great-uncle before that man leaves this world. For that, Etienne will thank her when he is older.

Chevy Platt left stern instructions that he wanted what he called a southern layout. The body is washed and dressed at home. Then it is laid out for a day of viewing—not on the bed where the living sleep,

but on a cooling board where the world-weary rest before returning
home to their Maker.

In Simms Corner, in the bedroom where Chevy had been ailing
for weeks, Etienne has taken a place beside the bed, between his uncle
Kiryl, who stands beside the head of the bed, and his cousin Yancy,
who stands beside the foot.

Kiryl's wife and her sister, before they left the house to spread the
word of Chevy's death, dressed the remains in the maroon suit Chevy
loved as a young man, when he lived in Glace Bay. Kiryl tells the boys
he remembers the southern layout ritual from the visits he made as a
child to Cape Breton to attend the funeral of former miners who had
come up from the southern United States.

"Hands and arms at the ready, young men," Kiryl says, motioning
Etienne and Yancy closer to the bed. "We will raise on my call."

Etienne slides his hands under the lower back of the body while
Yancy grips the ankles. Kiryl, showing the same dour face he had
worn when Etienne arrived, prepares to lift by the shoulders.

"Bring him up."

Etienne is surprised at how light the remains feel as they hoist the
body from the bed. In Chevy Platt's face, every sharp angle of bone
pushes out skin that looks as thin as wax paper.

The long table Etienne helped Kiryl haul up from the cellar now
sits covered in a silk cloth. With each steady step of the slow proces-
sion toward the cooling board, Etienne inhales more of the talcum
powder wafting off the body. But there is also another odor, like the
smell of burnt skin. Is this what death smells like? He has never been
this close to a dead person. But after they lower the body onto the
table, Chevy Platt does not look dead. He looks as if he has lain down
to take a nap.

The dark suit to dress the body for the funeral is hanging on a hook
on the wall near the cooling board. "Why does the undertaker have to
change the suit?" Etienne asks later, when Kiryl is pouring two glasses

of soda pop in the kitchen. "I thought you said your father is not having an open-casket funeral."

"Those are the man's instructions," Kiryl says. "We don't always know why a man does what he does. I could guess. So can you."

Kiryl Platt has not yet found the pictures of Omar he promised to give to Etienne. But he has found a few old letters that relatives in Halifax and across the bay in Preston received from the Platts in Mississippi.

"Your aunt tells me you need something to do while your parents are away," Kiryl tells Etienne as he hands over the letters. "Why don't you come work for me at the business? Your mother did, you know?"

Without acknowledging his uncle's offer, Etienne accepts the letters then insists he must go. "You don't have to drive me back," he tells Kiryl. "I will take the bus."

Did Luela know she was sending him to all of that, he wonders as he gets off the bus on the bluff. Was that more punishment for his being sent home early from the camp?

The Platts' business on the bluff is now called Platt's Hardware and Appliances. From the bus stop, Etienne wonders if any of the people he can see passing the building have heard the news. He is convinced that very little about working the cash register there would interest him. The one time he was inside, the few customers who came in seemed to recognize him but said nothing. One day he was certain he had seen one of the women who had been rude to his mother at the picnic.

Passing Basinview Baptist, Etienne almost turns to go by the cemetery to see the graves of his family. He did not know Chevy Platt but thinking now that soon the old man will be joining other deceased relatives there makes him sad. Etienne is about to leave the road when a thought occurs: there are Sebolts buried in the cemetery as well. But after attending to Chevy today, does he really want another visit with the deceased? He halts abruptly with an even worse thought:

his mother might be buried here soon. Trying to shake that thought, Etienne continues up Dempsey Road toward the Hindquarter.

Luela has waited until after Chevy Platt's funeral to tell Etienne she has news about his mother.

"Your parents are flying back from Italy today, directly to Montreal," she tells Etienne the next afternoon. "They are taking your mother to the hospital there this evening. She's not feeling well, but it could be just another cold. The hospital visit is merely precautionary. Your father says your mother is doing fine."

Etienne receives the news with a blank face. Later he is glad that Luela and Chamberlain have gone to work. He wants to be alone. After a while he takes a walk down the hill. There are a few boys shooting tin cans with their pellet guns over at the place they call the Bowl, but today he would rather walk to Nobody's Acre. It is quiet there. He likes it when warm breezes interrupt the cool air.

On Nobody's Acre he sits on a boulder trying to imagine his mother here. Did she bring him out here when he was a baby? If he tries hard enough, can he remember?

Thinking about the words on the postcard from Italy, he tries to imagine his mother happy, as she was the day the two of them walked together on Dempsey Road. But what he imagines instead is her being carried out of an airplane. She is lying in an ambulance that careens along a street in the Côte-de-Liesse, heading toward a trauma room at the Sacred Heart of the Lachine. He cannot imagine himself at her bedside, as he was the last time she recuperated in a hospital bed. At her request he sang a song imitating the Italian balladeer on a record Timothee's grandfather used to play when he lived at their apartment. His mother always said he had a nice voice. But that evening she could not have enjoyed his singing, plagued as she was numerous times by hacking coughs.

Two boys arrive carrying baseball gloves and bats. While one of the boys stands at home plate with a bat, Etienne directs the other boy to a position in right field. A few pitches and Etienne can feel his mind begin to clear. But when he is hitting fly balls for the boys to catch, his mind drifts back to thinking about his mother. Everybody is calm about her return, and he is trying to be. But it is difficult.

Heading back, Etienne imagines he will show his mother the letters he got from his uncle Kiryl. But not until she is feeling better. "You need to learn about the other side of the family," his aunt Luela had said. He knows more now, but what he knows does not please him. From the letters it is clear that despite Omar's requests, the family in Mississippi—including Omar's mother—had never wanted him to come down for a visit. If that was true, why on earth would Etienne want to get to know the Platts better?

Etienne decides he needs something else from Halifax to cheer his mother, because the letters might make her sad. Passing the Penn-campbell house, he notices a woman on the porch. Is that the mother of the girl in the picture with his mother at a county fair? He waves, but all she does is stare. He arrives at his aunt's house, recalling the day of the picture party, when his mother took him to the back of the family house to see the shed. "If I had a crowbar with me now," Kath said when they were inside, "I'd pull up one of these planks from the floor."

The interior of the shed smells damp as Etienne enters. In one corner, he kneels and touches several boards. He runs his fingertips over the brass square etched with the date the floor was laid. This would be a good board to take, but a better choice would be a board with etchings on the end.

When Etienne jiggles a board, a heavy nail pops up and hits him in the chest. He puts the nail in the pocket of his jacket and then pries the board loose. He carries the plank out of the shed. He will find a way to hide the plank from Shirley and George, and from Luela. He wants this to be his secret.

From the backyard he can hear people talking on Dempsey Road.

What happened to all the noise his mother says used to rattle the Hindquarter? Centervillage is noisy, but up here it is dull city. With the plank on the ground he uses a heavy rock and the nail to pound a row of punctures across the board. *Sixty or so days until he starts school in Montreal. By then his mother will be well again—that will happen.* After leaning the board against a small boulder, Etienne jumps high. When he lands, the board splits where he wants it to, sending a sharp thunderclap across the bluff.

Overdue Lessons

T he weather in Montreal near the end of July is sweltering. With no air-conditioning in the apartment, the heat irritates Kath, who gets out of bed thinking today is the day she will begin gathering material for her fall classes at Greeves Adventist Primary. How is it possible that, once again, it is time to prepare her lesson plans? Where on earth did those early summer months go?

That is a question she is not in a hurry to answer, Kath thinks, leaving the kitchen with her cup of tea. She slept well last night. And with several hours before she must go to her doctor's appointment, she enters the bedroom thinking over other tasks she could do. Her memory cabinet arrived last week from her parents' basement in New Jamaica. Cleaning out more drawers might be easier than working on her lesson plans. But just imagining the dust mites and mold that might erupt from that job gives her a fit. And besides, those drawers contain too many letters she is in no hurry to revisit. Why on earth did she save the letters from Oscar Mislick? She has heard he is now a high civil service commissioner in Ottawa. Who was the girl who let herself be taken under the spell of that man's words?

She sits at her desk, almost feeling the warm seawater of Gaeta on her feet. Before she fell ill, she and Timothee had explored the seaside town like a new couple. From rough wooden piers, they watched the sun redden behind gray clouds. In restaurants with low ceilings, they sipped spirits that gave their throats the most delightful burn. The small bedroom where they slept at Timothee's great-aunt's house had thin curtains for a door. Still, they somehow managed to find ways to be intimate. But the idea of any more fun ceased the day she woke up on the ground-floor hospital room in Naples, thinking her lungs were going to burst. The doctor there said the new fibrosis would be difficult to arrest. As each day went by, though, she began to believe her lungs would clear in time to make the trip to Morocco. But it did not happen, Kath recalls as she retrieves a folder of papers from a drawer in the desk.

"It's better in here," she told Timothee yesterday evening, when he came home to find that she had gotten Etienne and his friend Fabrice to move the desk into the bedroom. "This way Etienne and the boys do not have to listen to my hacking cough when they are in the living room."

In the folder with the material for her lesson plans is the speech she gave last year to begin her class. Icky, icky, icky, her new fourth-grade students would say if they knew how many times she had given this same speech.

After working a while, Kath slips on her low-heel shoes for another trip down to the lobby. Retrieving the mail is usually Etienne's daily chore. But just the sight of any document emblazoned with the gold-crusted crest of Saint Richelieu is enough to cause several hours of moping. What Etienne saw a few weeks back, and suspected was a fall tuition bill from the school, was a letter from the headmaster detailing his concerns about admitting Etienne for the fall. Timothee replied in long paragraphs expressing his admiration for the school and his fond memories of his time there. He also included half the payment for the fall tuition.

Money talks, Kath thinks at the bank of mailboxes, where she retrieves a large envelope from Saint Richelieu. Kath pulls more letters out of the mailbox, realizing she will miss her son in the fall, despite his moods. Etienne's gloomy face at dinner last night may have resulted from the discussion Kath and Timothee were having about today's doctor's appointment. At least sending him to school will prevent him from hearing his parents discuss more of those.

These low-heel shoes carrying her to the elevator will also do well for the walk to the medical school campus. "A woman surviving into adulthood with the type of dormant chest infirmity you are suffering is a medical rarity," her new doctor has said. She has been in his care for only three weeks, but already he has suggested several novel therapies. If the medical device he will fit her for today does not yield results, he will suggest another hospital stay. The stay, he says, will be solely for tests and observation, but she is not sure she believes that.

Another letter from Marcelina Higgins. Kath shakes her head in the elevator. This is the second letter she has gotten from Marcelina since returning home to Montreal. She left for Italy suspecting that Marcelina was not too happy with her for failing to complete her assigned task of bringing a project for the children in the monthly weekend academic program. To make matters worse, Marcelina was also not happy to see Kath agree with one of the neighbors who complained that Marcelina had not selected any children from New Jamaica to sing at the picture party. "Couldn't you have at least chosen one for the children's quintet?" Kath had asked.

The French make the best maps of West Africa. But the stack of maps Kath gave to Marcelina apparently did not spur enough ideas in the students or their teacher. *Help, help, help*, the letter from Marcelina begins. It ends with an invitation for Kath to come to Halifax one weekend and teach a lesson herself. *The children will learn plenty being taught by a college-educated woman who used to live on the bluff*, she writes.

The letter also includes a newspaper clipping from the summer

1953 issue of the *Colored Freeman*. The article discusses one of the towns in West Africa with inhabitants claiming to be descended from the men and women who, in 1823, waded ashore from the grounded HMS *Perspicacious*. For years, Shirley has been sending Kath similar articles from the *Colored Freeman*. One article about foreigners landing on the northern coast of Africa made Kath wonder about ancestors of hers who might have come ashore somewhere there. Today she imagines herself free of illness, driving in a convertible from the city of Mogador, Morocco, down the Pepper Coast toward Freetown, Sierra Leone. There she would walk the beach looking for items that her great-grandparents Ephram and Ivy Sebolt discarded as they waded ashore.

Mere rumor, her father says about the stories of former residents of Woods Bluff living in Africa. Both of those ships went down at sea, George maintains. But this newspaper article gives the name of a town in a northeast corner of Sierra Leone, where the boundaries of Guinea and Liberia meet. Families there have discovered old church records that prove a claim they have been making for years: that many families in the town have ancestors who once lived in Nova Scotia. Kath refolds the clipping, revising the dream she had of driving down the Pepper Coast. Now she would also turn inland, driving through flatlands and hills to the town the article says is called Halifaxship.

If that Marcelina is anything she is persistent, Kath thinks, as she slides the clipping back into the envelope. It will be a pleasure to write a lesson plan for a class using the information from the article. But she is not sure she will be able to return to the bluff to teach it herself.

Enough procrastinating, Kath tells herself as she opens the fat envelope from Saint Richelieu. Time to get to the real work today. As she suspected, it hurts a bit to read the words welcoming her son to the Saint Richelieu Cohort of 1953–1954. She hesitates a moment, but then signs the enrollment papers. After writing the check, she hides the envelope to be mailed back to the school beneath a pile of papers on her desk. All is well. Etienne will be away in the fall, she hopes, with plenty to keep his mind off worrying about his mother.

Just look at the time. It is nearly eleven. Instead of beginning her schoolwork, Kath rises from the desk and heads for the living room. She gives her orchids a misting, having decided to find a way to make these next few months easier for her husband. Timothee has offered to drive her home after her doctor's appointment today. But she will telephone his firm from the doctor's to say she will take a taxi. That will also avoid getting into another disagreement with Timothee about the woman she plans to interview tomorrow morning for help around the apartment a few days a week. Timothee insists that is unnecessary. He says that he will pitch in. But she is having none of that. She is doing this for him.

It is a few minutes to five in his twelfth-floor office at PMR Architecture and Construction, but Timothee has still not picked up the note his secretary placed on his desk several hours ago. He knows what Kath says in the note—*Don't bother coming to get me. I can make it home by myself.*

Perhaps he should have told Kath his plans for a leisurely walk home. Inviting her out for a stroll in the hot evening air would have shown her he is not ready to treat her like an invalid. He also wanted to take her for a glass of wine at the bistro where they ate on their first outing. He would tell her he remembered the colorful blouse she wore the day they dined. And he would tease her about the hose she wore, which had looked a bit ragged. She would make a face when he told her that back then she reminded him of the actress in the movie *Sexual Kitten*, the way she grinned and peeled off her gloves as she perused the menu. Talking about Italy could be tricky. He could mention the ocean voyage over and the moments during the flight back when they agreed that the happiness they felt during the first days in Italy would reignite after they returned to Montreal. Will it? Timothee wonders as he crumples the note and tosses it into the waste can.

In Gaeta, Timothee enjoyed the stories his great-aunt told about his grandfather's foraging for rabbits and wild cabbage in the woods, while the foreign soldiers slept off their night of drinking. When his great-aunt showed some of the stones her brother had collected, Kath started to cry. Timothee still does not understand that reaction. What could be so sad about a collection of rocks?

The shelf in Timothee's office holds awards his firm has won for projects he managed. Sometimes, when he is having a bad day, he picks up one of the framed certificates and wonders why he let go of his desire to make partner at one of the modish firms spreading out down in the warehouse district. He has been promoted from overseeing the financial aspects of building dams and bridges to overseeing the design and construction of airport terminals and urban medical complexes. There is some satisfaction in his work. Or at least there used to be.

The hallway, which at this hour is usually busy with chatter, is as quiet as an abandoned airport hangar. He will encounter plenty of noise soon, now that he has time to make a quick visit to his parents' house. His mother, Claire, will be in a huff when he tells her he will not allow Etienne to accept another bicycle. *What can I do?* he will say. The administrators at Saint Richelieu do not allow wheels of any sort. Claire hasn't put up an oversized fuss since the day Timothee told her he intended to marry a woman who not only was colored, but also already had a child. He had quickly added that the child's father had died. When his mother calmed down, she seemed happy when he told her that he and his wife planned to have more children. Claire has gotten over her disappointment about the failure of that goal. Just look at how she spoils Etienne. Timothee feels he has grown fond of the boy as well. Though nothing he does lately seems to convince Etienne of that.

It probably didn't help matters that the very evening Etienne returned home from Halifax, instead of answering any of the boy's questions about his mother's health, Timothee forced him to sit down and write a letter to the headmaster at Saint Richelieu, apologizing for his misbehavior.

Kath worries a bit about Etienne since he told her what the colored boy had said to him at camp to cause their scuffle. Something about questioning whether Etienne was colored. Situations like that are easy, Timothee told Etienne. When your grandfather was your age, he had to contend with real terror. Many of the villagers whom the invaders killed or raped in the Italian woods were not yet adults. Even today people do more than make rude comments to teenagers. They rape or murder them.

Saint Richelieu inculcates in its students the idea that new, uncomfortable experiences can help broaden a young man's thinking. Etienne's distress about having to go there in the fall could be softened if Timothee could only show his son that the decision is being made out of love. But where is the fortitude for that effort? The trip to Italy seems to have brought Timothee and Kath closer. For now, his efforts are spent thinking of ways to demonstrate his love to her. Doting on Etienne will have to wait until he has more energy.

The housekeeper Kath hired is not due to begin work until Saturday. This Friday evening, however, Timothee arrives home to find the living room floor mopped and not a single sofa cushion out of place. In the kitchen, the boy humming must be the one who has swept the floor, washed every dish, and wiped down every countertop.

"I can pick up mother's medicine at the pharmacy tomorrow," Etienne says as Timothee takes a plate covered with aluminum foil out of the oven. "There's no need for you to go."

"Your mother can pick up her own medicine," Timothee says.

"Oh," Etienne says. "I didn't realize she was going to do that herself."

While Timothee eats his plate of broiled halibut and kidney beans,

Etienne stands at the counter. As he flips the pages of a sports magazine, his eyes go back and forth from the kettle warming on the stove
to the stack of mail on the table, only partially visible from where it is
held down by Timothee's briefcase.

When the kettle begins to screech, Etienne sets a dainty cup and
saucer on the counter. "I think Mother will like this set," he says.

"Preparing tea for your mother and you straightened the living
room?" Timothee says. "I see that you are growing into a respectable
young man."

"Does this mean I get a new bicycle?"

"Must you always bring up the damned bicycle?"

"Cool yourself, Dad. I didn't mean to."

"I know what you want to ask me," Timothee says as Etienne pours
steaming water into the teacup. "But your mother has most of your
school clothes washed and folded."

"But nothing's packed."

Timothee reaches for the cup of tea, but Etienne picks it up first.

"I'll take the tea in to Mother," Etienne says.

"Your mother might not be decent."

"That's okay," Etienne says. "I'll knock."

The instructions on the medical device in Kath's bedroom say the
operator must ensure that the padded leather backrest is properly
affixed to a high-back chair before turning on the motor. A dining
room chair serves the requirement well.

Finally Kath has a proper diagnosis for the illness that plagues her.
It is not lung cancer, as her previous doctor had said, but a malady
called nonspecific internal pulmonary edema. This medical device,
like a few of the other palliative care remedies her new doctor has pro-
posed, seems just as odd as the name of the disease.

The first time Kath sat down to be strapped into the device, she was
glad Timothee was there to assist. This evening, alone in the bedroom,

she folds the front part of the apparatus over her chest with barely a hesitation and begins fastening the six buckles running up the side.

She once owned a suit jacket that fastened down the side. She discovered the item on a rack in a consignment establishment when she was strolling down a narrow side street in Côte-des-Neiges. Before she met Timothee, she was fond of flashy but cumbersome clothing like that.

The belts tightened, Kath presses the foot pedal to start the motor. The humming will soon rise to a noisy rattle. With her eyes closed she wonders if her face indicates how uncomfortable she feels with the device vibrating her upper body. She hasn't yet let her son see her strapped into the device. This evening it might be a comfort to hear him say she looks silly.

So far, a single five-minute treatment loosens most of the mucus gumming up her lungs. That she feels better immediately after every treatment is an added treat. A few more weeks of success and she might stand at the head of her classroom to welcome her new students.

"Why are you knocking?" Kath asks when she hears rapping at the door.

She expects Timothee to enter. But pushing open the door, holding a steaming cup with his face showing mild panic, is the person she loves most in this world.

"Come on in, my dear. Your mother won't bite."

Etienne enters thinking how much more loudly the contraption sounds than it did when he listened from the other side of the door. The rattling is even more annoying up close. After setting the tea on the desk, he helps his mother undo the buckles on the device, wondering if his parents have been telling the truth about her health. He reunited with his mother the day she was released from the hospital. She came to the car where he was waiting looking thinner than she had when she left for Italy. She did not criticize his wrinkled slacks, nor did she tell him he needed a haircut. Nor did she order him to give her a kiss. What was the matter with her? At the curb in front of the apartment building, her grip seemed weak as she held his hand on the walk to the lobby. In the elevator, she barely responded to a chatty neighbor.

"The doctor says you shouldn't do any schoolwork," Etienne says after Kath has returned to her desk. "He says you should take it slow."

"I'm not doing any hard work," Kath says. "And besides, my doctor is not a mother with two men to look after."

"I can take care of myself."

"I believe that more every day. But you are still my little boy."

The back of the floor plank Etienne pulled from the shed in Halifax has been outfitted with wire and screws but not yet hung on the wall. It had taken him a week to find the right moment to present the gift to his mother. "Do you remember the little clay figure you made in the third grade?" Kath asks, watching Etienne examine the mounting on the plank.

"It was a paperweight."

"You made several more nice clay items in the fourth and fifth grades. When you started high school, you made me hide your artwork so your friends would not see it."

"I like my friends. That's why I'd like to stay here in Montreal."

"Did you ask your father?"

"Yes."

"What did he say?"

"He said I should ask you."

While Kath sips her tea, Etienne walks to her memory cabinet placed near the closet. "Where is everything?" he asks, peering into one of the empty drawers pulled halfway out.

"You have to make room for new memories."

"What will you put here?"

"Letters from my son. Will you write to me every day?"

While Kath sips her tea, Etienne sits on the bed, stunned. The look on his face surprises her as she resumes writing. She assumed he had braced himself for the news that he would be going away. Just a few years ago, he loved to sit and watch her work. This year she fears all her lesson plans will be overdue. Apparently so is her work to prepare her son for the fall.

When Etienne bounds up off the bed and marches to the desk, Kath sets down her pen, pats her chest, and lets out a few mild coughs.

"My goodness, you are becoming a man now," she says as Etienne helps her rise from the chair. "Now, be a dear and let your mother rest."

Only on Nobody's Acre

A chorus of complaints erupts this hot August afternoon in the basement of Basinview Baptist. Colored pens are thrown, construction paper is tossed to the floor, and paintbrushes are banged against tabletops. While the teacher picks up the discarded school items, one of the girls playing patty-cake by the long worktable strikes the whale made by the children, sending it to the floor, where it bursts into a scatter of Popsicle sticks.

"But we don't want to paint Africa," one bespectacled toddler tells the young woman trying to settle down the students on this second day of the Weekend Academic Enrichment Program. "It's dirty."

When Kath arrived on Friday from Montreal, Marcelina told her that many of this young woman's neighbors in New Jamaica agree that she will become a great teacher with just a little training. But Kath does not see it yet. This is the third time today that Kath has had to come over from the groups she is teaching to help with the children the young woman is supposed to handle. Thank goodness she is enjoying a few days when her chest feels clear and her pills are giving her energy. During yesterday's class, the children in the young woman's care were even more boisterous.

"Everybody on your feet," Kath says. "That's correct, everybody stand. Now, raise your hands. And on the count of three, we are all going to scream. Ready? Arms up."

Standing with her arms crossed, the young teacher looks unimpressed as the students' hands fly into the air.

"One . . . two . . . th-ree!"

The children shriek their loudest, wearing mischievous smiles as they look across the room at the kids working quietly at the other two tables.

"Now then," Kath says, when the screams have ceased. "What we need is a larger work area. Come on, kids, let's put two tables together and make one big table. Wouldn't that be fun?"

"Yay," the kids say.

As the children arrange the chairs around the table, Kath talks to the teacher. "Have them do something else," she says.

"What?" the teacher asks.

"Oh, anything. Just keep trying. Something will work. They can make their maps of Africa later. I'll come help if you need me."

The noisy interlude has done nothing to disturb Kath's students. All have laid down tracing paper over a map and traced the outline of Sierra Leone. With the thick-tipped colored pencils, the students have begun to draw a line in the middle of the map to represent the road from the western coast border to the eastern border of the country.

Kath makes several more trips across the room to assist the young teacher. Later, after the children have gone, even though she should be heading to Luela's house to finish packing for her overnight train back to Montreal, she remains behind to help sweep the basement floor and put away the teaching materials. She agreed to come to teach in the program after Marcelina told her that several other girls had volunteered to help. Betty Addison had taught a class in July, something about the students pretending to be elected officials. What does Betty

Addison know about teaching that? A few years after beating Kath out for the college scholarship given by the Victorian Maternal Order, Betty got a job with the provincial government, where she has worked ever since. But all that girl does is push papers. Kath chose to come for one of the last weekends of the summer classes. She planned to have the kids finish with a bang.

And they have. Before leaving, she admires the maps taped to the walls. All have titles written with assured penmanship that say THE ROAD FROM FREETOWN TO HALIFAXSHIP. Along both sides of the thick crayon lines the students have glued on small pictures of kitchen items the travelers might have dropped or discarded on their journey inland—wooden spoons, an ice pick, a line of porcelain chickens. One kid even found a small pair of oven mitts.

The weekend of teaching has taken her mind off Etienne, whom she delivered to school last Friday before coming to Halifax. Later in the evening, she begins the long trip back to Montreal without her son or her husband. She does not mind, since this is a trip she has made before. She feels better, but with her health up and down she feels she needs some time alone. A few hours into the train ride back she begins to think about her life and what will happen this year. Not everything will go as planned. But isn't that life?

I n the fall, Marcelina Higgins offers her academic enrichment program every other Saturday. Toward the middle of October, she begins to regret relenting to the pressure from folks in New Jamaica, who made her keep their young neighbor teacher on the payroll. Too many times she has had to come downstairs from the church office to help calm the children.

Trying to give the stubborn young woman advice is useless. She listens to none of the other teachers either. Kath is the only one the young woman seems to heed. But Marcelina is reluctant to send another request to Montreal or even to place a phone call, especially since she knows Kath has been in the hospital again. Kath had seemed fine when she was on the bluff in August. In fact she seemed robust.

Oh, what could it hurt? Marcelina thinks several days later at her kitchen table, where she puts pen to paper. *The young woman needs advice again*, she writes to Kath. *Don't rush yourself. Call or write to her anytime. We are in no hurry.*

Two weeks later, having gotten no answer, Marcelina begins to worry. This is not like Kath, she thinks on her way to the Wales and London Hotel to see if Luela has heard from her sister.

But Luela is not at the hotel. Nor is she at her house in the Hindquarter.

This morning on the campus of Saint Richelieu, the headmaster enters the reception room in Divine Hall, followed by several boys in rumpled dark-gray blazers. The boys carry boxes and suitcases, which they place on the wide hearth of the fireplace.

"I assure you," the headmaster tells Luela, who is seated on a large sofa beside her husband, Chamberlain, "no one here wanted Etienne to hear the terrible news the way he did."

Luela shifts her body on the sofa. Each of the retreating boys has a miniature Oktoberfest pumpkin pinned to the lapel of his blazer. When one freckle-faced boy passes near her, she almost pats the smiling pumpkin as a gesture of thanks. But the pious-looking young man might be the devil that broke the news to Etienne that his mother had died. The headmaster says he believes the culprit was Tyrell Levesque. But somebody had to have told Tyrell. These past few weeks, whenever Kath was in the hospital, one of the Saint Richelieu mothers would call the hotel to report how Kath was doing. Had one of those mothers told her son the news?

Not a single employee at the hotel—not the floor maids or the uniformed security sergeants, not even Grandville, the concierge—had the backbone to give Luela the sad news. They all knew when she arrived at the hotel last night for a day shift that Timothee had called the hotel. How else to explain eight hours of encountering sagging faces and voices that went quiet when she approached? Not until her shift had ended did a supervisor call her into an office to mention Timothee's phone call. Luela was awake most of the night. And when she wasn't thinking about her trip here to give Etienne the news, she was hearing Kath's voice in her head. It was a voice that, on the drive to the campus today, gave her not one moment of peace.

Timothee arrives later. After conferring with the headmaster, he exits Divine Hall and chats with Luela at the curb while Chamberlain directs the boys who are loading Etienne's belongings into the trunk of the Regent.

"Seems like she just dropped her son off yesterday," Luela says.

Timothee nods and then turns to Luela to resume their discussion of the funeral arrangements. Luela is not happy with his decision to have her sister cremated.

"Sebolts' bones need to be somewhere the family can get at them if they want to," Luela tells Timothee. "That's how the family sees it."

"I've discussed these plans with Shirley," Timothee says. "She offered no objection."

"Shirley might have thought that you were not serious."

"I assured her I was."

"I want to see my sister's body. Shirley and George will, too."

Timothee nods. "They have a nice chapel at the facility. We could also have a service before the cremation. Will you help plan the service?"

Luela puts on her gloves, noticing the constellation of rust and yellow flowers on the nearby lawn. Flowers and an open casket is how things ought to be done. If Shirley agrees to go along with Timothee's distasteful plan, she can be the family representative at the service. Luela wants to say she'll have no part of it. She notices Timothee's eyes looking toward the dormitory down the hill. Etienne is there in the doorway shaking hands with the headmaster. She doubts Timothee will go down to escort his son to the car. He is not that kind of father.

Luela spots the streaks of gray in Timothee's hair. Was George correct to say that this older man had exerted undue influence on Kath to get her to marry him? After all, Kath met Timothee when she was still uncertain about whether she could raise her child alone. Luela has always believed she was much more accepting of the marriage than Shirley or George were. Was it a mistake to accept Timothee so quickly into the family? Perhaps her mind is not right today, but she does not like how easily he seems to discard a Sebolt family tradition.

I can't believe what I'm hearing," Marcelina Higgins says a week later in the lobby of the cremation facility in Montreal. "We came all this way to see Kath. Why can't we?"

Other neighbors from the bluff who have traveled from Halifax with Marcelina in a six-vehicle caravan stand nearby. Everyone looks first to Shirley and George and then to Timothee, who is speaking in French with a tall woman dressed in a bright-green suit.

"The manager says they are not allowed to bring out the remains once the chamber is locked," Timothee tells George and Shirley. "It's the law."

"Get the owner out here," Marcelina says.

"Forget the owner," someone else says. "Get a constable."

"And get one straightaway," Reverend Steptoe adds. "For all we know they have misplaced the body. Or sold it to the government medical doctors."

When Reverend Steptoe, Clemmond Green, and Dominion Penn-campbell begin moving toward the double doors leading to the firing chamber, the employee hurries past them. "I will go in first," the woman says, as she pushes open the doors. "Stay here, please."

There is a low grumbling while the crowd waits for her to return.

"All right," the woman says when she comes out again, "everyone will get a viewing."

Years ago, when the nice suit Kath had purchased for her first job interviews began to fray, she cut off the buttons and stored them in her jewelry box. For her thirtieth birthday, Timothee surprised her by having the buttons sewn onto a pale-blue suit. The body is now dressed in that suit and stretched out on a long steel table in the chamber. As the crowd approaches the table, a loud gasp rises from several visitors.

"If this is their idea of a cooling board," the Reverend says, "I am not here for it."

"They could have at least put her in the coffin the family paid for," Steppie Caulden says, holding Veronica Teakill's hand.

"Don't look like her at all," someone says.

Reverend Steptoe leads the crowd in the reading of a few Bible verses. One of the women sings a short solo. While the crowd is debating and fussing about how long to remain here, one of Marcelina's nieces tugs on the front of Marcelina's dress. "Who is she?" the girl asks.

When the girl asks more insistently, everyone looks at Marcelina. But she seems unable to fashion an answer.

The six-vehicle caravan travels back home from Montreal, stopping at a cluster of roadside picnic benches, where the neighbors quietly eat sandwiches while the children play. When a conversation begins it is low and not about the unsettling incident the group has experienced in the city. It is about the place to which they are returning. A few stilted laughs break out when several neighbors begin a friendly argument about how to characterize Woods Bluff. All nod in agreement about the neighborhoods that make up Woods Bluff: the Hindquarter, Centervillage, and, yes, New Jamaica. And do not forget the Bowl. But there is little agreement about the bluff's temperament.

Is the bluff impish and contrary like a three-year-old? Or is its temperament like a grown-up's—harsh and angry, with its hard rain and heavy snow steeling its residents for future struggles? Nobody agrees with one man who says the place is as moody as a child when the sky is overcast. The bluff, many say finally, is nurturing. Where else to be on a warm fall day when a lingering evening grosbeak with black-and-white wings can be seen streaking through trees bursting in reds and golds? And at the comment that the best months to be on the bluff are June and September, a chorus of hands rises in agreement.

Luela, still angry with Timothee about his insistence on cremation, had left Montreal before the caravan arrived. The day after it returned, when neighbors come by to tell her about the ride home, their words assure beyond a doubt that her sister's body is no longer on this earth. The sadness that overtakes her plagues her all through the winter. The following spring, at the picture party, when Marcelina Higgins approaches about having a memorial service for Kath in Halifax, Luela says, "Sorry, Marcelina, but I am nowhere near ready to discuss my sister."

A week later, however, Luela cannot keep quiet about the item Marcelina has brought with her on a visit. It is something M. T. Everson's son said he found wedged into the back seat cushion in one of his father's two cars, which carried the neighbors to the service in Montreal. Luela inspects the oblong button, which has a distinctive polished wood back and a gold-plated front etched with small crescents.

"This has to be a button from the blue suit that belonged to my sister," Luela says. "I know because I pressed the suit myself before it was put on Kath's body."

"What has the world come to?" Marcelina says. "Who the devil would have the nerve to take a button off a deceased woman?"

"Well, who was in the car?" Luela asks.

"The riders changed cars several times on the drive back," Marcelina says. "It would be near impossible to tell from whose pocket the button fell."

"But I'll bet M. T. Everson can tell me who rode in his cars," Luela says. "Surely he could give me the names of the people."

"Good luck asking them about that," Marcelina says. "Them Everson boys got a jitney service to operate. I doubt any of them will tell on a customer."

Luela puts the button away, barely able to contain her anger. Over the next year, whenever she has guests visiting, she leaves the button in a prominent place in her living room. But not a single former neighbor seems bothered at the sight.

On the afternoon of November 15, 1954, a year after the cremation ceremony, when Marcelina visits, Luela tells her that she has put away the button from the blue suit for good.

"Does that mean you are tired of grieving in the same way?"

"I suppose," Luela says. "I do know I was tired of harassing people about the button."

"Are you warming to the idea of having a memorial service for Kath here in Halifax?"

"Not yet. But I'm ready to give the idea a bit of thought."

After the visit, Luela learns that Marcelina is planning what she calls "a citizen's march" from Woods Bluff to city hall to urge the mayor and councillors to stop ignoring the needs of bluff residents. Every event Marcelina plans on the bluff seems merely to be an opportunity to talk about her march. Given the tepid response by people to this crusade, Luela is fearful that Marcelina will turn a memorial service into a recruitment event for the march. So she decides to plan the service herself. Feeling guilty about excluding Marcelina from helping to plan the service, Luela asks her to design invitations for the event.

A few weeks later, Marcelina arrives carrying a box of envelopes already stuffed with invitation letters. Reading one of them, Luela discovers that the invitation contains only a few of the sentiments she had drafted. Mostly the letter talks about the upcoming march.

"I want a small memorial for Kath," Luela tells Marcelina, "not an invitation to a protest."

"But the kind of work I do is trying to make things better for everyone," Marcelina says. "When I was in Montreal, it hurt me to hear my grandniece say she did not know who Kath was. Kath loved the bluff. Probably more than either of us. I've said so in the letter. We'll say so at the memorial. It will be good for the children. They will hear about her from her old neighbors and we will say that Kath would be happy that we are trying to get things to change on the bluff."

Marcelina takes a bite out of a haddock cake, looking at Luela as if not liking the silence. "There are two hundred invitations here," she says, wiping crumbs from her chin. "It's going to cost plenty if you have to print everything again."

Luela watches Marcelina take a sip of iced tea, her legs crossed at the ankles, her neck and wrists burdened with the clunky turquoise and faux-silver jewelry women in their forties and fifties are fond of wearing these days. Now that Kath has passed, Marcelina has been going around giving Kath credit for the colorful houses on the bluff. But before Kath died, Marcelina took credit for that. And if Marcelina or anybody else believes Kath spent a second of her life in Montreal missing the bluff, they are surely wrong. Once Kath moved away, her thoughts moved away, too.

"I'm sorry," Luela says, putting the letter back into the envelope. "I want invitations that honor Kath. These do not."

Near the end of winter, Marcelina presents an idea that Luela listens to without a hard face.

The upcoming Tenth Anniversary Splash of June Memory Celebration will present an excellent opportunity for a small half-hour ceremony in Kath's honor. Fund-raising for the celebration has been going very well. No doubt, the event will be well attended. There is even a gospel group coming up from Philadelphia.

Luela likes the idea and writes a note about her sister, which Marcelina includes in the invitations that go out at the beginning of March. By the middle of April, Marcelina notices a worrisome trend. Not a single person from New Jamaica has returned the RSVP card included in the invitation.

Called to Shirley and George Sebolt's house on April 14, Marcelina finds a tall stack of invitations on the coffee table. They are all from folks in New Jamaica.

"Serves you right that nobody over here is attending," George Sebolt tells Marcelina. "You have been disrespecting this neighborhood for years."

"I have not," Marcelina says. "Have I, Shirley?"

Instead of answering, Shirley picks up the unopened invitations and puts them into a paper bag. "My neighbors gave me their invitations because they wanted me to know they had no desire to disrespect my daughter," she says, handing the bag to Marcelina. "You know we were planning to honor her. But now, as I told my neighbors, we may not be able to attend the picnic this year anyway. George may need an operation on his hip at the end of May."

Marcelina accepts the envelopes, looking exasperated. "What can I do?" she asks.

"That's easy," George says. "Talk to more of your neighbors over here."

Marcelina leaves New Jamaica confused and frustrated. To an outsider, seeing the colorful houses all over the bluff, a visitor might think the area is a unified community. But if this stack of returned invitations is any indication, in some ways the bluff has never been so divided. When her aunt Oneresta was doing community work, she had only to consult with the community council, a few captains of the bluff, and the ladies club if matters were severe. But these days, if anyone wants to do anything important in the community, they also must consult the Centervillage Business Council and several young people's groups. Everybody on the bluff, it seems, wants to question every decision she makes on behalf of the community. She listened when residents of New Jamaica said they wanted more than one representative on the Woods Bluff Community Council. It was just that she didn't agree.

The next week, Marcelina visits every home in New Jamaica. Not a single complaint she hears makes sense to her. Except one—moving the picnic to Nobody's Acre. It makes sense because Nobody's Acre abuts the Hindquarter, Centervillage, and New Jamaica. A neutral spot if there ever was one.

The fund-raising Marcelina has been doing for her enrichment program is also going well—so well that the classes are now being taught by paid teachers. Since Kath Sebolt is being honored at this year's picnic, the children are once again doing the project Kath taught a year ago. This afternoon in the church basement, Marcelina has to fight back tears as she turns the pages in the scrapbooks the children have been filling with poems and writing and drawings about Sierra Leone. Marcelina hands one of the teachers a pack of letters that have come to the bluff from children at a school in the distant village of Halifaxship.

"For their lesson today, let's have our children write back," Marcelina tells the teachers.

Marcelina carries an armload of letters to the post the next day, noticing that each letter has a return address that says Halifax. But folks on the bluff don't really feel they are a part of Halifax. Perhaps there might be a bit of pride, however, in a name that unites the neighborhoods we have. Of course, New Jamaica residents will not want to say they live in the Hindquarter, and Hindquarter folks will not want to say they live in New Jamaica. What we need is a name that folks from all parts of the bluff will agree to.

The following Sunday, with a hard rain beating the windows of Basinview Baptist, Marcelina stands in the third pew, asking the congregation to consider a proposal: a single name for the entire bluff. "Something better than Woods Bluff," she says.

"What name though?" someone asks.

"Africaville."

Many in the congregation ponder and then nod their heads, but no one says outright they are behind the idea. Several days later, the postman attends a meeting of the Woods Bluff Community Council carrying a letter addressed to Oneresta Higgins in Africaville. In his presence Marcelina opens the envelope, which has no return address. Inside are three blank pages.

"I cannot deliver mail to an address that doesn't officially exist," the postman says. "I could lose my position."

After he leaves, Marcelina advises the men and women on the council how to modify the return address on the letters. "You should still write Halifax, Nova Scotia," Marcelina says. "Just write the new name on a line above that."

A week later an envelope with Africaville written on the front is delivered to Gussie Mills. Gussie keeps the insurance bill inside but gives Marcelina the envelope. Marcelina shows the envelope to Oneresta. But, having had another stroke, Oneresta is too confused to comprehend.

Few of the neighbors who see the letter are impressed. One letter got through. So what? The next ones may not.

But over the next few weeks more letters appear with the new name, including one that is placed in the mailbox of the Sebolt house. It is a letter Marcelina has sent while traveling. But it is not addressed to Luela.

At the Splash of June Memory Celebration of 1955, Marcelina passes around other letters that have made it to the bluff with only an Africaville address. One of Marcelina's nieces makes the honorary first visit to the picture board. The crowd watches the young girl tack up the map Kath helped her draw of Sierra Leone. But they burst into applause when she adds, below the drawing, a posted, unopened envelope addressed to Kath Sebolt, 68 Dempsey Road, Africaville, Nova Scotia.

PART THREE

Crowing

Lyons and Crows

Burlington, Vermont, November 1961

Why the hard face?" Luela asks Etienne as she exits the taxi in the driveway of his house. "Aren't you happy to see your aunt Luela?"

"Yes, I am happy to see you," Etienne says.

Waiting for her change, Luela notices that Etienne has put on a few pounds and grown a beard since she saw him at the Splash of June picnic more than six years ago. The tribute to his mother had already concluded when he drove his motorcycle onto Nobody's Acre. His hand bandaged from a motorcycle mishap, he seemed mature as he greeted the attendees, most of whom seemed elated that he had come to the celebration. "Pop wants me to go to college in Montreal," Etienne had told her later at the house. "But I'm going to school in America. It's going to be a flat-out nosebleed."

The sweatshirt that says WESTERN NEW HAMPSHIRE SWIMMING testifies that Etienne achieved that goal. In the threadbare pullover, he walks with hunched shoulders ahead of Luela along the brick path through a narrow tunnel of snow. Luela's steps are careful. She is annoyed at Etienne's grandmother, Claire, and does not want the distraction to cause her to lose her footing.

Other than his father, Claire is the only family member Etienne writes to regularly. The last letter Luela received from him arrived several years ago during his last year of college. She was surprised to get a call last week asking if she was interested in joining Claire and her husband, Jean-Yves, for a get-together down in Vermont with Etienne and his wife. She hesitated even after Claire offered to arrange a hotel room and any transportation she might need while she was in Burlington. She agreed to come only after learning that Etienne and his wife had a new baby. Luela had gone along with Claire's idea to let her arrival be a surprise to Etienne. However, the look on Etienne's face when he opened the taxi door was not surprise. It was shock.

"I realize you didn't know I was coming," Luela says when they reach the front door of the house. "But you could at least look happy to see me."

"I am happy to see you," Etienne says. "But, please, it's cold out here. Come inside."

Stacks of packing boxes lie about the living room. Etienne's wife, Jocelyn, narrow-faced with curly hair down to her shoulders, shakes Luela's hand looking flustered. "I apologize for the mess," she says as Etienne takes several boxes from the beige crushed-velvet sofa. "The movers will be here on Tuesday. Of course Etienne waited until the last minute to get the boxes we need."

"Claire and Jean-Yves said they would meet me here," Luela says. "Where are they?"

"They went to pick up the baby at my brother's house," Jocelyn says. "I took the baby there this morning because too much dust bothers him."

"Claire was happy to go," Etienne says. "She wants to spend time with the baby."

"I'll bet Claire also wanted to give Etienne and me time to spend with you," Jocelyn says. "Claire always has marvelous ideas."

While Jocelyn heads to the kitchen to get refreshments, Etienne carries Luela's coat to a rack in the front hallway. Luela unwraps her scarf and studies the line of framed pictures over the fireplace mantel. When Etienne returns, he tries to direct her toward the sofa, but she continues to study the photographs. She recognizes Etienne and Jocelyn, but the other faces in the frames are strangers.

"What will the two of you be doing down in Alabama?" she asks.

"Jocelyn and I interviewed for jobs at the same college," Etienne says. "I've already got an offer letter. I will be the director of student accounts."

"*Director.* That is quite a title for a young man. Congratulations."

"Thank you. How long will you be here in Burlington?"

"I'm catching a bus tomorrow morning."

Etienne rustles a soft-sided pack of cigarettes. "I don't know if I wrote to you about it," he says, taking out a bent cigarette. "But I stayed on to work at the college where I graduated. That's where I met Jocelyn. She worked in admissions."

"No I didn't," Jocelyn says, carrying in a tray that holds a teapot and several mugs. "I was temping in the bursar's office. Etienne has a terrible memory."

Jocelyn sets the tray on the coffee table and sits down on the floor. "I apologize again about the baby not being here," she says, dropping tea bags into the mugs. "But the doctor insists the dust could cause another sinus inflammation."

"I'm sure his grandmother's taking good care of him," Luela says. "But I can't wait to see him myself."

"In the meantime, I've got a photo you can look at," Jocelyn says.

As Luela finally sits, Jocelyn hands her a steaming mug, then a three-by-five picture of their newborn. "What's the child's name again?" Luela asks.

"*Warner,*" Etienne and Jocelyn say in unison.

Ordinarily even a picture of a child with Sebolt blood is cause for a fuss. However, Luela studies this picture, not yet sure what she will say. His grandmother, Kath Ella, couldn't wait to leave the bluff. And now his father plans to move even farther away than his grandmother did. This may be the last time Luela sees the child. What is the benefit of getting too close?

"Are there any pictures of your mother on this shelf?" she asks Etienne.

"I've moved so much," Etienne says. "I've never unpacked any."

"Not one?" Luela asks.

Etienne shakes his head.

Luela sips her tea, taking in Etienne's neatly combed brown hair and loose corduroy pants. For the moment, she will accept his explanation about the absence of images of his mother. The lack of visible photographs or other mementos of his mother may be his way of mourning her death. Then again, his mother left this world more than eight years ago.

After several sips of tea Luela heads for the bathroom. In the hallway, a face she sees in one of the framed photographs on the wall causes her to halt. The picture must have been lifted from Timothee's college yearbook. She looks closer, grateful that she has gotten over her anger at him for cremating Kath. She wants to chastise Etienne for smoking, but she may have other more serious complaints. There is no way to compare parental love, Luela thinks at the door to the bathroom. Nor does a child's love for his parents have to be displayed for others. But Timothee's pictures are displayed in this house and Kath's are not? What is going on here?

"Etienne went down to the cellar," Jocelyn says when Luela returns to the sofa.

"Whatever for?" Luela asks.

"I guess he wants to show you that he does have pictures of his mother."

Luela sips her cold tea, barely able to make conversation. So the cellar is where Etienne has hidden his mother? She drains the mug, finally putting together the pieces of why Etienne might be unsettled that his distant aunt from Halifax has come to visit. Left alone when Jocelyn carries off the tray, Luela begins to suspect that Etienne has been hiding his connection to his colored mother. She pulls her purse closer to her, angry that she has relinquished her coat. It took four payments to pay it off. And it may well be too nice a coat to have worn to a get-together at a house where her nephew has been doing the distasteful thing called crowing.

Y ou're a lying crow," children sometimes say to each other on the grounds of the newly named Africaville Elementary and Secondary. "You'd better stop fibbing, or you'll never be prime minister."

How long has it been since Luela thought about the origin of that put-down? It began during the turmoil of the prime minister campaign of 1933. Every day that year people all over Canada opened their local newspapers, eager to read the latest about a man named Lyon Arthur Crow. A successful lawyer in Montreal and head of the New Labour Party, Lyon Crow spent most of 1933 traveling across Quebec, Ontario, and New Brunswick, making newsworthy speeches critical of the prime minister, who was eager to get reelected. The most damning criticism Lyon Crow levied was that the prime minister had not done enough to help ordinary citizens during the financial crisis. Lyon Crow's favorite activity was to poke fun at the incumbent's 1929 campaign promise of a chicken in every pot. Early in the campaign Lyon Crow's road crew began letting a chicken wander around the outdoor stage. When Lyon Crow chanted the ridiculed slogan—"A chicken in every pot!"—his workers in the audience would shout in response, "Yes, but where's the pot?" By the time the campaign reached the western provinces, crowds had learned the call-and-response perfectly.

Lyon Crow claimed that he was half French Canadian, half English by birth. But two weeks before the election, several newspapers published a report—some said with research paid for by the prime minister—that Lyon Crow had been born in Latvia to German parents. Veterans of the Great War were horrified. Was Lyon Crow a spy of our former enemy now plotting revenge? Many angry veterans took up the prime minister's call and volunteered at the polls. Dressed in uniform, they handed out ballots, and many of them wore buttons that said HOW FAR TO DEFEAT? AS STRAIGHT AS THE CROW LIES.

Soundly defeated in the election, Lyon Crow returned to his law practice in Montreal. But for decades afterward, radio shows discussed him, and his name peppered the conversations of residents of Woods Bluff. Why had Lyon Crow lied? Would he really have done anything to become prime minister?

D amn it," Etienne says, shoving items back inside the third cardboard box he has opened since coming down to the cellar. "This is not the box I wanted either."

His frustration is understandable. The only markings on the boxes in this corner of the cellar are the grayish-green smudges from the asphalt dust and mold that stained every item stowed in the basement of the Peletier family apartment in Montreal. When his father's girlfriend called to ask if he wanted the boxes shipped, it was clear the only answer she would accept was yes. The second box he opened contained the items packed before he left home for Saint Richelieu. Several of his glass action figures were broken. His father's girlfriend must have heard them rattle. The least she could have done was repack that box before shipping it.

Two textbooks in this box, *Finite Mathematics* and *Strengths of Materials*, bring to mind his two fathers. He holds the books closer to the naked light bulb hanging from a fat ceiling beam. To which father—Omar Platt or Timothee Peletier—did each textbook belong? He knows his adopted father, Timothee, studied architecture. And his uncle Kiryl said that Omar—had he lived and had a better attitude— could have been the first black man accepted into Canada's Royal Civil Engineering Corps. A few engineering courses had been on Etienne's freshman schedule at Western New Hampshire. But he hated the assignments. He preferred to spend his Sundays with his friends instead of in his dormitory room completing onerous lab reports, which were invariably due at 8:00 a.m. on a Monday. To appease Timothee he decided to major in business administration, although he chose the easier concentration of retail management.

Etienne is examining a stack of sports magazines when he realizes that Luela has come down the cellar steps. You are not a teenager, he tells himself as she approaches. You do not have to explain yourself. Nor do you have to get along with her anymore.

"I know the pictures are here somewhere," Etienne says, setting aside the stack of magazines. "But where I do not know."

Luela peers into the open box. "Jocelyn is very nice," she says. "You did good with her."

"I hope you are not mad at me for not inviting you to the wedding. We went to the county clerk. I don't like big ceremonies. I guess I'm like my parents that way."

Etienne searches one more box, then looks at his watch. "Boy, look at the time."

"Aren't you going to open the last few boxes?" Luela asks.

"We don't have time."

"Yes, we do."

"Why does it matter whether I have a picture?" Etienne says. "She's dead."

"Not her memory."

"I doubt anything's here. Mother never gave me any pictures of her."

"Why wouldn't she do that?"

Etienne turns toward the cellar steps, where Jocelyn is calling down that it's time to go. He watches the steps a moment, not wanting

Jocelyn to come down. When he turns toward Luela he struggles to find words.

"Mother didn't like something I said to her one day," he says. "I don't remember what I said, but she didn't like it. I remember it was the evening before I was supposed to leave to go to school at Saint Richelieu. I had asked her several times if I could remain in Montreal. She said I couldn't. In my room she asked me where the photo album was with the pictures of me and the family. When I told her I must have thrown it out when I cleaned out my room, she got really upset and started to cry. I don't know why. There were only a few pictures of her in the book. I told her to stop crying, but she wouldn't. Some of my friends were there."

"She wasn't herself then," Luela says. "All that medicine. But you must have had other pictures."

"If she had any, she never gave them to me."

"She wouldn't have kept all the pictures," Luela says. "My sister wasn't like that."

"The sicker Mother got, the harder she was to get along with," Etienne says. "You didn't know that."

"Maybe that was her way of preparing you for her passing. Maybe she thought if she had the energy to be difficult with you, you wouldn't worry so much."

"What kind of logic is that?"

"I doubt she expected you to pretend she didn't exist. Do you at least talk about her?"

"I'm Canadian. Americans don't care about my parents."

Luela precedes Etienne up the steps, not sure what to say to him. He is no longer a teenager who gets kicked out of summer camp for fighting with his classmates. He is an adult now, perhaps fighting with the world. And there are no parents to return him to after she has chastised him.

Upstairs in the living room, while Luela puts on her coat, Jocelyn makes a big production of making sure Luela does not forget to take the picture of their newborn. In the car on the way to the restaurant, Luela spends a long time staring at the child's face. She studies the picture again the next day and for most of the bus ride across the Vermont countryside. She wants to see something of Kath's coloring in the child's plump cheeks. But the child's pink face only dredges up the memory of Etienne as a baby.

Changing to a different bus at the depot in Bangor, Maine, Luela thinks again about Etienne's comment that Americans don't ask Canadians about their parents. She is not sure she believes him, but as the bus crosses into Canada she decides not to complain about how her nephew wants to spend his life. Crowing can work, some residents of Woods Bluff pointed out during the weeks after Lyon Crow was defeated. Yes, the prime minister had stirred up old anti-German sentiment enough to win the election, but most Canadians were too young to remember a war that had been over for years. Lyon Crow returned to his law practice, making even more money than he had before the election. The public forgave him for lying about who he was, didn't they? What was the harm really? Many people crow about their past and nothing bad comes to them. What harm could it do to hide a little part about yourself?

And what sense did it make to put up a fuss about a child crowing about a distant grandparent? She may well have some white relative far in her past. Her nephew chooses to hide his mother? She might keep silent about it. But she is not yet ready to forgive.

No Colored Rider

Montgomery, Alabama

Etienne turned down the job offer from Montgomery A&M several years ago because he didn't see himself working in one of the college's cramped buildings downtown. Packed in one of the boxes that came in the moving van that brought his family's belongings down from Vermont last month was a color brochure of the new campus located on a sprawling former army base a short drive west of downtown Montgomery. The new campus was the realization of a plan announced in 1943 by members of the Alabama legislature. The legislature also directed the college to enroll an equal number of colored and white students. Since the announcement, the student population had never been more than thirty percent colored. On December 1, when Etienne arrived for his first day of work, he was told that his job was to ensure colored registration did not regress to its former low levels.

This morning, on the third day of the spring enrollment period, he sits at one of the long tables in the student union with the two colored work-study students he hired to help with registration. What could be keeping Deedra Cummings, the deputy director of student affairs, he wonders. Yesterday, he accepted Deedra's excuse for getting to work an hour late. Trees and traffic signs were toppled around the city by a rash of tornadoes that had struck. And many side streets were clogged with rubbish from overflowing garbage cans not emptied in days, because the Montgomery Sanitation Workers Union had declared a strike. But Deedra also said she had to get her child to the special school he attends because of his partial blindness. What excuse will she offer today, he wonders at ten past eleven when he spies Deedra walking through the front doors of the student union.

With barely a hello, she sits at the other long table. She chats easily with the students who visit the table. And when several colored students who had passed the table earlier bring their registration cards to her, they laugh with her as she checks the course codes on their registration cards against the listings in the printout.

"Sorry I got here late," Deedra says to Etienne later, as she gets ready to go to lunch. "The man driving me and the other women to campus was running behind."

Deedra has placed a paper on the table in front of Etienne.

"I saw this when it was in my in-box," Etienne says.

"I suspect you did," Deedra says. "Why haven't you signed it yet?"

Etienne studies the form, not a blue registration form for him to initial, but a vacation request. He heard about the bus boycott by the colored residents of Montgomery several years ago. And now the city has been slammed by a string of tornadoes, and a strike by the Sanitation Union. Does Deedra want a vacation to make herself scarce before any more trouble happens here in Montgomery? Or is this an attempt to leave him to flounder during a busy work period for the department?

"You know how busy we are in January," Etienne says.

"That's why I'm putting my papers in early."

"Why so many days?"

"I earned the days. I'd like to take them."

Etienne picks up his pen, feeling Deedra's eyes on him. Why is it that when he is angry with Deedra, he compares her to his aunt Luela? True, Deedra is roughly the age Luela was when he spent those weeks with her in Halifax. And Deedra has dark eyes and full lips like Luela. He declined to order the expensive desk Deedra wanted, but he did move her into a larger cubicle—one away from any windows, which she claims now scare her. He also agreed to let her come to work at ten o'clock so she could get her youngest son off to the special school. A little gratitude from her wouldn't hurt, he thinks, as he signs the vacation request form.

E verything all right with Deedra?" Etienne's boss, Livingston, asks the next day, when Etienne visits his office to discuss the vacation request.

"All right, if you discount the fact that she still wants my job," Etienne says.

"She's been working at A&M for more than a minute," Livingston says.

"But she's got no degree."

"Associate's."

"That's not competitive."

"Maybe not where you're from," Livingston says. "And Miss Cummings has a point that her fifteen years of working here makes up for that."

"You must not think so," Etienne says. "Or else you would have promoted her."

Livingston chuckles as he stands at the window, looking out at the former military parade ground. The first colored officer hired by Montgomery A&M, he took the position as vice president of administration after leaving a job with an even bigger title at a colored college in Tuscaloosa. Sitting back down at the desk, Livingston slides a paper toward Etienne. Below the bold heading that says POST-DISASTER REPORT is the word CONFIDENTIAL. There is a check mark in the small box next to the entry UNRULY, DIFFICULT, OR TRAUMATIZED STAFF. Etienne reads the comments written on the line next to the box and feels the muscles in his neck tighten.

"I wasn't unruly or difficult," Etienne says. "Far from it."

"You didn't nearly get someone injured in the supply closet during the tornado?"

"No, I did not. Deedra has never been happy about me getting this job. Now I guess she's got her own protest going."

"Right or wrong," Livingston says, "another report like this and you've got trouble."

Livingston runs a hand down his yellow tie. His bearing reminds Etienne of the preacher he saw on the news a few nights ago, telling residents of Montgomery to keep up the boycott. Several times over the last few months he advised Livingston that Deedra be transferred. And yet what has this seasoned college administrator done about that? Nothing.

"She's not happy with me either," Livingston says. "I hear she's talking trash about me for hiring you."

"I'll work on her," Etienne says.

"I'm glad to hear that," Livingston says as he slips the papers into a manila folder. "It wouldn't look good if I have to step in and try to help her get with the program."

In early January, during the first week Deedra is on vacation, Etienne visits the head of every department, talking at length about the assistance he wants to offer for Deedra's career. While many managers and supervisors offer appreciative comments about Deedra, a few give friendly but muted criticism. All agree that as loyal as Deedra has been to the college, she deserves every opportunity to move up.

"You wanted to see me," Deedra says on the afternoon of the day she returns from vacation.

It is a little after one, and she has come to the door of Etienne's office, holding a restaurant take-out box. She wears a smart outfit and has a new haircut, bangs in front, low in back. Dressing for a job interview, Etienne wonders, getting up from his desk. Or still after my job?

"You've hit the salary roof in this department," Etienne says, handing Deedra a job posting. "Thought you might want to see this."

"This job is in facilities," Deedra says.

"The pay is good."

"I'd be working for Jim Stockard. Jim can't keep anybody. Two people quit while I was on vacation." Deedra takes her eyes off the page. "Is this why they hired you, to get me out of the department?"

Etienne follows Deedra out of the office and into the open work area. He is about to say something to her but then he hears the quiet. Not a single typewriter is clacking as Deedra walks out. He returns to his desk hoping she will return later, having reconsidered. But she doesn't.

"I've already started looking for her replacement," Etienne tells Livingston the next afternoon.

"How did you manage that?" Livingston asks.

"Jim Stockard is hurting for managers. He says he'd be willing to sweeten the deal to the point where Deedra would be a fool to turn the job down."

"Do that and your budget might support the raise I said I'd look into when you came on board."

Deedra Cummings leaves his department in early April, but the promised raise does not show up in Etienne's paycheck until the end of June. With their baby, Warner, now walking, the one-bedroom apartment he and Jocelyn have been renting since they arrived in

Montgomery is starting to feel small. One afternoon in July, they take a ride on his motorcycle out to Autauga County to see a house one of Jocelyn's colleagues has been bugging them to come look at as a possible purchase.

"Why don't you go down and take a look at the creek," Jocelyn says, taking off her helmet as they pull to a stop in front of a two-bedroom house tucked among a group of mature pines. "I heard it's not far. I'll go inside to say hello."

Etienne takes his time getting the bike's kickstand into position. He told Jocelyn he did not want to look at houses this far outside the city. But after a short walk down the narrow, winding path, the view opens to him and he feels his head begin to clear. At the creek's edge, he estimates that it is a mere forty meters to the far bank. But that short distance is no longer an easy race for him. He watches the slow-moving gray-green water and with each passing minute he feels grateful that the long winter that followed their arrival from Vermont is well behind them. No snow but plenty of other difficulties. Every few weeks Jocelyn wondered if they had made a mistake moving to Alabama. But now summer is here. He always considered himself a city boy, but maybe he can appreciate a house in the country.

The house belongs to an uncle of Jocelyn's work colleague. Etienne returns from his walk to find Nathan Czerwinski, the colleague's husband, inspecting a motorboat on its trailer still hitched to the rear of a double-cab truck in the driveway. Nearing fifty, Nathan is taller than Etienne. He wears nice slacks and dusty work boots.

"I am not surprised to hear that you're ready to leave Montgomery," Nathan says, raising the cover off the motorboat engine. "You couldn't pay me to live there—especially now with the Nigras protesting and marching every other week. Christ, it's worrisome."

"Your daughter's probably marching right there beside them," Jocelyn says.

Nathan's tanned face tightens. "They say good sense sometimes skips a generation."

"How come you and your wife don't buy the house?" Etienne asks.

"Excellent point," Jocelyn says. "Your grandkids would love it out here."

"The two-bedroom townhouse we got is enough to look after." Nathan points his screwdriver at Etienne. "Do the two of you have any children?"

Etienne and Jocelyn exchange glances.

"We lost our first child," Etienne says.

"We don't talk about that much," Jocelyn says. "And now we have a healthy baby boy. His name's Warner."

Nathan lifts the battery out of the housing. "Don't know if my wife told you yet about our little request," he says, digging crud out of the connectors with the screwdriver.

"No, she didn't," Jocelyn says.

"My uncle asked us to make sure that anyone with serious intent to buy the house is white and Christian. I feel like we have to honor what my uncle wanted."

"Makes some sense, I guess," Etienne says.

"Not to me," Jocelyn says. "Seems a little unusual in this day and age. Why would you promise that?"

"Not that it's any of our business," Etienne says.

"It is our business if we're buying the house," Jocelyn says, looking at her husband.

"That's not what I mean," Etienne says. "I mean, we'd go crazy if we wanted to look into every little wish a seller has."

"Just doing what our uncle asked," Nathan says.

Nathan's wife, Rose, a thin woman with dyed-blonde hair, comes outside with a trayful of beers.

"I suppose I understand the Christian part," Jocelyn says, taking a beer off the tray and offering it to Nathan, "but how do you determine that somebody's colored?"

"What do you mean?" Nathan says.

"I mean what if one of us is colored?"

Nathan takes the beer from Jocelyn but seems reluctant to drink. He stares at Jocelyn's hair a long while. "I see my wife still doesn't know a helluva thing about picking friends," he says, handing the beer back to Jocelyn.

Heading home with Jocelyn on the back and mindful of the motorcycle mishap he had the previous spring, Etienne works hard to keep his attention on the road. He disagrees with Jocelyn that Nathan thought she was joking about one of them being colored. While Nathan continued working on his boat, Rose handled the walk-through of the house. He joined them later on the back patio, but he had little to say as they chatted over drinks.

Etienne didn't say much either.

If Jocelyn expects him to call Nathan later to say they are outraged over having to sign a covenant agreement, she is mistaken, Etienne thinks as he steers into the lot at their apartment complex. Any such remark will only cause Nathan, Rose, and the rest of their family to wonder why. He has lived in Alabama long enough to recognize that he is not ready to answer that question truthfully. That is the best strategy, since they plan to bring up their child here.

Dismounting the bike, Etienne wonders if Rose remembers the day she visited their apartment and put her arm next to his to show off her tan. When Rose asked if his mother's skin was lighter or darker than his, Jocelyn had turned from chatting with another woman to listen to his answer. When they were first married, Jocelyn used to say things like that to Etienne all the time. That day she gave him a look that said, Why don't you go ahead and say something about your mother? But he changed the subject.

"A realtor called the other day to say she has a perfect house," Jocelyn says several weeks later. She and Etienne are in the bathroom, fighting for the best spot in front of the mirror as they get dressed for work. "Are you ready to look at another one?"

"That depends on the house," Etienne says. "If it's got a bigger bathroom, bring it on."

The following Saturday afternoon, Jocelyn arrives home from a trip to the grocery store to find a brand-new motorcycle in their extra parking space.

"Didn't we agree not to make any expensive purchases?" she asks Etienne in the living room, where he is feeding the baby. "We want to buy a house, remember?"

"We don't need to buy one tomorrow. It can wait a while."

Jocelyn does not bring up the matter at dinner, but for the next few days Etienne can tell she is not happy. The following week, on Wednesday evening when she comes home from her pottery class, he can tell something is coming.

"Three times this week I have asked you to park that thing farther away from the car," Jocelyn says during dinner. "When are you going to move it?"

"I will," Etienne says. "Stop bitching about it."

Jocelyn finds plenty of other matters to complain about as the evening progresses. The next day, in her cubicle at the bursar's office, she finds herself cursing about the new motorcycle every few hours. This stealth purchase has made her recall how her mother avoided handling money. For twenty years her mother worked as a retail sales clerk, and for twenty years she turned her paycheck over to her husband. Jocelyn would watch her father sign her mother's name to the back of the check and then take it to the bank. "Look," Jocelyn said to her mother on a visit home from college, holding one of the deposited checks returned with the bank statement. "These days he just signs his own name."

In the staff lounge at a quarter of five, Jocelyn runs a soapy sponge over her coffee mug, realizing that she has no idea how much money Etienne took out of their joint account to pay for the motorcycle. She now resents the fact that he talked her into accepting the college's offer of the apartment just off the highway. She wanted an apartment in a nicer neighborhood.

"What are these?" Etienne asks several weeks later in the living room, when he finds a stack of bank forms placed on the sofa cushions.

"Application for a new joint account," Jocelyn says.

"We've already got a joint account."

"This one's different. The bank won't honor a withdrawal on this unless we both sign."

"You don't trust me?"

"For keeping track of our money, two heads are better than one."

Jocelyn gathers up the forms and presents them to Etienne. When he does not take them, she drops the forms into his lap.

"I'll sell the motorcycle, if you want," Etienne says.

"Go ahead and sell it, then."

Etienne does not sell the motorcycle. But on a hot September morning, with Jocelyn reluctantly aboard, he takes a drive out to a small town fifty minutes east of Montgomery. The small three-bedroom house sits near a paved road, but back a ways. The large backyard is lined with towering elms and oaks.

"It's for rent," Etienne says. "But the realtor says it might come up for sale."

"I suppose a house like this will do," Jocelyn says with barely a smile. "I wouldn't object to our renting it."

Out in front, Jocelyn studies the house a long time before getting back onto the motorcycle. The next evening when they are at a steak house with a couple they have become friendly with, she mentions several times how easy the commute to work would be from the house. In October, Jocelyn sends out change-of-address postcards filled with gushing sentences about the family's new house.

Quick, tell me," Jocelyn says to Etienne in early December. "How many months are there in a decade and a half?"

Etienne carries two bowls of ice cream into the living room of the house they have begun renting in Woodhaven, Alabama. "That easy," Etienne says sitting down on the sofa next to her.

"One hundred and eighty, right?" Jocelyn says. She holds a copy of the most recent edition of the *University Administrator* magazine. "Half the high school students who will be graduating in the class of 1963 who took this nationwide test got that question wrong."

"Oh, I doubt that," Etienne says. "Maybe it's because the question was worded funny."

"How do you mean funny?"

"Well, in a way the kids didn't understand."

"Oh, peacock," Jocelyn says. "The question was worded exactly like I said."

"Do you have an explanation?"

"Oh, I don't know, maybe bad parents."

"What about bad teachers?"

"Perhaps," Jocelyn says. "But I always figure most kids learn to count at home. I did."

Jocelyn takes her bowl of ice cream and resumes reading the article. A little while later, when Etienne turns on the television she sets aside the magazine. "Where did you put the letter you were reading earlier?" she asks.

"Over there." Etienne points to the top of the television.

"My French was never that good," Jocelyn says. "What does it say?"

"My grandmother Claire is having a birthday in a few months," Etienne says.

"How old will she be?"

Etienne laughs. "Grandmother has never told anybody her age. The party is in April."

"That's right around the corner. I assume you do not plan to attend?"

"Maybe."

"Well, that response is a surprise."

"You shouldn't be surprised," Etienne says. "I've told you how much I loved my grandmother when I was growing up."

The envelope contains a picture of Claire. Etienne holds it the following evening when he dials his grandparents in Montreal. He has trouble understanding his grandmother, and at first he thinks his French is rusty. But then he realizes Claire's speech is slurred.

"Just a mild stroke," Jean-Yves says when he comes back on the line. "She's recovering well. She will pick up super-duper when you come see her."

The next evening Jocelyn enters the kitchen to find Etienne about to cut up a new credit card that has been sent to her, unrequested. "Don't you dare," she says. "I've already charged something on the card."

"What?"

"Two airline tickets to Montreal. You do want to go to your grandmother's birthday party, don't you? And guess what? We can take the baby for free."

Etienne hands over the card without comment. But later he lies in bed annoyed at Jocelyn for purchasing the tickets without consulting him. He turns over in bed, recalling how young Claire looked when she sat for the picture that came with the letter. He tries to recall her voice as it sounded that year, or the year she bought him his first grown-up bicycle, or during the weeks he spent with her and Jean-Yves in the mountains the summer before he graduated college. But this evening, no pleasant memory can replace the memory of how weak and raspy her voice sounded the previous evening on the telephone.

In a bad dream he had a few days after moving to Alabama, he saw his grandmother Claire telling his father that he ought to marry again. In another dream Claire was asking Timothee if he had heard from her grandson. "I'm afraid our young one has disappeared into the wilds of America," Claire said. "Will we ever see him again?"

Can it be that his last visit to Montreal was for an uncle's funeral? he wonders as he tries to will himself to sleep. On that trip he arrived in the morning and flew out in the evening. But he will not chastise himself too harshly for not visiting his grandparents more often, he concludes, pulling the covers up to his neck. He comprehended enough of Claire's words on the telephone to have understood her to say that she recognized he has a new life down in Alabama, a life he must dedicate to his family.

On New Year's Eve, Etienne makes a resolution for 1963 to spend more time with his wife and son. On a warm Saturday at the beginning of spring, he loads his motorcycle onto the bed of a borrowed truck and takes the family on a day-trip out to a lake in Elmore County. While Jocelyn and the baby nap on a picnic blanket, he mounts his motorcycle for the three-mile loop around the lake.

To his surprise, navigating the rough patches on the gravel road is not fun today. The vibrations on these rough stretches of road produce uncomfortable jerks to his body. He has been riding for less than ten minutes but already he feels a headache coming. Gripping the handlebars, he races along the dusty road at speeds far lower than when he used to race down Mount Royal on his bicycle. The motorcycle Claire encouraged Timothee to buy won Etienne new friends. He liked that some of them used to drive down to visit him when he was at college in New Hampshire. A better grandson would have thanked his grandmother more often over the years. And when over the years has Etienne ever bothered to write to his grandfather?

Jean-Yves did not sound happy on the phone call last night, Etienne tells himself, entering a curve on the road. Perhaps Claire is in worse shape than Jean-Yves let on. Though he has not visited his grandmother since moving to Alabama, the thought of living in a world without her unnerves him now.

The gravel lake road has narrowed, looking like the one leading to the creekside house he and Jocelyn had considered buying. On a few other house-hunting trips, he learned that the conditions to not sell a property to a black person were often called no-colored riders.

Claire and Jean-Yves aren't the only Canadian relatives Etienne is remiss in contacting. What would his aunt Luela in Halifax say to him if they were close enough to discuss a no-colored rider clause attached to a house sale? Etienne lowers his head as the motorcycle accelerates into a long curve. He chuckles and leans with the bike as it accelerates further into the bend. He has been on this road before. He knows this curve. He is an eager rider. But is he colored? Astride the motorcycle, he finds the idea of a colored rider funny. *Colored rider. No colored rider.*

Back on the bank of the lake, Jocelyn lies on the blanket beside Warner, who is wrestling with his teddy bear. She occasionally looks up from her magazine. After a while she wonders why Etienne has not raced by. But she does not suspect trouble.

Jocelyn does not hear the skidding. Nor does she see the motorcycle buckle after hitting a hole in the road. She does not see Etienne hurtle from the motorcycle and slam against the trunk of a thick oak.

Two Hundred and Forty Months

Ever since Jocelyn read the question to him from her copy of the *University Administrator* magazine, Etienne has thought of the passage of time in terms of months. He and Jocelyn have silly moments in which they recount their lives in months. Sometimes the play is sexual. How many months since we did it in the car? How many months since we did it in a forest or in a dark movie theater?

This morning, doped up with painkillers in a hospital bed and barely conscious, Etienne tries to calculate the number of months since he brought his family down to Alabama. How many months has it been? Given the dull throbbing in his hip and his fuzzy mind, it is no wonder that he cannot finish the calculations.

Even in his stupor, though, Etienne has no trouble recognizing the voice he hears interrogating his doctor. He knows the man who asks why it was necessary for the surgeon to go in for a second time to clean out a troublesome section of his son's fractured hip.

"Was my father here earlier?" Etienne asks, when he wakes up from a nap and sees Jocelyn seated beside the bed.

"That was Timothee in the flesh," Jocelyn says.

"Was it something I said?"

"What do you mean?"

"Well, he didn't stick around long. Did his girlfriend call him home?"

"Come on, now, let's not talk badly about her again. Your father was here for two days."

"Did you and my father have a nice chat?"

"Yes. He wanted to call your aunt Luela in Halifax."

Etienne raises his head slightly. "Was I knocked out for that long?"

"You've been out for over a week. You shattered your hip badly."

Etienne closes his eyes. "There was no need to call anybody in Halifax."

"That is what I told your father," Jocelyn says. "But it was scary there for a while. We were worried about you."

Jocelyn closes the magazine lying open on her lap. "Pretty soon you ought to call your aunt. And you ought to mention her to our son."

"I plan to. When he is older."

Jocelyn raises a cup with a straw to Etienne's lips. "What's the matter?" he says, after taking a drink. "Don't you believe me?"

Jocelyn smiles and places a hand on Etienne's arm. "You look like you can hardly keep your eyes open. Let's talk about this when your head is clearer."

Etienne closes his eyes and soon drifts off to sleep. When he wakes again the nurse tells him that Jocelyn has gone to a meeting at the college.

"Your wife left something to keep you occupied until she returns," the nurse says.

A stack of envelopes sits on the bed near Etienne's arm. When his head clears a bit more, he realizes that he holds get-well cards. He checks a few return addresses, feeling uneasy. This stack of cards dredges up unhappy memories of the cards his mother got when she was ill.

One envelope that seizes his attention has a Halifax return address. Inside is a generic greeting card with every bit of white space filled, including the back. He opened the envelope thinking the card was from his aunt Luela, but the card is signed by his uncle Kiryl. He is not surprised to hear that the Platts are still doing business in Simms Corner and on the bluff. Nor is he surprised to read that his cousin, Yancy Platt, has not joined the family business and now works in a bank. When he encounters Luela's name he starts to worry. Is there bad news about her health? But the news is about his aunt and her Africaville neighbors. *Folks on the bluff are threatening to conduct protests like those you all have been having down there in Montgomery*, Kiryl writes.

Etienne sets the card down but immediately picks it up again. Do the people in Africaville know what a scary year 1963 has been here in Montgomery? The colored residents of this town seem angry about everything. A few have been injured in clashes with the police. Is his aunt going to join a protest march up there in Halifax? That could be dangerous.

Given the strained reunion he had with Luela before he moved from Burlington, he is not surprised that he has not heard any news directly from her. Of course, he could have telephoned her. Perhaps she would have told him what is happening in her life. But what would he have said to her?

The paragraphs on the back of the card concern his grandmother Zera Platt, in Mississippi. His uncle writes that prison officials there may move some prisoners out of state because of overcrowding. *Right now we don't know if Zera is one of the prisoners likely to be moved*, Kiryl writes. *But she may be. If you got any intentions of visiting her on the easy, you might want to get on it soon, nephew.*

Would Zera be shipped off to a faraway state, Etienne wonders. The places his uncle mentions in the letter—Utah or Colorado—would be costly places to visit often. But then, what is he supposed to do with this information? He does not even know Zera.

As he had earlier, Etienne tries to make sense of his family estrangement, which has been on his mind ever since he arrived in Montgomery, a city that seems a planet away from the one where he was born. Even more pitiful than his lack of contact with the family in Montreal is the sorry attention he has given to his family in Halifax. Why? Nobody in either city abused him as a child. He had no explosive arguments with his parents or his relatives. Why has he put such a distance between himself and Canada?

Did his desire to do so begin with the snickers he heard as a boy when his mother came to pick him up after classes at Greeves Adventist? Yes, he was taunted by kids who found out that he had a colored mother. But they were toddlers who thought a boy who looked white while having a mother who looked colored was worthy of ridicule. And he cannot recall the last time he felt any enmity toward the Saint Richelieu classmate who doubted the logic of his saying that he could be black if he wanted to be.

What, then, do more recent incidents tell him? Hours after his first surgery, he must have confounded the nurses with all his mumbling about colored riders. His mind must have been brooding over the trouble he and Jocelyn encountered during that first house-hunting trip last July. Would he have treated the idea that the house not be bought by a colored family so cavalierly if he had spent more time getting to know the colored side of his family?

Etienne puts the card from his uncle back into the envelope, thinking perhaps he might soon have the strength to write to his family in Halifax. But in the short term, he cannot imagine a visit to the prison where his grandmother is incarcerated. There must be relatives in Mississippi who can visit Zera. More important, as soon as he is well enough to walk, he must fulfill his promise to fly to Montreal for his grandmother Claire's birthday celebration. Any movement toward his family in Mississippi will have to wait until after that.

Often when exiting an airplane, Etienne checks out a distant tower or some other airport building, wondering if the firm where his father works designed or constructed it. This afternoon with his family, he walks off the DC-7 and enters the terminal in Montreal thinking only of his grandmother. He had wanted to fly up sooner, after he heard that her words had become incoherent. But until today he was still having trouble moving without the use of a wheelchair.

In the living room of his grandparents' apartment, a large birthday banner written in French hangs on the wall behind the sofa. However, Etienne and his family have missed the party by a week. Many of the relatives who attended have stayed on, and a few have assembled here today. In the bedroom down the hallway, there are only the remains of Claire, who died several hours earlier.

Jean-Yves comes in from the bedroom, insisting that Jocelyn remain seated on the sofa where the baby is asleep on her lap. But Etienne has already risen on his crutches. His grandfather looks heavier than the last time Etienne saw him. He looks tired.

After kissing little Warner, Jean-Yves makes an announcement in French. It sets a few heads around the room to nodding.

"He says everyone will get a look," Etienne tells Jocelyn. "The attendant is still washing and dressing her." Etienne gives a nervous smile. "He said Claire said she wanted to be presentable for the family."

Timothee arrives later with his girlfriend. She huddles close to Timothee, stealing all his attention, rarely letting him talk to anyone, including Etienne. Etienne's cousin, Berto, who sits in a comfortable chair, talks to Etienne a bit in French, then switches to English. "Do you remember that you used to make up games?" Berto looks at Jocelyn. "Your husband was always running around the apartment, turning things on and off—the hi-fi, the television, the radio. He was always running."

Jean-Yves laughs. "I also remember that you and Etienne didn't get along," he says to Berto.

"We got along," Berto says. "It is just that I did not see Etienne much after my family moved to Quebec."

"Remember those bad things you said about Etienne's mother?" Jean-Yves says.

Berto, who wears a light-blue suit, shakes his head and lights a cigarette. He is about to respond but notices that the room has gone quiet. Two women in white uniforms cross the living room. They speak with Jean-Yves as they pull on their jackets and then head out the front door.

"Etienne will go back for a visit first," Jean Yves says.

A superhuman strength seems to propel Etienne up from the sofa. His arms feel twice as large as he works the crutches that carry him down the hallway. He had hoped that during this trip he would tell his grandparents about his life in Alabama. He intended to thank Claire for taking him to his first symphony, Jean-Yves for taking him to his first hockey game. He pauses in the bedroom doorway. His eyes go first to the foot of the bed, where he once sat while Claire, feeling under the weather, crushed pistachio nuts and sang an old tune from her childhood.

The picture of San Giovanni a Mare Church still hangs on the wall. Timothee purchased that on his second trip to Italy. But where is the picture of Claire seated at the grand piano before one of her recitals at the conservatory? The trip across the bedroom seems to drain the last of Etienne's energy. At the bed, he stands on his crutches, trying to muster the strength to lower his eyes. His mother's death left him feeling that he might live his life perpetually unhappy. Now he lowers his eyes to take in the only person other than his mother who made him feel that an adopted boy could be loved in the world. Do you think my dead father would have loved me? he once asked Claire. Why he had not thought to ask his mother that question is still a mystery to him. He tries to recall her answer. Knowing Claire, the answer must have been yes.

"I want to come along," Jocelyn says in the kitchen later, where Berto has offered to give Etienne a ride to the apartment building where Etienne grew up.

"We'll go together next time," Etienne tells her as she hands him a glass of water and two pain pills. "This time I want to go alone."

The ten-story apartment building at 685 Guy-Mathieu Street looks smaller than Etienne remembers. And he does not recall the brick front being a dark-red color. How many months has it been since he was last here?

What seems familiar to him as he leaves his cousin Berto's Peugeot behind at the curb is the weather. The sun has a cast like it did the day they arrived back in Montreal, after his parents returned from Italy. His mother had gotten into the Regent with plenty of strength, but she was too weak to walk to the front door of the building without help. The sky that day was filled with the tiniest hint of clouds and a white-hot sun.

"Go on back," Etienne tells Berto, who has gotten out of the car. "I can manage."

An elderly woman holds the front door open for Etienne and he hobbles across the threshold. In the lobby he catches his breath, taking in the familiar white floor tiles, mirrored walls, and gold inlaid ceiling. Many evenings a strong smell of spice would waft out of apartment 1-E. Today there is only the scent of the carnations in the vase on the lacquered wood table. At the elevator he waits with the elderly woman, who breathes as heavily as he. Did he once know her?

The building's owner was from Scotland, Etienne remembers. And the residents were from many parts of the world. A few were well-to-do. Kath liked that the building was quiet, but he did not appreciate all the quiet during the days after his mother died. In the evenings, as he lay across his bed, the only noise was the housekeeper walking the apartment, trying to stay busy. For weeks after the cremation ceremony Etienne rarely saw Timothee.

Ringing the buzzer at 5-B, Etienne wonders what he would do if his mother answered. Could it be true? Could his memory of the day he learned of Mother's death be a terrible concocted memory of a day that never happened?

How clear is that memory anyway? The day he got the news of his mother's death, he had gone to the field on the back campus at Saint Richelieu with a group of boys, their backpacks full of oranges, beer, and bottles of cranberry carbonate. One of the boys carried two pints of vodka. And Tyrell Levesque, chewing loose strings on the sleeves of his glee club cardigan, kept tossing the oranges stolen from the dining hall over the fence, trying to hit the lacrosse nets on Alumni Green. Etienne cannot remember which of the boys started the joke. But he remembers how they began to look at each other, some with stiff faces, others laughing with their heads down. When Tyrell complained that he didn't know what everyone was talking about, one boy leaned over and cupped a hand over Tyrell's ear. At first it seemed he was about to whisper. Instead he yelled: "Etienne's mother died."

Etienne is ringing the buzzer at the apartment again when another sound in the hallway startles him. Has someone else come up on the elevator? He turns quickly.

"Mother?"

He rides the elevator to the tenth floor. At the end of the hallway the sign on the door says ATTENTION: *MAINTENIR CETTE PORTE FERMÉE*.

Etienne shoulders the door open, causing an alarm to go off. It will quiet after a minute. Before the roof became off-limits, he and his friends pitched bivouacs up here. The ledge is lower than he remembers. Even with his bad hip, it is an easy climb up.

The view from the ledge is familiar. His friend Fabrice lived in a tall white building down the block. He hated leaving Fabrice, but he made friends at Saint Richelieu. He remembers sitting with those friends one day and laughing during a talk by a priest—was he Korean? Vietnamese?—in the athletic field house. But he also remembers something from the lecture itself.

To the place where you were born, your spirit returns, always.

All those years, Etienne believed he had been born here in Montreal. Kath and Timothee sat like statues on the sofa when they told him he had been born in Halifax. That his name at birth was Omar. Not until the evening before his mother was cremated did his aunt Luela tell him all the details about how his biological father died when a truck he was in slammed into an apartment building in Halifax. Several times Luela made a point of saying that Omar was riding in a truck speeding too fast. Etienne himself had been speeding on the motorcycle as it rounded the lake. Was it the nature of father and son to be reckless?

What about the place where you die? Etienne wonders, looking down at the people gathering at a window on a lower floor across the street, one of them pointing at him. Does the spirit visit there, too?

"None of those people would miss me if I jumped," Etienne says aloud.

The door to the roof opens. A man in a light-blue jumpsuit sticks his head out. He starts speaking French but switches to English. "Out of bounds. Come down, please."

Six months later, during the press of fall classes at the college, Etienne talks with his cousin Berto, who has called with the news that death has taken Jean-Yves.

"My grandfather sounded so spry on the phone last week," Etienne tells Jocelyn over dinner. "I am still shocked."

Etienne flies up to Montreal alone for his grandfather's funeral. He returns to the campus in Alabama grateful for the time he spent with his relatives up north. And yet, recalling that his father, consumed as he was with his girlfriend, barely spoke to him, Etienne wonders what is left for him in Montreal. After several weeks, his mind turns to other cities—Halifax and Jackson—and to other families, the Sebolts and the Platts. No way does he have the energy to begin a correspondence with both families. He will contact one at a time.

"Well, it sounds like I'm hearing the voice of a long-lost nephew," Etienne's uncle Kiryl says the evening Etienne calls Halifax. "Boy, whatcha know good?"

"Got married and had a baby," Etienne says. "But you know that. I'm calling to catch up with the family up there. I heard Yancy got married."

"With a wife that is a bit too old for the boy to handle," Kiryl says. "But he seems to be making it work."

Some of the news Kiryl relates was in the card Etienne read when he was in the hospital. But when the talk turns to Luela, he begins to focus his mind. He listens, recalling the stiff hug his aunt gave him before she climbed onto the bus at the depot in Burlington.

"I've left several messages for her at the hotel," he says. "But no call."

"Why don't you try calling Africaville?" Kiryl says. "Two of the businesses on the bluff have telephones now. The one in the rooming house is your best bet. Somebody there will definitely get a message to Luela."

"I did call there," Etienne says.

The phone line is quiet for a moment. "Luela tells me you are down there crowing," Kiryl says.

"Doing what?"

"Crowing."

"What is that?"

"That means a colored person is passing for white."

Etienne grips the phone. "I am only living my life. That's all."

"I'm not going to tell you how to live," Kiryl says. "As my father, Chevy, used to say, them's your business."

Etienne continues the conversation, embarrassed about how curtly he answered his uncle. A glance around his living room reveals no pictures of his mother displayed. In fact, there are no pictures of any of his Halifax relatives. White is what everybody down here in Alabama thinks he is. Is that his doing?

"I've begun reading a few of the Mississippi newspapers in the college library," Etienne says. "I hear that the governor over there is trying to fix the overcrowding in the prisons."

"Does that mean your grandmother may remain in Mississippi?"

"Possibly."

"That's good to hear."

"I also plan on trying to locate some of the family over there."

"Do you still have those letters I gave you a few years back?"

"Somewhere."

"Well, take another look at them again," Kiryl says. "The Platts down there have been blaming Zera for years for getting Matthew Platt thrown in prison, where he died. Read the letters. That way you'll know what you are getting yourself into."

Etienne hangs up the phone, wondering what to make of his uncle's words. He will try to locate the letters. He also intends to check out the relatives on his own. So what if the family once disliked Zera? People change. He hopes to change himself.

A search of several closets in the house turns up no sign of the letters Kiryl had given Etienne long ago during Marcelina Higgins's picture party on Woods Bluff. The letters must be in the boxes he left in the basement of Jocelyn's aunt's house in Vermont, he decides.

When the letters arrive from Jocelyn's aunt several weeks later, Etienne rereads them, surprised by the nasty words the relatives have written about Zera. In one letter addressed to Chevy Platt, they are clear: Don't bother to send her son, Omar, down here to visit.

"I suppose what I thought about the family in Mississippi is still correct," Etienne tells Jocelyn one evening. "These may not be people I want to contact."

A few weeks later, though, out of curiosity, he dials a number given to him by his uncle Kiryl. "I've contacted one of my relatives in Mississippi," he tells Jocelyn one Saturday afternoon while the two of them are doing chores in the backyard of their house.

Jocelyn rises from where she has been pulling weeds out of her small herb garden. She takes off her work gloves, giving a tentative smile. "Have you spoken to anybody there yet?"

"Talked to a woman who married into the Platt family. But she didn't stay on the phone long. I asked to speak to her husband and she said she would pass on the message. But he hasn't called me back."

"Will you keep trying?"

"I guess."

Weeks go by with no result, and Etienne calls the prison in Mississippi where his grandmother is incarcerated. "You need to fill out the visitor permission forms," the clerk tells him. "You can come in and pick up the forms, or we can mail them to you."

Etienne is about to give the clerk his address, when he realizes that his call is being transferred to another department. Listening to the hum and static on the line, he thinks over his decision. It is not yet clear that his grandmother will be moved out of state, though she might be. But if she remains a few hours' drive away, what can he do for her? Her age makes him uneasy. She must be eighty by now. He hopes she lives for decades more, but she may not. As far as he can tell, no other relatives visit her. Would he be responsible for her funeral? And if he gets close to her, how will he feel about her death? Will it throw him as the recent deaths of his grandparents from Montreal did?

And what if his grandmother is a bad seed? The family she married into seems to think so. Where are her blood relatives? There must be some reason they do not visit. If his grandmother needs plenty of help, can he provide it? He has a family to look after. What's the rush? Etienne thinks, hanging up the phone. He can call back tomorrow.

The next week he reads a *Mississippi Clarion Ledger* article saying that no prisoners will be moved out of the state. Afterward, he lets the matter lie for several months. But then, reluctantly, he puts in a visitation request to see Zera.

Several months later a copy of the visitation request is returned to him. Stamped diagonally across the page in large blocky letters are the words DENIED BY INMATE.

The visitation request, along with copies of various articles from Mississippi newspapers, goes into a drawer of his desk at work. He resumes today's paperwork feeling relieved, but later in the day, he feels embarrassed to have no immediate desire to keep trying to see Zera. After all, she is family.

As the months pass, Mississippi recedes from his mind. Then the years begin to pass, and Mississippi remains merely a thought, coming up sometimes in the once-a-year telephone call Etienne makes to his uncle in Halifax. On the call Etienne reminds Kiryl that Zera is still a stubborn woman.

C an it be that soon you will have been on this earth for forty-five years?," Jocelyn says this evening. "How many months is that?"

It is Saturday, March 20, 1982. Jocelyn is driving the car on their return from the Barnraiser Steakhouse, where a group of work colleagues and friends had gathered to celebrate Etienne's upcoming birthday. Etienne, drunk from too much tequila, wants to play along with Jocelyn's game. But all he can think about is the fact that he will spend this coming Thursday, the day of his actual birthday, in the hospital recuperating from yet another operation on the hip he injured years ago in his motorcycle accident.

The day after the operation, Etienne wakes up several times eager to talk to hospital workers. He doesn't mention the birthday balloons hanging about the room. Instead he talks about the upcoming wedding of his son, Warner. "My son's engaged to a nice woman whose father is a banker," he tells a cleaning woman. "And his future mother-in-law is a TV news reporter."

Etienne drifts off to sleep with only one regret: that Timothee is not alive to attend. It took months to feel a release from the pain he felt because of his father's death several years back.

The wedding date has been set for a year from this coming May, a few days after his son and future daughter-in-law will graduate college. On the afternoon that Etienne is discharged from the hospital, he arrives home to find that Jocelyn has already begun gathering addresses for the wedding invitations to be sent to the future groom's family.

Later in the fall, in the living room, where Jocelyn is addressing invitations, she hands Etienne two light-blue envelopes.

"I wasn't sure about sending these," Jocelyn says.

One is addressed to Etienne's cousin Berto in Montreal; the other, to his uncle Kiryl in Halifax. Etienne scans a third envelope, which is addressed to his aunt Luela. Jocelyn's words suggest she knows that he might not yet be ready to invite any of the relatives from Canada. She sounds like she wants him to think the matter over.

Etienne puts the envelopes in his briefcase, wanting to remind his wife that they have not yet told their son that he has black relatives. Etienne feels a bit sorry about that. But if there ever was a proper time to fix the oversight, it has arrived.

Several weeks later, searching his briefcase for a work memo, Etienne realizes that all three invitations are still with him. If Jocelyn finds out that he has not mailed the invitations, the reasons will not be as she might conclude. He hesitates to invite his relatives from Canada not because he does not want them to come. He does. And it is not because he is ashamed of his colored mother. Jocelyn has heard certain comments spoken during visits with their future in-laws. She knows their son is marrying into a family that would be uneasy to learn their daughter is about to marry a man of another race. He has never heard his son's fiancée or her parents make explicitly bigoted remarks. But he has heard the unflattering things they say about the neighborhoods in Montgomery where the black people live.

When he first came to Alabama everybody used the term *colored* to refer to Negroes. People in Alabama seem slow to change to the term *black*. If he recalls correctly, the schoolboys at Saint Richelieu years ago used the term *black*. On matters of race, is the world moving forward or backward? Is his son, Warner, colored? Is he black? Does his son get to choose? He did. At least he thought he did.

Etienne decides not to mail the invitations. When Jocelyn finds out, he can tell she is disappointed with him. But with his son and future daughter-in-law over for dinner several months before the wedding, Etienne sees the prudence in his decision, especially having gotten the news of a coming grandchild.

A week after the wedding Etienne is rushed to the hospital with swelling in his side, a complication from his riding and his operations. "His body is not responding to the antibiotics in a way we had hoped," the doctor tells Jocelyn. "We're going to keep him at the hospital for observation."

Jocelyn takes a seat beside the bed where Etienne sleeps, her anger reigniting over his motorcycle obsession. After she sold the expensive model he bought ten years ago, he purchased another one. Why?

On her way home from the hospital to change clothes, Jocelyn stops by the offices of the *Montgomery Times* and places a classified ad: "Late Model Motorcycle for Sale. Very Good Condition." Two days later, she receives a handful of crisp twenty-dollar bills from a man who wants the motorcycle. Over Warner's objections, she also hands over the helmet, riding gloves, and the collection of handkerchiefs Etienne tied around his arm when he went riding.

No need for those things anymore, she tells herself over the long week during which the doctors work to get Etienne's infection under control.

The efforts by the doctors fail and on the evening of June 25, 1984, Etienne Omar George Peletier dies.

B y early August, Jocelyn has packed up the house in Woodhaven. The evening before the movers arrive to load her belongings for the trip back to Vermont, she sits in the quiet kitchen looking out at the backyard. She is grateful for the time she has spent out there, holding her infant granddaughter, but she will not miss constantly being reminded that the grassless spot at the back corner of the house is where Etienne parked his motorcycle. How would their lives have been different if she and Etienne had taken that creek house out in Autauga County? They had gotten to the point where they could laugh about the day they became acquainted with the term *colored rider*. She suspects Etienne felt as she did, that Nathan's comments had not been really that bad. He was trying to fulfill a promise to his uncle. What person doesn't have relatives who get them involved in family nonsense?

If they had bought the Autauga County house, she could have gotten rid of the redwood paneling and updated the den. When they were done with the house, they could have sold it to whomever they pleased. More important, Etienne would not have had the money to buy that motorcycle.

Jocelyn wonders what her Scottish great-grandmother would have made of the tornado that crashed through town the year she and Etienne arrived in Montgomery. Until her death, that elderly woman feared the arrival of what she called a North Sea bluster, like the one that drowned her father. Probably she would have said a weather disaster like that so soon after their arrival was a bad omen.

Can it be that two decades have passed since they moved down here? She almost begins to calculate the months, but today the old game depresses her. They hadn't been married long when they moved here. For the most part, it was a happy marriage. On several occasions she asked Etienne if it was time to consider moving back to Vermont. She will regret not having been more insistent a few years back, when the perfect time would have been the summer before Warner began high school. He, too, said that he was appalled by what some of the neighbors were saying about the fact that Woodhaven High was being integrated. Had she nagged, Etienne might have given in. Perhaps if she had, this bad thing would not have happened.

The Almost Gone

Burlington, Vermont, October 1984

On the wide lawn next to the aluminum-sided building that houses Olshanowsky's Lawn and Cemetery Ornaments, granite headstones stand in rigid rows like a platoon of foot soldiers.

"This one's pink," Warner Peletier tells Andrei Olshanowsky, who has brought Warner to a headstone in the third row.

"Not pink," Andrei says with a thick Ukrainian accent. "It's rose granite. The governor's statuary is this same stone." Andrei, whose thinning white hair nearly reaches the collar of his shirt, pats the top of the headstone with a hand crisscrossed by bluish veins. "Your mother says you will pick some nice words to put on it."

Warner drops to a squat and runs a hand over the surface of the headstone. Will the words he penned on a three-by-five card serve as a proper epitaph for his father? On the church grounds after the funeral in Montgomery, a string of Etienne's former acquaintances seemed eager to tell him something he did not know about his father. Despite the new knowledge, the man still seems as murky as the figure he sees reflected in the glassy surface of the monument.

"If you don't like that stone, I can get you another model," Andrei says when they are back inside the building. At the checkout counter, he opens a shiny catalog. "Now, these I don't have in stock, but it would be very easy to order. Look here, this one is nice. It comes with a solid base."

The price of the bluish-gray monument is three times the cost of the headstone already selected. "I don't dislike the other one," Warner says. "I just think the color is a bit flashy. My father wasn't a flashy man."

"Your mother picked it," Andrei says. "I suspect she knew him better."

"I guess."

Deep lines radiate from the corners of Andrei's mouth as he looks over several papers on the counter. "There's a mix-up," he says. "Pretty serious."

"What kind?"

"Now, the death certificate says Mr. Peletier was white. But the purchase form for the plot says he was black. There's a mix-up."

Warner reaches across the death certificate and picks up the other form. Nearby, two women who had been critiquing a terra-cotta angel have gone silent. "I don't imagine this is a king-size problem, is it?"

"Could be," Andrei says. "After a flood over in Stowe, a man washed up out of a plot with a headstone that had a woman's name on it."

"Not good."

"Bad for business. Several of the trustees at that cemetery went to jail. Do you have your father's birth certificate?"

"Somewhere."

"Good. Mail in the birth certificate and everything will be finished."

"My father was from Canada—just over the border."

Andrei hands Warner a refrigerator magnet with the shop's address and phone number on it. "Just the certificate and we are finished."

On the drive home, Warner decides to take a tour of the old neighborhoods. On his return visits here during the summers, he didn't
spend much time downtown. Today, however, as when he was a child
in a car going through town, he glances down the side streets at every
corner, hoping for a view of the expanse of Lake Champlain.

For a man whom Warner had never seen put a toe in a pool, his
father fancied himself an expert swim instructor. That proved somewhat true. Under his father's coaching, Warner and his cousin could
swim the widest stretch of Saint Albans Bay before they were in their
teens. But the lessons began with a rocky start. Warner still remembers the day Etienne heaved him into the chilly greenish water in the
deep end of the pool at the community center. While his father stood
along the edge doing nothing, Warner thrashed about to stay afloat.

Warner pulls his mother's Volkswagen Scirocco into the driveway at
her house and kills the engine, recalling how the pool water stung his
eyes each time he sank below the surface. "That wasn't so hard now,
was it, son?" his father said after he had fought his way back to the edge.

Yes, Pop, Warner thinks, it was hard.

A note on the door of the refrigerator says that his mother and his
wife, Minerva, have taken the baby for a walk in a nearby park.
After mowing the grass and clipping the hedges in the small front
yard, Warner goes to the garage in search of other tasks to clear his
mind. He finds the motion-sensor outdoor light that he sent to Jocelyn
last December as a Christmas present.

With Heavenly Narcissus blasting on the living room stereo, Warner
removes the old light switch near the back door and begins rigging the
new wiring. Nothing he has heard recently from his mother nor from
Etienne's former colleagues who attended the funeral in Alabama has
been on his mind as much as what he learned from his correspondence with his relatives in Canada. Minerva was with him the evening
he opened the letter with the Halifax return address. She pulled him

out of his stupor to tell him that a photograph had fallen out of the envelope and onto his lap. That evening he was still telling himself that he was not that bothered by the news that his relatives in Halifax were black. But the picture did something to his brain. A young black woman, whom he learned was his great-aunt Luela, stood in front of what the letter said was Basinview Baptist Church. Beside her, looking black herself, was the woman the letter said was his grandmother, Kath Sebolt.

Warner lifted his eyes from the picture and met the eyes of his wife, someone he had known since elementary school. There was an odd expression on Minerva's face. The expression cemented itself in a part of Warner's brain where he doubted it would ever be erased. It was the look of someone uneasy about an unfamiliar sight that has entered their view. Minerva's face twitched and the look vanished.

On this, his first return to Burlington since the burial six months ago, a faulty light in the backyard is not the only thing Warner plans to repair. On the many phone calls he has had with his mother since his father died, he has mentioned the relatives in Halifax but not once has he pressed the subject to ask why nobody told him about them sooner. Well, six months is more than enough time to respect a widow's period of mourning. He and his mother need to have a serious conversation. He finds it a bit odd that his uncle Berto in Montreal never mentioned that the relatives in Halifax were black. But then he never asked. And why would he have? His father is no longer here to confront. There is only his mother to explain why no one told him. And Warner has decided that she has some explaining to do when it comes to her part in the deception.

I'm sorry he didn't tell me about this problem sooner," Jocelyn says, sitting with Warner at the kitchen table after dinner.

"What problem are you talking about?" Warner asks.

"The problem with Andrei at his cemetery. That business."

"Oh. I thought you were talking about something else."

Jocelyn is quiet for a moment. Then she shakes her head. "And what is Andrei asking for now, a birth certificate? I tell you, the way that man runs paperwork through the business can be exhausting for customers. Just ask my aunt Sylvia."

"Through the mail, it will take six weeks to get Pop's birth certificate," Warner says. "But if I show up in person I can get it in a day."

"I don't expect you to spend your vacation days chasing down paperwork."

"I've been thinking I need to get off my butt and take a drive up to Halifax," Warner says. "Now, I'll finally meet Luela."

Warner unfolds a map of Nova Scotia, feeling the last bites of corned beef and cabbage turning in his stomach. The bag he packed for the trip sits by the sofa. Minerva will not be getting up at four in the morning to accompany him on the drive. Though the baby is no longer bawling, Minerva insists the baby's not feeling well enough to travel. Thank God he did not start another argument with her before dinner. He now thinks it is better if he goes alone.

Another reason he kept his tongue earlier was because he knew Minerva was still angry with him for hiding the fact that he has been job hunting in Vermont. Jocelyn must have heard their argument yesterday in the backyard. He was turning a bratwurst on the grill, irritated to hear Minerva suggest for the tenth time that he ask her father for a job at the bank in Montgomery. And for the tenth time he said he wasn't interested in working for her father. After she spat out the news that she knew about the job interviews he was trying to set up in Vermont, the discussion rose to shouting.

Warner studies the yellow insert on the map showing the streets of Halifax. Why bring up the subject of an interview for a job he might not get, he wonders, as he orients himself to downtown Halifax. And besides, Minerva has kept her own secrets. They agreed she would remain on birth control pills until after they were married. Yet two months before the wedding, he found her vomiting in the bathroom.

"Has Andrei changed all the paperwork to say Etienne was colored?" Warner asks, refolding the map.

"Heavens, no," Jocelyn says. "Everything's been changed to white."

"How did the forms get mixed up in the first place?"

"Who knows? Your father purchased those plots a long time ago."

"Did you agree with Pop when he decided to not talk about his family in Canada?"

"I've told you many times, your father felt his family was his own business."

"There's nothing wrong with having colored relatives."

Jocelyn brushes aside a few strands of her wavy, just-starting-to-gray hair. "Your father being colored—or black—wasn't the problem," she says. "The problem was your great-grandmother. She's in prison."

"Up in Canada?"

"No, in Jackson, Mississippi."

"Have you visited her?"

Jocelyn shakes her head.

"What's her name?"

"Zera Platt. She sent her son, Omar, your grandfather, up to Canada to protect him. Your father was trying to protect you, too. Your father said that if your playmates knew you had a relative in prison, they would have teased you."

"But look at the trouble we're having now," Warner says. "The cemetery here in Burlington is white-only, isn't it? We're lucky Andrei's willing to fix the paperwork. Do you think he considered moving Etienne out of the plot?"

"Certainly not," Jocelyn says. "This is Vermont, not Alabama."

Up in Halifax, Luela enters her living room, where Chamberlain is watching the evening news. "That was Eh-tinne's son on the phone again," she says, sitting down on the sofa.

"Where the devil is he?"

"Nearby, so he says." Luela holds a teacup with a dollop of freshly baked rice pudding in it. "I told that young man I wasn't feeling well," she says, stabbing the pudding with a spoon. "Like his father, he doesn't seem to have any sense of other people's time. If he doesn't get here soon, I'm going to bed. You can direct him to the spare bedroom."

"Must be dying to see you if he drove all this way."

Luela studies the television screen with temperature forecasts for the next few days. "Yesterday he told me he was bringing his family. Now word is Minerva and the baby have stayed back in Vermont."

"The baby's ailing, you said."

"A baby can travel with a head cold. They could have left the child with the grandmother, too. Wonder what the real reason is that Minerva's not coming."

"You're not going to bother him about that, are you?"

"I will if I can work it into the conversation."

The bite of pudding feels cool on Luela's tongue. Why didn't she set the cup in the warm oven with the lamb stew while she took the call? Warner is no longer in a rush to get his father's birth certificate. So what on this planet does he want in Halifax? When she mailed the letter sending her regrets about not attending Etienne's burial, she sent him everything she was willing to part with. She sent along his grandmother Kath's college yearbook and the two *Lucy Kirchner in the Mountains* books. Clearing out the house in New Jamaica after her mother, Shirley, died, she cried for a solid minute when she discovered those items. She might part with the photograph of Kath and Timothee at their tenth anniversary dinner, or the church announcement of Etienne's birth. But no way is Warner getting any of the money Kath left.

Kath didn't actually leave Luela the money. Luela found it inside the lining of a hatbox that arrived in a trunk six months after her sister's funeral. Tacked against the wall of the hatbox were rows of fifty-dollar bills. The haul was five hundred dollars. Timothee insisted Luela keep the money as payment for the months she spent taking care of Kath's baby while Kath finished her degree.

Reluctantly, Luela had acquiesced to Timothee's generosity. What she did not tell Timothee was how much she loved the weekends she spent on the bluff taking care of her sister's boy, little Omar. Here was another person in the world, she had told herself, who would be eager to carry the Sebolt family's history. A pity that when the boy grew up, he had other ideas.

When Warner had called from a pay phone to say that he was running late, Luela sounded annoyed at him for keeping her waiting. Now, after she has fed him several helpings of her lamb stew, she sits before him on her living room sofa with only a slightly more pleasant demeanor. His great-aunt looks older than he imagined. In the green-and-gold dress, smelling faintly of perfume, Scotch, and mouthwash, she hands him a stack of photograph albums with barely a smile.

"It's hard when all you have are a few photographs," Luela says as Warner leans in to look at one picture. "But that is the only way you will get to know your grandmother Kath and your grandfather Omar. And, of course, Shirley and George."

"I am starting to feel like I am getting to know them well."

"That's because they are what we call the Almost Gone," Luela says.

"What does that mean?"

"It means the persons are deceased. They are gone. But there are still people walking the earth who knew them well. People are like that for a while."

"Like my father."

"Like a lot of people."

With the sound of Chamberlain's light snoring wafting in from the bedroom down the hallway, Luela studies her corduroy house shoes. She gives a slow nod and for some reason thinks of Clemmond Green, another former neighbor now among the Almost Gone. One year she tried hard to get him to notice her. But the only person on his mind then was Kath.

"Every few years or so I go over to the cemetery in Montreal," Luela says after a while. "I carry a bouquet of bugnets. Those were Kath's favorite flower. Our mother, Shirley, tried to grow them behind the old house, but the soil was all wrong."

"I'll go with you to Montreal the next time you visit," Warner says. "I'd be happy to buy the flowers."

Warner has barely lifted the cover of the next album when Luela sets down her drink. From the very first page she takes a picture out of its plastic sleeve and presents it to Warner. It is of two baseball teams gathered on Nobody's Acre.

"On this side of home plate, those were members of the Hindquarter Rockets," Luela says. "On the other side are the New Jamaica Wildcats."

"Did we have any family on the teams?"

Luela shakes her head.

"I only ask because you look a bit shook up."

"I guess that is because I wish I had been there. Those boys are getting ready to play the last game before—"

"The last game before what?"

"The last game on that field. The last game before hard trouble began in Africaville."

"I want to see Africaville."

"Not much to see anymore."

"Be nice to see what's there."

Luela picks up her Scotch and ginger and sits back in the sofa. Can a town be an Almost Gone, too? Foolish is what she must be to think that way about Africaville. The place is down, but not yet out.

Two houses still breathe on the bluff—the same number of houses that were there when the town began in 1792. That counts as life, not death. Doesn't it?

"Your father was born there. But he didn't care too much for the place. Did you know that?"

Warner nods. He sets down his beer and takes a sheet of paper out of his pocket. "There's plenty more I want to do in Canada," he says. "Do you want to see my list?"

Warner unfolds the paper and hands it to Luela.

The family in Halifax.
The family in Montreal.
Shirley and George's graves.
Grandfather Omar's grave.
Apartment in Montreal where Pop grew up.
Pool in Montreal where Pop learned to swim.
The cemetery in Montreal where Kath and Timothee's ashes are interred.

"I also want to bring my daughter to see Saint Richelieu," Warner says. "Etienne had lots of good things to say about the school."

"Did he now?"

"Yes, but I figure that can wait until she is older."

Luela gives a chuckle; then her face looks serious again. "The first time he went to the school, Etienne stayed with me. That was the summer Kath and Timothee went to Italy. His parents were glad to leave the angry boy behind."

"They were probably happy to be going on a vacation."

"True. Although they were having a few problems then, as I recall."

"Problems?"

"In their marriage."

"Every relationship has some trouble," Warner says. "Minerva and I have a few. I imagine you and Chamberlain sometimes have problems, too."

Luela lets the comment go without a response. Most of the remaining pages in the last album are of people from the hotel. While Warner looks at it on his own, Luela goes to the spare bedroom to turn down the covers. She folds a fresh towel at the foot of the bed, feeling put off by Warner's remarks about her marriage. Did he know about the months she and Chamberlain lived apart? He's a bit brash, like his father. Yet as an adult, Etienne would not have come right out and asked a rude question like Warner had. The young man has been in Halifax less than a day, but already he has the nerve to eat her lamb stew and rice pudding, and then criticize her marriage.

"Come here and look," Luela tells Warner when he enters the bedroom. She points at a nick in the bedpost. "Your father did that."

"How?"

"That's what I asked him."

"What'd he say?"

"Said he knew how he did it. Then he said he wasn't going to tell me."

Warner throws his head back in a big laugh and now Luela is finally ready to take him in. His hair has fewer waves than Etienne's. And his eyes are light brown instead of grayish blue. He's a few inches shorter and perhaps thinner than Etienne was in his early twenties. But while Etienne's laugh was always guarded, this young man just let out a good one. If Warner is carrying any worries, you'd never know it from that laugh.

That Saturday afternoon in the fall of 1968 on Nobody's Acre, the victorious Hindquarter Rockets shook hands with the defeated New Jamaica Wildcats in front of the largest crowd ever gathered to watch a baseball game on the bluff. When the spectators left the field, they crowded into Basinview Baptist to await the arrival of a representative from the Halifax Regional Council. Many in the crowd held copies of the newspaper with the headline "Regional Council to Hold Hearings on Urban Renewal: Africaville High on the Agenda."

"Forget urban renewal," Marcelina Higgins-Pitts roared from the pulpit. "This upcoming hearing is about urban razing, specifically, tearing down Africaville."

One of the Steptoe brothers led the crowd in the singing of a Negro spiritual when the city representative entered the church. As the official came up the aisle, the youth brigade in their green-and-red jumpsuits leaped to their feet and began a shout that continued for several minutes.

"That newspaper article is pure hogwash," the representative said when the crowd finally let him speak. "We have no plans to evict residents from the bluff, no plans to tear down Africaville."

By the end of the following week, however, three houses had been abandoned in New Jamaica. The following Tuesday Luela was awakened at three in the morning by a rumble so loud she thought a battalion of military tanks was invading the bluff. The next morning, eight bulldozers sat in the yard of one of the abandoned houses. Four had huge hydraulic arms and gaping metal jaws that seemed capable of chewing up anything in their way.

The newspaper article had shown a picture of the house before it was abandoned. Few on the bluff could deny that it could have used a coat of paint. That was true of many houses in Africaville. But most residents had decided that new exterior paint on their houses would have to wait until more pressing repairs had been made. The week before, the Africaville Yard and Garden Club had held a yard sculpture contest open to the students at the elementary and secondary school. All over the bluff, the children had made wonderful entries out of found rocks and fallen branches. Why didn't the newspaper cover that?

The bulldozers sat quiet for two weeks. In the meantime, teams of men visited the bluff. Each man carried a bucket of small, paint-filled latex sacs. From the yard of designated houses, a man would throw a sac with a pitcher's precision, hitting a mark just above the entry. At first they marked only abandoned houses. Soon, they did not care if the houses were empty or not.

The evening Luela returned home to find her house desecrated, she was unable to leave the porch for several minutes. The dark paint had streaked down her front door. Up close the metallic flecks in the paint looked grayish or dark blue. She entered the house hearing noises—the memory of her father George whistling in the back room, of Shirley washing Kath's hair on the back porch. Having let go of her desire to have a child, Luela felt this house—the Sebolt home—was her legacy. Property her ancestors had earned protecting the city of Halifax. That evening she did as Marcelina instructed and searched for her ownership papers. The next day she carried them down to the regional housing office, determined that she would not be leaving her house no matter what.

The next evening the sound of breaking wood jolted Luela awake. She dressed quickly, but by the time she got to Centervillage the old schoolhouse was a pile of rubble.

Neighbors who walked along Dempsey Road and saw the demolition were too stunned to speak. So this was how the notices came now? No warnings in the newspaper about plans to build luxury hotels or expand the rail yards. No notes in mailboxes or slipped under the door with weak offers from the city. Just a splatter of paint to say good riddance.

Misdemeanor summonses got some residents to leave. The threat of a felony citation ran off several more. But most residents stayed. For several days people sat on their porches, daring the work crews to displace them. When a bulldozer entered one yard, a group of teenagers climbed onto it. The driver made a few jerky turns then killed the engine and walked off the bluff. People took turns sleeping in Basinview Baptist. Whenever a public official visited or a constable car patrolled, people chanted, "Where is the electricity your bosses promised? Where is the running water? Where are the paved roads? Where? Nowhere."

At both ends of the bluff, large signs were put up reading LAST VILLAGE IN NORTH AMERICA.

Luela was sitting on her porch the day a constable handed her a notice to vacate. "Take me to jail," Luela told him. "This is not right."

And off to jail Luela went, along with Marcelina and a dozen others. There she sat for five days. It felt odd to return to the bluff to find the Penncampbells' old house gone. With a constable at every turn, Luela had no choice but to consider packing. Now, if a bulldozer crew showed up and found a resident on the front porch, they simply went around back or to the side and started their destruction there. One neighbor managed to carry out only half the family possessions before his house went crashing to the ground.

Luela had never wanted to pack up the house she was born in, the property where her father had been born. She did not want to leave the land that had been home to every Sebolt man who had ever set foot in Canada. Before leaving with the last of her belongings in the truck, she went out back looking for the footprint of the shed. Surely there was some sign here of Ephram or Ivy or the elder George. Or even of her father. But there were only weeds.

The memory of that long-ago carnage—a ragged swath of busted house siding and roof material, upended refrigerators and stoves, splintered window sashes, and overturned cars—weighs on Luela's mind this evening when she finally climbs into bed beside Chamberlain.

Shirley and George are gone. Kath is gone. The Sebolt house is gone. All that is left is the family story. Her nephew, Etienne, made it plain he did not want to hear it. Warner says he does. But does he?

How Marcelina raised the money to hire an expensive lawyer is anybody's guess. It had been worth it, since the two Higgins houses withstood years of legal threats by the city. Nobody is home at the larger house, so Luela peeks through the window into the dining room. Each year the renters who inhabit the houses seem less responsible. In what had once been one of the most impressive dining rooms in the Hindquarter, there is now grime in every corner.

The sight of the unkempt dining room stays with Luela as Warner drives them down Dempsey Road. The cemetery is still here, but rumor has it that the city has commissioned a study to see if it makes sense to move it. Shirley and George, Mordechai, Pallis, Coreletta, Testafera, Kipbo—the cemetery holds a gathering of the Sebolt family. Luela has heard no plan from Marcelina about saving the cemetery. But Marcelina is getting up there in age, with little of her youthful organizing energy. If the cemetery is destroyed, what proof of Africaville will be left?

"Jocelyn is letting me select words for Etienne's grave marker," Warner tells Luela when they arrive at the weathered headstone marking Omar Platt's remains.

"What did you choose?"

"Rest Ye O Man of Measure," Warner says. "I'm thinking maybe I should put Pop's full name on the headstone. Now that I know it, I mean. Etienne Omar George Peletier." Warner turns from the grave. "I'm embarrassed to say I'm sorta mad at him."

"What about?"

"He told me he didn't know his mother's family. Don't you think that's bad?"

"I used to."

"Well, now I have to deal with it."

"I don't exactly know what you mean by 'deal with it.' If you mean deal with being colored, that's not something you deal with. Being colored is something you are."

"I know," Warner says. He is quiet for a while, looking around at the other graves. "I asked my mother why Pop was estranged from this side of the family. Her answer was that a man is allowed to live his life like he wants."

Luela frowns. "What about a man's children? They ought to know where they're from."

"That's why I'm here," Warner says. "That's why I'll be visiting Zera at the prison in Mississippi."

Luela shows Warner a few more graves, keeping her voice pleasant. Aunt and great-nephew are quiet later walking to the car. Warner drives slowly down Dempsey Road, as if fearful that a bluff child might cross in front of the car any minute and be struck dead in midstride.

Trains to Glace Bay

PART FOUR

Sons and Daughters

Sons of Canada

Montgomery, Alabama, November 1984

I f the Canada-bound trains that came through southern Alabama
in 1889, in 1908, and in 1933 had come through again in the
1960s, very few men would have been waiting at the station in
Montgomery, hungry for a mining job in Cape Breton. By 1960, the
Cumberland Mining Corporation already did brisk business in Dallas and Perry Counties and was opening in several other areas near
Montgomery. Not only was Cumberland Mining hiring more men, it
was also using company profits to support educational institutions all
over southern Alabama.

The corporation's Cumberland Mining Trust funded the move
Montgomery A&M made from its cramped offices downtown out to
the former military base. Nearly a decade after Warner's mother and
father accepted jobs at the college, the trust made a $20 million grant
to the school. In exchange for the donation, Montgomery A&M was
renamed Cumberland College.

In the years since the donation, construction on the campus has been proceeding at a brisk pace. This afternoon, on the grounds of the former pistol range, a tall fence surrounds the work site of the seventy-thousand-square-foot Elizabeth Tutwiler Cumberland Science and Technology Hall. Warner looks through the open gate to where Deedra Cummings, in an inexpensive-looking business suit and a bright-yellow hard hat, directs a photographer who is taking pictures of the four-story, beige brick building. She heads toward him showing the same dour face she wore last June, when the vice-provost told Warner and Jocelyn that Deedra would be organizing the college's ceremony to honor Etienne's years of service.

"You're not authorized to come in here without a hard hat," Deedra says, approaching Warner. "You're going to get me in trouble."

"She's not wearing one," Warner says, pointing at the photographer. "Why should I?"

Before she can reply, Warner presents a large manila envelope with pictures of Etienne and other items Deedra said she might use to prepare a press packet.

"I can't look at these here," Deedra says, not accepting the envelope. "Wait over in the parking lot, please."

Deedra's light-blue Nissan is parked beside the work-site trailer. On the back window of the car is her burnt-orange-and-white Cumberland alumni sticker. Hanging on the wall in the office Deedra inhabits as Director of Minority Affairs is the Cumberland diploma that Etienne used to say she did little to earn. Last summer she had assured Jocelyn that she would call early in the fall term with a list of documents she would need for the press packet. Why is Deedra so testy with him? Warner wonders. Jocelyn is the one who complained to the vice-provost that Deedra had not returned any phone calls.

Across the road is the last open field on the campus. The former pistol range is now the future site of a new athletic complex. Only one more semester of classes and Warner can claim his diploma. Yet, despite the advances made to the campus, he's not yet ready to sit in a classroom—too many memories of running into his father in the student union or the bursar's office. He did not even enjoy his visit earlier today to the administration building, which took him down the carpeted hallway past his father's former office. The trip reminded him too much of the hallway in the hospital ICU room where Etienne lay still as a sleeping cat. The strange buzzing he heard when he entered the room made him fear that a nurse had gone out and left a piece of equipment running. One of Etienne's hands lay outside the bedsheet, in a slight curl. When he grabbed the hand, it felt warm. But somehow he knew there was no life left.

Deedra dumps the contents of the manila envelope onto the dusty trunk of her car. "Facilities will mount a plaque on the bulkhead outside one of the lecture halls in the new science building," she says, sifting through the items. "The plaque will read 'The Etienne Peletier Lecture Hall.'"

"I was hoping to get Pop's name on something bigger," Warner says. "Maybe a wing of a new building."

Deedra's lips, covered in lipstick that matches her rust-colored blouse, give not the slightest hint of a smile. They are pursed as she scans an article published in the college newspaper the year Etienne took the job as head of student accounts. "I guess we could use this picture," she says, holding a photograph of Etienne in a suit and tie. "I like the plain background."

The photographer approaches and hands Deedra a form. Using the photographer's back as a surface, she signs her name on it. "Wasn't Etienne from Canada?" she says, noticing another clipping as she shoves items back into the envelope. "Maybe we can interview one of the relatives."

"Dad wasn't close to that side of the family."

"Are you?"

"Not yet."

"I don't understand why my office was assigned this commemoration," Deedra says.

"Probably because you knew Etienne the longest."

"But it isn't like Etienne's relatives are minorities."

"A few of our relatives are colored."

"I mean close relatives."

"So do I."

"I mean blood relatives."

"So do I."

Deedra looks puzzled for a moment. Then she lets out a loud laugh.

"Did I say something funny?" Warner asks.

"You did if you want me to believe you're a minority."

"I never said I'm a minority. You asked about Etienne's relatives. I'm telling you the truth about them. Never mind that. Etienne deserves to be honored. He should be appreciated."

Deedra opens her car door and tosses the envelope onto the passenger seat. "Etienne was appreciated," she says, closing the door. "Appreciated more than I've been. Matter of fact, Etienne's bosses did nothing but appreciate him ever since he first came down here."

A s compensation for the extra work the other clerks at the Kwik Mart had to do while he visited Vermont and Halifax, Warner has been given the job of the daily cleaning, including swabbing, of the bathroom. He also has to hang all the holiday decorations. He was not surprised to get the extra jobs on his return. But he was surprised to hear the rumor that the owner of the Kwik Mart might be selling the store and fifty acres of surrounding forest—and soon.

Customers come to the Kwik Mart in Woodhaven to buy what they can't find at stores in the Plaza or in Montgomery: Prince Albert tobacco in a portable tin, Vienna sausages in tomato sauce, a can opener that lasts longer than a year. When customers complain that bars of Octagon soap cost twice as much here as they do at the Plaza, Warner likes to think he's patient, even tries his best with the one or two colored customers who still come in. He likes working here.

Still, the only reason he turned down the job at McKenny Shoes several months back was because Udall Nicholson, the owner of the Kwik Mart, had promised to make him assistant manager. Last week, when Jocelyn began to nag him about returning to finish his last semester of college, he reminded her that Udall had promised to teach him inventory and ordering, how to manage the suppliers, the store, even the arrangements he'd worked out with the banks and contractors. Losing this job would put him in a bind, Warner thinks, as he carries a stepladder up the store aisle. Have any of the other employees pumped Udall about the rumor, he wonders, setting the ladder down near the head of the aisle.

"It's a little late to hang those," Warner says to Gerrick Gilroy, the storeroom helper, who sets a box of Halloween decorations on the floor beside the stepladder. "Where are the ones for Turkey-Day?"

Gerrick brushes dust off the front of his oversized T-shirt, which reads AUBURN PHYS. ED. His Afro is much shorter than the one he wore the year he and a dozen other black kids integrated Woodhaven Junior High. "I haven't found them yet," he says. "But Udall says you got to hang these, too."

Warner wants to check that with Udall, but this may be the only chance he gets to talk to Gerrick. "You need a ride home?" he asks.

"You plan to stick around till I get off work?" Gerrick asks. "Why is that?"

"Everybody knows that Monte Carlo of yours still ain't working," Warner says, pulling a cardboard cornucopia on a string out of the box. "I'll betcha Udall will let you off a little early today knowing you need a ride home."

"You can read Udall's mind now?"

"I plan to swing by the hiring office at Platinum Paper on the way home. We could both snatch up a job application."

"Didn't I hear you tell Udall you wouldn't work for the paper plant?"

"I only said that because Udall seemed so pissed about the plant buying up land. Can't a man change his mind?"

Gerrick gets a Nehi soda from the chest cooler. "Udall ain't told me nothing about the store being sold," he says, heading to the back, "if that's why you're being friendly."

Up on the stepladder, Warner tacks one end of the string on a cardboard pumpkin to the ceiling. Not for a minute does he believe Gerrick. The other clerks have already spilled the news about Gerrick driving Udall's Buick to the post office to overnight correspondence from Udall to the paper company's lawyers. The boy knows something.

But if Gerrick does have news about a possible sale, would he tell Warner? Ever since finding out that Warner tried to get the storeroom job for his best friend, Randy, Gerrick has been cold to him. And yet Warner's not the least bit sorry about wanting the job to go to his friend. If Randy were running Udall's errands, by now he would have told Warner what he knew about any plans to sell the store.

After his visit to Canada, on the drive from Halifax to Burlington, during which he had to take a detour down a long, unfamiliar country road, Warner was certain he could feel the Canadian border tugging at him, trying to pull him back up north.

On the highway now, heading for the offices of Platinum Paper, he wonders if Gerrick Gilroy has also felt the same tug. "Since you both have distant relatives above the forty-ninth parallel," their ninth-grade history teacher had said to Warner and Gerrick years ago, "it would be good if the two of you would cooperate on a paper about Canada."

Gerrick asked no questions about what Warner was gleaning from the stack of library books about Montreal. And he told Warner nothing about what he learned from the single encyclopedia volume he combed for information about Glace Bay, where one of his relatives had gone to work in the mines. On the day the report was due, Gerrick stapled his two handwritten pages to the four pages Jocelyn had typed for Warner and dropped the report on the teacher's desk.

The personnel office for Platinum Paper occupies a small white building with a freshly paved parking lot. "Would you look at all these questions?" Warner says to Gerrick back in the car as he unfolds the application form over the steering wheel. "Filling out this monster will require three hands."

He turns the application over, glancing at the form still lying in Gerrick's lap. "Those envelopes you've been taking downtown for Udall," Warner says. "I know you been reading 'em."

"All sealed, fella."

"Not the outside. They were being delivered to the paper plant's lawyers in Birmingham, correct?"

"That don't mean Udall is selling the store to 'em."

"Then who is he selling to?"

"Search me."

A noisy group of men, all in dusty work clothes, walk in front of the car, their faces beaming as they climb onto the back of a cordwood truck. "If you wanna know what's up with the store," Gerrick says, "why don't you ask Udall?"

"Udall's not talking." Warner puts his job application in the glove compartment and slams the small door. "If he sells the store, the new owners will probably let us go."

"You think we can stop 'em?" Gerrick fans his neck with his application. "Looks like you and me are stuck in the same boat, fella."

"Not when it comes to getting hired at this plant. I suspect you haven't opened that application because you're worried the company won't hire you."

"They sure will."

"Not as long as your granddaddy Sibelus is sitting on land the paper company wants. Acting all big like he's the shah of Iran or something."

"That's him, not me."

"Platinum's a big company. Do you think Sibelus will get to stay in his house?"

"The lawyer with the NAACP thinks so. Colored gal. Real smart."

Warner starts the Camaro and shifts into reverse. It's true. He is in the same predicament as Gerrick. But hearing Gerrick say it makes it sound worse.

"You need to stop doing every little thing Udall tells you, Gerrick," Warner says as he backs the car out of the parking space.

"Soon as you start paying me cash money," Gerrick says. "That's when I'll do what you say."

G errick was absent from school the day their teacher handed back the history report he and Warner had completed. From Gerrick's pages Warner learned that in the summer of 1889, when workers from a Canadian mining company visited southern Alabama looking to hire men for the mines in Cape Breton, only a few men from the town of Pathview made the trip. But in 1933, when the third Canada-bound train departed Montgomery, twenty-three men from Pathview were on board, including Gerrick's great-uncle Percy.

Gerrick's pages also said that the dirt road running through Pathview was once one of the widest in Lowndes County. Today, a single car can barely squeeze along its length. The postmaster is a saint for making biweekly trips down this horror show, Warner thinks, steering his Camaro across another shallow crater in the road.

Since working on the history report that earned him and Gerrick a B-minus, Warner has rarely thought about Gerrick's life in Pathview. And he has never seen the house where Gerrick lives. Parked on the road near the Gilroy mailbox, he watches Gerrick walk up the long driveway, thinking his eyes are deceiving him. A brick house in Pathview? But he then notices places where the imitation brick tarpaper shingles have peeled away to reveal weathered gray planks. The two chinaberry trees in the front yard must once have been well pruned. The same for the spruce hugging one side of the house. But the front steps and the porch railing look as shabby as the rusted tin roof.

How in the world can Gerrick believe that the two of them are in the same boat? Does Gerrick not recognize that the lawyers for

Platinum Paper might well succeed in evicting him and his grand-father from that house? And that the people in the personnel office might refuse to accept his application? If Gerrick loses his job at the Kwik Mart, he will have far more to worry about than Warner will.

But not everything Gerrick said earlier was without merit, Warner concludes when he is back on the blacktop. In fact, he may soon need to ask for the particulars of the NAACP lawyer Gerrick's grand-father is hiring. The idea came to him the day he decided it was time to get serious about visiting his great-grandmother Zera at the prison in Mississippi. Prisoners are always in need of lawyers. He imagines Zera would require a special one. His desire to visit his great-grandmother had intensified in Halifax, when his aunt Luela showed him the weather-beaten grave marker of his grandfather Omar. He made the decision, however, when he held his daughter, Jennifer, near the shiny headstone that had been installed at Etienne's grave in Vermont. He wants to make sure his daughter knows her rel-atives, even the colored ones.

Etienne had always claimed that the problem he had with Zera had nothing to do with the fact that she was colored. The problem was that she was a well-known prisoner in Mississippi. According to a few of the articles Warner has read, she may still be well known. Neverthe-less, Warner wants his daughter to learn that family is family. Will she want to get to know her colored relatives? Or will she rebuff them, as her grandfather Etienne had done?

His great-grandmother must be eligible for parole by now. Had any-one ever tried to help her obtain it? The only trepidation Warner has about asking Gerrick about the NAACP lawyer is that Gerrick might ask why he wants the information. That he feels uneasy about that surprises him. He was quick to criticize his father for keeping family matters to himself. But now he finds that, outside the family, he is not yet ready to talk about this new part of his life. There are too many facts he still has to hunt down.

Warner passes the first neat houses in Woodhaven feeling the weight of his journey to learn more about his people. His father's death closed off one avenue he had to learn about himself. But a new avenue has opened. Still, what if he meets his great-grandmother at the prison only to learn that she is a despicable person, one neither he nor his daughter will want to associate with? What if he learns that Etienne was right: some family matters are better left buried?

The Dilemma

I f the television forecasts are to be believed—and Warner doesn't doubt them—the monthlong interlude between Thanksgiving and Christmas will be the hottest on record. The entire week after Thanksgiving, the temperature in Montgomery hovers in the high eighties. And this Saturday afternoon in early December, with his head still briny from all the rum shots he downed at a buddy's house, where a party gathered to watch the Alabama-Georgia football game, Warner arrives home so wilted from baking in his Camaro that he doesn't respond to what Minerva has said.

"Didn't you hear me?" Minerva asks. "I said I forgot to tell you that Deedra Cummings called here for you yesterday."

"What did she want?"

"She didn't say. She wants you to call her back."

Warner carries in three large shopping bags filled with Christmas gifts and wrapping supplies, which Minerva left in the trunk of the Camaro the last time she borrowed it. The look on her face suggests she may have delayed giving him this message. She knows he is never happy talking to Deedra.

"Jocelyn called me this morning," Deedra says the next day, when Warner returns her call.

"Probably wanted to check up on me," he says. "That woman's a worrywart. I hope you told her that I delivered the package you wanted."

"That is not exactly why your mother was calling," Deedra says.

"Well, what else did she want?"

"She wanted to talk about you."

"What about me?"

"Your mother feels it would be a dishonor if she comes down here to a ceremony for Etienne at the college where his son has failed to graduate. She wants me to hold off on any ceremony to honor Etienne until after you have graduated. She told me to call you to find out if you will be registering for the spring. Will you?"

"My mother knows I don't have the money right now to finish school."

"Your tuition's free."

"Books and gas aren't. Plus, I have to work. I've got a new baby."

"What's the problem?" Deedra says, her voice rising. "I finished my degree raising two grandchildren. What do you want me to tell your mother?"

"I'll call her myself, damn it."

From the pause on the other end of the line, Deedra must be surprised, as she was on campus when he told her about his colored relatives. Warner hangs up, wondering what Deedra will do with that information.

Deedra Cummings is not the only person in Alabama who knows that Warner has colored relatives. The only other person, outside of Minerva, is his best friend, Randy. When he broke the news, he noticed the way the gold flecks erupted in Randy's slate-colored eyes. "That's some crazy stuff you should keep to yourself," Randy said.

Why did he tell Randy, Warner wonders this evening, getting out of the Camaro at the Lucky Lounge bar. That boy's mouth is as big as Texas.

The usual Tuesday night crowd is here: members of the summer softball league and old classmates from high school, including Millicent Agnos, one of the other clerks at the Kwik Mart. At the bar, while Warner orders a beer, Millicent tries to keep Randy's hands off her pack of cigarettes sitting on the bar.

"Randy, if you be a sweetie and fetch me some pop-pop," Millicent says, holding an empty teak bowl, "I might let you have a smoke."

Randy walks to the popcorn maker while Millicent catches Warner up on what happened at the Kwik Mart during the afternoon shift. "Gerrick's daddy is in town," Millicent says. "Betcha didn't know that, did you?"

"That beer's got you tipsy," Warner says. "Don't you know Gerrick's daddy is dead?"

Millicent raises her chubby arm and wags a finger. "My daddy saw him. He swears it was Gerrick's daddy."

Warner pays for his beer, confused. Why would Gerrick lie about that?

"So what if he saw Gerrick's daddy?" Warner says to Millicent. "What's that to me?"

"I'm just spreading gossip is all. Speaking of which, I hear Udall's wife doesn't think it will be good for business to promote a colored man at the store."

"Udall's never going to promote Gerrick."

"I'm not talking about Gerrick, sweetie," Millicent says. "I'm talking about you."

"Who said I was colored?"

"Randy."

Randy, who has come back, sets down the bowl of popcorn onto the bar. "Didn't your daddy teach you to keep other folks' name out of your mouth, Miss Millisecond?" he says, grabbing the pack of cigarettes from Millicent's lap.

"Like you kept Warner's name out of yours?" Millicent says. "Come on now, Randy. Ain't that what you said? Didn't you say Warner's daddy had a colored mother?"

"No, ma'am, it ain't what I said."

"Well, that ain't my point anyway," Millicent says. "What I was saying is that if it's true that Warner has a colored grandmother, then he's colored enough for Udall and his wife to have a problem." Millicent chuckles and offers Warner some popcorn. "I suppose we can tease you about your little problem," she tells him, "because we know you."

"You think having a colored relative's funny?" Randy says. "I don't."

Warner washes down a mouthful of popcorn with a swallow of beer, looking at Randy. Who else has his friend told? Any advice Udall got about not promoting a colored man probably came not from his wife but from Millicent. She started a rumor in high school that Warner and Gerrick had the same relatives in Canada. And when she heard Udall was thinking about hiring Gerrick at the Kwik Mart, she asked him not to schedule Gerrick when she was working. Now, whenever Gerrick attends a clerks' meeting, Millicent interrupts him every time he tries to speak. Of course, she may dislike him for reasons that have nothing to do with his being colored. That's possible. Warner's not too fond of Gerrick himself.

The front doors of the Lucky Lounge swing open, letting in more of the warm December air. Hearing a familiar laugh, Warner scans the bar. Is that Millicent's sister, Pinky, playing darts with the VFW softball team? He caught up with Pinky yesterday when she came by the store. A toenail clipper, a bottle of Mercurochrome, and a box of peanut brittle are much cheaper at the Plaza. So why had Pinky driven the extra miles to the Kwik Mart?

"I know I don't have big tits," Randy says to Warner, "but could you pay attention?"

"Did you say something important?"

"I said where has Gerrick's daddy been? Shouldn't he have come down here sooner to see about his son and his father?" Randy shakes his head. "Niggers, I tell you."

Randy takes a drink of beer, looking embarrassed about his slipup. When Millicent's boyfriend walks up, Randy heads to the bathroom.

Millicent's boyfriend takes the half-full beer out of her hand and drains it in a few gulps. After setting down the bottle he shakes a set of car keys.

"That's my cue," Millicent says. She slides off the bar stool and follows her boyfriend out of the bar. Warner remains, and when Randy returns from the bathroom their conversation is not as easy as it usually is. Warner is deep in thought when Randy taps him on the shoulder.

"Are you still mad at your daddy?" Randy asks.

"I was never mad at my daddy."

"You said you were. You said your daddy kept a lot of secrets."

"Nobody's perfect."

"Is that the colored in you talking?"

"Boy, give that a rest."

Randy uses the butt of a matchstick to prod the wick on his cigarette lighter. Warner watches him work, wondering what became of the crazy idea Randy had that the two of them lease a docking station at one of the garages in Woodhaven. They both had been recently laid off from their jobs at the Montgomery Hotel and Conference Center. Warner had worked his way from parking lot attendant to concierge. Some days he wore a tie for work. Minerva liked that. These days, Minerva likes nothing he does. It is well past eleven. If he does not leave right now, she will be in bed when he gets home, and tomorrow there will be trouble.

"Not ready to go home yet," Randy says when Warner produces the keys to the Camaro.

"You are if you want me to give you a lift."

Randy looks toward the back of the bar. "You hear Pinky?"

"Who'd miss a girl with a laugh like that?"

"Not coming back here after you drop me, are you?"

"Now why would I do that?"

Warner slides off the stool, feeling a pleasant rush of heat down his face and neck. His thoughts of Pinky's laugh are disrupted by the stifling air outside and by his irritation—not at the distasteful things Randy says about colored people, but at his nerve for suggesting that Warner is still mad at Etienne. Obviously Randy was too drunk to remember he had asked that question several days ago.

Warner opens the car door, thinking about the news that Gerrick's father has come home. Even in high school he detected anger in Gerrick toward his father. Odd, he thought at the time, to carry around hate for a man who was dead. But if he is alive, the anger was clearly for a different reason. Is it because his father was absent for so long? He wonders again why Gerrick lied. Whatever Gerrick wants or needs from his father, with the man still alive at least there is a chance to get it.

Warner is not so lucky. Whatever gifts he wished to continue getting from his father will never arrive. At least not in a form he expects. He can only search out traces of his father in Halifax, Montreal, and Mississippi. Angry? Hardly. Last month in Vermont he looked through boxes in Jocelyn's basement for hours until he found the articles and old photographs his mother thought Deedra Cummings might need for the college's planned tribute to Etienne. And he delivered them all to Deedra eagerly. Are those the acts of a son angry with his father?

R egistration for seniors ended yesterday," Deedra's voice on the answering machine says. "I see that you have not signed up for classes. I guess this means we will not be doing the ceremony for your father this spring. Tell your mother I'm putting away the paperwork. Let me know when you're ready to proceed. Next year, maybe?"

Warner hits the stop button on the answering machine, shaking his head. There is no way he is going to call his mother with that news. He had not realized that the deadline for winter registration had passed. Surely Deedra knows that he can register late. It is obvious she could care less about any celebration honoring Etienne.

The desk in the spare bedroom used to belong to Minerva's grandfather. Everyone in her family talks about the man as if he had been a professor at a fancy college, but Warner knows the facts: he substitute-taught one college course at a so-called industrial junior college. Most of his teaching was of physical education and civics at a high school up in Limestone County. Warner retrieves the Cumberland College Catalog of Spring Courses from the desk drawer, certain that there's no sense in complaining to Minerva about the message from Deedra. "I don't expect you to understand my predicament," he told her months ago, when all the news—the death of his father, meeting Luela, finding out about Zera—was piling up in his brain. "Nor do I expect you to fully understand what I am trying to figure out about my life."

Minerva had nodded and said, "You're right, I don't understand your predicament. But what I do understand is that your predicament might improve if you finish your schooling while you run around trying to understand yourself and chase down family stories and mementos."

Inside of an hour Warner has written down the course codes for all four classes he will register for tomorrow. He closes the catalog, not yet able to see himself receiving a diploma at a June graduation. And the little satisfaction he feels about completing this task is tempered by the fact that the job application he picked up from the personnel office at Platinum Paper is still sitting on his desk.

He promised Gerrick that he would deliver both their applications to the company office. His is only half completed, but he has not been fretting about the delinquency. For one thing, the woman in the personnel office said the hiring managers would not come over from Germany to look at applications until the beginning of April. That is still three months away. And for another, he did not think Gerrick would ever complete his application. How could Gerrick concentrate with all the turmoil at his house? His grandfather is getting sicker but still re-fuses to leave home. And now Gerrick is trying to reunite with a father he has not seen for a decade. Warner thought Gerrick would surely drag his feet on filling out the job application until well into spring. But as Warner left work last week, there was Gerrick's completed ap-plication sitting on the front seat of the Camaro.

Better finish mine, he thinks, taking up the application again. Most of the boxes to be checked are preceded by explanatory sentences, all ending with a question mark. At the top of the first page of the application is the one-word query to which Warner has yet to offer a response.

RACE?

In the past such inquiries never caused him the slightest trepida-tion. He would check the box that said WHITE with barely a thought. But now he wants to think over his answer. When he notices that the form says this information is optional, Warner decides to leave the box unchecked—although he suspects that if he is called for an interview, he will be asked his race. He might say that his father was adopted and he doesn't know his race. That is technically true—enough. If pressed, he could insist on leaving the matter at that. He is from up north, he can say. We don't have such rigid views on race.

But is that true? He attacks another question, recalling a few de-rogatory comments he has heard over the years about colored people. During his yearly visits to his grandparents in Vermont and New Hampshire, he cannot recall them voicing many slurs against blacks, but he does recall a few. Before leaving Vermont last month, he asked Jocelyn if, during the months before her marriage, she knew that Etienne was colored. She said she did. But there had been a moment of hesitation.

Deedra Cummings may not be happy that his registration has put her back to work planning his father's commemoration, Warner thinks, as he leaves his morning class and heads to his afternoon shift at the Kwik Mart. But most certainly his wife and mother are elated that he is back on campus.

Warner gets out of the Camaro at the Kwik Mart to find Gerrick beaming over a letter from Platinum Paper. "The letter says I need to come into the personnel office again," Gerrick says. "They tell me I need to fill out some more papers."

"You and a hundred other guys, no doubt," Warner says. He skims the letter. "Industrial technician? What is that?"

"Don't know," Gerrick says. "But I'll bet it pays better than Udall. Did you get a letter?"

Warner shakes his head. "But I'm putting in for something better than technician. Maybe they are still reviewing the job application for those types of jobs."

"If you say so."

"It says here that they won't bring on any new hires until August," Warner adds. "That is a long way off."

Warner reads the letter again, feeling a bit jealous. Where is his letter? There were boxes to check that asked the types of jobs he thought he was qualified for. He had checked most of the boxes beside jobs that required a college degree. Were the people in personnel unimpressed with his application?

"I heard your daddy was in town," Warner says, handing the letter back to Gerrick.

"Bad news travels fast, I guess," Gerrick says.

"That's no way to talk about your daddy. I've been meaning to ask you, why did you tell everybody he was dead?"

"Because he might as well have been."

"But he wasn't."

"He was to me."

Something tells Warner to keep at it, but what good will that do? "Your old man must be proud to see you getting on."

Gerrick shrugs. "I remember meeting your daddy when I was a kid.

Mr. Peletier picked me up off the ground and held me over his head. Scared the shit out of me. One time he called me a Bluff Boy. Couldn't tell you what he meant."

"You probably reminded him of a boy from Halifax."

Gerrick looks puzzled as he slips the letter into his back pocket. "Pinky came by the store yesterday," he says, a smile returning to his face.

"Looking for her sister, no doubt."

"If she was, she didn't tell anybody," Gerrick says. "Soon as that girl heard she had just missed you, she was out the door. She didn't even pay for the MoonPies she put on the counter." Gerrick laughs. "If I didn't know better, I'd say you got trouble."

Warner laughs, too, though he heads into the store to start his shift knowing he shouldn't. His friend Randy has already mentioned that Warner was seen standing awfully close to Pinky in the parking lot of the Lucky Lounge the other night. If word is getting around, he ought to cool his mischief. But all he was doing with Pinky was talking.

The first weeks of classes pass in cool but pleasant fall-like weather. But later, as heavy, frigid air lingers over Montgomery during February, the term starts to drag on. At home in the evenings, Warner hardly sees Minerva. During her months of part-time work at the hospital, where she is a rehabilitation therapist, she spent her off-hours absorbed with the baby. And now she is busy studying for her Physical Therapist II certification exam. When they are not passing the baby off to one another, they rarely talk. And they are not having sex.

In early March, with a string of exams approaching, having finished a double shift at the Kwik Mart and attended a review session on campus, Warner arrives home to find Minerva and the baby asleep and his textbooks on the kitchen table. With his plate of cold pork chops on the table, he opens his Intermediate Macroeconomics textbook with a loud exhale. Despite what he's been telling in-laws and friends, he does not particularly like this class. After reading a long section, he scans the ten questions assigned, unable to answer a single one. It looks like the answers to questions seven through ten will require extensive graphs.

Had he majored in pre-law, as his father had advised, his final months on campus would have been loaded with easy afternoon classes. He also ignored his father's suggestion that he take a summer job in the mailroom at a private law firm. Instead he took an internship at the county courthouse. He would have been able to file court transcripts faster if he spent less time reading them, but he couldn't help himself. Though he had quibbled with a few of the indictments, every verdict seemed right as rain. Do the crime. Do the time. Sometimes prison is a good thing.

But since the runaround he has gotten at the correctional facility in Mississippi, he has been developing a different attitude. Not only is the staff rude, but nobody there even believes he is the great-grandson of Zera Platt.

Warner hardly believes it himself. He stabs at the green beans with a fork, recalling the frustrating telephone calls he has made trying to locate Zera's relatives in Mississippi. He started with her family, the Bradenburgs, in Sunflower River. The problem is not that there are no Bradenburgs living in northwest Mississippi. It is that there are too many—twenty-nine listings alone in the Sunflower County phonebook. He reached two people who claimed to be relatives of Zera, and both agreed to come with him to the prison. But after he asked them to bring proof of their relationship to her, neither would take his calls. His job would be so much easier if the married couple in Jackson would cooperate. They are Platts for sure. But they will not return his calls.

Warner rakes the remnants of his meal into the trash can, glancing at the clock on the stove. The Tuesday night regulars at the Lucky Lounge will probably wonder why he is absent again tonight.

On a sheet of paper he draws a set of intersecting axes. Price on one axis, quantity sold on the other. That is the easy part. He reads

the question in the economics text again. But now the words blend together. After another minute, he closes the book and gets up from the
table, wondering where he put the keys to the Camaro.

W arner exits the parking lot of the Lucky Lounge with Pinky
on the front seat next to him. On the highway, he feels a presence behind him in the back seat of the Camaro. Yet his urge to turn
around is not as strong as his interest in each approaching set of headlights. Every time he meets a car on the road, he imagines the unseen
driver suspects his mischief.

Pinky, who stuttered as a child, sounds steady and assured now.
She's telling Warner about her time in California.

"Of course I've seen a walnut tree," Warner says. "We have walnut
trees here in Alabama, you know."

"Not as many," Pinky says. "In Modesto, I saw an orchard that
took up more land than Woodhaven. Even if you count the colored
section."

The headlights illuminate a telephone pole riddled with small round
reflectors. Nothing's going to come of this, Warner tells himself, turning into the driveway at Pinky's house.

After he dropped Randy off, he drove back to the lounge telling himself he just wanted one more rum and Coke. He remembers the feel of
Pinky's freckled arm as he helped her off the bar stool, and again as she
got into the front seat of the Camaro. Her skin felt as soft as new grass.
Just being friendly, Warner thinks now, with the car rumbling along the
rocky driveway. A quick detour before the ride home.

In the dim light, Pinky looks fifteen. "Don't see Millicent's Dodge
in the yard," he says.

"That girl's on the way to Opelika with that storytelling boyfriend
of hers," Pinky says with a laugh. "She won't be back here tonight."

Warner kills the engine, and before he realizes it he is kissing her.
He undoes the top buttons on Pinky's blouse. When the porch light

comes on, he takes his hand out of her blouse. A tall cedar blocks his view of the front porch.

"It's my daddy, Rayford, turning on the porch light," Pinky says. "More'n likely he's on the way to bed."

Warner reaches back into Pinky's blouse again. "You on anything?"

Pinky shakes her head, pressing her lips tightly. "Don't imagine you'd have some rubbers. You being married."

"We don't have to do anything that might get you in trouble," Warner says. "We can just have a little fun."

Warner unzips his pants. Feeling Pinky's warm mouth over his penis, he lays his head back on the car seat. He is trying not to think about Minerva, but when Pinky's hand starts to work his penis, his thoughts begin to blur. After helping Pinky lower her jeans, he puts a hand inside her panties. The softness and warmth make him dizzy.

Kissing Pinky's shoulder, he inhales her strong perfume. Blue Wind, she calls it. A thought causes him to lift his head quickly. Upholstery cleaner will mask the smell, but Minerva knows when a stranger has been in the car.

"What's wrong?" Pinky asks.

"Let's get in Rayford's car. We could have more fun on those large seats."

Pinky puts her hand on the door handle, looking like she is considering whether Warner is worth any more trouble. Warner has his own trepidations. He will have to get up at four o'clock if he is to complete those last few economics problems before morning. He pushes that thought out of his mind. He kisses Pinky again. This time he is more tender, hoping Pinky realizes that, despite his half-hearted attempt to pay attention to her, he really does hope he can give her pleasure.

Colored Enough

A pleasant sprinkle of March rain hits Warner as he strolls the parking lot behind the economics department building on the campus of Cumberland College. His final midterm exam completed, he is looking forward to a weekend at the lake house owned by Minerva's parents. To his surprise, Minerva says she is also looking forward to the trip. It will be their chance to stop ignoring each other as they have been over the last few weeks.

The next day he is unbothered that the rain looks in no hurry to let up. At a quarter to five, as he unpacks items from an overnight bag, Deedra Cummings calls.

"The trustees have approved another way to honor Etienne," she says. "Instead of naming a lecture hall, we're going to plant a little tree grove. Isn't that awesome?"

"How many trees?"

"Two. Oak saplings, so they will grow mighty tall."

Warner shifts the phone to the other ear, continuing to listen but hearing nothing of interest. "Both of Etienne's biological parents were colored," he says. "You're the director of minority affairs. Shouldn't you be working hard to make sure the college does right by him? A couple of saplings? I don't believe that's an adequate honor."

"Well, when I told the vice-provost that Etienne has decided to identify as a colored man—"

"Decided?"

"Now, listen, young man. I admit I was not that fond of Etienne. But I am serious about my job of helping minority students."

"But you are doing a poor job."

Deedra's voice gets quieter. "Maybe you should have kept your mouth shut about your father being a colored man."

"That's odd talk coming from someone in your position."

"What do you mean?"

"I mean shouldn't you be encouraging white folks down here in Alabama to stop denying their heritage? Wouldn't that make your job easier? Maybe some of the so-called white trustees are colored. In any event, I may have to contact a lawyer."

"What good will that do?"

"I'll let you know after I talk to one. I've already got a lead on one with the NAACP."

"Calm down, young man. Remember, this is Alabama. I've been living here my whole life."

"So have I."

"But not as a colored person."

"One day the trustees want to honor my father," Warner says, "the next day they don't. The lawyer will at least make them explain the slight to my family. I'm sure Jocelyn will want that, too."

"Listen, Warner."

"Oh, so now you know my name?"

The line is quiet for a long while. When Deedra resumes, her voice has cooled, almost to a soothing whisper, as she tells Warner a few things about her experiences at the college. "I have been here a long time," she says. "Any lawyer you get will not be able to change what the white trustees of the college decide."

Warner hangs up, but it takes several hours before he starts to calm down. Why was he so angry, he wonders as he watches the evening news. Lying in bed later, he considers the tone in Deedra's voice. She has never sounded like that in his presence. There was a softness to her voice that now soothes his brain. Maybe she really is trying to help.

Despite what he has said on the phone, he does not yet know an NAACP lawyer. But the conversation with Deedra has reignited his desire to ask Gerrick for the name of the one helping Sibelus fight Platinum Paper. A lawyer could also help with any problems that come up after he has visited his great-grandmother Zera.

"Why do you need to talk to my lawyer?" Gerrick asks a few days later at the Kwik Mart.

Warner has come to the front corner of the building, where Gerrick is using the air pump to inflate a leaky tire on his Monte Carlo. "A distant relative is in some nasty trouble with the prison authorities in Mississippi," he says. "I figure the NAACP helps the down-and-out."

"They help the colored down-and-out."

Gerrick takes a business card out of his wallet. "You could call her," he says, handing the card to Warner. "But I doubt she'll help a white man."

Warner takes the card, surprised that one of the clerks has not said anything to Gerrick about him being colored. But then none of the clerks know Gerrick that well. He could tell him. Well, maybe at a later date.

C an we reverse the college's decision concerning your father's commemoration?" the lawyer from the NAACP says, when Warner calls. "Can we do that? Perhaps. Am I optimistic though? Not too much."

"But will you at least contact them to try?"

"Of course. I'll be happy to put in a call to the college."

Warner talks to the lawyer from a phone booth at the Plaza. Looking out through the murky glass windows, he feels uneasy about the people that pass on the covered sidewalk. They all seem lost in their own troubles.

"I guess it's premature to talk about my great-grandmother," Warner says. "Being that I haven't met her yet."

"That's correct," the lawyer says. "Moreover, whatever legal issues come up with your great-grandmother's incarceration are best handled by our sister office in Mississippi. I'll give you the telephone number."

The following week, inside a plain brick building several blocks from the central business district in Jackson, an elderly man with graying blond hair and blue eyes welcomes Warner. "Before you ask," the director of the NAACP office says, "yes, indeed, I am a colored man. Very nice to meet you, young man."

What kind of situation is this? Warner thinks, taking a seat in the office. Whatever it is, it is one he has never been in before. Why has the man just announced right off that he is colored? Is there some unspoken understanding among people like the two of them, men without the slightest features that anyone would consider colored? When did this man learn the news about himself? Has he known his entire life? All these questions flood Warner's mind.

The director seems eager to talk about Zera Platt. But when he does, all he offers is a long list of barriers to getting Warner's great-grandmother out of prison. The warm optimism that grew in Warner on the long four-hour drive from Montgomery cools with every word he hears. But he tells the director that he has no intention of giving up.

When the meeting ends, the director gives Warner a three-by-five card with the name of a lawyer in Jackson. Then the director shows Warner several faded mimeographed letters.

"Look here," the director says, pointing to a faint signature at the bottom of one letter. "Even the Reverend Doctor couldn't get Zera paroled."

From the NAACP offices, Warner takes a short drive to a house on Farish Street. On a brick patio at the rear of the house, the man who admits to being a relative of Zera Platt's does not look pleased that his wife has extended an invitation for Warner to visit.

Bald and heavy and sweating in a green apron that says KISS THE CHEF, Icarus Platt waits until the chicken thighs he is tending to on the charcoal grill are sizzling to his satisfaction before he picks up the letter Warner has placed on the small table near the grill.

"Every decade or so, some man or other wants to write a story about Zera," Icarus says, opening the folded letter. "And now you're here. What are you writing?"

"I'm not a reporter," Warner says. "I'm family."

"Why don't you visit her then?"

"I've tried," Warner says. "But the folks at the correctional facility won't approve my visitation request. The problem is that my father, Etienne, was adopted. That and the fact that he was born in Canada. The paper trail, you know?"

One of the newspaper articles Warner read on the microfiche machine in the college library said Icarus's eyebrows were cinnamon red. Today his brows are steely gray. The letter he holds is the one that Zera Platt wrote to her in-laws in Canada back in 1923, asking them to take in her son, Omar. Icarus holds the pages at arm's length, his chin jutted.

"I'm amazed at what calm words Zera wrote," Icarus says and places the letter back into the envelope, "especially knowing any minute she might have a rope thrown around her neck. She must have been quite a young gal."

"I imagine she still is quite a gal," Warner says.

"Her brother-in-law, Thomas Platt, was the closest relative I had up in Canada—he and Chevy Platt. There was a great-aunt up there, too, somewhere. They are all dead, of course. All the family I had heard talk of in Canada are dead. There is not a soul down here in Mississippi who knew Zera well."

Icarus's wife, Gussie, comes out of the back door. Her short, gray Afro is half hidden beneath a floppy hat. The features of Gussie's face suggest to Warner that she is colored. But as with her husband, her skin is as pale as Warner's. "I don't know why they keep putting my husband's name in the damn papers," she barked at him the first time he talked to her on the telephone. "Icarus has never had anything to do with Zera Platt and he never will." Warner is glad that he wore her down.

"Y'all go ahead and eat," Gussie says, placing a box of assorted doughnuts on the patio table. "Don't wait on us."

Gussie says she needs to pick up their grandson at tennis practice. Unlike the hard face she wears out here, in the living room she was cordial as she showed Warner magazine covers with pictures of their grandson. Last year, she said, he reached the quarterfinals of the US Open. At the table, Warner spoons potato salad from a plastic tub onto a plate, doubting that Gussie will return in time for him to meet the young man.

Warner bites into a chicken thigh, feeling the warm smoky juices coat his tongue. It has been a long haul from that first phone call to this meal. Minerva believes this visit will be another waste of time. She also says perhaps it is premature to talk about getting Zera paroled. Who said anything about getting Zera paroled? he reminded her. He just wants to visit the woman.

"I'm going to see a lawyer when I leave here," Warner tells Icarus, as they sit down at the table to eat. "He's going to help me get visitation rights to see Zera."

"Don't tell me you're trying to get her paroled."

"Everyone's been asking me that. I'll cross that bridge when I get to it."

"If you see her, you'll try to help her," Icarus says. "You wouldn't be the first person to fall into that rabbit hole. A whole mess of pro bono lawyers have tried to get that gal paroled. But Zera is still incarcerated. You get what you pay for, I reckon."

"Will you come with me to see her?"

"Gussie told me that was what you wanted."

"Don't you want to hear what Zera has to say?"

Icarus's lips tighten and his shoulders slump. "Me and Gussie will feed you, nephew," he says, pushing the platter of chicken closer to Warner. "But we don't want to hear any foolishness Zera might be talking."

A cross town, a secretary escorts Warner into a corner office on the tenth floor of a gleaming building in downtown Jackson. The lawyer he is here to see, Eldridge Littlejohn, stands at his desk with the telephone pressed to his ear. Eldridge nods and directs Warner to a seating area with two burgundy wing chairs and a cherry coffee table. Seated, Warner looks around at the walls, which hold framed replicas of gold records; NCAA championship plaques; and pictures of men posing in suits inside sports arenas, jazz clubs, and theaters. Eldridge Littlejohn is in every picture.

"Heard you've been poking around over at the prison," Eldridge says, after hanging up the phone. "Handling the paperwork over there for Zera will be my job from now on. Have you found me a family member here in Mississippi?"

"Well, I've told you about my uncle Icarus Platt and his wife, Gussie."

"Are they willing to talk to me?"

"Working on that."

Eldridge sits in the armchair facing Warner. He is as dark as Gerrick Gilroy but probably twenty pounds heavier. He has a fresh military haircut. "If we don't find a cooperative local family soon," he says, "I'll have to hand off the case to an associate."

"You said you were the lawyer to help."

"But I have to argue the benefit to the firm to keep me on the case pro bono."

"Getting Zera paroled will get your name in the newspaper," Warner says. "My uncle says you're always in the newspaper."

"Why didn't you bring your uncle?"

"His wife won't let him come." Warner glances at the crystal paperweight shaped like a football on the corner of Eldridge's desk. "My cousin is Byron Edgecomb."

"The tennis boy?"

Warner nods. "Though I don't imagine he wants this kind of publicity."

From a pocket of his double-breasted suit, Eldridge takes out a small notebook with a tiny pen attached. Several times as he and Warner talk, he chuckles to himself as he makes a note.

"We need the warm body of one Mississippi relative," Eldridge says later, shaking Warner's hand at the elevator. "I'll be in touch to talk about incentives to get your uncle on board."

On the long drive back to Alabama, Warner feels good about his recent accomplishments. Midterm grades will not be posted until the end of March. But he is certain he did well. And tomorrow, despite the nonsense Millicent has said about Udall not wanting to hire a colored fella, he will be offered the position of assistant manager at the Kwik Mart.

Still, his mind is heavy the next morning as he unlocks the back door to the store. This is the first morning he has arrived to work not planning a way to steal time at the counter to study. Instead he is thinking about Pinky. It was a mistake during the first months of the school term to believe that cramming for exams and taking trips to Mississippi would keep his mind off her. Walking the dim aisle of the Kwik Mart, he recalls how his chest swelled two nights ago, when he heard her approaching in her father's Ford on the gravel road behind Moffet ball field. He climbed into the Ford and the temperature seemed to rise twenty degrees as Pinky undid her blouse. He knew the risk. But by the time Pinky slid naked underneath him, his desire had grown well beyond his ability to resist.

Despite the lapse with Pinky, Warner feels he has made some effort to be a good husband, a good father. A few weeks ago, he skipped a class to take his daughter to the pediatrician. And last Saturday, after he fed Jennifer a small jar of creamed carrots, the two of them dozed for several hours on a blanket in the backyard.

At the counter later, Warner studies a page in his marketing text-book, determined to put Pinky out of his mind. But thoughts of Zera take her place. Every newspaper article he has read brings up new questions. As do the letters he shared with Icarus. He has read each letter several times. Yet he still does not know if Zera ever laid eyes on her son, Omar, after she sent him to Canada. And what will Zera think of him?

He is halfway through his second can of soda, but no sugar rush has arrived to boost his concentration. At the kitchen table last night he was also unable to keep his mind from thinking about the sex with Pinky. Before he knew it, midnight was on him. Minerva was snoring lightly when he climbed into bed. He placed a hand on her hip, and, to his surprise, she turned toward him. When he rubbed her back, she came in closer. After a few minutes of holding each other, they began to kiss.

The orgasm was even more intense than the one he'd had the pre-vious night with Pinky. This morning when he reached for Minerva again, she stroked his arm for a while and then slipped out of bed. But Pinky was there—at least the thought of her. It felt good to take off the briefs cramping his stiff penis. He pumped his hard penis for less than a minute before he spattered all over his stomach.

Warner's the one I'm promoting to supervisor," Udall tells the three clerks assembled in the back office. "Now this meeting's over, and I don't want to hear nothing more about that."

While the other two clerks leave the office looking none too happy, Warner remains behind, feeling a bit disappointed. He expected a better title.

Udall is wheezing as he closes the door. "Gerrick's outside on the phone again," he says, his face in a cloud of smoke as he lowers his seventy-year-old body into the desk chair. "That is some nerve, given how many days the boy's called in absent."

"His granddaddy is not doing well," Warner says.

"Oh, I am well aware of that," Udall says. "But I got a business to run. I got kids who'll do the stocking for half of what I'm paying Gerrick. Somebody's got to give Gerrick the news that we have to let him go."

"That's a job for somebody with a big title," Warner says. "Like assistant manager."

Udall puts out his nub of a cigarette in the ashtray and picks up his pouch of Prince Albert tobacco and rolling papers. "I made you a supervisor," he says as he starts to roll another cigarette. "I need to see how you do that job before promoting you higher."

"Gerrick's car is back in the shop."

"That piece of junk always is."

"He's put in a job application at the paper plant."

"Hell's liable to freeze over before them foreigners decide who they want to hire. From what I hear, even for one of them no-account, low-paying jobs Gerrick would be qualified for, hiring's going as slow as molasses."

Warner imagines his own job application stuck in a bucket of molasses. "Do you have to let him go right away?"

Udall chuckles. "Are the two of you buddies now?"

"I'm just saying it might be a nice gesture to keep him on until that piece-of-crap car of his is fixed."

After lighting his cigarette, Udall places two checks on the edge of the desk. "I believe there's enough here for Gerrick to get a start on fixing his vehicle."

Warner stands, without reaching for the checks. He looks down at the check with his name on it. He likes what he sees. Gerrick's check is for twice as much.

"If you don't want to tell Gerrick he's being let go," Udall says, "say so and I'll see if one of the other clerks wants the extra responsibility."

Warner picks up the checks and walks out. Back at the counter he wishes people would stop asking if he and Gerrick are buddies. He's not upset that Gerrick is being laid off. The boy has been absent a lot. But there are more decent ways to handle the task.

"If Udall don't have the money to keep paying me," Gerrick says later, "then how come he's paying his grandsons to come to the store and do nothing?"

"Search me," Warner says. "I'm just delivering the news."

Warner sets a carton of cigarettes on the counter next to Gerrick's check. Gerrick picks up the check, and at first Warner is afraid he is about to tear it in half. But he puts the check into his pocket. If the money has appeased him, he does not show it as he grabs the cigarettes off the counter and heads for the front door.

Two days later Millicent calls in sick, forcing Warner to work a double shift. The next day, Thaddeus, the other clerk, does the same. This need to work extra hours could not have come at a worse time for Warner. He is behind in his assignments and needs to begin studying for his final exams. Several days later, halfway through yet another double shift, he looks up from reading a handout from his behavioral science class to see one of the contractors coming through the front door.

"What're you gonna do with all the time off?" the contractor asks Warner at the counter.

"Udall's not giving us time off," Warner says.

"He'll have to," the man says. "For the renovations—the place will have to close for at least several months."

Warner spends the rest of the day barely able to contain his anger. He had believed Udall's story that he was only threatening to do renovations to be in a better bargaining position with Platinum Paper, to show he is not pressed to sell. But why didn't he mention that the store would have to close?

"Will there be any work for us during the months they're doing the renovations?" Warner asks Udall in the hallway the next day, even before Udall has unlocked the door to his office.

"If I can find some," Udall says. "And I'm going to try."

On Monday, Millicent calls in sick again, forcing Warner to work another double shift. On Wednesday, the contractor arrives with a note from Udall asking Warner to hand over his key to the back door. Driving off the lot, Warner sees two workers install a steel cage over the front windows of the store.

I wonder if Millicent was right, Warner considers on the drive home. Was he indeed colored enough for Udall—colored enough for Udall to have no intentions of keeping him on at the store? He starts to recall the Platinum Paper job application and the box in the section that asked about race, the box he left unchecked, but he pushes the thought out of his head. Is that how his mind will work now, always vexing about some situation involving his being colored?

He recalls the day he first heard the term *passing*. It was in his freshman sociology class. For several days afterward he would look around the room, trying to see if he could guess which of the other students was colored. It never occurred to him that the other students were doing that, too. Did any of them guess right about him?

This pleasant April afternoon, Minerva places a large bottle of ibuprofen on the checkout counter at the Rexall, thinking the headache she has had all morning is now jumbling her mind, causing her to see things that are not there. Through the front window, there is no mistaking the red-and-gold golf shirt she sees. It is one of the shirts she gave Warner last month as a pregraduation present. Could that be him way over there on the other covered walkway?

Minerva is certain that Warner told her that he had to drive like a madman after his class today to make his visitation meeting at the correctional facility in Mississippi. What is he doing here at the Plaza? And why is he standing so close to Pinky?

Minerva exits the Rexall noticing that Warner and Pinky have reached a green-and-white van parked next to the Photo Hut. Pinky's ponytail is swinging as she climbs into the van. After glancing around, Warner steps around the door and leans in. The flash from a passing station wagon interrupts Minerva's sight. But that was most certainly a kiss.

"That filthy bastard," Minerva says on the road home. "I'm going to put a real hurting on him." Thank goodness Jennifer is in the crib at her parents' house, she thinks, and not in the car with her now.

Later, back at the house, Minerva begins packing several suitcases. She will not be here when Warner gets home from Mississippi. Seeing him working hard to prepare his Wednesday night meal of runny corned-beef sandwiches or warming up another soggy apple pie from the upright freezer at the Kwik Mart might stop her from confronting him. Or worse, she might believe his lame story that what she saw was not a kiss.

Having dragged her suitcases to the car, Minerva sits at the kitchen table and goes through the mail. She first looks over the bank statement. When Warner suggested they ask her father, Clayton, for a line of credit to redo the floors, cabinets, and countertops, she thought, Why not? Now she wonders if it was a good idea.

Another bill from the lawyer? Minerva reads the front of the envelope, wondering about the several hundred dollars Warner took from their line of credit to settle the last bill. So what is this? She thought the lawyer was doing the work pro bono. Minerva rips open the envelope with a ballpoint pen, sorry that she did not confront Warner about the previous bill as soon as it arrived last month. But she had come into the bedroom with the bill to find him on the bed, studying hard. Before today, she believed that he missed none of his classes. Come to think of it, when she'd seen him with Pinky he was supposed to be still on campus. Had the scheming bastard lied about everything?

When Minerva was upset with Warner back in high school, she didn't bother to confront him to his face. She simply stopped taking his phone calls. A few weeks after one particular argument, when they were speaking again, she said she wasn't sure the two of them wanted the same things. Does Warner want the same things she does now? Minerva wonders, dropping the bill onto the table. She wants to buy another house. He seems content in this one. She dreams of living in the arid Southwest, like her cousin. He sounds as if he wants to move to Vermont. He admitted as much in a family counseling session several weeks ago at the church. When he said he had set aside his desire to move up north, his voice had the same earnestness it had a few weeks back, when he explained why he had given Pinky a ride home from the Lucky Lounge. It was a favor for Millicent, he said.

Her stomach a bit queasy, Minerva goes in search of the bag of items she purchased at the Plaza. Ibuprofen and antacids were not the only things Minerva had gone searching for at the Rexall. The checkout girl told Minerva the store didn't yet stock the new home pregnancy tests. This evening, however, Minerva does not need any confirmation. She is certain she is pregnant. Warner had taken a while to embrace the child they have. Despite wanting to see his face when he learns another baby is coming, she will not stick around for the experience.

Lucky Peace

Warner's great-grandmother Zera Platt did not believe in apparitions—at least not until she got to college.

In September of 1915, the year Zera Bradenburg began her first term at Payne-Oglethorpe in Jackson, Mississippi, her roommate dropped onto her bed in the dormitory room one evening, claiming that she had seen a strange woman leaning against the window in the dining hall. A month later, Ava-Marie Sessions—the richest and most popular girl at the school—said she had also seen the woman. With each passing week, more girls reported having seen her. During November, the woman was spotted on the stairs humming and eating a slice of peach-chester cake. During winter exams, she was seen on the lawn putting new laces in a pair of ice-skating boots. Later, someone said they had seen the woman in the choir room practicing the alto parts to the popular song "Two-Step Girlie."

Someone said the woman's name was Ruth, but by spring everyone agreed with Ava-Marie Sessions that the woman's name was Gertrice, that her singing voice was mezzo-soprano, that she wore nice hats but her jewelry wasn't ladylike, that she kept her own key to the powder room on the ground floor of Norwood Hall, that her curls fell down to her slender brown neck—and that Gertrice never carried a Bible but could recite Nehemiah 8 or Ephesians 4 almost as quickly as Reverend Graham.

When Zera went home to Sunflower and sat on the porch, listening to the creek that flowed down to the river, she knew better than to admit that she, too, believed she had seen Gertrice. Danger comes in the flesh for us women, her grandmother Althea had taught Zera. No need to worry about spirits. Althea had waited at the house years earlier with baby Zera while her son-in-law, Floyd, carried Zera's mother, Patience, in the wagon to find a doctor to stop the bleeding from childbirth. When Floyd returned in the afternoon, he carried the remains of Zera's mother in the wagon with a blanket laid over the body. That evening Althea sat next to the cooling board for hours, reading the Bible and talking to her daughter's lifeless body.

When Zera went off to college, Althea helped Floyd pay the cost for one of the better dormitory rooms and for nice shoes and undergarments. Zera's deceased mother had wanted to be a teacher, and if Zera wasn't going to be a teacher herself, the least she should do at Payne-Oglethorpe was concentrate on getting a good husband. When Zera came home from college, Althea wanted no talk about movie theaters with organ players in them or about fashionable ladies' scarves. And she certainly was not working two jobs so that Zera could waste her time discussing foolish things like a darkie walking the dormitory halls. What potential husband would put up with that kind of talk?

Zera didn't tell her suitor, Matthew Platt, about the apparition until her last year at Payne-Oglethorpe—and only after Matthew had invited her to the second spring dance. A month before the wedding, when Matthew told his parents Zera's story about the apparition, they didn't comment on it, mainly because anything they said about Matthew's choice of a bride seemed to lead to arguments. Matthew's mother, Adelle, thought Zera was the right color—light enough to pass—but Zera was from too small a town. Matthew's father, Stetson, who taught at the colored high school on Farish Street, where Zera had been a summer activities counselor, said the problem was that Zera had a mouth on her: strong opinions from a future wife were not something a Platt man was obligated to put up with.

"We told them to be careful, but did they listen?" Adelle Platt said to her husband after learning that Matthew and Zera had been arrested for mischief at the governor's houseboat. "Now look what happened."

The judge took less than an hour to decide the death sentence for both Zera and Matthew.

While Adelle and Stetson waited on the appeal of the death sentence, Adelle could hardly contain her anger at Zera. Why hadn't Zera corrected her lawyer when he told the judge that Matthew had talked Zera into going to the governor's boat? Heavens, no, Matthew had been a perfect child, dutiful with his music lessons, excellent at schoolwork, a little gentleman. Why hadn't they sent him to one of the more conservative schools in Tuskegee, Nashville, or Washington, DC? If they had, perhaps their son would not have met *her*.

Stetson Platt said he regretted not letting Matthew get aboard the steam train along with his uncles C. C., Tommy, and Chevy. At the time, he'd felt Matthew was too smart for digging coal. But what lapse of thinking compelled Matthew to join those crazies, the New Confederates, on a lark to vandalize the governor's houseboat? There had been a previous lapse that led to a shoplifting incident during his first year of college. But since then, Matthew had been a model son—until he met Zera.

The day after the governor commuted both death sentences, Adelle walked the three blocks down Farish Street and put the long key in the front door of Zera and Matthew's two-bedroom bungalow. The sleeve patches and written material from the New Confederates were thrown in the trash cans, but the rest of their belongings were distributed to the few relatives still speaking to Adelle and Stetson. With each item handed over, Adelle reiterated her opinion—Zera was the bad influence. How else to read the matter? Remember all that talk of apparitions? That nonsense should have been a big clue that Zera's head wasn't sitting right on her shoulders.

W arner drives off the rental car lot at the airport in Jackson, eager to finally meet the person who has for months been a near phantom for him, an image conjured up from letters and two short phone calls. Several hours later, in Unit 6-C at Peace Correctional Facility, seated on the green two-cushion sofa wearing a thin cotton dress is his great-grandmother—Zera Bradenburg Platt in the flesh.

Her silver hair is pulled back and held with a plastic hair clip. With her ankles crossed and tucked close to the sofa, she looks much younger than her ninety or so years. "I'm afraid I can only give you a few minutes," she says, "I'm old and tired, you know?"

"You don't look old and tired," Warner says, from the small kitchenette, where he dumps the bag of apples he has brought into a bowl on the Formica-top table. "You look good to me. You must be eating well."

"Too well, if you ask the governor."

Is she being serious? Warner wonders as he searches his book bag. Or is she just being as difficult today as she was on both phone calls they have had since Eldridge Littlejohn made the breakthrough that allowed them to meet?

The guard has completely disrupted the contents of the bag Warner packed before leaving the house this morning. Zera's copy of the legal engagement letter is here, but two other documents are missing. He probably should not have been short with the guard during the security search. But his nerves were still frayed from the argument he had with Minerva before he left the house. That woman has been quite irritable lately.

"I had some more papers for you to look at," Warner says, taking a document out of the bag. "But it looks like they've gone missing."

Zera uses a hand to smooth back a few errant strands of hair. "I don't accept the lawyer's phone calls," she says. "Is that why he keeps sending me papers?"

The coffee table holds two saucers next to a small bowl of cantaloupe cubes. Zera spoons a few cubes on a saucer. "I'd offer you a fork," she says, handing him the saucer of cantaloupe, "but all I have is plastic. The forks are so flimsy you may as well use your hands."

Warner picks up several cantaloupe cubes and drops them into his mouth. "You know I'm Omar's grandson," he says, chewing on the fruit.

"So you tell me."

"It's the truth. You know I'm married and that I have a daughter. Tell me something about you."

"Didn't you read about me in the papers?"

"I read somewhere that red and gold were your favorite colors. I thought of that this morning when I put on this shirt. See, it's red and gold."

"What else can I tell you?"

"When were you born?"

"Too long ago to remember."

"Where did you grow up?"

"Here in Peace Correctional."

"All right, then, I imagine you won't like this question, but I'll ask it anyway. Why did you go with the men to the governor's boat?"

"You expect a ninety-year-old woman to remember that far back?"

"You're not yet ninety. I'm only asking because I'd like to understand."

"You would understand if you were colored and lived in Mississippi when I grew up."

"I am colored."

Warner can see Zera's tight jaw slacken, and a few of the sharp lines around her gray eyes seem to melt into her pale skin. She's not as light as he is. If he had been asked to guess where she was from, he would have said Eastern Europe. He takes a photograph out of a small compartment of the book bag, thinking he needs to choose his humor carefully. Had Zera appreciated his joke about being colored? Or is she getting ready to tell him it is time for him to leave?

"My daughter, Jennifer, gets an odd rash on her neck," Warner says, handing the photograph to Zera. "You can almost see it here. Don't know what it is."

"Sunflower measles," Zera says. "My son Omar used to have outbreaks. Folks used to say it came from river water."

"Jennifer's a lake girl," Warner says. "And I don't remember my pop ever having a rash like that."

Zera leans over and touches a spot near Warner's elbow. Warner inspects his arm. "Well, what do you know?"

"The next time the child breaks out," Zera says, "tell your wife to put a warm damp rag on the baby's neck."

Warner takes out another set of papers. He does not believe that Zera agreed to see him simply because he is her great-grandson. If she had cared that much about her male heirs, she would have sent for Omar or made an attempt to contact her grandson, Etienne. Her feelings for her deceased husband are another matter. The stapled pages he holds are for Zera's cemetery plot. Eldridge Littlejohn says Zera is eager to sign them because she wants to be buried next to her husband, Matthew. Eldridge had the brilliant idea to tell her she had to sign them in Warner's presence. "Warner could contest the decision after your death," Eldridge told Zera, "and not put you next to Matthew. You do not want that." But if Zera is so eager to be near her deceased husband, Warner thinks, setting the papers on the coffee table, why then has she not mentioned him once?

"Did you know I'm the oldest resident of any correctional facility in America?" Zera says, accepting a ballpoint pen.

"Yes, ma'am. You told me that on the telephone. You didn't say too much else."

"On my seventy-fifth birthday, two reporters came to talk to me.

The colored gal was country-sounding, pretty without a stitch of powder on her face." Zera inspects the pen, as if she has never seen one like it. "I didn't answer a single one of the gal's questions, but she claimed I did. On the television that heifer stood right in front of the cameras all made up—Afro all puffed out, eyeliner, lipstick—and said she had a long conversation with me. Said I was doing well and that I said I was sorry. I told her no such thing." Zera shakes her head. "I guess I won't have to worry about any of that after they put me into the ground."

Warner is reaching for another cantaloupe cube when a knock at the door startles him. One of the friendly guards, no doubt. Still, Zera seems startled, too. After looking around the room, her eyes harden again. "Why do you keep at me?"

"I won't need to come here as often if you return the papers the lawyer mails to you. Will you agree to do that?"

"Depends on the papers."

"I mean the ones that's got your name on them."

Zera laughs and rises from the sofa. Her shoulders are pushed back, but her head is bowed as she leads Warner to the door.

"I'm going to try to get you released," Warner tells Zera after he has stepped outside onto the cement landing.

Zera points at the female guard nearby. "Did you hear that, Nadine?"

"I heard, Miss Zera," the guard says, scratching her chin with a long, painted fingernail. "I heard Eldridge Littlejohn's on the case. With that man working for you, something just might happen."

The women inmates in Peace Correctional rarely report seeing apparitions walking the halls. But that is not to say Peace is without other oddities. In the dining hall, an inmate never places her spoon on the table before placing the plate. Inmates never fight following a day when it rains while the sun is still out. And never, under any circumstances, does a woman at Peace sign the first set of papers presented to her by a lawyer.

Over the years, Zera has come to believe she had a good lawyer during her trial. The trouble was that the judge barely listened to him. But the judge seemed enrapt by the prosecutor who argued that Zera had in fact pushed the man who drowned in the lake off the pier. Ridiculous, Zera tells herself, carrying the papers Warner left to the chest of drawers near her bed. She was not even on the pier when the man fell off and drowned.

Inmates also say that even if a sibling or a parent has ratted you out to the authorities, you should never place a family photograph facedown in a drawer. Putting the papers in the top drawer, Zera recalls that the photograph of Warner's daughter, Jennifer, is somewhere in the drawer. She remembers putting it there but has no idea of how the photograph lies. When she put the photograph of her great-great-granddaughter in the drawer, she was distracted, trying to recall the last time she held a baby girl. While she was pregnant, she'd been certain she was carrying a girl. Throughout the long nine months she dreamed of bringing a girl into the world. When the midwife presented her newborn, she almost spoke the name she had selected: Patience Althea Platt.

But the child was a boy.

Zera has no pictures of Omar as a baby. But she had a few photographs of him as a young man. The photographs came to her in the short letter from Halifax, written by the wife of Chevy Platt. Zera had them in her possession for barely a day before a former cellmate scratched Omar's face on both photographs. For years, she would stare at the pictures and reconstruct the face of her son. There were times when she wanted to tell him to come see her. But she knew that was foolish. His life was better where he was.

Zera's maternal relatives were scattered around the South, living nowhere she could find them. And though her father never liked his wife's family, during the trial Zera wrote to those relatives anyway, asking if any were willing to look after her son. The only letter she got back was from her cousin Naomi, who lived in Arkansas. *I wish I had a better answer,* Naomi wrote, *but we don't have room to take in Omar.*

That was when she reconsidered the Platts. She knew it was useless to ask any of the Platts in Mississippi to care for Omar, and after getting no answer to her letter to Matthew's relatives in Trinidad, she wrote to Canada.

Zera appreciated the letters Chevy Platt and his wife wrote from Canada, saying Omar had graduated from the Adventist school, and later that he had been accepted at Fundy Technical School. She had done the right thing sending her son up to Canada. She never kept any of the letters he wrote to her, nor did she reply. Years later, when another letter arrived at Peace from Chevy Platt, Zera opened it near the mail pickup, intending to toss it into the aluminum trash barrel when she was done reading. But after she scanned the first few paragraphs, a word caused her to hesitate—*accident?* He drove a truck into a building in Halifax? How had that happened?

Confused, she studied the postmark. Was this old news she had read about in another letter? In the hallway, she leaned against a wall and read the perplexing sentence again. When it finally made sense, she almost fell to the floor.

Zera walked back to her quarters thinking of all the letters her grandmother Althea said she wished she had been able to read. But letters carry bad news, too. In her quarters, Zera searched for something that had once belonged to her son. There were only the photographs. She held them in bed that evening, trying to remember the last hug she had given her son. She told herself she was not disappointed at not having a daughter. She really had wanted Omar.

Now Zera has a new baby picture. She wants some new thoughts to add to those about Omar and Etienne and Warner. Thinking about all these fathers and sons hurts her brain. Warner seems nice enough. Something about him may even have broken through the iron cage around her heart.

But Zera doesn't know Warner well enough yet to want to get close to him. Oddly, she feels she might have gotten along better with Warner's father. She never met Etienne, but she has little trouble believing he was her flesh. Warner told her Etienne hid the fact that he had relatives in the colored community in Canada. And what Warner had not said was that Etienne had also not visited his grandmother. Zera had no trouble with that. Etienne was sensible, like her. Etienne didn't see the world as he wished it to be, as Warner and Omar and even Matthew had. Etienne saw the world the way it was.

Heat wafting out through the back door of the house hits Warner in the face even before he has stepped through to the kitchen. After a cool shower, he finds a note taped to the refrigerator door.

Minerva has gone to her parents? Why?

"Minerva was here," Pat says when Warner calls his in-laws' house. "She's gone up to the cabin. She said she needed a few days to herself."

This is becoming a habit, Warner thinks, hanging up the phone. In the living room he tries to watch television but cannot concentrate. Just before ten, he climbs into bed, suspecting that he and Minerva need to have another talk. What he will say, however, he does not know.

A few days later, Warner sees Minerva's car parked in the driveway at Pat and Clayton's house. When he calls the house, though, Minerva refuses to come to the phone. The next afternoon, while Minerva is at work, he rings the doorbell at her parents' house.

"I'd like to let you in to see the baby," Pat says, leaving Warner standing on the front porch. "But Minerva would knock me into next week."

"She doesn't need to act like this," Warner says. "We're still married."

Pat pushes the screen door further open, looking out at Warner like he's a stranger. "Does Pinky know that?"

A few days later, after Pat tells Minerva that Warner has been by the house again, Minerva purses her lips and says, "I'm not surprised. The crazy fool called my job. To shut him up I agreed he could come see Jennifer."

"He didn't ask to see Jennifer," Pat says.

"Why did he come then?"

"He was after some boxes he says you took when you were over at the house."

"I'll give everything back," Minerva says. "It's all junk. Why would I want any of it?"

The box that Warner wants to reclaim sits in the garage at his in-laws' house. The next afternoon, Minerva lifts the flaps on the box, feeling numb, not unlike how she felt when she drove off after seeing Warner with Pinky. The box contains items that Warner has been collecting from his trips to Halifax and Mississippi. She looks at a few things and then closes the flaps. She does not want to see anything Warner has deemed suitable to collect.

But she does not deliver the box to Warner that day or the next. A few days later, she examines the contents more closely. Inside are two small boxes, one marked PELETIER and the other marked SEBOLT. A large manila envelope marked MISSISSIPPI is filled with copies of newspaper articles about Zera Platt. Minerva tries to read one of the letters sent to Etienne from one of his relatives in Montreal, but her French is too rusty. She puts the letter back and takes out a few more items. She has never seen the swimming medals, the pictures of Kath and Timothee in Italy, or the yellowed announcement of Kath's memorial service in Halifax. Where did Warner learn to be this organized?

Sliding back the top of the marbled wooden candle box, Minerva half expects some little genie to jump out and tell her another story of her husband's infidelity. She closes the top, reminded again of why she moved out. Yes, she was angry about the affair with Pinky. But there was more. Right or wrong, she had concluded that Warner isn't that interested in their family.

A noisy truck comes by on the road in front of the house. It's one of the sanitation trucks now operating in Woodhaven. Minerva arrives at the window only in time to see the rear of the truck as it races away.

Clayton says the truck will return a little later. She carries the box of mementos outside to the side of the road, agreeing with her father that Woodhaven is better than that colored town in Nova Scotia. At the road Minerva places the box near the garbage cans. Those pathetic bluff people probably never had this kind of garbage service.

These latest decisions about her marriage have come on so quickly, Minerva has hardly had time to think. From the window, she watches a sanitation worker peek inside the box before tossing it into the garbage truck. As the truck rumbles up the road, Minerva has no misgivings about what she's done. Warner seems to care more about those papers from Halifax and his trips to Mississippi than he does about his wife and daughter.

With all the work Warner has had to do writing papers and cramming for final examinations, he has not had time to fret about the box of mementos Minerva took by mistake from the house. Several days before graduation, when he listens to the telephone message from his mother-in-law, saying she inadvertently threw out the box with the trash, it takes him a moment to figure out what box she means. When he does, the news hits him like a train wreck.

That's bullshit, Warner thinks, stopping the message before Pat has finished her long, rambling apology. Pat did not throw out that box. Minerva is the petty cunt who threw out his belongings.

Warner waits until several days after his last final exam to call his in-laws' house again. "She's coming," Pat says, returning to the phone after leaving Warner waiting for at least a minute.

"About time," Warner says.

"I agree she shouldn't have thrown away your things," Pat says. "But you ought to go easy on her. You know she's pregnant."

The receiver nearly slips out of Warner's hand as he hangs it up. In what seems to be barely a minute later, he arrives at his in-laws' house, shocked that the Camaro did not get pulled over on the highway by a county sheriff for speeding. Without knocking, he pushes the front door open and enters.

Neither Pat nor Clayton is home. The house is quiet.

"Just a minute," Minerva calls from the back.

Warner settles on the sofa, realizing he has driven here having no idea what he will say. Minerva's pumpkin-colored hair is fixed in a single long braid. Watching her enter the living room, he realizes that the casualness in her walk suggests that Pat has not told her that he knows she has thrown away his mementos.

"I suppose you're here to see the baby," she says, handing Warner a beer. "She'll wake up from her nap pretty soon." Minerva sits down cross-legged on the other edge of the sofa. "I heard you've been up in Vermont."

"Who told you that?"

"Randy. I guess this means you'll be able to vacate the house by the end of the month, like you said you would."

Warner snaps open the beer can. "I didn't come here to talk about me moving up to Vermont. I came here to talk about the news I got from Pat."

Minerva shifts on the sofa. "I'm sorry I threw away the box."

"Not as sorry as I am."

Quiet prevails in the living room for long moments. There have been similar chilly pauses during past arguments, but the two of them have now entered new territory. He wants to rail at her for throwing away his things. She knew what they meant to him. Warner takes a sip of beer, glancing at Minerva, who is staring at her feet. His sorrow is not something she cares about right now. Pointing out that she has hurt him by throwing out his family mementos is not something he can use against her now—especially if she is thinking about Pinky.

"Pat told me you're pregnant," Warner says. "Is that true?"

Now Minerva looks uncomfortable. "I don't think the news changes much. Do you?"

Warner dislikes the taste of beer from a can. Still, to cool the flush of heat coming off his chest and neck, he takes a long drink. "Have you been wanting another child?" he asks.

"Have you?"

"I asked you first."

"I know, but I always go first in situations like this."

A Betrayal

A few weeks later, when Warner arrives at Pat and Clayton's house to drop off Jennifer, he finds a note taped to the door.

Taking Minerva to the hospital. —Pat

Probably nothing that serious, Warner thinks, returning to the car. By the time he gets home there will no doubt be a telephone message from Pat saying everything is fine. Before turning the ignition, he reaches into the back and touches Jennifer, still asleep in her car seat. If he leaves now, he could get to the prison before visiting hours end and still deliver his daughter back here. But there will be hell to pay if he takes Jennifer to Mississippi.

"She's a little shook up about the stomach cramps," Pat says when she calls at a few minutes before four o'clock. "The doctor wants to keep her at the hospital to monitor her for the rest of the evening."

"Is there a chance she might lose the baby?"

"Oh, I'd rather not talk like that," Pat says. "Let's keep things positive."

But several days later, near the end of another visit to Peace Correctional, Warner is barely able to keep his voice steady as he delivers the bad news to his great-grandmother: the baby has died.

"I am sorry to hear that," Zera says. "No mother wants to lose a child."

Zera has little to say as Warner tells her how much he feels the loss. "I wanted another child," he says. "And the reason was not just so Minerva and I could get back together."

After Warner leaves, Zera wishes she could have found more soothing words to say to him. Her recollection of the gloom she heard in his voice keeps her awake the entire night. By morning the bad news feels even more personal. Her own blood has died in a hospital room in Alabama. In the cafeteria she has no appetite for any of the breakfast dishes warming on the steam trays. She picks at her scrambled eggs and grits near a group of young women, alert to every word said about their children. For a moment she considers walking over to the bank of phones in the hallway to put in a call to Warner. But what would she say? Would she ask Warner to tell Minerva that his great-grandmother is very disturbed by the news about her lost baby? How would that be a comfort? Minerva does not know her.

For years Zera hated the fact that her birth had led to the death of her mother, Patience. It was not a stretch to believe that her life had also led to the death of her son, Omar. Yet during all the years of being incarcerated, most days Zera has been glad to be alive. What she wishes she had said to Warner yesterday was that he and Minerva should be glad to be alive, too. The two of them are lucky to have a child who continues to breathe on this earth.

Perhaps during one of Warner's visits she will admit that she would be happy if he brought Jennifer to see her. After he left yesterday, she wondered why he had waited until it was time to leave to give her the news. Did he think it might upset her feeble constitution?

Zera wishes she didn't feel so strongly about the fact that her great-grandson has lost a baby. Each day that passes she feels worse. The few women to whom she confides her sadness say they sympathize. But two or three others tell her to take it on the chin and shut up about it. "Shit happens," one of the inmates says. "Be glad that you are alive."

"That is such a sad way to live in the world," Zera tells her friend Davida in the recreation and education annex, where the two are sorting through fabric odds and ends. "Some of the women in here have hearts as hard as lump coal."

Davida is several years younger than Zera, and her eyesight is better, so she digs through the old army duffel bag for remnants that might suit today's project: either pincushions or pot holders. "You ought to know better than to talk about that with some of these women," Davida says, holding up a checkered pillowcase. "It will just get you upset."

"I suppose."

"Besides, you're not that close to your family."

"Don't mean I don't care about my great-great-grandchild."

"Making yourself sick about it won't help though."

Zera looks at the blouse Davida has pulled from the bag. Her cousin Naomi wore a dress in a similar gaudy maroon to Zera's wedding. Though she never said another word to Naomi after the gal refused to take in Omar, some days she misses her cousin. Death will do that to family.

"That's one thing about Peace I have never liked," Zera says. "After many years, there is always somebody who will never accept their own humanity."

Davida begins picking up the remnants on the floor. "Did you eat too many fried eggs for breakfast?" she asks, stuffing the castoffs into the pillowcase. "You know eggs make you philosophical."

Zera lets out a laugh. Davida is right about one thing. She should not have eaten that third fried egg. Her stomach is tight now. But in

Peace, how many times a year does a woman get to taste a runny yolk? Zera is about to say the maroon blouse would make a nice Halloween design when she notices Davida's head leaning back.

Hearing a light snoring, Zera wonders whether she should let Davida get in a short nap. But Davida had returned recently from a two-week hospital stay. And it's anybody's guess whether the stay was for Davida to rest while doctors monitored a mild seizure or to recover from being accosted by another inmate. Davida wouldn't say. And now she might be ill again.

Zera goes into the hallway and turns to head for the infirmary. Hurrying to get the medic, she hopes all her complaining did not worsen whatever is ailing Davida. Knowing Davida Coleman has been one of the few pleasures Zera has had in Peace Correctional. She met her the year the annex began offering cosmetology classes. Zera was inhaling the smell of plum-scented pressing oil when she turned the corner and bumped into her. Zera tried to step back, but Davida took hold of her blouse. "Why don't you come to the beauty class tomorrow?" Davida said, her hair smelling fragrant. "The teachers will show you how to put some color in that gray on your head."

Zera never attended any cosmetology classes, but she got to know Davida when the two of them were assigned to latrine detail. Zera liked her, even if sometimes when they parted Davida held her a bit longer than Zera thought was decent. Davida had also attended a college, and the two of them laughed about having to march to class or to Bible study in pairs and threes. Over the years, sometimes Davida slipped notes into Zera's pockets, saying their friendship meant more to her than life itself.

Zera's chest feels heavy as she watches the medic push Davida down the hallway in a wheelchair. Davida has a strong body. How else had she been able to endure the years of whippings at the hands of her husband? If the verdict is to be believed, Davida fed her husband a poison-laced gumbo that froze his heart and lungs. Living in

peace is better than wasting away on a decaying, used-to-be planta-
tion, Davida has said more than once.

Zera rips up a few shirts, wondering if the rumor is true that the
black-and-blue marks she's seen on Davida's arms and shoulders are
the work of the ladies Zera has seen following her to and from the cafeteria and the rec room. Complaints Davida has made to the guards
have proved useless.

Zera long ago stopped wanting revenge on her cousin Naomi for
refusing to take in her son. And when was the last time she woke up
angry with the men who told lies about her at her trial? Still, it is a
mystery to her how Davida, a woman with plenty of reasons to dislike
her dead husband, can still preach restraint when it comes to saying bad things about the man's evil brother. Everybody knows that
her brother-in-law—an inmate named Brapper Coleman in the men's
facility—is behind some of the trouble the other female inmates have
caused Davida.

The next day, after Davida loses her footing in a stairwell, she is
rushed by ambulance to the hospital. In the rec room Zera sits doing
nothing, certain that the woman who pushed Davida down the stairs
did so on the word of Brapper Coleman. Angry about that, her first
thought is to ask a guard, Chester Olms, to bribe one of the cooks
in the men's facility to put roach poison in Brapper's oatmeal—just
enough to tear up his stomach for a few days. On the walk from the
cafeteria this afternoon, Zera waves at Chester. He's at the exercise
yard, watching several young women play tetherball. Zera has known
Chester for nearly twenty years. Many times over the years she has
handed him a pocketbook or wallet left in the bathroom by an absent-
minded visitor. The last time they rummaged through a nice purse
together, Zera wanted the expensive lipstick. All Chester let her take
were two emery boards and a packet of breath mints.

· Despite her years of knowing Chester, to trust a white man in a plot
to harm another white man on the say-so of a colored woman could be

tricky, even in Peace. Better to wait until Randell Payton comes back from vacation.

*D*o me a solid. *Do me a solid.* Randell Payton used to say that often when he was a rookie guard, wanting a favor from the more experienced staff. Often the solid Randell asked for was a violation of a department of corrections rule or two. Near the exercise yard now, having no compunction about asking for her own outrageous solid, Zera approaches Randell, who sits atop a picnic table.

Before Zera speaks, Randell checks to make sure the two-way radio strapped to his belt is turned off. He is thirty-nine now and has been in correctional work as long as Mrs. Gobe, the deputy warden for women. Like her, lately he is always bragging about retirement. As he listens, Randell moves his hand to the radio several times, causing the dull gold chain on his thick wrist to shift. Word is, he once broke an inmate's neck with pressure from that wrist.

"Rough up Brapper Coleman before the warden's concert?" Randell says. "Any guard foolish enough to do that has to have marbles for brains."

"Rough him up after the concert then," Zera says. "And could you kill him?"

"Come on, now, Miss Zera."

"Then break a rib or something."

"That I can do."

"I'd be grateful. And be sure to tell him why."

"Not wise," Randell says. "Might get back to you."

Zera nods, studying the laces in his heavy boots. "Well then, tell Brapper some of the women in Peace hate his voice."

"That'll work."

Randell looks down to check the radio again, the muscles in his thick neck bunching. "Was that a new color television I saw in your room, Miss Zera?"

"My great-grandson sent me that," Zera says. "Don't work worth a damn."

"Fill out a W-5, and I'll come take it off your hands."

Randell pushes off from the table and lands on his large feet. Zera holds her breath, hoping he doesn't ask for her record player. The player would be a small loss, but she does not want to give up the stack of classical records she's been collecting for thirty years. Randell seems to be looking in the direction of the motor pool. Last month, a female inmate keeping time with a guard had a baby behind one of the minibuses. By the time Randell got there, the young woman and the baby were being carried off to the hospital. Zera suspects she may never hear what became of mother or baby. That's how things happen in Peace.

Several days later, Zera is summoned to the office of the deputy warden for women.

"Sit down, Zera," Mrs. Gobe says from behind the large oak desk where she sits signing papers.

"I'd rather stand, ma'am, if you don't mind."

Mrs. Gobe, looking thin and underfed, signs another document from the hefty stack resting on the leather desk pad. Zera had pushed the heavy oak door open, certain she was being summoned to hear bad news about Davida. The guard doesn't wear a heavy face. Still, you never know.

Organizations that pushed for years to retry and secure death sentences for former members of the New Confederates—the activist group Zera had joined and whose members were now scattered in prisons around the state—were elated when Sherry Gobe was hired. With skin even thinner than her predecessor's, Mrs. Gobe often complained that the head warden, a do-gooder from Biloxi, was responsible for allowing inmates like Zera to have apartments. Mrs. Gobe allowed the women to do quilting. But the women had to rip the cloth with their hands and teeth—no scissors. And to check out a needle, you had to fill out three forms at the armory. At least Mrs. Gobe no longer orders those beatings behind the mechanic's shed. Mrs. Gobe even plays nice—sometimes.

"I need somebody to clean Davida's room," Mrs. Gobe says, picking up a sweating can of cola.

"She can do it herself when she gets back, can't she?" Zera says.

Watching Mrs. Gobe's mouth tense as her lips clench the straw, Zera feels her shoulders stiffen. She waits for more details. When none come, Zera leans against the chair. "Usually the guards clear out the cells," she says, "when an inmate will not be returning."

Zera added the last statement hoping she has misinterpreted Mrs. Gobe's comment. She waits for her to say that Davida is simply being moved to quarters closer to the infirmary. But all the woman does is take another sip from the can of cola. What is she, sixty now? Another two years will make twenty years in corrections. Retirement time.

When Mrs. Gobe first took this job, she stated publicly that she thought Zera should have been hanged. Today she knows the bad news she is hinting at about Davida must eat at Zera. Over the years, the deputy warden has made tactical adjustments to her punishment arsenal. Her blows are no longer physical, but sometimes they hurt twice as much.

D avida's quarters are much smaller than Zera's, just a room. Zera arrives to find that the guards have already combed the place. Nothing has been put back neatly the way Davida would have done. Framed pictures of Davida's daughters and her grandchildren are tossed in a cardboard box.

"Don't bother to wrap anything," the guard tells Zera from the door. "Just get everything packed."

Zera waits until all the other personal items are in boxes before opening a drawer in the cardboard chest of drawers. Years ago, a young woman in C-Unit started the rumor that Davida had been keeping a diary, scribbling bits from Zera's life for the deputy warden to pass on to the parole board. When Davida denied that she was the snitch, Zera believed her.

Zera opens the first drawer and tries to recall what personal information she has divulged to Davida. It's been too many years to remember everything. Probably she had shown Davida one or two of the letters she helped other inmates write to their congressmen. Had she told Davida about the man she stole away from her cousin Naomi? Had she mentioned the butcher knife she once hid in her mattress? Had she told Davida the names of the two young men who had been on the houseboat with the others but who had not been arrested? Had she admitted to Davida that it was she, not Matthew, who suggested to the other New Confederates that they throw paint on the governor's boat and that they leave a dead lamb on the dock? Surely she told Davida that she had testified truthfully when she said she didn't know a bomb had been left on the boat. She learned about that only at the trial.

The bottom drawer is full of small spiral notebooks. Zera opens the one dated 1979—the first year women were allowed to handle threading needles. Some pages cover a day, some a whole month. Early that year, she and Davida worked for a full month on a quilt now pictured on a line of postcards that are still sold in several Mississippi museums. Odd, there does not seem to be anything written about the quilt in the notebook entries for January, February, or March.

The notes written in the margins of some pages are definitely in the ink of the deputy warden's fountain pen. Several notes say NICE WORK. Having found a page with her name written on it, Zera sits down on the bed to read.

A while later, Zera is reading her fifth notebook. The guard enters and yanks it from her hands. "Whatcha waiting on, gal, Christmas?" the guard says, tossing the notebook into the box. "Git a move on."

For the next few days, Zera wakes every morning wishing she had not read those notebooks. She has had some mean thoughts about Davida over the years. But she has never written them down. Could those words have been what Davida thought of her? That she was selfish, cow-headed, stupid? What hurt the most was reading that Davida considered her a sad Ruthbeth.

No way does Zera think she is that elderly woman from the Testaments who drank water at the desert cistern, unconcerned that the flesh of her malnourished children, grandchildren, and great-grandchildren was being picked at by vultures. It's bad enough that Davida had twisted her words to get in good with the deputy warden. But are those other nasty entries really what Davida thought of her?

Zera is thankful she did not show Davida the most recent letters Warner wrote from Vermont. How distasteful it would be to read those letters again if that woman's arthritic fingertips had tainted the pages. Instead, the letters are a comfort today, especially the pictures Warner sent in his last one. Zera had asked for the pictures. That means she cares about something, doesn't it? That means she is no Ruthbeth.

The note on the back of one old picture says the young woman standing beside Omar at some outdoor event in Halifax is Kath Ella Sebolt. Warner says this is his grandmother. Zera has heard of her but has never seen a picture of her before. The bracelet on Kath Ella's wrist in another picture is the reason Zera keeps returning to the letter. This morning in the prison chapel, using the lighted magnifying screen that swivels over the large Bible, Zera examines the picture further. That has to be the herringbone bracelet she gave Omar. Chevy Platt must have given that to the young woman after Omar died.

Flipping pages in the Bible, Zera can feel the years unravel in her head like thread from a faded spool. What was the Bible verse she quoted there in jail after telling her son to take the bracelet with him to Canada? What a fool she is, thinking she might remember that. And what a fool she has been these years for refusing to see a resemblance between Omar and Warner. As a mother she ought to have seen the likeness. But her son was barely six years old the last time she saw him in person. And when had she ever seen a picture of Omar as a young man? If she is starting to believe that Warner is her flesh, what is she starting to feel about his daughter, Jennifer? There are feelings other than revenge buried there, somewhere. She loves her babies. All of them. She is no Ruthbeth.

O ver the next few days, Zera wakes up some mornings barely able to contain her anger at Davida. Several weeks later, calling again to see Mrs. Gobe, she arrives at the office, missing her friend badly.

"Did you have anything to do with Brapper Coleman getting his head bashed at the motor pool, Zera?"

When offered a seat this time, Zera drops down into the hard chair. "Why would I know anything about that, ma'am?"

"I heard Randell Payton had a television in the trunk of his car the other day when he left the grounds," Mrs. Gobe says. "One that belonged to you. Now why would you give Randell a brand-new television?"

"Thing wasn't working."

"Don't play with me, Zera. Not today."

Zera rubs her hair back with her hands. No use trying to look more presentable though. She hasn't washed her hair regularly since Davida left the compound. She heard about the scuffle between Randell and Brapper in the motor pool lot. Word was, Brapper nearly got the best of Randell before slipping and busting his head against a truck bumper. If Randell is as smart as she thinks he is, he has already sold the television. It will be a stretch to connect her with the fracas.

"I'm going to ask you again, Zera. Did you put Randell up to that devilment?"

"No, ma'am."

"What if I told you Randell said you did?"

"Man in the big house makes guards and inmates say what he wants them to."

"Why must you women insist on continuing this nonsense about some big house?" Mrs. Gobe says. "There is no big house. There is only me."

"And the head warden."

Mrs. Gobe pushes roughly back from the desk and stands. Years ago, terror would shake Zera's body when that fiery auburn-haired woman made the trip around the desk. Something else frightens Zera now. The gray-headed Mrs. Gobe sits in the vacant chair next to her. With her arms crossed, Zera glances at the guard. She's a pretty young blonde—too junior to suspect the warden is probably lying about what Randell has confessed.

"Your hotshot lawyer has gotten your parole request moved to the governor's desk," Mrs. Gobe says, pinching the pleats in her skirt. "Did you know that?"

"Been there before."

"If Randell is telling the truth, that lawyer's work will come to nothing. And you will lose some privileges. Do you want to lose your nice living unit?"

"Thank you for your concern."

"Do you want to die in here, Zera?"

The tart smell of dry-cleaning chemicals wafts off Mrs. Gobe's blouse. Zera's silence seems to irritate her. What Zera wants to do is chuckle. Too many administrators have asked her that question. She knows the deputy warden would like nothing better than for her to die in prison. Then again, Mrs. Gobe seems different today. Might have something to do with the story circulating that the girl inmate and the newborn from the motor pool both died at the hospital. Another inmate told Zera that Mrs. Gobe cried on hearing the news. Now that would be a first.

One thing that has come out of all this talk of Randell and Brapper is that Zera believes there needs to be less talk of fathers and sons. Thank goodness she has turned her mind instead to Kath Ella and Minerva. And she has done a deed to show her fondness for her great-great-granddaughter Jennifer—and for another mother and daughter, Davida. She herself, the warden, the guard—every single prisoner in this facility is a daughter. What about them?

"I used to fear dying in here," Zera says. "Not anymore."

Saplings for Jennifer

Because he did not want to deliver the bad news over the telephone, Warner had waited until he picked up his mother at the Montgomery airport to tell her that Minerva had lost the baby. At the time he thought it was a good idea to wait until she flew down for his graduation. But now, the day before graduation, at the tree-planting ceremony on the quad, it is obvious that the news has saddened Jocelyn, who is still struggling with what she considers an insult to Etienne.

After the saplings are planted and the speeches are done, Minerva's parents take Warner to a gathering at their house, while Jocelyn remains behind to voice her disapproval directly to the vice-provost.

Fuming at the vice-provost seems to have improved his mother's mood, Warner thinks later, when Jocelyn comes through the front door of Pat and Clayton's home. She wears her first smile since he picked her up at the airport. With her sunglasses sitting rakishly on the top of her head, Jocelyn surveys the living room as if amused by how it is decorated.

Warner hoped Jocelyn's entrance would shut up Steve, a loudmouth who is married to Minerva's sister. But as Jocelyn says her hellos, Steve ups the volume as he continues boasting to Clayton about all the time-shares he's sold since Easter. In a side chair, sipping Scotch, Clayton nods agreeably to every point Steve makes.

"But you're not selling anything real," Warner tells Steve.

"It's as real as what you're selling at the Kwik Mart," Steve says. "By the way, the Kwik Mart used to be owned by someone living right here in Woodhaven. But now Udall's gone and sold the business to the paper company."

"That's not true," Warner says. "He hasn't sold the store."

"Not yet," Steve says. "If the newspaper is correct, production at the plant will require lots of men. What kind of job you putting in for, Warner? Machine operator? Cooker?"

"Anybody can cook pulp," Warner says. "I'm after one of the manager jobs."

"I believe you'd need an MBA to get into management at a foreign company," Steve says. "Although I myself would never work for a foreign firm."

"Platinum Paper will be hiring American workers to pulp American trees," Warner says. "And the firm's money ain't foreign."

Minerva's mother, Pat, enters carrying a platter of salmon mini-croquettes. When she's not delivering news at the television station, Pat wears little makeup. The platter she carries rests on a thick mitten covering the prosthetic hand she's had since a car accident a decade ago.

Warner puts a dollop of sour cream on a croquette, waiting for Steve to begin performing for his mother-in-law also. Before asking permission to marry their daughter Evelyn, Steve opened a checking account at the bank branch Clayton manages at the Plaza. Warner didn't open an account at Clayton's bank until several months ago. Steve's account comes with all sorts of bells and whistles. The account Clayton opened for Warner has monthly fees and earns half the interest, with no overdraft protection.

When Jennifer starts to cry, Jocelyn carries her around the room humming. "A few of Etienne's relatives from Canada came down to Vermont for Etienne's burial," she tells Clayton, when she sits again with the quiet baby. "Did Warner tell you that?"

"Probably," Clayton says.

"I learned a little more about Etienne's mother," Jocelyn says. "I don't know how in heaven she managed in Montreal. She probably didn't speak French well, I mean, being from Halifax."

"Probably spoke little good English either," Clayton says.

"Not true," Jocelyn says. "She graduated college. And tomorrow her grandson Warner will, too."

Instead of smiling like the others in the room, Clayton picks up his drink. "I heard said the town Warner's grandmother grew up in isn't there anymore."

"It was called something really quaint," Jocelyn says. "What was it, Warner, Africatown?"

"Don't sound too quaint to me," Clayton says.

"Well, it wasn't exactly that," Jocelyn says. "Whatever the name, I imagine it was a small town like Woodhaven."

"You can't compare that place to Woodhaven," Clayton says.

Steve returns to the sofa with another beer. "From what Minerva told us," he says, "Warner's folks living up there in Halifax were mostly squatters."

"I didn't say that exactly," Minerva answers, her voice rising. "Why do you say that, Steve?"

"It's what I remember you saying," Steve replies.

"Folks up there didn't have things nearly as good as we've got here in Woodhaven," Clayton says. "Why, Woodhaven's practically incorporated."

"Africaville was just people trying to make a living," Minerva says.

Clayton turns to Jocelyn and points off in the direction of the black-top. "If you want to compare the town in Canada to one in Alabama, a better comparison would be to the colored quarters—Pathview, Union, Cooksville."

"You don't get what Minerva was saying," Jocelyn says. "That town was like this one. It was just folks trying to make a living."

"Well, it's gone," Clayton says. "There's a difference."

"No place is ever what it was," Jocelyn says. "Including Wood-haven."

Clayton draws in his narrow shoulders and sits back in the chair, the color rushing to his face. "Those were some awfully scrawny saplings donated by Platinum Paper. Do you think they'll grow?"

Getting no answer from Jocelyn, Clayton turns to Warner. "Etienne never mentioned that town nor his relative in jail," he says. "Do you think he was ashamed of all of that?"

Even though Jennifer looks comfortable in Jocelyn's lap, Warner lifts her up and carries her back to the love seat. "Etienne's not here," he says, sitting with his daughter held to his chest. "And I wouldn't pretend to know what he thought."

With the stress of classes over, Warner turns his attention to trying to work on his marriage. Minerva still lives with her parents. But by the end of June she has been coming by the house several times a week. Still, despite a few romps in bed, he recognizes that she has no intentions of moving back in.

"I'm having good luck with the job hunt up here," Warner tells his mother on a trip to Burlington in July. "It looks like I might be coming back."

Warner returns to Alabama, still a bit unsure about his decision to go up to Vermont. One evening, though he is in no mood for another drinking session in which Randy criticizes the mistakes in Warner's marriage, he decides to go to the Lucky Lounge. It is better than sitting in the house alone.

"I can't believe it," Warner says, sitting at the bar next to Randy.

"Well, believe it," Randy says. "Gerrick Gilroy's dead as a doornail."

"No way."

"Swear on my daddy's grave."

"Your daddy ain't dead."

"Well it's the gospel truth anyway."

"How?"

"Car accident. The brakes went out on that old piece-o-car he had. Can't say I'm surprised."

"Wonder who's taking care of Sibelus. He's over there at that house alone now."

Randy's head jerks back. "Boy, ain't you heard? That house burnt to the ground. Ain't nothing but ash and cinder. I heard Gerrick did it—the only way he could get the old geezer out of that shack."

Warner finishes his beer, unable to believe the news. He orders another beer, trying to recall a happy time he spent with Gerrick in high school. The only memory that comes to him is of the times he and Gerrick clowned around the year they both went out for the junior varsity baseball team. He has recalled that memory before, but now it has a different cast.

Having relatives in Canada is something he and Gerrick had in common. But now one son of Canada has died. Is that what bothers him?

Before Gerrick lost his job at the Kwik Mart, Warner had entertained the idea that he might one day introduce Gerrick to his great-aunt Luela. Now that will never happen. But maybe his sadness is really guilt. He was, after all, the one who fired Gerrick.

Near the end of September, Warner packs up the house and moves to Vermont. Over the next year and a half, he returns to the South often to visit his daughter, each time making courteous talk with Minerva. On one visit she agrees to let him bring Jennifer back to Vermont for a visit.

"Can you believe Platinum Paper has sent Randy's butt over to Germany?" Minerva says during a visit, as they drive from the airport. "Davey Michelson went over, too, for nearly six months with the college guys."

"Sounds mighty nice," Warner says. "And I hear the money's good."

When Minerva suggests they stop at the Kwik Mart, Warner agrees. It is no longer a secret that Udall was pretending to do substantial renovations on the store to be in a better position with Platinum Paper. But after the company succeeded in getting Sibelus off his land, they called Udall's bluff and stopped the negotiations.

Inside the Kwik Mart, Warner looks around at the revamped interior while Millicent, back at the counter, fills him in about all the fighting between Udall and his wife. Through the window Warner sees Minerva at the car, showing off Jennifer to a young woman he does not recognize. Several coal trucks rumble by on the road. Millicent giggles as she rings up Warner's purchases, but he can tell she is slightly offended that Minerva hasn't come in with his daughter.

"Don't imagine you're coming back to live in Alabama," Millicent says. "Ain't it better for you up there?"

"My mother's up there," Warner says. "But my kid is down here."

Millicent drops two tins of sardines into his bag but holds the carton of Salem cigarettes in her hand. "This looks like what Gerrick used to buy for Sibelus."

"I'm going to stop over to see him, give my condolences about Gerrick to him in person."

Millicent takes a draw on her cigarette. "To dust everything shall return, they say."

"That's the first time I've heard you quote the Bible."

Millicent chuckles and hands the bag to Warner. "Don't be a stranger, stranger."

"Couldn't if I wanted to."

Warner climbs into the car, looking back at the store. "I'm taking a ride over to see Sibelus later," he tells Minerva. "I'd like to take Jennifer, if that's all right."

Minerva thinks a moment. "Why don't we take a ride over there now?"

W arner had called Sibelus some months back to say he would come by to see how Sibelus was doing. Now, Warner enters the house in Cooksville where Sibelus rents a room, wishing he had followed up on that promise sooner.

Sibelus sits in an overstuffed chair by the window, peering into the bag of items from the Kwik Mart. His face has filled out since Warner last saw him. So have his shoulders, which no longer look bony. Finally he looks like a man in his late sixties.

"You wouldn't believe all the development in Woodhaven," Minerva says, when Warner has difficulty breaking the silence. "New folks are moving in right and left. I put a hook-and-eye to the back screen door. Don't want anybody just walking in. Of course, I would have done it anyway, to keep Jennifer from sneaking out on me."

Warner remains quiet. He looks around the room. A bold-print bedspread covers the bed and two cane-bottom chairs sit along one wall. A picture of Sibelus and a woman is on the bureau. But no sign of anything that reminds Warner of Gerrick.

"It was awful what happened to Gerrick," Warner says.

"It put a hurt on me, too," Sibelus says. "And on Gerrick's daddy."

"Is he doing well?" Warner asks.

"Well enough, I suppose."

Sibelus takes two MoonPies out of the bag. "Gerrick probably told you I liked these," he says to Warner. "But most of the MoonPies that boy bought was for hisself."

"The Kwik Mart's been done nice," Minerva says. "You wouldn't recognize it."

Sibelus picks up a glass of iced tea from the windowsill. While he drinks it with his MoonPie, Warner catches him up on his life in Vermont. Seated on the floor, Jennifer pretends to pluck the flowers painted on the linoleum.

"I've been wanting to ask you something," Sibelus says when Warner and Minerva are about to leave. "What did my grandson do wrong at the store?"

"Nothing," Warner says.

"Well, he got let go."

"The store was closing."

"It ain't closed though."

"He was a good worker," Warner says.

After a long breath, Sibelus looks at Jennifer, now hiding behind Warner with her arms around his thigh. When Sibelus waves, Jennifer giggles and patters over to Minerva at the doorway.

"Pretty, isn't she?" Warner says.

"Sure is," Sibelus says. "But you better watch out. They grow up before you know it."

At his office in downtown Jackson, Eldridge Littlejohn opens a folder, feeling frustrated at the scant cooperation he has gotten from Zera over the month he has been working with her. Not a single letter has the stubborn woman written on her own behalf.

He knows Warner is not that happy that he has been unable to get Zera even a hearing for parole. He assured Warner that his friendship with the new congressman who represents Jackson was going to help with Zera's case. And while his connections with the congressman and the new lieutenant governor have managed to secure Zera treatment by a renowned heart specialist, she remains in Peace Correctional, despite the help of an army of law associates, interns, college professors, philanthropists, and the staff at the Southern Law Center.

"Perhaps it's time to quit Zera's case," Eldridge's wife had said. "You're a partner now. Didn't I hear you say that if things improved at the governor's mansion or the state legislature, you would hand over Zera's case to one of the young associates? Maybe it's time."

Perhaps he took up Zera's case too late, Eldridge tells himself, drawing circles in the margins of one document. Had he gotten to Zera in 1934, when prison life was harder, or in 1964 during the demonstrations, or perhaps in 1979, the year before she moved into better quarters—maybe.

The human resources manager—the only other black employee at the firm when Eldridge joined over a decade ago—used to say that too many stalled cases was a sure way to get you off the senior partner track. But this is not an admission of defeat, Eldridge tells himself, placing a file into the box that will soon be on its way to a young associate.

"Are you ready for Mr. Peletier?" the secretary asks from the doorway. "Or do you need a few minutes?"

Eldridge raises his hand with his fingers spread.

"Okay, five minutes," the secretary says.

Eldridge reaches for the folder containing copies of the paperwork for Zera's burial plot. There are no plots at the cemetery in Jackson where Zera's deceased husband, Matthew, and his parents are buried. Nor is there any space under the large oak at the cemetery that shades the graves of her parents, Patience and Floyd Bradenburg, and her grandmother Althea. And now Warner says this other cemetery claims that the plot Zera has purchased has already been spoken for.

"Eldridge Littlejohn here," Eldridge says into the phone, reading the note clipped to the document. "From Strum and Pearsons. I hear you're claiming that Zera Platt's burial plot is spoken for. Well, sir, my client doesn't see it that way. I'm looking at paperwork that says Zera owns the plot. Sure, you can call me back, but you're going to need to also call Congressman Levitt. He wants an answer, too."

After hanging up, Eldridge almost puts the folder back into his inbox. When he realizes what he is doing, he drops the folder into the box sitting on the floor.

V isiting Minerva at her parents' house the next morning, Warner sits at the kitchen table for several minutes before he notices the samples of resin-based countertops and pictures of oak and maple cabinet doors.

"These two look the same to me," he tells Minerva, holding up two peach-colored tile samples from a box.

"They're not exactly the same," Minerva says. "Look close. The tile in your right hand has more blue in it."

Warner doesn't check out too much in the living room as he maneuvers past Jennifer's playthings on the cluttered floor. He does, however, notice a new framed picture sitting on the television. In it, a man leans against the hood of a brand-new truck. Is he the fella from Crenshaw County he heard Minerva started seeing a few months back? Randy says the fella graduated a few years ahead of them at Woodhaven High, but he doesn't look familiar.

"I hear you've been seeing someone," Warner says, accepting a beer from Minerva.

"It was a while ago," Minerva says. "What about you?"

"Been busy with the job," Warner says. "Not to mention my trips down here. Saw Eldridge yesterday."

"Zera, too?"

Warner shakes his head. "She's not feeling well. It would be nice if our daughter got to see her, while Zera still knows who she is."

Minerva reaches into a drawer at the counter. She returns to the table, not with a bottle opener as Warner expected but with the bill from Jennifer's preschool. "I'm making myself a sandwich for lunch," she says, handing Warner the envelope. "You can have one if you like."

Warner nods, thinking his daughter will be up from her nap soon. But Jennifer sleeps through their lunch and, to his surprise, he and Minerva seem to enjoy the stolen time together. In the bedroom later, Minerva's naked body is another thing in the house that feels unfamiliar. So does the taste of her neck and shoulders. After a few minutes of kissing, Warner climbs onto Minerva, inhaling the aroma of a lotion she uses on clients at the rehabilitation center. Even before he enters her, Warner believes the sex will be good. After a few minutes, he is about to finish when he thinks of the last pregnancy. "Should I pull out?" he asks, continuing to thrust.

Before Minerva answers, Warner empties himself with a shudder.

Lying on the bed beside her for several minutes, Warner fails to come up with something new to say. He gets up and dresses quickly.

On the way to the living room, he looks in on Jennifer, asleep in the second bedroom. Perhaps someday when he looks at his daughter he will not think immediately of her lost sibling. He was adamant he didn't want to know the sex of the lost child. He thought that information would only increase his mourning. But during one conversation, Minerva lets the news slip—a daughter.

Warner has tried to break out of his depression over losing the baby by throwing himself into his new job. He still thinks of the child often during work at the appliance store in Burlington. But lately, each time a customer signs their name to a new sales receipt or warranty, he has felt a renewed sense of accomplishment. Last month he got a bonus as the employee with the top quarterly sales. Successes in Vermont haven't erased all his missteps in Alabama. But they have helped.

Outside, three pecan saplings stick out of the bed of the truck Warner borrowed from Randy. "There are saplings growing for Etienne," Warner says. "I figured why not plant a few for Jennifer."

Since Minerva looks pleased, Warner carries the trees to the backyard. Just before the tree line he paces off three spots he figures are fifteen yards apart. "The two saplings there are for Jennifer," Warner says, dumping a bucket of water onto the dark soil at the base of the third sapling. "This last one is in memory of our other daughter. We don't have to mention that to Jennifer, if you don't want."

"Jennifer will appreciate that, when we decide to tell her," Minerva says.

Driving to the airport later, Warner checks the Alabama roadside for more saplings. But he gets distracted by all the newly cleared lots. Soon he is content to let the scenery pass. He thinks about the divorce papers he saw sitting on the bureau in Minerva's bedroom earlier. Minerva did not dwell on the matter during this trip. When he peeked, he saw that the papers were still unsigned. Would it make sense to try to patch things up with her? It is hard to believe that the relationship could reignite, especially after seeing the man in the picture in the living room. The picture he can ignore, but not the colorful men's T-shirt he saw in the hamper in her bathroom.

He told Minerva he wasn't seeing anyone. But a few months back, he had met an older woman. It was raining the day he and Jocelyn were driving back from dinner at a new Italian restaurant in Winooski. Maneuvering around a car stranded next to the road with a flat, he ignored Jocelyn's advice to keep on driving and stopped to help the woman driver. Dating her, and a few other women, has required a lot of hustle—but perhaps not as much as trying to find a way back to Minerva.

When he first saw the word *dissolution* on the divorce papers, it sent him to Jocelyn's basement to seek out the heavy dictionary he hadn't used since college. On many occasions up in Vermont, he would be chatting up potential customers, sitting in a bar watching a baseball game, or lying on the sofa eating fries and a burger when his mind would grow numb, trying to name the many threads that had unraveled during his marital catastrophe. Was he too young to marry, as Etienne had once said? Was he too preoccupied? Had he ever loved Minerva? Of course, he loved Minerva. Why else would he still feel so scarred?

Warner had planned to drive by the new paper plant. But that exit is miles behind him now. He thinks again of the saplings on the Cumberland campus and those he planted for Jennifer. The adolescent trees will one day be as tall as the adult pines along the roadside. When the pines thin out, Warner has a momentary sense of knowing where he is. But too soon the familiarity falls away. There are red clay hills where he thinks the land should be flat, new townhouses where, as a child, he imagined the trees would always rule.

Who Is North American?

PART FIVE

Tract East 128

A Northern Aurora
on the Bluff

Halifax, Nova Scotia, March 1992

This morning downtown, city workers arrive to find a small two-bedroom trailer parked on the lawn of city hall. A hand-painted sign leaning against the trailer says CITY DISPLAY: NO ENTRY WITHOUT PERMISSION.

Throughout the morning, staff and visitors who arrive at the building heed the words. However, around one o'clock, a facilities clerk inspects the front and rear doors of the trailer and finds that both are secured with padlocks. A van carrying four constables arrives several minutes later. One of the constables knocks out a front window on the trailer and drops in a canister of tear gas. After the smoke has cleared, the constable cuts both padlocks on the front door. But when he attempts to step inside the trailer, he can move in only a foot or two. The front room is packed—floor to ceiling—with household belongings.

"We've towed the trailer out to the facilities lot," the chief of staff in the mayor's office tells Marcelina Higgins-Pitts when he telephones her home in Simms Corner. "It might be one of the trailers from the bluff. Can you break away and take a drive over and look at it?"

An hour later, on a gravel lot at the public works facilities complex, Marcelina climbs the cinderblock steps to the front of the trailer and looks inside. A strong smell assaults her nose and she steps back.

"Where are the contents?" she asks, holding a wad of tissue to her nose.

Bradford Nesbitt, the mayor's chief of staff, stands down on the gravel, sweating in a dark suit. He points with his cell phone in the direction of an aluminum-sided warehouse. "One half of the trailer had furniture in it," he says. "And the other half, just random stuff. Most of it looks like mining gear. There was nothing in the trailer to identify the owner or tell us who owns the material."

"Somebody out on the bluff ought to know who the trailer belongs to," Marcelina says.

"If they do, they are not talking."

"Can we go take a look?"

"Facilities might not let us into the warehouse—at least not until the inventory's done."

"They may if the mayor gets here," Marcelina says. "Where is he?"

"En route."

Bradford bounds up the steps without spilling a drop of coffee out of the fancy take-out cup. At twenty-nine, he is three years younger than his boss, the recently elected mayor. "You called the mayor several times last week," he tells Marcelina, "but you never told the secretary what you wanted."

"The mayor knows why I was calling."

"Can you tell me? Maybe I can help."

Though her elderly knees are giving her trouble, Marcelina does not accept Bradford's arm to help her descend the steps. She agreed to come out here only because Bradford said the mayor would stop by on his way to the airport. But for all she knows, the mayor could be in the air heading to Ottawa. Since she was appointed co-chair of the city's housing task force—the first black woman to hold the position in the history of Halifax municipality—she has gone right to the mayor, rarely needing to bother with his chief of staff.

"The city manager is still giving me the runaround about the repairs to the apartment building at 920 Gottingen Street," Marcelina says, when she reaches the gravel. "Residents want to know when they can move back in."

"The ruptured water main flooded an entire floor," Bradford says. "That's a lot of work."

"A little bird told me the repairs are finished."

"The mayor was hoping there might be room at 920 Gottingen for some of the people living in the trailers," Bradford says.

"Unfortunately, there are building residents ahead of them on the waiting list."

"Perhaps not all the displaced residents will want to move back into their apartments."

"Young man, do you really believe what you're saying?"

"The mayor might hurry the release of the repaired apartments if you will stop fighting his plan to move the cemetery off of Woods Bluff."

"I have nothing to say to the mayor about the cemetery. A judge will settle that fight."

"Weeds are invading the cemetery."

"You haven't visited the cemetery lately, have you, young man?"

"We would be respectful when we transport the remains."

"The judge will decide if you can haul off even a single headstone."

"The district court's been very supportive of municipalities," Bradford says. "It may well decide in the city's favor."

"The Friends of the Cemetery has a good lawyer, too."

Marcelina steps off for a tour around the trailer. The deferential look on Bradford's face as he made his arguments was a surprise. If he is showing respect for his elders, Marcelina thinks, it's a rare occurrence in this town recently. Her term as co-chair of the housing task force concludes in a few months, but not a single colleague has encouraged her to run again. She's well into her seventies, but that does not mean her opinions are no longer of value to the city.

Marcelina has said plenty downtown about Basinview Baptist cemetery ever since a military plane crashed on the bluff several years ago, flinging debris that mauled half a dozen headstones. When sinkholes disturbed eleven graves, nobody cried foul when city officials offered to put the caskets in storage until the sinkholes could be investigated. But then three of the caskets came up missing. During the recent mayoral campaign, candidate Jonathan Maryse demanded the missing caskets be found. Since becoming mayor, however, he hasn't mentioned them once.

What the mayor will not shut up about, Marcelina believes, is his economic development plan. Halifax has no chance at hosting the Olympics. But the city's bid to host a future North American Sailing Regatta could be bolstered by the addition of a high-end hotel and retail complex on the bluff. The alternative is a high-tech industrial park. Either project would mean making a final clearing of the area city officials now call Tract East 128.

Tract East 128? The first time Marcelina read that description of her former neighborhood in one of the city's planning memorandums she wanted to throw the document into the basin. But now, as she reaches the backside of the trailer, she thinks, why not let the city move the cemetery? Despite what she said to Bradford, the cemetery could use a bit of sprucing up. Reliable volunteers for weeding and pruning are getting harder to rustle up. It is true that members of her family, not to mention her former neighbors—the Sebolts, the Penn-campbells, the Ovitses, the Cauldens, the Delarojos—are buried in the cemetery. But do the dead complain?

A metal plaque on the back corner of the trailer has rusted, but on close inspection the manufacturer's name is faintly visible: Northern Aurora.

Marcelina had written the name in a leather-bound day planner years ago. But when she arrived in the Hindquarter on that afternoon in 1986, the trailer she found parked near the Higgins family home had a beige exterior. She almost called the constable to evict the family from her property, but was dissuaded by the sight of three girls playing out in front of it. It also helped that the occupants offered to pay a seventy-five-dollar-a-month hitching fee to be allowed to run an extension cord from the trailer to her house. For years she feared an electrical fire might scorch the house. Instead it was a skillet-oil fire. The kitchen was only slightly singed, Marcelina recalls now as she moves farther along the side of the trailer. City officials didn't have to condemn and demolish her house.

At the far side of the trailer Marcelina looks up at a bedroom window. If there were a face peeking out through the grimy panes, she doubts she would recognize it. Years ago she had written down the information on the plaque at the back of the trailer in case the family took off with the unit still owing back rent. But after her family home burned down and the city claimed the land, what reason did she have to keep up with the trailer?

At the front of the trailer, Bradford has his arm outstretched, showing his open cell phone. "You expect me to read the writing on that tiny screen?" Marcelina says. "What does it say?"

"It says that the trailer was rented to a man named Bartholomew Eatten. Do you know him?"

"Of course."

"Do you know where he might be?"

"I could make a phone call to try to locate him."

When Bradford offers his phone, Marcelina shakes her head. She's too embarrassed to ask how to operate the thing and, besides, she doesn't want Bradford listening in on her conversation. "You need to keep your phone open in case the mayor calls," she says. "I'll make a call from the office." The facilities department's office building looks like a rustic structure in a Canadian national park. At one of the desks, Marcelina lifts the phone receiver, perplexed. She knew the busted water main at 920 Gottingen had forced Bartholomew Eatten and his father, Jessup, to vacate their apartment. But the last she heard, Jessup Eatten was residing with relatives, and Bartholomew was renting at the Battleship Inn. In a blue moon, Bartholomew might stop by the bluff to help chop weeds in the cemetery. But she cannot imagine he would store any of his possessions on the bluff. Not out there with those strangers.

"Bartholomew did use the trailer for storage," the woman on the phone tells Marcelina. "He had to put a double lock on the door to keep those Trailerheads from bothering his property."

"Where's Bartholomew now?"

"Don't know."

"Is that the truth?"

"If I knew where he was, I would say."

"Tell him to come see me at my house," Marcelina says. "Tell him that if he knows what's good for him, he'd better show up."

Marcelina hangs up the phone not certain she believes any of what she has just heard. In the small bathroom she washes the stink of the trailer off her hands, thinking she ought to have admonished the young woman for using the term *Trailerheads*. She is a community worker after all, trying to bring people together, peddling the notion that we are all the same. Accepting talk like that doesn't help that work.

The bluff community now comprises ten trailers, eleven if you count the empty green-and-white one-bedroom shell sitting on the facilities lot. That trailer has changed occupants many times since Marcelina dealt with the family that first dragged it onto the bluff. She leaves the bathroom unable to think of a single family out there now that she knows well. And, these days, given how often the evening news shows the flashing lights of constable cars parked out on the bluff, she must agree that sometimes the term *Trailerheads* has merit.

Former residents of Africaville say the trouble in the trailer park goes back to the years those colored men boarded the trains in Mississippi and Alabama, arriving in Glace Bay with little more than their thin coats and thick country voices. Marcelina's relatives say that if the men had watched their money better or gotten more learning, the families now living in the trailers might have remained in Glace Bay after the mines closed.

Marcelina could not agree more. True, some Glace Bay families do own houses across the basin or down the coast. And few would deny that one or two Southerners—Chevy Platt and the Wilson boys from Georgia—had moved from Glace Bay and done well in Nova Scotia. But two or three up-and-comers do not make up for the failures of a hundred shiftless.

Bradford is not waiting in front of the facilities building when Marcelina comes out. Looking in the direction of the warehouse, she can see that he has reached the entrance. But who is the woman with him? When Bradford and the woman turn to see Marcelina heading toward them, they disappear inside the warehouse.

Marcelina picks up her pace. She could not make out the face of the woman, but she recognized the light-blue business suit. No doubt the woman wore it when she accompanied candidate Jonathan Maryse on several of his visits to prominent black churches in the area. Bradford said access to the warehouse was restricted until the mayor arrived, Marcelina recalls as she nears the entrance. But somehow Eva Cannon is getting a peek? Access when Maryse became mayor was what Eva Cannon wanted. And now she is getting it.

I nside the warehouse, the trailer's contents have been laid out on the concrete floor in two long rows. Bradford and Eva are already up the far row, so Marcelina heads down the nearest. There are stacks of mattresses, several kitchen tables, two sofas, six televisions, a stack of portable radios, and two refrigerators. Nothing looks familiar.

By the time Marcelina heads along the second row, Bradford has moved to a side door, where he stands with his cell phone to his ear. "Carbide," Eva says when Marcelina catches up to her. "That's the nasty smell."

"It's nice that you know that," Marcelina says. "But I figured Bradford let you in here because he thought you might know who owns these items. Do you?"

Eva moves her bangs out of her eyes and adjusts the thick-rimmed tortoiseshell glasses that frame her light-brown face. "I don't know who owns the trailer," she says. "But whoever moved it downtown may have been angry about the eviction notices."

"What eviction notices?"

"The ones the city sent to every house on the bluff."

"If the city was sending out eviction notices I would have heard about it," Marcelina says. "I doubt what you're saying is true."

Eva hands Marcelina an envelope and, without waiting for her to read the letter inside, continues up the row in a clatter of heels on concrete. Moments later, realizing that she has walked by several items without checking them out, she takes a few steps back. It was rude to walk off leaving Marcelina looking shocked and confused. But it feels good to have done so. When has anyone ever gotten a bit of juicy community gossip before Marcelina Higgins-Pitts? Bradford had also looked stunned when she told him about the eviction notices. Of course, he could have been pretending.

Neither Bradford nor Marcelina has the proper respect for the people living in the trailers, Eva believes. Perhaps they might, had they come to know the community as she did during the months before she started dental school, when she lived in her aunt's trailer. Last year, when she suggested to her boss that the dental practice offer free teeth cleanings to children living on the bluff, she had no idea the activity would yield such useful community information. This morning, when a young mother who brought her child in for an exam mentioned the eviction notices, Eva knew she had to call Bradford. She had planned to make the call as soon as she finished the exam. He did not have to call Marcelina Higgins-Pitts.

Eva feels she has expressed plenty of gratitude to Marcelina for helping her find her first apartment in Halifax. But two years ago, after she was elected president of the minority business coalition, she was hurt to hear that Marcelina was telling people that the girl from Glace Bay was getting too large for her skirts. A worse indignity was the apathy Marcelina displayed last year as Eva attempted to get her aunt's housing application moving. It took months of nagging to get Marcelina even to make a telephone call to check on the application. And by the time an approval letter for a city apartment was shoved under the door of the trailer, Eva's aunt had been dead for two weeks.

"It's a shame about these eviction notices," Marcelina says, handing Eva back the envelope.

"It is more than a shame," Eva says. "It's criminal. Some of these people have been living on the bluff for years."

"Nothing's permanent."

"An apartment in the building in Simms Corner would be permanent enough."

Getting no response from Marcelina, Eva resumes her inspection of the mining equipment. "I saw a man demonstrate a contraption like that at a county exposition when I was a girl," she says, pointing to an item lying on a paint-spattered tarp. "It's spring-loaded. It launches things into hard-to-reach crevices."

"One of the teenagers was messing with one of these out on the bluff a few months ago," Marcelina says. "Hit a man in the chest and sent him to the hospital. Those teenagers from the bluff are nothing but trouble."

Eva frowns. "The owner should not have been keeping dangerous equipment in the trailer."

"I don't think Bartholomew owns any mining gear," Marcelina says.

"Did he drag the trailer downtown?"

"I doubt it. Bartholomew is too old for that kind of foolishness."

A facilities clerk approaches and says that Bradford would like to meet them outside in the parking lot. Marcelina steps off first.

There she goes, Eva thinks, watching Marcelina near the side door, the woman who is always eager to convince everyone that only she can get to the bottom of any trouble that involves a black Haligonian. But Marcelina didn't know about the eviction notices. Her days as a well-connected community leader are definitely on the wane.

Well, good riddance, Eva thinks, slipping the folded envelope into the pocket of her suit jacket. And good riddance to the trash Marcelina and her neighbors have been talking about the current residents of the bluff. The fact is the trouble on the bluff sprang up long before the trailers arrived. One could count on one hand the number of Glace Bay families living on the bluff during 1968, the year the *Halifax Herald* wrote weekly articles saying the community was plagued by filth, overcrowding, and petty crime. The trouble did not start with the families whose grandfathers came to Canada from the United States aboard the mining company trains. The eyesore that Africaville became began when those Jamaicans—or were they from Trinidad or Haiti?—landed in Halifax in the 1800s. When the mines of Cape Breton closed down, at least the Glace Bay families had the sense to leave a place that wasn't working for them. Years before Africaville was demolished, young activists talked big about heading to the so-called ancestral town of Halifaxship. Big talk, but where was the action? Back then, Sierra Leone was probably no worse for a black person than Canada. Parents in Africaville had the opportunity to help their sons and daughters take the village on Woods Bluff home to Africa. Why didn't they?

The mayor has postponed his trip to Ottawa," Bradford says when Eva arrives at his black SUV, where he waits with Marcelina. "He's on his way back from the airport."

"Because of the trouble on the bluff?" Eva asks.

Bradford nods.

"This is quite a mystery," Eva says.

"Not a tough one though," Marcelina says. "It's just a matter of time before we know who owns the belongings."

"What about the person who dragged the trailer downtown?" Eva says. "You say this man Bartholomew didn't do it. Well, who did?"

While Marcelina thinks, Eva steps closer to Bradford. "If the mayor has any more questions, he can call me," she says. "I'll relay any info to Marcelina."

"Why would the mayor call you," Marcelina says to Eva, "when he can call me directly?"

Eva folds her arms with a slight smile. "It's too bad Miss Oneresta is no longer living and working for the community," she says. "She would have had all this mess sorted out hours ago."

Bradford climbs into the SUV, and Marcelina steps to the open car door. "Which one of us is the mayor going to call on this matter?" she asks Bradford. "Me or this woman who knows so little about the city?"

"I'll have the mayor call you," Bradford says to Marcelina, "but only if you promise to be open to talking with him about the cemetery lawsuit."

"You can forget that," Marcelina says.

But then Marcelina steals a glance at Eva, who stands looking smug and confident. Her comment moments ago still stings. The nerve of this gal thinking she knows anything about the work of Marcelina's aunt Oneresta. Marcelina thinks another long while before she turns to Bradford with a reluctant nod. "All right," she says. "I'll discuss the cemetery with the mayor."

Bradford looks back and forth between Eva and Marcelina and then gives Eva a disappointed look. "Marcelina can probably get to whoever owns the trailer before you can," he says, reaching for the door handle. "I think it's better if the mayor calls her about this matter."

Putting Eva in her place at the facilities parking lot was a necessary task, Marcelina tells herself back at her home in Simms Corner. But why then does the victory feel so hollow?

She wonders if she was convincing earlier when she told the chief of staff that she could find Bartholomew Eatten. She had declared with such confidence that Bartholomew never lived in a trailer out on the bluff. But is that the truth?

She's at her kitchen sink, washing her hands again, and the warm soapy water reminds her of how often she washed her hands during the visits she and Steppie Caulden made out to the bluff years ago to tend to Rosa Penncampbell. With every new snowstorm that winter, Rosa seemed to get sicker. Yet she refused to go back to the hospital. On the last trip Marcelina made to the Penncampbells' house, she saw Bartholomew Eatten standing on Dempsey Road. She tried to see if anyone else was on the road with him. But the end of Rosa's porch that would have afforded a better view was in bad shape and had been cordoned off. Bartholomew was probably there getting the news that Rosa had died earlier in the day. His mother had died the year before. Thank goodness Mrs. Eatten had not lived to see the mess her son was becoming with all the drugs he was taking. The man was in such bad shape that he missed his mother's funeral. What is he into now? Marcelina wonders, as she watches Bartholomew get out of a car idling in her driveway.

She opens the door to find the car gone and Bartholomew sitting on her front steps. "I heard you've been asking after me," he says.

"Is that your gear they took out of the trailer downtown?" Marcelina asks.

"Half of it is," Bartholomew says.

"And the rest?"

Bartholomew shifts on the steps, watching the traffic. His shirt is clean but wrinkled and his pants are faded. With his face unshaven, he looks every bit like a man on the other side of fifty. "The other crap belonged to the fellow renting the other half of the trailer," he says. "I go in through the front door. He goes in through the back."

"Who is the other fella?"

"Don't know his name. Only met him once. We were both at the trailer a few weeks ago. Somebody had been trying to jimmy the padlocks. I phoned the constable, but I could tell he wasn't listening."

"That's not a reason to run the trailer down to city hall."

"I didn't do that."

"Who did then?"

"I'd put money on it being one of those Trailerheads."

"If I was you, I'd get downtown and tell the constable that."

"It's what I plan."

Marcelina opens the door wider and steps out onto the landing. "Have you eaten?"

"A hard roll this morning."

"I can fix that."

In her kitchen Marcelina stands a moment feeling the cool air drift out of the open refrigerator. She heard recently that Bartholomew was still using drugs. In the time it takes to make a sandwich, she could summon a constable. She might do that but first she wants to find out what drew Bartholomew back to the bluff. Surely not the memory of the neighbors he knew as a child. By the time he was a teenager, his parents had moved away.

On the way out front with the sandwich, Marcelina pauses to pick up an envelope with an invitation to this year's remembrance picnic. Last year, she had told a group of angry attendees not to lose a night's sleep worrying about whether the cemetery, that last piece of Africaville, would be there next year. Was it wise to have spoken with that much bluster about a fight whose outcome she cannot guarantee?

"I would have sent you this by post," Marcelina says on the steps, where she hands Bartholomew the invitation. "But I didn't have your address."

"I might just show up this year," Bartholomew says. "Bring the little gal I'm spending time with."

While he takes a bite of the sandwich, Marcelina notices the soft-sided hat resting on his knee. It reminds her of the elderly men who used to gather on Saturday afternoons in front of the Africaville post office, discussing past events few of them remembered the same way.

"Did you see the note I stuck into the envelope with the invitation," Marcelina inquires, "asking for volunteers to help tidy up the cemetery?"

"I do like passing the cemetery when I am out there," Bartholomew says. "I could help clean up the area. But nobody has asked."

"Well, now I am asking," Marcelina says. "My husband could help, too."

"What about you?"

While considering Bartholomew's question, Marcelina notices a flock of swallows alighting on the crown of an old oak. Birds like those have nested in the trees on this street for over a century—and will long after Marcelina is gone. She wants the cemetery to survive. But she also must accept that it may not. What would be wise is to show her old neighbors that she appreciates the place now. "Pretty soon I'm going to have plenty of time on my hands," Marcelina says. "I guess I could get my hands dirty doing some different work on the bluff."

The New
New Confederates

Jackson, Mississippi, April 1992

As a descendant of persons buried in Basinview Baptist cemetery, Warner promised the lawyers helping the Friends of the Cemetery fight the city that he would be in Halifax this week to give a deposition for the case going to the appeals court. But more pressing matters have brought him to Jackson: a possible decision by the governor of Mississippi to pardon his great-grandmother Zera.

"I've been moved by the affidavits of three former members of the New Confederates, who swear that Zera Platt was not on the pier when the man guarding the houseboat drowned," the governor told the group of reporters that accosted him several weeks ago as he was leaving the state capitol building in Jackson. "I also believe that she had no knowledge of the bomb that police found on the former governor's houseboat. I have not yet made up my mind about the pardon. But rest assured I will terminate my days as governor of the great state of Mississippi with my conscience clear about the matter of Zera Platt."

The next day—Tuesday, April 14—the governor is due to fly to Washington, DC, to serve out the eighteen months remaining in the term of Mississippi's recently deceased senior senator. What departing action will leave the governor with a clear conscience? Warner wonders, as he drives off the rental car lot at the airport. Will he leave office pleased about signing Zera's pardon? Or will he depart satisfied about deciding to leave her to spend her last days in prison?

The most prominent voice in the chorus of politicians urging the governor to pardon Zera is Mississippi's newest black congressman, Eldridge Littlejohn. "I never thought I'd get another meeting with you," Warner tells Eldridge in the wood-paneled office in the federal building as he arrives for his 10:15 a.m. appointment. "Especially now that you're a big-time congressman."

Eldridge sits at the desk, where a young aide arranges folders sent over by the pro bono attorneys now handling Zera's case—the third firm to take up the case since Eldridge's former firm bowed out. His muscular face is still youthful, though his sideburns are tinged with gray. "I wish we could have had this meeting sooner," he says, opening one of the folders. "But I understand you don't get down here too often now that you've moved up to Vermont. I trust the family is doing well."

Warner nods, feeling the chill in his legs, stiff from the walk from the parking lot through the cold April rain. Usually he is eager to relay news about his daughter, who was up in Burlington last month during school break. If pressed he might even admit that his brain is still drunk with the news that his ex-wife, Minerva, is having a baby with the man from Crenshaw County. But today he isn't interested in making small talk with this man who once made plenty of tall promises. Watching Eldridge trying to decide which document he wants to examine first, Warner feels a resurrection of the anger that racked his body years ago when a legal assistant called to say Eldridge was passing Zera's case on to a younger associate. Letters asking State Representative Littlejohn and later State Senator Littlejohn to assist with Zera's parole case were answered with form letters saying the office was looking into the matter. What a shock to get a telephone call several days ago saying the congressman wanted to meet. But with Zera in the hospital again, Warner did not come to talk about anything but her. Watching the congressman struggle to make sense of the papers on his desk, Warner wonders how serious Eldridge is about helping now. Why does Eldridge look confused? Hasn't he already reacquainted himself with the case?

"Any word from the grandnephew, the tennis boy?" Eldridge asks, examining a document.

"He's playing in a tournament somewhere in Europe," Warner says. "He can't get away. He says he will help Zera financially."

"She won't need his money if she doesn't get released. Can we call the boy?"

"I have already," Warner says. "You must have a copy of the letter he sent to the governor."

Eldridge shakes his head. "A letter? That's the best he can do? He has been a disappointment."

"Zera has other supporters," Warner says. "Half the congregation from the church in Sunflower is willing to drive down to speak on her behalf. Members of the city council here in Jackson have been calling the governor about her. And now you are on the case."

Eldridge's face shows a bit of pride as the aide directs his attention to a note sitting on the desk. "I expect the governor will return my telephone call soon," Eldridge says, picking up the note. "Who knows, he may call while we are sitting here."

Eldridge frowns as he studies the words written on the tab of another folder. "I thought we settled the matter with Zera's burial plot years ago," he says. "Don't tell me the cemetery owner has put another body in Zera's plot."

"I'm afraid so," Warner says. "After we got the notice that the plot was being sold, we fought it. But we got whupped. The entire cemetery's full now."

"Is the occupant of the plot at least a deceased relative of Zera's?"

"Not a close one. A cousin by marriage, I believe."

"Have you told Zera yet?"

"I want to see if it is possible to get her plot returned to her. Can we sue?"

"Evicting a body from a plot's a tall mountain to climb. I would not be optimistic." Eldridge drops the folder back onto the desk, shaking his head. "I advise you not to tell her just yet. We don't want to send her into a tailspin. Better to wait until we get her released to discuss this matter."

Eldridge sits back in the chair with a long exhale. "I wish I'd known sooner about the new trouble with the burial plot."

"I left a bucketload of telephone messages for you," Warner says. "Nobody in your office ever called me back. I don't fault you for that. You had work to do, especially those campaigns to run."

Eldridge shrugs then hands Warner a page with a list of names. "Plenty of constituents in Jackson are willing to talk with the governor on Zera's behalf. Anybody on the list worthy?"

Warner scans the list, disappointed that his great-uncle Icarus Platt and Icarus's wife, Gussie, are not still alive. He had come to like them.

"Every time Zera is hospitalized, one of these imposters shows up at the hospital, telling lies to reporters," Warner says. "Zera doesn't know a single name here. And none of these clowns knows Zera."

Eldridge lifts a yellow sticky note off another document in the folder. "Well, I'll be a monkey's uncle. Is this really a letter from Sherry Gobe?"

"The deputy warden herself. She's retired now."

"Still, I never thought I'd see the day that woman would write something nice about Zera."

"My great-grandmother's gone a near decade without an incident at the prison."

"That's bankable conduct when it comes to consideration for clemency."

"The big one this time," Warner says. "A full pardon."

When the aide tries to explain the contents of another folder, Eldridge silences her with a wave of his hand. The confusion and tentativeness he displayed earlier have disappeared. He pores over the documents in the folder, chewing the end of a pen, his gaze focused as it used to be when he was an up-and-coming young partner.

"Clemency petitions are usually typed," Eldridge says. "But the governor wants a handwritten document from Zera. He says he wants to read Zera's own words."

"Something he can show the newspapers, too, no doubt."

Eldridge holds up the single page, which is blank on the backside. "A simple but powerful document. Lot of clean white space at the bottom, so Zera can write plenty."

After Eldridge hands over the form and a few other documents he wants Warner to take to the hospital, he escorts Warner through the reception area, gesturing grandly as he used to when he was a hotshot entertainment lawyer bolstering his community credentials with pro bono work. His most important compatriots back then were the head of the local NAACP, several prominent black businessmen, two members of the city council, and too many well-known Mississippi activists to count. And he bragged with the most fervor about the dozen or so law students he had recruited to work for Zera's release. "We are the New New Confederates," he had said during one of Warner's previous visits. "All of us are working hard to do what's right. Not just for Zera. For all the wrongly convicted."

"It will be a struggle to get her to write anything," Warner tells Eldridge while they wait for the elevator doors to open.

"Surely you can motivate her to write a sentence or two."

"I hope I can. But you know Zera."

B ack then, Warner tells himself as he reaches the second floor of the Jackson City Hospital and hands his driver's license to the uniformed state guard seated by the elevator, Eldridge and his fellow New New Confederates proved to be a lot of bluster. Their previous effort was a bust. The question is, will Eldridge and his cohorts succeed this time? Maybe. As in the past, their success will depend on Zera.

"Did you hear me, Great-granny?" Warner says from the doorway of the hospital room. "I was saying it's good to see you."

"I think they heard you in Tennessee," Zera says. She sits in a wheelchair on the other side of the room, looking out the window. "Why all the shouting?" she asks as Warner approaches. "Nothing's wrong with my hearing."

When Warner reaches her, Zera points at the window. "See the dirt daubers' nest on the wall out there?" she says.

"Afraid I don't."

"Right over there below the window ledge. A mother wasp works fast as slick lightning to build a home for her eggs. Of course, I doubt there are any eggs in the home now. That nest looks abandoned."

Warner leans toward the window, still unable to see the nest. But, then, the bars on the window distract him. After a two-week hospital stay, Zera sounds like her old stubborn self. He hopes that another health scare has gotten her to consider the chance she has for freedom. By the time another governor sympathetic to her case sits in the state mansion, she may not be alive to benefit.

"Are you happy that you are being discharged today, Great-granny?"

"Not really. The iced tea is better here at the hospital."

"They do not serve iced tea to patients."

"They do to an old woman who asks nicely."

"I've been told we've got a bit of time before your discharge paperwork is done. What say we take a gander at some of the things I
brought."

Zera frowns. "Papers?"

"We'll get to those. First I want to show you a few pictures. I'll lay
them out over on the bed."

Warner unlocks the tires on Zera's wheelchair and pushes her
toward the bed under the eye of the guard now seated in a chair by
the doorway. That is another sight that should make Zera eager for
freedom. He has heard enough now from her to understand some of
her pain. She blames herself for her son dying up north, where she
sent him after her foolish mistake. She probably also blames herself
for the fact that her husband, Matthew, was killed in prison. But
there are reasonable periods of purgatory after which a person has
atoned for their mistakes. Even the Mississippi governor recognizes
that.

At the bed Warner unzips a laptop computer case, the makeshift
briefcase he uses to carry Zera's documents. "That is a lot of looking,"
Zera says as he takes out a stack of pictures.

"It would have been taller," Warner says. "But I rushed out of the
house first thing this morning for my flight and forgot a whole other
stack. You've already seen enough pictures of my girlfriend, but I hate
that I forgot the new pictures I had of Jennifer."

Warner places two pictures on the bed. One is a wide shot of a section of the cemetery in Jackson where the Platt family is buried. The
other is of a single burial plot. The name on the headstone is Matthew
Ornell Platt.

Zera leans over the bed and stares a long time at the picture of the
headstone. "Matthew had not been dead but a few years before his son
left this earth, too," she says. "I'd like to believe father and son are now
together in heaven."

"I've got more pictures," Warner says. "But first I'd better tell you that I've got some not-so-good news about your cemetery plot here in Jackson."

"Go right ahead."

"They've put another family in there."

Zera considers the news a moment, her fingers pinching the thin cotton of her drab, checkered dress. "I guess that means I have no need to worry about where I will lie."

Warner hands Zera another photograph. "There may be room in the cemetery where this woman is resting. Take a look."

Three lines are carved on the face of the tombstone in the picture:

Patience Frances Bradenburg

Faithful wife of Floyd Aldolphus Bradenburg

Mother of Zera Josephina Bradenburg

Warner detects a slight tightening around the corners of Zera's gray eyes. Is that pain? As she mumbles a few low, unintelligible words, he notices that the guard has left the room and gone into the hallway. On his return, the guard hands Warner a note.

"The congressman wants to see me again," Warner says, reaching for his bag. "When I return, I have a few more pictures you definitely need to see."

"Your great-granny is happy to look at pictures," Zera says. "But tell the congressman not to send me any more paperwork for a pardon. I am still not inclined to sign any."

Eldridge does not get up to greet Warner when he enters. He remains seated at his desk, playing with his necktie.

"What's the matter?" Warner asks, taking a seat. "Has something come up?"

"The governor wants to meet with Zera," Eldridge says.

"When?"

"Before she leaves the hospital. Has she started to write the pardon request?"

Warner shakes his head. "I was getting ready to show it to her when I got your note asking me to come back here. I will get her working on it when I go back. I hope she agrees to meet with the governor."

Eldridge hands the aide a note and she rushes out of the room.

"I'll bet you noticed those state guards strutting the hallway at the hospital," he tells Warner. "Those Mississippi boys will sit Zera in front of the governor in shackles if need be."

"She cannot refuse to see the governor," Warner says, "but she can refuse to fill out the papers that will allow her to accept a pardon. That is messed up."

"Don't look at me. I'm no longer a lawyer."

"But you are a lawmaker."

Eldridge rises and closes the door. When he returns to his desk, he takes a seat on the front edge. "The head of clinical psychology at the hospital is a supporter of mine. A few phone calls and—"

"I do not want to go there again," Warner says. "I'm not about to declare Zera incompetent."

"Nobody would fault you."

"Zera would."

"Not after she's inhaled a lungful of freedom."

"If I ever gave you the impression that I wanted to force Zera to do something she doesn't want to do, it was probably because I was angry with her."

Eldridge checks his watch. "The governor finishes his meeting at the statehouse at four. Then he will head over to the hospital."

The aide returns and hands Eldridge a document. "You know, after this brief stint in the Senate, the governor plans to retire," he says. "I suppose dreaming about lounging on the porch of his beach house has made him soft. He no longer cares if Zera handwrites her clemency request." Eldridge holds up a typed form. "The governor will not question the paragraphs we have written on her behalf saying why she wants to be pardoned. But the man wants some political cover, if only on the temporary. There will be no deal if Zera does not sign."

"That's all she has to do?"

Eldridge nods. "Will she?"

"I hope so."

"Work on her. Maybe this long hospital stay has made her more cooperative."

"You mean more compliant?"

Eldridge circles the desk and returns to his chair. "Your great-grandmother is healthy now," he says. "But with every passing day her chances of staying well enough to enjoy any freedom will get slimmer and slimmer. That is a bit of logic for you and Zera to chew on."

Warner hoped that the short walk from the federal building back to the hospital might clear his head. But the chilly drizzle that seeps through his thin jacket and corduroy slacks disturbs his thoughts. Perhaps this journey south is yet another folly.

He enters the hospital room intending to get right to the paperwork. But maybe it would be best to first show Zera two more photographs.

Zera studies the first photograph with a tight mouth and tense brow, as if both curious and fearful. And for the first time since he began visiting her, he imagines he can tell what she might have looked like as an inquisitive young woman.

The name on this tombstone is Omar Jedediah Platt.

After what seems like several minutes Zera exhales a long breath of air. "My mother-in-law gave my son his middle name to honor Omar's grandfather," she says, her eyes still on the photograph. "That man was one of the first colored congressmen to walk the halls of the Capitol. All the Platts had similar aspirations for Omar."

Zera seems reluctant to hand the picture back to Warner. "You've been hauling yourself around visiting cemeteries in Jackson, up in

Sunflower, and way up there in Halifax," she says. "What will you do with yourself when I am dead and gone?"

"Let's not talk about anybody dying."

"If you didn't want to talk about dying, why did you bring me pictures of tombstones?"

Warner sits down on the bed. "There's a space in the cemetery in Sunflower," he says. "I've been told there is one plot that can fit two family members."

"There is just one of me," Zera says. "I don't need a plot big enough for two."

"You will if we need a place for Granddaddy Omar's remains."

"Stop your foolishness, boy. My son is buried up there in Canada."

A state guard comes to the doorway and waves to Warner. "He's telling us that the governor has left the statehouse," Warner says. "He'll be here directly."

"Coming here?" Zera says. "Why?"

"He wants to meet with you," Warner says. "Decide if he wants to help you get released. He says he will help but only if you ask to be released."

"Like I've said in the past, I'm not inclined to do that."

"I don't understand you, Great-granny."

"Then you have not been listening to me. I already told you that you do not need your granny walking out free, reminding everyone you know that you have a felon in the family."

"Everyone I know already knows about you."

"Boy, stop the lying."

Warner hands Zera another picture. "Here you can see the entire plot where Granddaddy Omar was buried. As you can see, the plot's been damaged."

"Did another airplane crash into the place?"

"No, ma'am. Sinkholes this time. That hole you see is where Granddaddy Omar's casket used to be. He's been moved."

"What's become of him?"

"He's at a funeral home in Halifax."

"He can't stay there."

Warner reaches into his bag and takes out the clemency papers. "As a free woman, you can choose where you and your son are laid to rest," he says. "If you leave it to me, I may not do what you want."

"I don't have many days left," she says. "And maybe there is some virtue in going to the grave because of something I believed in once."

"I noticed you said *once*."

Warner lays the form down on the bed in front of Zera and places the pen down next to where Zera should sign. "We should hurry."

Zera studies the document, looking even younger. There is strength there alongside the bit of ache, as with a child who has decided today is the first day she will endure the pain of a bruised knee without tears.

A soon as Zera picks up the pen Warner starts to gather his belongings. She holds the pen to her chest, thinking. "Aren't you going to wait to see if I sign it?" she asks, as Warner heads out of the room.

"Nope."

Heading down the hallway, Warner is surprised to see an open door. Inside, a body lies in the bed, but no guards or nurses stand nearby. Did the inmate in that bed die? And how many other inmates being tended to on this floor will never see freedom? Was it a mistake to leave Zera alone with her papers, alone to face the governor? Perhaps. But today he had to try something different.

Zera's Gift

Epoch: Canada's Daily News Magazine Digest

Thursday, June 4, 1992

P roperty-rights advocates all over the province of Nova Scotia rejoiced today when the Appellate Court dismissed the city of Halifax's appeal of a lower court's decision to deny the Halifax Community Development Department the right to seize a city parcel known as Tract East 128.

"Naturally us local folks are also happy with the decision," says Marcelina Higgins-Pitts, who has relatives in the Africaville village cemetery, which would have been relocated had the city prevailed. "But the fight is not over."

Higgins-Pitts was referring to the announcement today by the Halifax City Council that it will meet next week to debate whether to support the mayor's desire to take the case to the Supreme Court of Canada.

On the following Tuesday morning, in the annex room at Jameel and Sons Funeral Home on Gottingen Street, shiny caskets stand about the light-filled space like colorful luxury vehicles in an automobile showroom.

"I have taken a liking to this one," Warner says, inspecting a model with a burnished oak veneer finish. "What's your opinion?"

Warner looks to his right and for a second is astonished at the sight of the woman in a tan-and-green dress heading toward another casket. Since Zera's release from Peace two months ago, there have been plenty of moments when the sight of his great-grandmother signing her name on a prescription refill form at a drugstore counter or sitting in the waiting room of a doctor's office seemed an odd vision—a woman out of place in spaces built for the nonincarcerated. It surprised him earlier at the hotel to see her dressed at seven thirty and eager to visit the breakfast buffet, especially since their flight from Jackson last night was delayed and did not land in Halifax until one in the morning.

With Jameel and Sons offering significant deals on caskets to families whose deceased relatives were moved out of the cemetery on the bluff, Zera insisted on getting to the showroom early. They arrived promptly at nine, yet most of the models already had large red tags on them that said SOLD. Zera doesn't seem bothered. Examining a model she passed earlier, she looks like a woman who has no plans to be dissatisfied today. Thank goodness. On the drive here, for a while he feared that she was sinking into the quiet and sullen mood he witnessed during the four days he spent with her in Jackson after her release. In the car he reassured her that today's visit to the funeral home would be completed quickly. They would have the rest of the day to spend with the Platt relatives who seem eager to meet her.

Zera has laid a hand on a silver model with a two-piece lid. "I like the color on this one," she tells Warner.

"Likewise," Warner says.

"The shade of gray matches my son's eyes," Zera says. "At least as I remember them."

Zera rubs the brass handle on the model and then presses on the pillowy-white lining inside. She closes her eyes as if imagining a sleep of unimaginable eons. "I've decided to bury my son in this one."

One of the Jameel family granddaughters, who has been waiting by the door, approaches swiftly in a light-green pantsuit. At the casket she drops to a knee and shines a penlight at its underside.

"I understand that you want your son returned to the cemetery over there on the bluff," the young woman says.

"I do if the city will permit it," Zera says.

"I hope the ground does not give way again," the granddaughter says.

"If you mean the sinkholes," Warner says, "the underground stream that caused the trouble has dried up. Even the old well near the church no longer gives water. I believe we have seen the last of the sinkholes."

After making notes in a pad, the young woman places a hand on Zera's shoulder. Her hair, pulled into a bun at the back of her head, glistens under the fluorescent lights. The smile she wore earlier is gone. "Mrs. Platt, would you like to see the remains?"

This trip to Halifax is not the only journey Zera has made to visit family remains. Last April, on the day she left Peace Correctional, the moment she saw the road marker for the city of Jackson, she told Warner to drive her directly to the cemetery behind Farish Street Methodist Church. Near the grave of her dead husband, Matthew, she tried to recall a few happy days of her marriage into the Platt family. But all she could recall was the cool reception she got the day she met her future in-laws. Adelle and Stetson Platt chatted with her in their fussy parlor with tilted heads, not yet convinced that she would be good enough for their son. It was not a surprise when the two refused to take in their grandson Omar. That memory did not bother Zera at the cemetery as much as the jealousy she felt about the Platt family member who had been buried in the plot next to her husband. That was her place.

Zera's mood was better a month later, when she rode with Warner to visit the graves of her family, the Bradenburgs. She gave a chuckle as she looked out the side window of the car at the houses on the road leading into Sunflower, Mississippi. She remembered houses of unpainted pine plank, but these were covered in nicely painted particleboard siding. Only weeds and brush grew on the site of her old homestead, but the Baptist church still stood. It looked smaller than she remembered. The front door was locked, but a young man tending the grounds climbed in through a window and opened the church for them.

Inside, Zera sat with Warner in a rear pew, telling amusing stories about family she had not talked of in decades. They laughed about the letter she had gotten recently from her great-nephew Byron Edgecomb, who lives in France. He wrote that he had run through most of his tennis earnings, but he could send a little money if need be. Zera had only to let him know.

Zera didn't need her great-nephew's money. The state of Mississippi paid her rent. Volunteers did her laundry and brought in meals. Twice a week, she and several other residents at the Saint Agnes Senior Housing Facility in Jackson ordered delivery dinners: chicken, fried shrimp, spaghetti with meat sauce, or her favorite—ham with mustard greens. A patron sent her dresses that were plain enough to wear when she sat on the concrete porch of her apartment without the neighbors thinking she was living too comfortably. The walk to the cemetery was easy in the nice pair of wedge-heeled shoes sent to her by a female advertising executive from Chicago.

But Zera was not prepared for the pain she felt as she walked past the graves of her grandparents, Althea and Henry, and the grave of her father, Floyd. At the grave of her mother, Patience, she stood for several minutes racked with the same grief that plagued her as a child, a heavy guilt about the fact that her mother had died bringing her into the world. The only comfort came from the gratitude she felt that the family buried there were all resting peacefully.

And now her son must be returned to a proper resting place. Her desire to help make that happen had been the reason she signed the paperwork petitioning the governor to grant her a pardon. She left the cemetery recalling the day she heard about the accident that killed her son in Halifax. To live with that grief she had contrived the circumstances under which she might see her son again. If they met in Canada there would be a cool wind, and the sun would be a pale silvery blue.

Those whimsical dreams about her son were on Zera's mind again yesterday when she boarded the plane in Jackson for Halifax. She arrived at the showroom in the funeral home this morning, not wanting to believe that the bones being kept here were the remains of her son—far better to believe that her son had not died, that he had survived the truck accident. Perhaps he walks the earth with a scrambled mind, not knowing who he is? She might well run into him here in Simms Corner, or on the bluff. Seeing her, he will regain his senses, surely. What son does not recognize his mother?

"I don't want to see my son's remains quite yet," Zera tells the young woman in the funeral home. "I don't want to see them until I know where he will be buried."

"When will you know?"

When Zera hesitates, Warner takes her hand. "If the city council supports the mayor tomorrow," he says to Zera in a low voice. "You do recognize that the case could drag on for months."

Zera turns to the young woman. "If that happens, Warner and I might make sooner arrangements."

"What do you mean?" she asks.

"We might return my son's remains to Mississippi, where he was born."

W arner helps Zera onto the front seat of the rental car, feeling out of sorts. Zera looks tired, but moments ago in the funeral home, a local woman reminded him and Zera about the Friends of the Cemetery meeting this morning at ten o'clock. He had been certain the meeting was scheduled for tomorrow, but of course that makes no sense. Members of the city council are meeting tomorrow, June 10. The Friends of the Cemetery have to meet today to prepare for that.

Warner had promised Marcelina Higgins-Pitts he would bring Zera to the meeting to decide who will speak on behalf of the Friends of the Cemetery at the council meeting. He steers the car down Gottingen Street, still surprised that Zera accepted Marcelina's invitation to attend the meeting. Perhaps Zera had been swayed by Marcelina's opinion that the council will lend a sympathetic ear to their cause if Zera is in the chamber tomorrow. Marcelina added that the arrogant young mayor had so alienated the councillors that none seemed inclined to back his plan to take the cemetery fight to the Supreme Court of Canada. "Zera is an elderly woman who was unjustly imprisoned down in the States," Marcelina said. "Elderly and not in the best of health, she will have traveled far to return her son's remains to the cemetery where he was buried. Her presence at the council meeting will be a big help."

The group assembled in the reading room at the Simms Corner Library is about the same size as the one that attended the deliberations by the appeals court of Nova Scotia last week, barely twenty people.

"We have got to have a better turnout at city hall tomorrow," Marcelina says. She wears a dark-blue jacket with a colorful blouse and skirt. The corner of an African-print handkerchief peeks out of the pocket of her jacket. Seated nearby at one of the long study tables is Eva Cannon.

"Eva is going to bring a few of the people who used to live in the trailers to the council meeting," Marcelina says, gesturing for Eva to stand. "That will help fill up the room with our supporters."

"You and Eva have gotten awfully chummy lately," a man near the front tells Marcelina. "Are the two of you paying those Trailerheads to come to the meeting?"

"We are not paying anybody," Marcelina says.

"Well, then, those people are coming only because you and Eva found them somewhere to live when they got kicked off the bluff. Do they really give two hoots about the cemetery, about Africaville?"

Heads nod around the room.

"Let's not get into any of the old fights," Marcelina says, raising her hands.

"Nobody's fighting," the man says. "We're just saying what we think. That's how you get someplace."

"To get someplace we needs bodies downtown tomorrow," Marcelina says. She points at a table in the back of the room where Zera sits beside Warner. "We have a few visitors who have come a long way to be with us. We will be adding their names to the list of aggrieved parties in the lawsuit."

"Will the city vote to appeal the ruling?" a woman asks.

"Hard to say," Marcelina says. "But Zera Platt's name should be added to the list of respondents if the city does appeal."

Marcelina passes around copies of newspaper articles about Zera's long imprisonment. A man near the front takes a copy with a frown. "I hear you that Mrs. Platt has come a long way," he says. "I agree that she ought to be in the council chamber tomorrow. But now you're saying she ought to speak?"

"None of us has been asked to address the council," an elderly woman says. "Do you believe what that woman might say is more important than what local folk have to say?"

"Thomas Eatten will address the council tomorrow," Marcelina says. "So will a few of the Caulden brothers. And Matilda Green said she would speak."

"But where are they?"

"They will be there tomorrow."

"I don't believe it."

Marcelina drops her shoulders, looking exasperated. "Mrs. Platt isn't more important than the rest of us," she says. "But this mayor is determined, even though the appeals court ruled in our favor. Our fight needs new momentum. Zera is someone the council has not heard from before."

A rumble of low voices erupts in the crowd. When Zera rises to her feet, the room gets quiet.

"I did not come to Halifax to right a wrong," Zera says. "I am old enough to recognize the foolishness in that. I came here to return my son's remains to the earth. Regardless of what the council decides tomorrow, I intend to do that. I hope the Africaville cemetery survives. I am more than willing to tell the politicians that tomorrow. But do not think for a minute that we all won't keep on living if it doesn't."

In the evening, the national news runs a segment on Africaville with video narrated by Marcelina Higgins-Pitts. There are pictures of Africaville Elementary and Secondary and of Platt's Hardware, the rooming houses, and the cemetery. But there are no pictures of houses in New Jamaica, and the only pictures of the Hindquarter are of the two houses Marcelina's family used to own.

The next day newspaper reporters and television news crews from as far away as Toronto enter the chamber of the Halifax City Council. Zera's testimony comes near the end of the hearing, and by the time she is seated before the council the chamber is packed with attendees, many of them standing in the aisles. The councillors do not seem inclined to press Zera on any matter. Most spend their allotted time telling her how grateful they are that she has traveled so far and how pleased they are to welcome her to Halifax.

One young councillor, however, sits sternly as she adjusts her rostrum microphone, looking eager to confront Zera. "Why did you agree to add your name to the lawsuit?" the councillor asks.

"Because I was asked," Zera says. "And because the plot in the cemetery where my son rested has been bought and paid for."

"Not with cash."

"No, but with the sweat of the men who cleared the land."

"Are you sorry you sent your son to Halifax?"

"I sent him here to keep him out of danger. And for most of the time he was on this earth, he was."

"But he died up here."

"My son didn't die over there in Africaville," Zera says. "The bluff was kind to him. On the bluff he met the woman he loved."

After the council chairwoman announces that the matter will come to a vote, a quiet falls over the chamber. "All those in favor of leaving the cemetery where it is, please say—no, let's do it different," the chairwoman says. "All in favor of supporting the mayor in his quest to move the cemetery, raise your hand."

The mayor's chief of staff and the other aides around him stop their conversations to listen. Several photographers in the aisle move in closer and raise their cameras.

Not a single hand goes up.

The rectangular container resting on the wide shelf in the back room at Jameel and Sons Funeral Home is made of plywood. The blocky letters stenciled on its lid say MISTER OMAR PLATT.

The funeral home employee assisting Warner and Zera today is a short, stout, middle-aged man. The dark suit he wears has sharp creases, but looks one size too small. He smells of disinfectant soap, as though he washes his hands too often. He unzips the oilcloth bag inside the container and waits for nearly a minute. But neither Warner nor Zera steps forward to look inside.

Warner thinks it best to let Zera have the first look. But she does not seem yet inclined to do so. After another moment, Warner walks to the container, takes a glimpse inside, and then steps back.

"You don't have to look," Warner says with a hand on Zera's elbow, "if you don't want to."

"No, sir," Zera says. "I came here to see the remains, so I intend to see them."

Zera steps toward the container with her hands crossed at her chest, her jaw sagging. Her palms feel coated with the talcum she rubbed on her son's bottom during the weeks after she brought him home from the hospital. Her nose recoils at the stout scent of the camphor jelly she rubbed on his feet at bedtime. She can hear Omar's heavy breathing as she leads him down Farish Street on his first day at the elementary school. Those are memories she wanted to enjoy in her forties, when she was sad about being beyond childbearing age. But in prison, whenever she had tried to sit and think deeply about her son, the attempt only brought pain.

The gathered bones seem strange to look at, an odd ash-gray color. She studies them a long while, wanting to recognize them. Does she? She reaches inside and touches a few of the bones. They feel dry and brittle, like a bit of old house paint.

The employee steps to the shelf, looking as if he wants to chastise Zera for reaching into the container. But he lets her step away unbothered, as he zips up the bag.

Zera returns to a spot near Warner. "Do you think it might be possible to locate a bit of spring water?" she asks.

"What for, Great-granny?"

"To douse the bones."

The employee shakes his head. "Only staff is allowed to clean the remains," he says.

"I don't plan to clean them," Zera says. "Not even give them a full rinse. Just a douse."

"How much water?" Warner asks.

"They used to say a handful was all you need," Zera says.

The employee thinks a moment. After returning the lid to the container, he steps close to Warner. "We cannot allow any interference with the remains," he says, his voice low. "I imagine there will be a pouring of libations at the graves. That's allowed."

"But that is not how we handle a reinterment in the place where I have folks buried," Zera says.

The employee shakes his head. "I apologize. But we could get into trouble with the law."

Warner steps to the container again and reads his grandfather's name on the lid. Though he is not sure why, the employee's denial of Zera's request angers him. He waits a moment to calm down before he responds.

"But it means so much to my great-grandmother," he tells the employee, hearing the exasperation in his voice. He is about to speak again when Zera pulls at the sleeve of his shirt.

"I heard the man," she says. "If there is one thing I do nowadays, it is obey the law."

Of the three caskets that went missing after remains were removed from the Africaville cemetery because of sinkholes, only one has been found. On Friday afternoon Warner, Yancy Platt, and four young men have nine graves to redig. The reinterment ceremony will happen tomorrow, Saturday, June 13, at noon. A few hours later the annual Africaville Remembrance Picnic will commence.

For the pouring of libations, each family will bring their own water in a container with some family history. Former Africaville residents insist the pouring must be done with clean spring water from the bluff. Only that will do.

It won't be easy, as both underground springs in the former Centervillage area have dried up. "A spring still runs in the former Hind-quarter," Marcelina tells Warner, after the graves have been dug and he has wandered over to Nobody's Acre. "But you have to beat back the weeds to get to it."

Marcelina smiles broadly as she directs the crew bringing in long tables and large trash cans, to be left overnight for the remembrance picnic. She still looks pleased that the city council has, since rebuking the mayor, issued a proclamation declaring the Africaville cemetery a Halifax landmark. "The councillors didn't help the cemetery out of love for it," Marcelina says to Warner. "They only did it because they did not want to look bad in the newspapers."

Marcelina has also been chatting with Zera, who rode with her to the bluff today. Zera sits in a folding chair. Warner stands near her, trying to sort out his thoughts about being on the bluff again. He is happy that his uncle Yancy Platt and his family will join him and Zera for the festivities tomorrow. It also pleases him to see Zera and Marcelina ignore him as they continue talking like old sisters. He wishes his great-aunt Luela had lived long enough to meet Zera. Luela and Zera might well have gotten along.

"Why is it that you haven't taken your great-grandmother to the cemetery yet?" Marcelina asks Warner.

"I haven't wanted to go yet," Zera says. "I will see it tomorrow morning. Soon enough."

Marcelina looks at Warner's hand, and he raises it to show a metal container. "One of the relatives gave me this," he says. "It's an old field-engineer's canteen. I heard Granddaddy Omar used to wear it as a kid, hanging from a rope tied around his waist."

"We'd better get to finding the spring," Zera says. "Before the early evening catches us."

One of Marcelina's helpers approaches with a tall stack of plastic tablecloths. After telling the helper to take the cloths back to the truck, Marcelina is quiet a moment. "May I have a word with you, Zera?" she asks.

Warner stands a moment, confused, and then walks off, leaving the women alone.

"Where will you be buried?" Marcelina asks Zera.

Zera shrugs. "The space near my husband, Matthew, has been taken. The cemetery where my mother and father are buried is full."

"I suppose this is what happens when you live a long life," Marcelina says.

"Especially when you've lived too much of your life apart from family."

"There are spaces up here in Halifax," Marcelina says.

"Where?"

Marcelina points in the direction of the cemetery. "We could put you there," she says, "next to your son."

Zera remains quiet and looks over at Warner, who stands at the edge of Dempsey Road. He seems to be staring off in the direction where they've been told the spring runs. Marcelina does not seem inclined to rush Zera to answer, as if she knows why the words will not come.

"Take your time if you need it," Marcelina says. "There is no rush."

Zera nods at Marcelina, rises, and heads over to join Warner. During the slow car ride to the old Hindquarter, she glances about. Behind her is the place where she has been offered a space to spend eternity beside her son. In front, Zera imagines she can see the land where the Sebolt house had once sat. Omar and the girl from the bluff had produced her grandson, Etienne, who was born in that house. *Kath Ella?* Yes, that was her name. What a shame that she was buried in Montreal and not here on the bluff beside Omar.

Even before getting out of the car, Zera can tell that the path to the spring has been well trod already today. As they approach the path, Zera takes the container from Warner. "No need for you to come," she says. "I can fill it myself. But I would like you to pour."

Warner gives in to her, but as Zera picks her way down the path a short distance, he begins to follow. Then he stops and turns back to the road.

With no weeds to brush back, the trip is short, and she soon reaches a small hill. Out of a crack in the jagged rock at the base of the hill, a thin stream of water trickles. After filling the container, Zera can see that someone has beaten the path farther through a line of tall bushes. She recalls Marcelina saying that the spring was a short walk from a clearing with a wonderful view over the basin.

Beyond the bushes the weeds give way to low tufts of grass. People say Zera is spry for her age. The container feels heavy and she is tiring; still, she keeps walking. In earlier times she might have lifted her dress hem, picked a spot along a far tree line—perhaps a silver hemlock, a needle-thin ash, or a showy birch—and raced toward it, laughing at some happy news or merely for fun.

The air is different here in Halifax. Perhaps it is the height of the bluff, or perhaps it's the south-flowing winds bringing clean arctic air, not yet tainted by the grit of cities. She had once hoped to visit a few cities up north. But she had married a man from a family whose attention was along the Gulf Coast or out in the Caribbean. Still, a few Platt men had taken the trains north. Her son had gone up the coast by bus. He was laid to rest beside a few Platts who had traveled north by train. Perhaps he had been laid near a distant ancestor who had come to this land by sea?

At the edge of the clearing, she is surprised at how near the water is, an easy task to toss something into it. After reaching into the pocket of her dress, she opens her hand. At first she can hardly believe what lies in her palm. Is this piece of bone from her son's thumb, elbow, or toe? She is certain the man at the funeral home wanted to honor a mother's wish to douse the remains of her son. But he needed to keep his job. The law is the law.

Zera likes the feel of the cool water that she pours over the bit of remains in her palm. For a long while she stares at the drenched bone. At first she thought she would keep this part of her son with her only a short while. Then she would place it in the casket or drop it in the grave. But now there is talk of rejoining her with him here in what had once been Africaville, a reunion of mother and son. She will be with him soon enough. No need to give up this part of him yet. She will keep it with her for as long as she can, perhaps until she dies. Before her mind goes soft, she will confide the thievery to Warner—and then hand over the gift to him.

Acknowledgments

Over the nearly twenty years since I began writing *Africaville*, many people have helped nurture the novel to publication. Many thanks to my early readers Victor LaValle, Brian Hall, Marita Golden, Colum McCann, and especially Tom Jenks of *Narrative* magazine, where an excerpt of the novel was published. Thanks, also, to Bridgett M. Davis, Min Jin Lee, Sameer Pandya, Lorraine Berry, Maria Kennedy, Mildred Ehrlich, and Juanita Bobbitt. To Ayesha Pande, my brilliant literary agent, who provided years of feedback and encouragement. Patrik Bass, my smart and astute editor, who has worked diligently to improve the book and has been a tireless champion. The amazing marketing, sales, and publicity team at HarperCollins USA, especially Paul Olsewski, Tara Parsons, Mary Beth Thomas, Josh Marwell, and Andy LeCounte. My Canadian editor Iris Tupholme. Sally Arteseros, Randy Rosenthal, and Holly A. Hughes, whose critical eye and commentary on later versions of *Africaville* helped me tremendously to improve as a writer. Juanita Peters, Managing Director of the Africville Museum. Brenda Steed Ross, former resident of Africville and leader of the Africville Genealogy Society. The research staff at the New York and Halifax public libraries. A special thanks to Amina Iro, editorial assistant at Amistad, who guided me with tremendous aplomb through the many deadlines in the publication schedule. I am grateful to have attended residencies at Cuttyhunk Island Writers Residency, Vermont Studio Center, Provincetown Fine Arts Work Center, and Hambidge Center.